Fugitive Six

PITTACUS LORE

PENGUIN BOOKS

PENGUIN BOOKS

UK | USA | Canada | Ireland | Australia
India | New Zealand | South Africa

Penguin Books is part of the Penguin Random House group of companies
whose addresses can be found at global.penguinrandomhouse.com

Penguin
Random House
UK

First published in the USA by HarperCollins 2018
Published in Great Britain by Michael Joseph 2018
Published in Penguin Books 2019
001

Printed and bound in Great Britain by Clays Ltd, Elcograf S.p.A.

A CIP catalogue record for this book is available from the British Library

ISBN: 978–1–405–93425–1

www.greenpenguin.co.uk

MIX
Paper from
responsible sources
FSC® C018179

Penguin Random House is committed to a
sustainable future for our business, our readers
and our planet. This book is made from Forest
Stewardship Council® certified paper.

CHAPTER ONE

DUANPHEN
BANGKOK, THAILAND

DUANPHEN WATCHED THE BEGGAR AS HE SCURRIED
through traffic with his bucket and rag. The boy couldn't
have been more than twelve, small, with a mop of greasy
black hair. He picked his cars smartly—shiny ones with
tinted windows and drunk passengers. He splashed dirty
water on windshields and stretched across hoods to inef-
fectively clean up, mostly smearing around more grime.
Drivers rolled down their windows to curse at him but usually relented, shoved a note into his hand to make him go
away, and turned on their wipers.

It was after midnight and Royal City Avenue still pulsed
with life. Motorcycles weaved through the traffic. Drunk
clubbers stumbled into the street. Neon lights flashed in
unison with their bars' competing bass lines.

Duanphen rubbed the handcuff around her wrist, which attached her to the executive's briefcase. The metal irritated her. Just like this place.

Three months since she was last here. She hadn't missed it.

The beggar spotted Duanphen and her limo. Well, not *her* limo, precisely—it belonged to the executive; she was only watching over it. The black stretch was double-parked obnoxiously in front of a club where go-go dancers gyrated in the windows. The executive had been so excited when he saw the place that he was practically drooling; they just *had* to pull over. The rest of the executive's security had gone in with him, but not Duanphen. She was too young.

"Sweet ride," the beggar said in Thai as he stopped in front of her. He held out his rag threateningly. "Dirty, though. For a few bucks I'll wash it for you."

Duanphen regarded him coldly. "Go away."

The kid stared up at her, as if trying to decide if he should press his luck. At seventeen, Duanphen wasn't that much older than him, although her steely gaze made her seem it. She stood a shade over six feet tall, her long-limbed body like a switchblade. She kept her hair buzzed and wore no makeup except for some extra-dark eyeliner. Her petite nose was a crooked zigzag; it looked like it'd been erased and redrawn.

"I know you," he said.

"No."

"You're a hooker," he said with a laugh. "No! That's not right. Where have I seen you?"

2

"Doesn't matter," Duanphen said. "Get lost."

The beggar hopped in the air as the realization hit him. "You're a fighter!" he said, shaking his rag at her. "I know you! You're the one who cheats. The one—"

As if by magic, the boy's bucket tipped towards him and spilled water down the front of his pants. He gasped and shut up, staring at Duanphen.

Not magic. Telekinesis.

"If you do know me," Duanphen said, "then you know what I will do when I run out of patience."

The beggar looked at her wide-eyed, then took off into the crowd with a yelp. Duanphen pursed her lips. Calling her a cheater. What did that little idiot know about anything?

Duanphen had been doing Muay Thai fights since she was fourteen, a necessity to supplement the pittance she got working sixty hours a week at the garment factory, all to pay her rent at a roach-infested boardinghouse. Before her Legacies kicked in, Duanphen had lost more fights than she won, often getting her face smashed to a bloody pulp by girls twice her age.

Telekinesis, she discovered after the invasion, made the fights easier. An assisted leg-trip here. A deflected punch there. She went on a winning streak. She began to bet on herself. The competition got tougher, but her telekinesis got stronger, too.

It wasn't until an opponent managed to get her in a choke hold and Duanphen's electrified skin unexpectedly triggered that the fight promoters got wise. They called what she'd been doing "stealing" and gave her a choice: work off the debt or die. She considered fighting her way out, but they had a lot of guns, and blocking punches wasn't the same as stopping bullets.

Word soon got out that the local mob had a Garde for hire. That was how the executive found her. He knew a lot of people. He was a talker. An excellent negotiator.

That's what made him so valuable to the Foundation.

The Foundation paid off her debt and gave Duanphen a fresh start. They gave her more money than she could hope to earn in a thousand fights, plus clothes and a splashy apartment in Hong Kong. All she needed to do in exchange was watch over this smarmy executive and carry around his briefcase.

Not a bad deal at all, she'd thought. At least until she got to know the executive better. Men liked him, of course, because he was always making gross jokes and buying drinks. But, to Duanphen, he was a middle-aged creep, the kind of tourist she'd encountered a million times in Bangkok. He was always complaining about his cold wife and his kids who didn't talk to him.

The executive sauntered out of the club surrounded by a phalanx of brutish bodyguards. He had a lot of security—more added in the last few weeks, for reasons no one explained to Duanphen. The muscle cleared a path on the sidewalk, shoving aside gaudily dressed revelers as they escorted the executive to his armored limo. People craned their necks to catch a glimpse of what kind of man commanded such an entourage. The executive didn't look like much—a thatch of thinning blond hair, short, a potbelly, his designer suit wrinkled from the humidity, his salmon-colored shirt damp with sweat. Not famous, the onlookers probably thought, disappointed. Just some rich jerk. Bangkok was full of them.

Duanphen opened the car door for her rich jerk. He pinched her cheek affectionately and she died a little inside.

"Missed a banging good time, Dawn," he said, his words slurred from too much champagne.

"Mm," Duanphen offered noncommittally. She despised his butchered *farang* version of her name.

The executive interpreted Duanphen's murmur as encouragement. "One of these days you'll be old enough to make a proper piece of arm candy," he told her.

Duanphen smiled mirthlessly and clenched her fist. She slid into the backseat beside the executive, one of the other bodyguards taking the wheel.

"Meant to ask you," the executive said. "Happy to be back home?"

"No," she replied. "I hate this place."

"Really? I've always loved Bangkok." He waved his hand airily out the window. "Although it's more fun when you aren't bloody surrounded."

Duanphen knew the executive chafed at the extra security. His bodyguards weren't just the average bruisers anyone could hire around Bangkok; they were highly trained mercenaries. The Blackstone Group detachment had been his wife's idea—or, rather, his wife's command. She was in the

Foundation too and seemed to wield more power than her husband. That, at least, cheered Duanphen.

The rest of the executive's security piled into two cars, one behind and one in front. The executive sighed as his ungainly security force began the journey through the crowded streets back to his hotel.

The executive checked his watch. "Ah, running a bit late." He wiggled his fingers at Duanphen. "Let's get to business, shall we?"

Ostensibly, the executive was in Bangkok to sign some paperwork on a hotel he'd invested in. But while that work had made the executive rich, it was no longer his true occupation.

Duanphen offered him the briefcase. The executive unlocked it with his thumbprint, then lifted out its contents—a sleek tablet computer. This, too, the executive unlocked with his fingerprint, followed by a nine-digit code that he kept hidden from Duanphen. The tablet connected to a secure server via satellite uplink. The executive settled back, waiting to connect.

"A good turnout," the executive said approvingly. He liked showing off, so he didn't mind if Duanphen peeked at the tablet.

There were twenty people waiting for the executive in the e-conference. They were represented by icons—an infinity symbol, a snarling fox, a silver-and-blue star that Duanphen thought was the logo for an American football team. The mundane avatars of the very rich people in the executive's club.

A slithering blob of shadows appeared among the icons. That represented the executive himself. That was always how the auctioneer looked during one of these Foundation events.

"Good evening, all," the executive said, after unmuting his side of the conference and activating his voice modulator. "On the block tonight, we have the services of Salma G., for the weekend of January third through the fifth."

The executive called up Salma's picture and sent it out to the bidders. The girl had wavy brown hair that was long and unruly, plus a thick unibrow that made her look like she was deep in thought. In the image, Salma wore a tangle of scarves that were nearly indistinguishable from her billowy dress, patterns upon patterns. She sat cross-legged, fingers pinched together like she was meditating, her eyes gazing into the middle distance.

He muted the conference so he could smirk at Duanphen. "Nice costume on her, eh? The lads in marketing thought it'd be clever to give her a sort of gypsy fortune-teller vibe."

"I see," Duanphen replied.

"Don't need any of that when you're on the block, eh? Your face conveys exactly what you're for."

Duanphen touched her crooked nose but didn't reply. The executive had already unmuted the video conference and was again speaking to his international audience.

"The following specs were included in your dossier, but I'll summarize. Salma is sixteen years old. Moroccan. Speaks fluent Arabic, passable French and passable English.

No health concerns. Buyer must provide a halal diet. Salma's telekinetic control remains middling at best, so, if that's what you're interested in, we've got better assets available. Her real allure is her precognitive ability. She's perfect for a visit to the track or the casino, although we don't recommend attempting to use her Legacies to choose stocks or other long-term investments. Salma is geo-restricted; you've already been provided with lists of approved locations. Bidders are also reminded that you are purchasing *only* the use of Salma's Legacies and that any behavior viewed by the Foundation as untoward or detrimental to the asset will result in swift expulsion from the organization."

Duanphen knew that expulsion, in this case, meant death. It didn't matter how wealthy and powerful the Foundation's members were; if they broke the rules, they'd be punished.

"Righto." The executive cleared his throat. "As there's a great amount of interest in dear Salma, I believe we shall start the bidding at five million euros. Do I hear five million?"

Immediately, a handful of the icons logged out of the conference. The price was too high for some, but not all. The bidding went back and forth. Each time one of the icons pulsed, a little beep sounded and the bid increased by 250,000 euros.

Five minutes later, the auction was over. A weekend with Salma had gone for 10.6 million euros. The executive checked his account. The payment had already come through.

"Bastard'll probably make that back in a night." The

executive sniffed. He handed his tablet back to Duanphen and she returned it to the briefcase. "We ought to take a percentage of what the girl makes them at the tables, eh?"

"It is a lot of money," Duanphen said, in awe of the price the Moroccan Garde commanded.

"Eh." The executive shrugged. "Not so much."

They arrived at the executive's hotel. It was a lavish place, where the staff wore silk vests and bow ties and were always underfoot with warm towels and glasses of rose water. The executive loved it. He had the penthouse suite all to himself. Well, not quite all to himself. Duanphen slept in an adjoining room and a handful of the other bodyguards were always camped out in the hallway.

Some of the guards stayed in the lobby to keep an eye on things; the rest piled into the elevator with them. When they reached the top floor, they met two more bodyguards who were stationed outside the executive's suite.

"Keeping watch on an empty hallway," the executive groused. "What a great use of our resources."

But, as he neared his suite, the executive suddenly began to whistle a jaunty little tune. Duanphen raised an eyebrow. The little man was practically swaggering, swinging his arms back and forth like he was in a wonderful mood. Maybe he was drunker than she thought.

"Aw, you lads are just doing your jobs," he said. "I don't mean to be such a bastard. I just made a tidy pile of quid tonight, y'know? Ought to spread the wealth, as the poors love to say." He stopped abruptly in the middle of the hallway. "Come on, ya blokes," he said. "Gather round, eh?"

The guards did as they were told. Normally, they were a stoic bunch, but now they looked as upbeat as the executive. Some of them grinned as they formed an impromptu huddle. Duanphen arched an eyebrow. The Blackstone mercenaries were usually much more professional.

"It isn't easy work, what you do. I want to show my appreciation." The executive pulled out his overstuffed money clip and started slapping high-denomination Thai baht into the outstretched hands of his security guards. "Bangkok's a damn fine place for strapping bucks like you lot. Take the night off. Go out and enjoy yourselves. On me, of course."

As if the money wasn't enough, the executive handed over his Black Card to one of the guards, then tossed his entire wallet to another. He winked and waved them off, watching like a generous father as the hardened mercenaries jostled their way back to the elevator, arm in arm, laughing and cracking jokes.

Duanphen watched it all happen with her mouth half-open in disbelief.

"What . . . ?" She sounded bewildered. "What the hell are you doing?"

The executive grinned at her. "What's the matter, Dawn? You sure you don't want to join them? Go on, then. Have fun." He slapped his pockets. "Afraid I'm out of money, though . . ."

Duanphen stared into his eyes, which had a wide and spacey quality. "You're—" She gave up on the stupidly

grinning executive. "Hey, wait!" she called after the mercenaries, but the elevator was gone. Had they all gone crazy?

"Sir," Duanphen said, balling her fists. "You're acting
strange."

"Nonsense," the executive replied. He swiped his key
card and pushed open the door to his suite.

Immediately, Duanphen could sense something wrong.
The air was warm and sticky, not meticulously temperature-
controlled like the executive preferred. And where was that
breeze coming from?

The executive stopped suddenly and pinched the bridge
of his nose. He shook his head as if he were coming out of a
dream.

"Dawn, what— Did our boys just rob me? Or—what came
over me?"

The answer stood right in the middle of his suite.

The young man was slender, his brown hair combed
from the side into a meticulously gelled swoop. He wore
expensive clothes—gray slacks, a black vest, a white dress
shirt. Duanphen thought he looked almost like a magician;
appropriate, as he'd somehow slipped in past the executive's
security. The broken glass from the balcony window probably explained that . . . although how had he managed to
climb all the way up here?

The executive was frozen. "You."

"Not easy, putting you in a generous mood while making
those Blackstone morons go all frat boy," Einar said. There
were dark circles around his eyes and he was out of breath,

like he'd just greatly exerted himself. He held up a finger. "Give me a minute, will you?"

Duanphen didn't hesitate. Clearly, this Einar boy was a threat. Maybe even the reason for the executive's added security. She charged towards him, the executive's metal briefcase held over her head as a weapon.

Wumpf! She didn't see it coming. A second intruder slammed into Duanphen's side, trucked her clean off her feet and sent her crashing through a coffee table. A burly and hunched figure in a dingy gray sweat suit, the hood pulled up.

Einar sat down in a plush armchair and stretched out his legs. He smiled at the executive. "You aren't the only one with a bodyguard. Shall we see how this plays out?"

Duanphen snapped back to her feet, facing down the looming figure in the sweat suit. He was big, but she'd fought bigger. She triggered her Legacy. A field of electricity crackled across Duanphen's body. One Taser-like blow from her packed enough voltage to put down an ox.

She had longer reach than the brute in the sweat suit and threw a series of quick strikes at his face—a jab followed by a vicious swing of the briefcase. He bobbed backwards on his heels, keeping his distance as Duanphen's lightning-charged punches crackled right in front of his nose. Duanphen was merely testing him though, gauging her range.

"Ha!" She unleashed a vicious arcing roundhouse kick. The sweat suit barely managed to get his forearm raised in a haphazard block.

Duanphen screamed and flopped to the ground, her shin bent at an impossible angle. She'd broken her leg on her attacker's forearm. It was like hitting a brick wall.

The pain caused her to lose control of her Legacy. The sweat suit was on her fast. He grabbed Duanphen around the neck and lifted her off the ground with ease, his fist cocked back.

"Stop!" Einar yelled. "Don't kill her! You weren't even supposed to *break* her!"

As ordered, the sweat suit dropped Duanphen. She writhed on the floor, whimpering, body curled around her broken leg.

Einar looked at the executive. "Him, on the other hand . . ."

Duanphen saw it happen. The executive managed, at last, to turn and run. But it was too late. Sweat suit grabbed him by the back of his neck, lifted him up and then—*crack*— down, slamming the executive spine-first over his knee like a dead branch.

There was a moment that Duanphen knew from her many losing fights, that sensation right before a knockout, when all the pain was erased by welcoming blackness. The pain in her leg was shrieking and intense. Too much to bear. She let herself slip . . .

And then she was being not so gently slapped awake. How long was she out? Seconds? Minutes? She was still in the hotel room, the breeze from the broken window somehow chilling her despite the humidity. With every slight shift of her body, new shards of pain broke free in her shattered leg.

Duanphen wanted to retreat from the agony, but she sensed that if she passed out again she might never wake up.

Einar crouched over her. He stopped slapping her once her eyes focused.

"Hello again," he said. He held up the executive's tablet. "How do I access this?"

Shakily, she pointed at the executive's body. "Fingerprint."

Duanphen felt a sticky heat beneath her, warm and spreading. Was that . . . ?

"Yes, I know fingerprint. We already took care of that." Einar held up the executive's severed hand.

Duanphen gagged. She was lying in a puddle of blood swiftly spreading from the executive's body. In a moment of panic, she checked her own wrists, was relieved to find them intact. They'd simply ripped open the briefcase with telekinesis.

Behind Einar, the sweat suit wiped his gore-stained hands on a bedsheet. There was something wrong with his skin. Duanphen squinted, but Einar snapped his fingers in her face.

"Do you know the code?" he asked.

She shook her head. "Only he did."

Einar frowned. "Well. Got a bit overzealous, didn't we?" He stood up. "So here is the situation, Duanphen. Did I say that right?"

She nodded. "Yes."

"We're like you. Garde. I'm sure you noticed how your

coworkers suddenly started behaving strangely out in the hallway. That was me. I can control emotions." Duanphen flinched as Einar reached out, but all he did was touch her gently on the nose. "But I'm not doing that to you, dear."

"Wh-why?"

"My new policy is that I don't use my Legacy against our own kind unless absolutely necessary. I don't kill them either. Good news for you, yes? But you still have a choice to make. Option one: you deliver a message for me. Tell the Foundation I know who they are and that I'm coming for them. We leave you here, the guards will likely be back soon, they take you to a hospital, fix your leg, and then you find out what the Foundation does to assets who fail at their jobs."

Duanphen glanced at the executive's mangled body. This failure was not something the Foundation would forgive. "Option two?"

"Option two," Einar continued, "is you come with me. Help me out with what I'm doing."

Duanphen already knew which option she would choose, but she still had to ask.

"What . . . what *are* you doing?"

"Simple. I'm remaking the world."

CHAPTER TWO

NIGEL BARNABY
UNDERGROUND
THE HUMAN GARDE ACADEMY—POINT REYES, CALIFORNIA

"WHAT YOU WANT TO DO IS GET A PROPER SLOUCH on," Nigel said, demonstrating as he scrunched down in his metal folding chair. "Like your balls are too big for your trousers."

Opposite him, Taylor Cook raised an eyebrow. "Not your most relatable advice, Nigel."

"Ah, don't get all hung up on the equipment, love," Nigel replied. "It's more a state of mind."

Taylor tucked a strand of blond hair behind her ear and then did her best to copy Nigel's disaffected posture, one arm slung over the back of her chair, legs spread out obnoxiously.

"Not bad," Nigel said. He reached into his vest pocket and tossed Taylor a pack of sour-apple gum. "Now, chew a couple of pieces of that with your mouth open. Do it like you kinda hate the gum."

Taylor did as instructed, sneering at Nigel around a glob of neon green. He laughed.

"Brilliant, that's brilliant," he said. "Looking at you, I'm not sure if I want to slap your face or be your best friend."

"Thanks?" Taylor replied, sitting up a little.

"Back at my prep school, I had a prof who used to hate when I'd do the gum thing. Drove him up the wall. Called me *insouciant*."

Down the table from them, Isabela Silva looked up from her English flash cards. "*Insouciant*," she repeated, enunciating. "What does that mean?"

"It means ya don't give a shit about nothing," Nigel answered.

Isabela studied Nigel for a moment, then yawned. "Yes. A good word for you. Especially in matters of clothes and hygiene."

Nigel smirked and flattened out some wrinkles in his moth-eaten Misfits shirt. Maybe he wasn't the most polished guy at the Academy, but he didn't think of himself as insouciant, not anymore. He cared.

He cared about being Garde.

Back during the Mogadorian invasion, Nigel had been the first human to answer the Loric's call for help. After the war was won, Nigel had been one of the first students enrolled at the Academy. It hadn't all been fun and games. There were boring classes to endure, exhausting training, a lot of sitting around. Oh, and also new friends slaughtered by evil aliens, religious zealots who wanted to burn them at the stake, and a psychotic fellow Garde who nearly caused Nigel to drown himself.

He'd been through some crap, that was for sure. And he had the nightmares to prove it.

But he wouldn't trade it. Especially not now that he and his friends had their first real mission: secretly plotting the takedown of an über-rich cabal devoted to kidnapping and exploiting the talents of Human Garde. That was something he could get behind.

Not to mention, as secret hideouts went, theirs was pretty badass.

They were underneath the training center, down among the inner workings of the sadistic obstacle course Professor Nine had constructed. They accessed the place via a hatch hidden in the back of the rock wall. Above them, the ceiling was all a massive gear-work of shining titanium, the pulleys and belts and racks and pinions that drove the various death traps that waited on the floor above. There was an array of glowing control panels and fuse boxes, nests of wires and cords, and a few purring engines.

Also, Kopano's legs. They were sticking right out of the ceiling. That gave Nigel a pause and he had to blink his eyes.

Kopano was using his Legacy up there, distorting his physical mass or whatever. Nigel still couldn't quite wrap his head around how it worked, even after watching the high-powered-microscope images that Malcolm Goode—their science teacher and adviser—had recorded. The footage showed how Kopano could separate his atomic particles to glide through solid matter or, alternatively, tense up those same particles so that his skin was basically impenetrable. Kopano had saved Nigel's life with that power.

He'd also entirely stopped using the door to their suite, instead opting to pass right through it.

"You find it?" Professor Nine asked Kopano. He was on the ceiling too, using his antigravity Legacy to hang from there, holding on to Kopano by the ankle. That was something Nigel knew Kopano had been working on—keeping some of his body solid while the rest of him went intangible.

A second later, Kopano popped his top half out of the machinery, breathing hard and sweating. He held up a twisted piece of metal—a broken gear.

"Found the blockage," he said, and let the scrap clatter to the floor below. "You got a replacement?"

"Down there," Nine said, pointing to a toolbox on the floor below them.

Kopano sighed and levitated the gear up to them. Professor Nine never missed an opportunity to train them.

No one outside their group knew this place existed. Ever since their run-in with the Foundation, they'd been sneaking down here at least once a week, always when the rest of the campus was asleep. Which didn't mean that Professor Nine went easy on them. Even after secret meetings, he still woke them up at five a.m. for their training sessions, part of their punishment for sneaking away from the Academy in the first place.

The hatch in the ceiling opened and Ran Takeda climbed down. She'd saved Nigel's life just as much as Kopano had. At night, often after one of his bad dreams, Nigel found himself rubbing his breastbone, where he could still feel a phantom ache whenever he imagined Ran exploding his heart back to life. He wanted to hug her pretty much every time he saw her.

Ran nodded at Nigel and took the seat beside him. "Did I miss anything?"

"Haven't started yet," Nigel said. He waved a hand at slouching Taylor. "Just giving Taylor here lessons on how to be a proper delinquent."

Taylor snapped her gum in response.

It was all part of their plan.

"I see," Ran said. She looked down the table. "I think one of the guards on patrol might have spotted me coming in."

"He didn't," a woman's voice answered from behind an array of laptops. "I saw him, too. Monitored his radio. He didn't call in."

That was Lexa.

Nigel had seen the woman around campus a few times before the trouble with the Foundation started. Of course he recognized her. She had been piloting the Loric spacecraft that rescued him and the other Human Garde from Niagara Falls during the invasion of the Mogadorians. He knew she was from Lorien but didn't have Legacies like the Garde— she was just one of those *average* extraterrestrials. However, the rest of the students and faculty weren't aware of Lexa's origins, and after a brief conversation with Professor Nine, Nigel had no problem keeping that bit of info to himself. To the rest of the Academy, Lexa was simply the school's cyber-security expert and one-woman IT department.

Whenever their group called a meeting, Lexa made sure their sneaking around campus wasn't recorded on any of the cameras mounted around the Academy. She put the security feeds on loop, the process seamless and impossible to detect.

Dr. Malcolm Goode and Caleb Crane were the last two to descend via the ladder. Seeing them enter, Professor Nine and Kopano broke off from their repair work and joined the others around the table.

"Anyone for tea?" Malcolm asked as he ambled over to the small stove and microwave they'd installed down there. Ran raised her hand. Nigel snorted and rolled his eyes. Tea. Such a fussy British thing.

Taylor snorted and rolled her eyes, copying Nigel.

Caleb sat down next to Taylor. Nigel's duplicator room-mate looked tired, with dark circles under his eyes.

"You look straight knackered, mate," Nigel said.

"Our eyes feel like they're going to fall out of our heads," Caleb replied. "I mean—"

"Got it," Nigel said. "Plural pronoun *not* intended. So did you find anything?"

Under the guise of an independent study course, Caleb and Dr. Goode had been spending a lot of time going through the online archives of every major news source, dark-web message boards and even conspiracy theory blogs searching for any mention of the Foundation or its mega-dorky full name—the Foundation for a Better World. Caleb was uniquely suited to the task; his team of clones could skim through six times the material in the same amount of time as anyone else.

"We were focused on the Blackstone mercenaries tonight," Caleb said. "Put a timeline together of their last few years of operations."

"And?"

"I grew up around the military, but that stuff?" Caleb shuddered. "They've basically been one step ahead of international-war-crimes charges for years."

"They seemed like such nice guys when they were trying to shoot us," Taylor said.

Caleb smiled in her direction and started to say something else, but then Kopano flopped down in the seat next to Taylor. "I may be a mechanical genius," he declared, cleaning his hands off on a rag.

Taylor turned in Kopano's direction and wiped a smudge of grease off his cheek. "Aren't you the same guy who needed my help printing his literature essay earlier?"

"They never covered paper jams in our training," Kopano said.

Nigel couldn't help but notice the way Kopano looked at Taylor. It was the same way Caleb looked at Taylor. Both of them staring at her with those smitten googly eyes. Straight guys. So obvious.

"All right," Professor Nine said. He clapped his hands, which sounded vaguely cymbal-like on account of his metallic arm. "We all here? Let's get started."

Dr. Goode returned with his tea, pushing over the whiteboard with his free hand. All the information they'd managed to gather about the Foundation was taped up there. Nigel had seen it all before—had practically memorized it—and still his eyes devoured the mystery, seeking something he might have missed.

There was a grainy picture of Einar—the mind-controlling Garde who nearly murdered Nigel—taken by a red-light camera in Los Angeles just days before he orchestrated an attack by the Harvesters to kidnap Taylor. Written on a Post-it note next to Einar's head: *Emotional manipulation. Gone rogue? Douchebag.*

Einar wasn't alone in the photo. Next to him in the car was Rabiya. She'd been ditched by Einar, abducted and beaten by those Harvester loons and then taken by Einar again. Written next to her: *Teleporter. Location unknown. Brother = Prince?*

Attached to that last note was a picture of a handsome young Arab prince and a news story about his miraculous recovery from leukemia. Taylor was pretty sure that was the guy she'd helped heal in Abu Dhabi.

There was a photo of Vincent Iabruzzi, the healer who the Foundation had kidnapped while he was on a mission with Earth Garde in the Philippines.

Some players they didn't have images of, so those names

went on the board as index cards. Taylor had identified two other healers working for the Foundation—Jiao, a Chinese girl who seemed to be a willing asset, and a nameless disabled boy who the Foundation appeared to have tortured into compliance. And then there was the mysterious "B" who had reprimanded Einar via video chat and, in all probability, sent Taylor the thank-you note she received after she escaped from Iceland. The note was pinned to the board, too. According to Taylor, who had heard her voice, she sounded British.

Figured. Most of the Brits Nigel knew were total wankers.

"We've actually got good news for once," Professor Nine said. "Well, if you consider us having a Foundation rat living close by good news. Lexa? You want to tell them?"

Lexa looked up from her laptops. "At the most recent meeting of the Academy administrators, I mentioned how because of a recent hack attempt we were relocating all of our student data to a new secure server."

"Thrilling," Isabela said, shuffling her flash cards.

"This hack—did they get anything?" Kopano asked.

"There wasn't actually a hack," Lexa said. "Not a new one, anyway. I only gave the info about the new server out to the other administrators."

Nigel could see where this was going. He grinned. "Bloody cookie jar. Tell me that worked."

Lexa winked at him. "Oh, it worked."

Malcolm set down his tea and began to tape a new set of pictures to the board.

"Sorry," Caleb said, raising his hand. "I'm lost."

"It was a test," Lexa said. "A trap. We wanted to see if someone would try to hack this new server—which didn't contain any actual info. They didn't even wait twenty-four hours."

"The mole is an administrator," Ran said.

Taylor looked at Nine. "I thought you said this was good news? You think it's *good* that the Foundation corrupted someone so high up at the Academy?"

Nine shrugged. "It's good that now we can bust their dumb ass."

Malcolm had finished taping four images to the board. All mug shot–style photos from Academy staff IDs.

DR. SUSAN CHEN. DEAN OF ACADEMICS.

COLONEL RAY ARCHIBALD. HEAD OF SECURITY.

DR. LINDA MATHESON. HEAD OF HEALTH AND WELL-BEING.

GREGER KARLSSON. EARTH GARDE LIAISON.

"One of those people," Lexa said, "is working for the Foundation."

"We just need to find out which one," Nine said. He glanced at Taylor. "And then we spring our trap."

Nigel rubbed his hands together. "Hell yes," he said. "Let's go hunting."

CHAPTER THREE

SWEAT BEADED ON RAN'S FOREHEAD AS SHE LET the energy pour out from her palms and into the slab of concrete. She had probably used her Legacy more than a thousand times and yet the sensation still surprised her. It tickled. How was it possible that something so potentially destructive could tickle?

Charged up with her energy, the stone gave off a crimson glow, its molecules vibrating. Ran sometimes wondered where the energy came from. It was a destabilizing force and, apparently, she possessed an unending font of that deep within her.

What did that say about her?

She had spent time with some of the other kinetics—the students whose Legacies allowed them to produce energies and elements from nowhere. There was Omar Azoulay, who could breathe fire. There was Lisbette Zabala, who could create and manipulate ice. These Legacies made sense to Ran. They weren't inherently violent. Fire could keep someone warm in the winter, and ice could keep them cool in the summer. The chaotic energy that Ran produced simply blew up, no matter the season.

It came from nowhere. And it produced nothing.

Ran could feel it under her fingertips. The charge in the concrete was growing and growing. If she took her hands away now, Ran would have about five seconds to get cover. Then, the stone's destabilized molecules would become permanently repulsed from one another and fly violently apart. The stone would explode, shards would go everywhere, and bystanders would be hurt.

But that didn't have to happen.

"That's good, Ran," Dr. Goode's voice issued over a loudspeaker. "I've got my reading. You can stop."

The scientist watched from an adjoining room, protected by a window of blastproof glass. He monitored her activity through a powerful set of lenses that recorded data on a variety of spectrums. Next to Malcolm sat Lexa. As usual, she had a laptop open in front of her, although her eyes were currently locked on Ran's glowing block. Lexa didn't normally come to these sessions, but she'd been sticking close since the midnight meeting a couple of days ago.

Ran grunted, focusing on her work. She gritted her teeth. "I will . . . pull it back . . . now."

"Be careful."

Ran nodded. A dark strand of her chopped black hair stuck to her sweaty cheek. This was the hard part.

She pulled her energy back into herself. It didn't want to return; it wanted release. This part didn't tickle—it burned. Like swallowing back a mouthful of vomit with her entire body.

If she put just enough energy into an egg and then yanked it back, she'd have a hard-boiled egg. She got tired of eating those things weeks ago.

If she desperately poured her energy into a British guy with a stopped heart, Ran had learned, then yanked it back, she had a best friend who was alive again. She'd learned that trick back in Iceland. But that wasn't a trick anyone wanted her to do on the regular, not after seeing the bruises on Nigel's sternum. She wasn't going to be replacing a defibrillator anytime soon.

So if she poured her energy into concrete, what would happen then? Something useful? She was about to find out.

The only problem was that her energy—her inner chaos— it still needed release. All that violence had to go somewhere.

The glow dimmed. The concrete was drained. Ran's hands trembled and she braced herself.

It felt like a great hand made of fizzy bubbles reached down and slapped her. Ran was thrown off her feet, her body jerking and twitching. They'd done this experiment before with different inanimate objects, so they knew what would happen and had positioned a net behind Ran to catch her.

That didn't mean exploding didn't hurt like hell.

Like every previous time, Malcolm rushed out of his safe area and came to her side. "Ran! You okay?"

Her clothes prickled with static electricity, and when she opened her mouth to answer, a plume of smoke rolled off her tongue. Her hands—where the energy had come and gone— were badly bruised, already turning purple and swollen, like she'd slammed them in a door over and over. She'd have to go see Taylor.

Ran nodded as Malcolm helped her up. "I'm fine."

"That was more—you expended more energy than we talked about."

"I wanted to see what would happen," Ran said.

Malcolm adjusted his glasses up the bridge of his nose. "I know Nine likes to teach that pushing your limits is the best way to grow your Legacies, but in your case . . . we ought to be cautious, is all I'm saying."

Ran looked down at her hands—slender and long-fingered; she had taken piano lessons in Japan when she was younger. The veins stood out now, dark and angry. She wondered, not for the first time, what would happen if she completely unleashed. She'd never come close to reaching this "limit" Malcolm described. How much energy was within her? How much destruction was she truly capable of?

She forced this thought aside. She didn't want to find out.

Lexa poked her head out of the safe room. "You good, Ran?"

"Fine," she repeated.

Shaking out her aching hands, Ran approached the concrete block. She prodded it with her toe. A puff of brick dust shook loose, but otherwise the stone still felt solid.

"Any change?" she asked, turning to Malcolm.

The scientist produced a hammer and approached the block himself, striking the stone with a few sharp blows. He knocked loose a few chips, then glanced down at a tablet held in his other hand.

"Not really," he told her. "You charged the atoms, as usual, but when you withdrew the energy, the concrete settled back to its inert state. Apparently, your Legacy only has a transformative effect on organic tissue and even that is . . . hard to quantify."

The corner of Ran's mouth twitched. "Useless."

"Well, we know that's not entirely true," Malcolm attempted to console her.

"I can cook an egg. I can jump-start a heart as an absolutely last resort. These things are not . . . they aren't valuable, Dr. Goode. How am I supposed to help people with this Legacy? I'm essentially a bomb with a brain."

"Hmm." Malcolm swiped through some readouts on his tablet, then came to stand beside Ran. "There's this."

The tablet displayed an infrared image of the concrete block, recorded by one of the many lenses Malcolm had trained on the test area. It looked like nothing more than a glowing blob to Ran, at least until Malcolm traced his finger across a dark slash in the cube's middle.

"You see this? Where there's none of your energy accumulating?"

"Yes?"

"It's a crack," he explained. Malcolm led her in a circle around the concrete, where there were no visible flaws in the rock. "It's a crack *inside* the concrete. That happens sometimes, when air gets inside the pour. If we were to exert enough pressure on the stone—a *lot* of pressure, mind you—that's the fault along which the concrete would break."

Ran studied the thin shadow in the image with her lips pursed. "Earthquakes in Japan were always a worry. My father is—" She cleared her throat. "My father *was* an engineer, in charge of checking buildings to make sure they would stand. Maybe . . ."

"Maybe that's something you could use your Legacy for," Malcolm finished her thought, brightening. "Your energy—or the absence thereof—could potentially be used to highlight structural weaknesses that can't be detected by more traditional means."

Ran's expression soured as Malcolm grasped for a silver lining. "And if I should make a mistake . . . what? I destroy a building? Blow it up?"

Malcolm's smile disappeared. "Well, of course, we would have to approach the process with caution . . ."

"The safest course of action is to just not use my power at all," Ran replied.

"Safe? Or selfish?"

Ran and Malcolm turned towards the voice. Greger

Karlsson leaned into the training center's entryway, an insufferably smug smile on his face. As usual, the Earth Garde liaison wore a designer suit, his hair brushed meticulously, everything about him exuding a confidence that bordered on arrogance. Ran had been so wrapped up in her testing, she hadn't noticed him standing there.

Greger often came to watch Ran train. From the corner of her eye, she noticed Lexa disappear back behind her laptop.

"Excuse me?" Ran replied to Greger.

"Greger, maybe this isn't the best time . . . ," Malcolm said diplomatically.

Greger waved this objection away as he walked farther into the room, approaching Ran.

"I'll admit that there's something admirable about your insistence on pacifism, Ms. Takeda, but I do think you're being somewhat obtuse."

Ran's lip curled—admirable and obtuse. A compliment followed by an insult.

"You needn't strain yourself in here or deny what you are. There's much good that could be done using your Legacies as they were intended."

"Hmm. I hardly think we can know what the Lorien entity intended for these Legacies, Greger," Malcolm replied.

Ran didn't feel like approaching the issue as some kind of intellectual debate. Before Greger could get too close, she snatched the hammer away from Malcolm, charged it, and thrust it in the liaison's direction.

"Show me," she said sharply. "Demonstrate how you

would use this for good."

Greger shied away from the glowing object. He reached inside his jacket and took out his phone, eyes never leaving Ran.

"I will," he said. "A moment, please."

While Greger navigated to an internet browser, Ran tossed the charged hammer into the nearby obstacle course's sandpit. It exploded with a small burst of debris.

Greger held out his phone to Ran. On the screen was a headline from the *Guardian*. "AUSTRALIAN SOLDIERS MASSACRED IN YEMEN."

"This happened last week," Greger explained. "An Australian helicopter was flying routine reconnaissance over a terrorist stronghold. Funny, isn't it, that after an alien invasion and a complete shift in the bounds of reality that such petty human differences as religion and borders should remain a dire issue, hm?"

"Hilarious," Malcolm replied dryly.

Without asking permission, Ran took Greger's phone. She started scrolling through the article, even as Greger explained the contents.

"After an engine malfunction, the helicopter was forced to make an emergency landing," Greger continued, speaking more to Ran than to Malcolm. "The enemy had the Australians pinned down on all sides. Their positions were deeply dug in. Traditional air support—missiles and such—were deemed too risky. Extraction was impossible. And so, these brave young men and women were left to their fate."

Ran looked up and locked eyes with Greger. "What could I have done that the military couldn't?"

"A young lady with your abilities could have detonated enemy barricades with more precision than traditional ballistics," Greger explained. "Your controlled explosions could have saved these soldiers, while minimizing damage to local infrastructure and civilian casualties."

Ran flicked a look in Lexa's direction. The movement was subtle, but she saw it—Lexa nodded once. Ran shoved Greger's phone into his chest.

"You still do not understand," she told him. "My explosions—they are not always controlled, not always predictable."

"Frankly, I think you sell yourself short," Greger replied. "I've watched your training. Better yet, I've seen videos of you in the field. You're incredibly skilled."

"An expression comes to mind," Ran answered coolly, deflecting the compliment. "When your only tool is a hammer, every problem looks like a nail. I've told you before, I don't want to be Earth Garde's hammer."

Smirking, Greger glanced at the shrapnel left from the hammer Ran had just detonated. "An apt metaphor, I suppose. Nonetheless, my recommendation to Earth Garde remains unchanged. You are ready, Ran. You should be fast-tracked for graduation and allowed to begin your service to the world. Inherently destructive as your Legacy might be, it would ultimately save lives."

Ran suddenly felt tired. This was the same discussion she

had with Greger any time he popped up around the Academy. She was tired of it. There were only so many ways to tell a foolish man that you wouldn't blow people up for the greater good. She turned her back on him and touched Malcolm's arm.

"Thank you for working with me, Dr. Goode. Can we resume our testing tomorrow?"

"Of course," he replied with a sympathetic smile. "Go see Taylor and get yourself patched up."

Ran nodded. Without another word, she stepped pointedly around Greger and stalked towards the training center's exit. She could hear them talking about her as she pushed through the door.

"One day," Greger told Malcolm, "she will have to come to terms with what she is."

"I think," Malcolm replied icily, "that's exactly what she's doing."

"It was easier than I thought it would be," Ran told the others that night, when they once again gathered underneath the training center. "He handed his phone right to me."

"With Greger connected to the Wi-Fi and not paying attention to his device, I was able to gain access," Lexa said. "I downloaded his contacts, his emails, everything."

"Find anything suspicious?" Kopano asked.

"Unfortunately not," Lexa replied.

"Prick could have a second phone, though," Nigel said with a glance at Ran. He knew the pressure Greger put on her and didn't like it. Ran appreciated his being so protective, but said nothing. She didn't think it was likely that Greger was their mole. He was almost too overtly sleazy to be hiding even more sleaze.

"Oh, a guy like that definitely has a second phone," Isabela put in, blowing on her nails. "One for business and family, one for all his affairs."

"Dude's not even married," Professor Nine said.

Isabela shrugged. "You'll see."

"There was one strange thing," Lexa said, "although I don't necessarily see a connection to the Foundation."

Ran leaned forward. "What is it?"

"There were calls, both incoming and outgoing, to some encrypted numbers. It took some work, but I managed to trace them back to the CIA." Lexa notice Isabela's blank look. "The United States spy agency."

"Oh," Isabela said.

"You know, like Jason Bourne," Kopano added helpfully.

"Who's that nerd?" Isabela asked.

Taylor spoke up before they veered too far off-topic. "Greger is Swedish, right?"

"Swiss," Nine said.

"No, he is indeed Swedish," Malcolm corrected.

Nine threw up his hands. "This planet has too many countries."

"Why would a Swedish guy be talking to the CIA?" Taylor asked. "That's a little strange, right?"

"Could be related to his work for Earth Garde," Caleb

said. "A lot of different organizations are probably interested in us."

"Too many," Taylor said.

While the others talked, Nigel got up and sauntered over to the whiteboard. He picked up a black marker and drew a speech bubble next to Greger's head. Inside, he wrote: *Am I evil?*

That actually got a laugh from Ran, probably louder than Nigel's drawing deserved. It felt good—a pressure release almost like when she charged an object.

Evil or not, Greger was wrong about her.

She would show him. She could do more than blow things up.

CHAPTER FOUR

"NEW TECH, LADIES AND GENTLEMEN," COLONEL
Ray Archibald announced. "Just came in."

The Academy's head of security, commander of the sizable detachment of UN Peacekeepers tasked with keeping the students safe, paced back and forth at the front of the mess hall. Except for those currently on duty, all of his soldiers were present, packed onto the benches to listen to the weekly briefing. Archibald was as stern as ever, his cheeks razor-burned, his uniform immaculate.

Lieutenant Halima Ouma, a twentysomething Kenyan soldier who had just rotated in with the Peacekeepers, stood at the back of the room near the door. It was actually Halima's day off, but no one thought it was odd that she'd come in for the briefing. That kind of dedication always scored points with Archibald.

The real Halima had actually gotten up early that morning, using her off day to take a drive down the coast to explore California. Isabela had watched her go. That's why she had decided to borrow Halima's face in the first place. She wouldn't miss it.

"This here is the Inhibitor 3.0," Archibald said. He held up what looked to Isabela like a simple silver button, albeit with a needlelike prong poking out of one side. "Obviously, this is meant for more close-quarters deployment than the previous shock-collar version. Once implanted in a Garde's temple, the Inhibitor emits a signal that disrupts their Legacies. Sydal Corp is working on a delivery system to turn these into smart projectiles, but apparently that's not ready yet."

Isabela's ears perked up at the mention of Sydal Corp. Her friends talked about them, down in their secret lair. They were the weapons manufacturers who supplied both Earth Garde and the Foundation with anti-Garde technology. Their CEO, Wade Sydal, with his baby face and bad goatee, even made an appearance on their bulletin board.

Did they have incriminating evidence against Sydal? Proof of his double-dealing? Isabela couldn't remember. She didn't pay much attention in those meetings. They felt like extra homework. She much preferred the exciting stuff.

Like sneaking into the barracks to get Archibald's data.

"Truth be told, I'd rather us not have to use these things," the colonel said as he tossed the new Inhibitor onto the table in front of him. "Our job here is to make sure nobody harms these kids. Sometimes, that means making sure they don't hurt themselves or each other. If we can't de-escalate a situation without shocking their brains, then we've failed at our mission."

Isabela reconsidered Archibald. When they did the Wargames event against the Peacekeepers, he had seemed proud of the way his soldiers dismantled the young Garde— at least until Isabela and her friends tricked their way to a victory. Isabela still savored the memory of Archibald's surprised face when she'd held a tranquilizer gun under his chin. Listening to Archibald now, she wondered if he really did have it out for the Garde, or if that whole training scenario was just his way of teaching the students—and their cocky professor—a hard lesson.

"We were supposed to be getting a new student to the Academy tomorrow." Archibald continued his briefing. "But the Italians are keeping her, on account of the incident in the Philippines. If any press contact you about Italy's participation in Earth Garde, you have no comment."

Isabela zoned out. Was Archibald just an uptight military goon or did he harbor the kind of anti-Garde sentiment that would make him a perfect mole? Isabela would find out soon enough.

"We've got the holidays coming up," Archibald said, oblivious to Isabela's scrutiny. "The Academy's headshrinker wants us to be aware that this can be a tough time of year for young people, especially considering most of them won't be allowed to leave campus for home visits. Let's be aware of students acting out and potentially trying to sneak off campus. We don't want a repeat of our recent lapse."

Isabela allowed herself a small smile. As if they could keep her here if she really wanted to escape.

Archibald opened up a folder on the table in front of him. "As for those home visits, if I call your name, you've been assigned to one of those detachments."

That was enough spying for Isabela. With a telepathic nudge, she pushed Archibald's folder off the table. With an annoyed grunt, the colonel bent to pick up the papers, and Isabela ducked out the door.

With as many times as she'd snuck off campus, Isabela knew the layout of the Peacekeepers' base well. The mess hall, the barracks, the armory, the fence that cordoned off the Academy, the gatehouse that led to the road and the outside world, and the private trailer where Archibald stayed.

Pff. If Isabela was a big-shot army guy, she would've demanded a much nicer house.

As everyone was in the briefing, no one noticed Halima Ouma approach Archibald's trailer. Isabela popped the flimsy lock with her telekinesis and slipped inside.

The colonel's abode was as dull as Isabela expected. His bed was made with such tight precision that Isabela imagined she could hear the mattress squeaking in anguish from the choking hospital corners. There were four books stacked on the nightstand, all of them biographies of US presidents. The man's vitamins were lined up in a row ordered by size next to the trailer's small sink. The entire room smelled like piney aftershave. Archibald's laptop sat on the dust-free linoleum-topped table next to a tin of unsalted peanuts.

Isabela powered up the laptop—background a waving American flag, of course—and inserted into the port the USB drive Lexa had given her. Immediately, some computer stuff started to happen—numbers and progress bars, that kind of crap. Lexa had told Isabela that all she needed to do was plug the drive in for a few minutes and let it do its work.

In the meantime, Isabela ruffled Archibald's bedcovers. Because why not?

The portable drive emitted a sharp beep when it finished mirroring Archibald's hard drive. Isabela slipped it back in her pocket, paused, went on the internet, found an image of some hot guys playing volleyball in very small eighties bathing suits, and changed Archibald's desktop wallpaper.

"Mission accomplished," she said to herself.

Isabela popped out of Archibald's trailer and immediately bumped into a soldier rushing towards the mess hall. Both of them nearly fell over from the collision. Isabela cringed. She should've peeked out of the trailer first. Was this what Professor Nine meant when he called her impetuous?

"Ouch, Halima, damn," the soldier said, rubbing his face where it had clipped Isabela's shoulder. He was young, American, his uniform sloppy. The name on his chest read *Pvt. Rhodes*. "You late for the briefing, too? My asshole bunkmates turned off my alarm."

Isabela formed Halima's lips into a sheepish smile. "Yes," she said. "I overslept, too."

"Well, let's . . ." Rhodes trailed off. He squinted at Isabela, realizing where she'd been coming out of. "Wait. What were you doing in the XO's . . . ?"

Isabela grabbed Rhodes's upper arm and squeezed. "Please, don't say anything," she said. "It was just a fling and I don't want to get Ray in trouble."

Rhodes looked supremely uncomfortable, like he regretted ever bumping into Halima. Isabela smiled inwardly. Good thing that she'd picked a woman to impersonate. It wouldn't have been so easy to explain away her carelessness if she'd been posing as a male soldier sneaking out of the colonel's trailer.

"Hi, guys!"

The awkward silence between Halima and Rhodes was broken by Caleb's chipper greeting. Not Caleb, Isabela could tell immediately, but one of his duplicates. The clone stood there with its unblinking stare, grinning stupidly at the two soldiers.

"I'm Caleb's sense of adventure and spontaneity," the duplicate declared. "Do you guys want to shoot some guns or something?"

Rhodes took a cautious step back from the clone. Before he or Isabela could say anything, the real Caleb appeared on the other side of the fence, waving his arms.

"Hey, sorry!" Caleb called. "I lost control of that one."

Isabela grabbed the duplicate by the arm. "I'll escort this . . . thing back to campus," she said to Rhodes. "You can still make the briefing."

Rhodes nodded, relieved to be away from both Halima and Caleb. The clone went silent as Isabela walked it towards the nearby gate where Caleb waited. Isabela ground her teeth, not wanting her annoyance with Caleb to show.

"Escorting this stray back to campus," Isabela said to the Peacekeepers at the gate.

They waved her through. Caleb absorbed his duplicate and sulked alongside Halima until they were out of sight of the gate. Only then did Isabela shape-shift back into her true form. They walked back to campus side by side, like they were just out for a stroll.

"I had that under control," Isabela said sharply.

"Oh," Caleb replied, rubbing the back of his neck. "I thought that soldier was going to bust you. Figured I could provide a distraction."

"I had a juicy cover story all ready to go," Isabela said, her eyes shining. "The boring-ass colonel is having a secret affair with Halima."

"Um, that would be really inappropriate," Caleb countered. "You could get Archibald in a lot of trouble if that got out."

Isabela rolled her eyes. "Don't be so uptight. Besides, if we find out he's the mole, the dirty rumors I made up will be the least of his worries."

"I don't think Archibald's our guy," Caleb said.

"Of course not. You love your army men."

Caleb frowned at that. "Just because I grew up on a base doesn't mean I think everyone in a uniform is a saint. But my uncle told me when I first came here that Archibald was a good man. That I could trust him."

"This is the same uncle who Nigel curses to this day because he stole his pet raccoon?"

"Our Chimæra, yeah," Caleb replied, looking off into the distance. "They needed to quarantine them, I guess. Not saying my uncle's always right but . . ."

"And this is the same uncle who pulled some strings so you can go home for Christmas this year while the rest of us are stuck here," Isabela added.

"I didn't ask for that," Caleb replied. "I don't even *want* to go home."

"Sure."

Caleb looked over at her like he might defend himself further. Instead, he blew out a sigh and fell silent. The two of them walked back to the dorms without speaking. Isabela wasn't sure why she felt the need to pick on Caleb so much. He'd just been trying to help and she even agreed with him—Archibald probably wasn't the mole. He was too boring for that.

"Well, sorry I got in your way back there," Caleb said flatly when they reached the dorms.

"Apology accepted," Isabela replied with a huff.

Caleb trudged into the dorms while Isabela continued on towards the faculty building to deliver the USB drive to Lexa. She pursed her lips, feeling bad for how she'd spoken to him. Oh well. He'd get over it. Hopefully.

"This teamwork shit," Isabela muttered, "is not for me."

CHAPTER FIVE

NIGEL BARNABY
HEALTH AND WELLNESS OFFICE
THE HUMAN GARDE ACADEMY—POINT REYES, CALIFORNIA

THE NIGHTMARE ALWAYS STARTED THE SAME. NIGEL was barefoot, in the cozy pajama pants he used to wear as a kid, his arms shoved inside his T-shirt sleeves and crossed over his stomach to keep warm. His breath misted in a cloud in front of his face. His toes were numb, but he could still feel the brittle ice beneath him, cracking and buckling with his every step.

He was back in Iceland. Out on that frozen lake.

Nigel looked over his shoulder. There should've been land behind him, a cabin, but there was nothing. Nothing except for ice in all directions.

So, he staggered onwards, unable to do anything else. His teeth chattered. The sound of the ice snapping echoed in his ears. A snow flurry blew across his face and he could feel snot frozen to his upper lip.

There were shadows in front of him. People, barely visible in the gloom. If he could just make it to them . . .

But then he heard their voices, their cruel laughter. Mocking him for his stupid pants. They were the boys from the Pepperpont Young Gentlemen's Preparatory Academy. His old school, the one he'd left behind when the invasion happened, when he leaped at the opportunity to become someone else. The old dread came over him. He wanted to hide, but there was nowhere to go.

They were coming towards him now. Some of them brandished lacrosse sticks and riding crops.

Nigel gritted his teeth to stop them from chattering. He wasn't weak anymore. He had Legacies. But somehow, he knew, they wouldn't work out here. Not on the ice. He couldn't decide whether to run back the way he had come or submit to whatever humiliations the prep schoolers had in mind.

It was in that moment of painful indecision that Nigel fell. Always the same. The ice parted underneath him and the dark water swallowed him up, freezing cold as it rushed into his lungs.

"And then I wake up, gasping for breath," he told Dr. Linda. "What do you make of that, eh? Used to be I dreamt about cool shit, like the one where I'm running round the burbs, busting windows with Siouxsie Sioux."

Dr. Linda stared at him blankly, her pen poised over her notebook.

"Siouxsie Sioux?" Nigel reiterated, aghast. "Siouxsie and the Banshees? Bloody hell, Linds, weren't you alive in the seventies?"

"Yes, Nigel, I was alive."

"Don't sound like it," Nigel replied. "Anyway, what're we going to do about these nightmares?" He ran the back of his hand across his pockmarked cheek. "Not getting my beauty sleep."

Nigel sunk deeper into the cozy couch in Dr. Linda's office, his gaze flitting around the room. Her office was cluttered with tchotchkes from all over the world; the little objects served as conversation pieces for Dr. Linda to break the ice with some of the foreign students. On the walls were variations of the same multicolored splotchy painting, which, considering Nigel still had to come here at least once a week, he was totally sick of looking at.

"It isn't unusual for two traumatic experiences to bleed into each other, particularly when they share a unifying theme—"

"Huh?"

"Your experience in Iceland and your background at the prep school," Linda explained patiently. "There are similarities."

"What're you on about?" Nigel replied. "Buncha pricks who tormented me for years got nothing to do with drowning."

"Is it the drowning that frightens you?"

"Drowning sucks, don't it? I was playing would-you-rather

the other night with the lads and we had total agreement that we'd all rather burn to death. You'd think that would hurt more, right?"

"Nigel."

"But the thing of it is, you pass out from the smoke long before your actual skin gets to roasting."

"Okay, Nigel. That's lovely." Dr. Linda sighed. "The point I'm trying to make is that, despite your close call, you don't have anxiety about drowning."

"Says you," Nigel replied. He put his combat boots up on the coffee table. He'd been meeting with Dr. Linda often enough that this no longer got even a raised eyebrow from the woman.

"The similarity, Nigel, is your feeling of powerlessness," Dr. Linda said.

"Whoa now. Aren't we skipping the part of the therapy where you ask me what I think the connection is and gradually lead me to that conclusion?"

Dr. Linda smiled dryly. "I've learned that a direct approach works better with you."

Nigel gazed out the window, the California sky crisp and blue, bright even in this so-called winter. He made a fist and kissed the first knuckle, thinking it all over.

"That why I'm thinking about revenge all the time? Against those assholes from Pepperpont once in a while, but more often against that fancy-dressing mind-boy who brainwashed me?"

"Revenge, I think, can be a lot like thin ice, Nigel," Dr.

Linda said. "It won't hold you up for long."

"Wow, Linda, that's a heroic reach for that metaphor, eh?" Nigel turned and smiled coldly at her. "Thing I still can't figure, all these weeks later, is how that Icelandic wanker knew so much about me."

Dr. Linda met Nigel's eyes for a moment, then looked down at her notebook. She tapped her pen thoughtfully.

"If you're truly having trouble sleeping, I could prescribe you something."

"Now we're talking, love. Something that I can get a solid buzz off, yeah?"

She looked at him levelly over the rim of her glasses. "Obviously not."

"Then never mind," Nigel said with a wave of his hand. "I'm right as rain, Linds. As always."

◇ ◇ ◇

Nigel had been suspicious for weeks. After the first time he had the nightmare—Einar and the Pepperpont boys, the great villains of his life uniting to torment him in the middle of the night—he'd lain awake wondering.

How did Einar know?

The thing was, Nigel actually liked Dr. Linda. He'd felt dumb for spilling his guts to her, but it was nice to have an adult take an interest. So, he'd buried that suspicion. Hadn't wanted to believe.

Not until they were sure the mole was one of the administrators. Once they knew that, there was no way to keep denying it. He didn't need to make a copy of her hard drive or hack her email like the others were doing with Greger and Archibald.

Nigel could see the guilt in Dr. Linda's eyes.

In the empty hallway outside her office, Nigel clenched his fists and let loose a scream. With his Legacy, he could've amped that scream up loud enough to break all the windows on the floor. Instead, he muted himself. The rush of air left his lungs soundlessly—all the catharsis of shouting, none of the noise.

He knew.

That night, beneath the training center, Nigel stood in front of their board of clues and suspects, glaring at Dr. Linda's picture.

"Lady looks me right in the eye," Nigel growled. "Right in the eye and pretends she doesn't know."

"Did you give it away?" Ran asked. "You are talking like you gave it away."

"No," Nigel said sharply. "At least, I don't think so. Not bloody easy for me to be so chipper with her."

"I know."

"Like to scream at her smug ass until she goes flying out her window."

"Perhaps," Ran said evenly, "that would be too far."

"Evil crone," Nigel grumbled. He grabbed a marker and doodled devil horns on Dr. Linda's forehead. "Gotta sit there and let her bloody *treat* me when . . ." He shook his head. "Think she even cares that her big mouth about got me killed?

Not to mention the violation of her freaking sacred oath!"

Ran bumped her shoulder against Nigel's affectionately. Her voice was as coolly dispassionate as ever. "I know it isn't easy, but we must maintain appearances. We can do more harm to our enemies when they think we are ignorant."

"Bloody Sun Tzu over here," Nigel replied. "*You* didn't almost drown."

"No. I was only shot in the leg by a sniper and then had my chest compacted by telekinesis." Ran eyed him. "Also, Sun Tzu was Chinese, but I have read his book. It's a little dry."

"Yeah, yeah," Nigel replied, and he smiled in his wild way at Ran. "I'm just saying, I'm not a revenge-served-cold type'a bloke. I like it hot and I like it often."

"Mhm, we know," Ran replied, used to Nigel's bravado.

Their group gathered once again around the conference table. The data they had hijacked from Archibald and Greger came back clean. Lexa, meanwhile, had simply been able to hack Dr. Chen's email and hard drive without any assistance from the students—Chen had the lax data protection of an innocent person. That left only Dr. Linda, who Nigel laid out the case against, limiting his curse words as much as possible.

When Nigel was finished, Nine looked over at Malcolm and Lexa.

"I'm sold," he said. "But then, I've been told that I don't always think things all the way through. What do you two think?"

Malcolm grimaced. "I really wish it wasn't her, but the evidence seems to add up."

Lexa nodded in agreement. "I think it's time for phase two," she said.

"Let's see how Linda handles a terrible student who wants to escape the Academy," Nine said.

All of them turned as one to look at Taylor.

She slouched in her chair just like Nigel had showed her, eyes drooping like she was about to fall asleep, loudly chewing gum. With a toss of her hair, she sat up slightly, glaring at her friends.

"You bitches talking about me?" Taylor asked.

CHAPTER SIX

TAYLOR COOK
THE HUMAN GARDE ACADEMY—POINT REYES, CALIFORNIA

Dear Taylor . . .

. . . hope this letter finds you well . . .

. . . give us a second chance . . .

*By saving one life, you have saved thousands
more.*

I look forward to working with you again . . .

A letter of apology. The Foundation had sent her a freaking letter of apology, one that doubled as a come-on. Taylor couldn't believe the nerve of these people. They had kidnapped her and almost gotten her friends killed, and their response was to break out the good stationery and calligraphy pens.

Taylor still remembered the anger she felt that day, weeks

ago. She'd burst into Nine's office and practically thrown the letter at him. She wanted to do something. Anything.

"They've got moles here," Taylor said. "Maybe we should get some there."

"How do you suggest we do that?"

"Let me go back," Taylor replied. "Let them recruit me. I'll be a double agent."

Nine leaned back in his chair, toying with one of the joints on his mechanical arm. "You're a student. Not even graduated to Earth Garde. I can't assign you some dangerous mission."

Taylor stared at him. "Seriously? But you said—"

Nine held up his hands. "Okay, you talked me into it. If Malcolm asks, we argued about it for way longer before you wore me down. We need a plan, though. Two plans. One to keep you safe and one to make the Foundation believe you really want to be there. Because if you run away again and let them scoop you up, they might not believe you're really with them. You could end up like that poor kid you told us about. The vegetable."

Taylor swallowed hard at the memory of the wheelchair-bound Garde she'd met in Abu Dhabi. "I made my feelings about them pretty clear," she said. "How do we convince them that I've changed my mind?"

Nine picked up his tablet and accessed Taylor's academic record. "Let's see. Says here that your grades are good and your instructors call you a joy to have in class. You're kind to your fellow students and seem naturally predisposed to being a healer."

"So?"

"So, for starters, you're going to have to cut all that shit out," Nine said. He leaned forward. "Taylor, it's time for you to discover the dark side."

It hadn't been easy.

In the student union, two days after they decided Dr. Linda must be the mole, Taylor grimaced at her economics textbook. She couldn't figure something out. The concepts she understood—business cycles, bubbles and booms, recessions and depressions. What she couldn't wrap her head around was when she'd ever get a chance to use this information.

She glared at the first question on her homework. *Imagine that you own a supermarket . . .*

Taylor snorted. What were the odds of that happening? But okay—imagine she *did* own a supermarket. Then, if it didn't get burned to the ground by a bunch of crazy religious fundamentalists who sincerely believed Taylor was some kind of devil spawn—*big* if *there*—she could set up a kiosk in the pharmacy aisle and heal sick customers, charging them . . . oh, how about everything they owned? That would be the Foundation's business model, anyway. Maybe she should write about that. Capitalism in a post-Garde world. How to exploit Legacies for money.

A rip formed in her notebook paper where Taylor had been angrily scribbling. Taylor took a breath and set down her pen. She had always been a good student, was one of those kids who whipped through her work as soon as she got home, who asked her teachers for extra credit when assignments felt too easy. Taylor liked school, and the classes at the Human Garde Academy were more interesting and challenging than anything she had taken back in South Dakota.

But now, after weeks of tanking tests and being rude in class, even Taylor's inner thoughts were turning cynical. She couldn't look at her economics homework without feeling the whole thing was pointless.

With a tired sigh, Taylor looked up from her books. It was lunchtime, so the student union was busy. Kids from dozens of different counties carried trays of food back to tables and booths, had laughing conversations, or engaged in a telekinetic battle to change the channel on the student union's one big-screen television.

Strings of red and green lights were draped from the ceiling and wrapped around the second-floor bannisters. There were paper cutouts of candy canes and snowmen taped to the walls, and a glowing menorah in the middle of the room. Someone on the faculty had really gone all out decorating for the season.

Taylor bit the inside of her cheek. This was going to be the first Christmas she'd ever spent away from home. She tried not to imagine her dad there all by himself, but couldn't help picturing him sitting in their living room beside a droopy

Christmas tree. In this depressing fantasy, the place was trashed, her dad sitting under a broken ceiling beam while melting snow dripped through the open roof and ruined their old couch.

She shouldn't have left him there by himself.

And then, she shouldn't have involved him in their plan . . .

Taylor shook her head, forcing herself not to dwell on what was already done.

It wasn't like Taylor would be the only one stuck at the Academy for the holidays. Most of the students weren't allowed to visit home. Apparently, for security reasons, the Academy only felt comfortable letting a handful of them go, and even those lucky Garde would be bringing small armies of UN Peacekeepers with them. The students who were allowed to leave were chosen based on their Legacy control, time elapsed since their last visit, grades, and recent behavior. So if someone snuck off campus and ended up in the midst of international chaos, they probably weren't getting a trip home. Unless that someone was Caleb.

She'd heard kids crying in the dorms. The emotional breakdowns that inevitably occurred in such a high-stress environment had doubled lately. So had the lines for the phones and the public computers. Taylor wasn't the only one having a tough time, although she was the only one having a tough time *and* pretending to be a jerk who hated everyone.

"You're always staring at her."

"You should just go talk to her. I read that American girls

admire the direct approach."

"While you're there, ask her what it was like to kill people."

Taylor pretended that she couldn't hear the loudly whispered conversation taking place at the table next to hers, but her flushed cheeks gave her away. She put her head down, let some hair fall into her face and peeked over. They were a foursome of boys, none older than fifteen. They were all tweebs, meaning they'd only developed their telekinesis so far, no primary Legacy. They were the bottom rung on the Academy's social ladder and tended to stick together. Taylor was pretty sure that a couple of them had arrived at the Academy after her; she didn't even know their names. Crazy. To think that she wasn't such a newbie around here anymore, even though she'd only been here like four months.

"She didn't kill anyone," said the tweeb who the others were trying to cajole into hitting on her. "She's a *healer*."

Taylor realized that she did know that guy. His name was Miki. On her first day at the Academy, she had seen him send Isabela's old boyfriend Lofton flying across the training center. Even then, his telekinesis was rumored to be more powerful than anyone else's on campus. He was only fourteen and small for his age, barely over five feet tall, with dark hair and almond-shaped eyes. But his features had hardened a bit over the last few months, some of the Inuit boy's baby fat chiseled away. He was like king of the tweebs now, Taylor surmised.

"I'd let her heal my wounds, if you know what I'm saying," said one of the other boys.

"*Of course* she killed people, dude," said another. "They all did. They fought like a hundred of those Harvester people."

"That's not what I heard."

"What'd you hear?"

"That they got drunk in San Francisco and made up the whole Harvester thing to get out of trouble."

"You guys gossip too much," Miki said, shutting down the discussion. He flashed Taylor an apologetic smile—he knew that she'd overheard them. She sneered in response and looked away.

Hushed conversations like that tended to happen around Taylor lately. She had a reputation. The other kids called Taylor and her friends the Fugitive Six. The nickname made Taylor roll her eyes.

Suddenly, the tweeb boys stopped talking about her and got real interested in the trashy talk show on the TV. A second later, Isabela plunked a tray of food down next to Taylor's homework. A crouton bounced into the middle of her economics textbook.

"Lunch is served," Isabela said as she put her own tray down on the table and pulled out a chair. "The line was so long, I almost died of starvation. You're welcome, by the way."

Taylor flicked the crouton off her book and glanced over at the tweebs' table. If they didn't have the courage to talk to Taylor, they definitely wouldn't last a second with Isabela, and by the looks on their faces they all knew it. The dark-haired Brazilian had a more outlandish reputation around campus than Taylor. She was also known for saying whatever was on her mind, no matter how cutting.

"Those boys were straight ogling you," Isabela declared loudly. "Ogling. I learned that word today. It means gross eyeball from horny pervert."

"Close enough," Taylor replied. She nudged the plate of food Isabela had brought her. "Hey. What is this?"

Isabela smiled, always happy to practice her quickly developing English.

"Too easy," Isabela said. "That's a salad."

"No, I mean—I *know* it's a salad. Why'd you bring me it?"

Isabela shrugged. "To eat?"

"I told you when we got here that I wanted pizza."

"They were out of pizza."

Taylor looked down at Isabela's plate, where two greasy slices of extra cheese glistened. Her stomach growled.

"You've got pizza," Taylor said icily. "A *lot* of pizza."

"Yeah, but . . . how to put this?" Isabela blotted the grease off one of her slices with a napkin. "I am a shape-shifter, yes? So, there are some things I don't have to worry about. Like, for starters, I stay skinny, no matter what."

"What're you trying to say?" Taylor asked through her teeth.

"The salad is me watching out for you," Isabela replied. "You look . . . I don't know. A little puffy."

"You're saying I'm fat." Taylor's voice had gotten loud. Now the tweebs were looking at her again. So were some of the other tables.

Isabela blew out her cheeks. "Are puffy and fat the same? Maybe it's my English. Let me check my dictionary."

"I'm tired of your shit all the time," Taylor snapped at her roommate, her voice getting louder still. "It never stops."

"Fine," Isabela said, rolling her eyes. "You can have the pizza."

"It's not. About. The pizza," Taylor growled, and, with one telekinetic swipe, cleared off their entire table. The pizza flew into the tweebs, and Miki had to react quickly with a telekinetic deflection to avoid the tray bonking him in the forehead. The plate shattered on the floor, eliciting a chorus of *oohs* from the other students. Now, everyone was watching.

Good.

"*Puta, esta tu louca?*" Isabela cried sharply, her hands raised to brush flecks of sauce off her shirt.

"I dare you to say that in English," Taylor replied.

And then, before waiting for a response, Taylor used her telekinesis to shove the table out from between them. The other students jumped up and away to avoid the flying furniture. Taylor lunged forward and grabbed Isabela before she could even stand up.

There was shouting all around them now, but Taylor couldn't make out any of the words. Probably telling her to stop. She was in a tangle of limbs with Isabela—scratching and tugging at one another. Isabela tried to push her away with telekinesis, but Taylor pushed back. The pressure in the air cracked a floor tile under their feet.

In the scramble, Taylor managed to get a hand free, cock

her fist back, and punch Isabela right in the nose.

Isabela fell onto her butt with a stunned yelp, blood already coursing over her upper lip. She stared up at Taylor with wet eyes, at first too shocked and hurt to react. Then, she started bawling.

"My nose!" she cried, nasally and hard to understand. "You broke my nose!"

Taylor loomed over Isabela, her fists still clenched, not sure what to do next. Everyone was staring at her.

Right on cue, Taylor was lifted off her feet, her arms telekinetically pinned to her sides. Someone with more tele-kinetic power than she could muster had hoisted Taylor up and floated her towards the doors of the student union.

"Goddamn, Taylor. What the hell is the matter with you?"

It was Professor Nine. His face was grim as he set Tay-lor down in front of him. Nine's arms—the real one and the metallic prosthetic—were crossed over his chest. This was Nine's stern look. She stared at Nine defiantly. The student union was still mostly silent, except for the sounds of Isa-bela's snuffled sobs, everyone trying to hear what would happen with Nine.

"I asked you a question," Nine said.

"Do you aliens even understand human emotions?" Tay-lor asked with a sneer. She tossed her hair over her shoulder. "Quit pretending like you care and just send me to Dr. Linda like you always do."

"Have it your way," Nine said. "Get out of sight."

Taylor was shaking as she pushed by Nine, the whispers

of the other students following her out. She wanted to cry.

It all felt so real. Especially the anger.

"What's gotten into you, Taylor?"

"Nothing."

"Do you realize this is the third violent outburst you've had in the last month?"

"I don't know," Taylor replied, one corner of her mouth curled up in a sneer she'd gotten from Nigel. "I haven't been keeping count."

Dr. Linda tapped her pen against her chin as she studied Taylor.

"Well, I have been," she said placidly, after an agonizing few seconds of staring at Taylor. "Your teachers, your fellow students—we've all noticed, Taylor. Even if no one can precisely understand what you've been through, we all empathize. You know that we're here for you, right?"

Taylor groaned. "I know. I couldn't get away from you people if I wanted to."

"An interesting choice of words," Dr. Linda replied. "Do you want to get away, Taylor?"

Taylor stared back at the older woman in resentful silence. With her prim bob of graying hair and large-framed glasses, Dr. Linda looked more like someone's sweet aunt than a corrupt mole.

"Yes," Taylor said finally. "Now can I go?"

"It's my job to be honest with you," Dr. Linda replied.

"So that's a no."

"And I have to say, your personality has changed greatly since you first arrived here."

"Uh, yeah," Taylor replied. "Maybe because some alien entity that we humans can't even begin to comprehend gave me superpowers. Think that could have anything to do with it?"

As usual, it was impossible to get a reaction out of Dr. Linda. "All the students here have Legacies," she intoned. "Not all of them are prone to such violent outbursts, particularly not the ones like yourself, who have no history of aggression."

"Uh-huh, well, maybe it's because some shadowy organization kidnapped me and basically sold me to a Saudi prince. The geniuses at Earth Garde filled you in on that, right? They basically let it happen. Security around here sucks. Not to mention I'm just supposed to do whatever the government tells me, no questions asked—but if my family needs help? No, they don't care about that. That's outside the *purview* of the program."

"That's a lot to take in," Dr. Linda said diplomatically. "A lot of resentment."

"No shit."

Dr. Linda continued like she hadn't heard her. "I'd like us to try to get in touch with that old Taylor. I want to know what she would think about your recent behavior. Surely, back at your old school, there were conflicts with peers."

Taylor folded her hands in her lap. If she was being honest, her old school seemed like a million years ago. Her normal friends without Legacies . . . she could hardly picture them anymore.

"Yeah," Taylor replied. "Okay. So?"

"Would you have ever resolved one of those conflicts by hitting someone in the face?"

Taylor looked down at her hand, where the knuckles were scuffed and raw. She touched the reddened skin and healed herself—a brief pulse of warm energy in her fingers, a cold draining exertion deep in her stomach. The give-and-take of using her Legacy.

"I didn't even hit her that hard," Taylor said sullenly.

"Before our next session, I want you to really reflect on who you were before coming to the Academy," Dr. Linda concluded, closing the notebook in her lap. "I want you to think about that old Taylor and tell me what you miss about her and what she might think about who you've become."

Taylor rolled her eyes. "I don't need to think about that," she said. "I already know."

"Oh?"

"I never wanted Legacies and I never wanted to come here," Taylor said measuredly. "The old Taylor was too chickenshit to say anything. I just went with the flow and did what you people told me. And look what that's gotten me. Imprisoned here, basically. My dad's whole life ruined—"

"I heard about the difficulties with your father," Dr. Linda said. "Some things are beyond even a Garde's control, Taylor. We could talk about that—"

"All you people ever do is talk. Talk and train me to be

one of your foot soldiers." Taylor shook her head. "It's crazy, but you know what I realized not too long ago? I was probably better off with those Foundation people. I could've had a nice house and enough money to take care of my dad and I wouldn't have to clean the cafeteria as a life lesson or spend another minute with your lame ass."

Dr. Linda leaned back. "I see," she said evenly.

Had she bought it? Taylor couldn't be sure. But the trap was set.

That night, beneath the training center, Taylor sheepishly endured a standing ovation from her friends.

"Yes, yes, everyone clap for the pizza bully," Isabela said with mock dismay. Her eyes were purple with bruises, a bandage over the bridge of her nose. "Ignore poor Isabela and her devastating injury."

"Bravo!" Nigel yelled. "The whole bloody Academy's talking about you two! Isabela, you've never looked lovelier."

Isabela smiled sarcastically at the scrawny Brit. "All for effect, dum-dum," she said, and the bruises melted away, her pretty face restored as she shape-shifted. Even though she'd changed her appearance, Isabela's voice was still nasally, her breath whistling in her nose.

Cringing, Taylor wrapped Isabela in a hug. "Are you okay?" she asked. "Let me fix it."

Isabela brushed her hands away. "I've had worse," she replied. "Save it for tomorrow. You can heal me in peer mediation and we'll have a good cry."

"I'm so sorry, Isabela."

"Psh . . . please. You should really be apologizing to poor Professor Nine. His face when you called him an alien!"

"An *emotionless* alien," Nine corrected, from where he sat at the head of the conference table.

Taylor lolled her head back in disbelief. "It was all part of the act—"

"Words hurt, Cook," Nine replied with a wink. "That's all I'm going to say about it. Words hurt."

"This man-baby," Isabela said scornfully, waving a hand at Nine. "I can't believe Earth Garde would put such a whiner in charge."

Lexa and Malcolm exchanged a look at that and both of them burst out laughing. Nine simply glared at Isabela and she glared right back. Kopano finally broke in, pulling out the chair next to him so Taylor could sit down.

"So, tell us, tell us," he said, smiling at Taylor. "Did Dr. Linda buy it?"

"I might've laid it on a little thick," Taylor told Kopano and the others. "But I think I definitely got across how much I hate it here. Hinted that I liked it better when I was with the Foundation."

Lexa tapped her computer screen. "Linda already filed her incident report. She mentions that you're feeling isolated and angry. Conveniently leaves out any mention of the Foundation."

"All we can do now is wait for them to approach you again," Nine said.

"I hope it happens soon," Taylor replied, pushing a hand through her hair. "It's not easy being disruptive and grumpy all the time." She looked at Nigel. "I don't know how you do it."

"Hey! Disruptive, maybe . . . but I am *not* grumpy."

"What if they don't come for Taylor?" Ran asked. "What if we've been wrong about Dr. Linda?"

"We are *not* wrong about Linda," Nigel stated.

Nine blew out a sigh and glanced over his shoulder at their board of leads and suspects. "Then we keep hunting, keep digging, until we find another way in."

"And if the Foundation does come?" Caleb asked, with a sidelong look at Taylor. "We're sure it'll be safe?"

"The hero's journey is never totally safe," Kopano interjected, putting one of his hands on Taylor's shoulder. "But she can handle it."

Taylor looked up at him and rolled her eyes. "God, you're corny."

Malcolm leaned forward to answer Caleb. "We've taken precautions. We'll be prepared this time."

"What about the other Loric?" Caleb asked. "Couldn't they help with this?"

"Six is doing what she can," Nine said. "As for John, Marina, and Ella—I don't know what the hell they've been up to. Some secret project. We're on our own."

"I thought there were others," Kopano said.

"No," Nine replied brusquely. "All the others are dead."

The meeting broke up shortly after that, the students

leaving in a trickle to sneak back to the dorms. Even though Taylor had to wake up early for chores—she'd lost track of how much extra cleaning she was being forced to do for punishment—she lingered in the basement until only she and Professor Nine remained.

"Something on your mind?" he asked.

Taylor looked down at her hands. "It's hard, you know? Pretending I don't like it here. Acting like I hate my friends. I don't actually mean any of that stuff."

"We know that, Cook."

"But sometimes, I feel so angry, like really angry," Taylor continued. "And I'm worried that I'm screwing my whole life up for nothing."

"We're doing the right thing," Nine replied. He put a hand on her shoulder, realized it was his cold, mechanical one, and switched it up. "The world will be a better place when we're finished, Taylor. I promise. It'll all work out."

She looked up at him, uncertainty in her eyes. "It better."

CHAPTER SEVEN

TAYLOR COOK
THE HUMAN GARDE ACADEMY—PORT REYES, CALIFORNIA

A KEY PART OF THE FUGITIVE SIX'S PLAN HAD nothing to do with the Academy. It was the piece that made Taylor feel sick to her stomach whenever she thought about it, especially since she was the one to suggest the idea. She had made it happen. If their plan failed to bust the Foundation, she'd have sacrificed a lot for nothing.

And the sacrifices weren't all hers.

About a month ago, her dad had come to visit.

"You sure you want to do this?" Professor Nine had asked.

Taylor took a deep breath, steeling herself. "I'm sure I want to get the Foundation. But this part of it?" She shook her head. "No. I'm not sure at all."

It was the Tuesday after Thanksgiving. Taylor bit her lip,

thinking about how she'd almost forgotten to call her dad last week. When she first came to the Academy, she'd called him every chance she got. As she settled in and got used to her strange situation, Taylor scaled back the calls to like once a week. And then—well, she obviously couldn't call her dad from Iceland, where she'd been kidnapped to, but, even after that, she was calling less.

"How much did you tell him?" Nine asked. "About what happened to you?"

"You probably already know. Don't you guys record all those conversations?"

"Pft, you think I want to listen to that shit?" Nine scoffed. "Not enough hours in the day."

The two of them sat on a picnic table in the visitation area outside the Academy. There were a few quaint little cottages spread out here, all of them stocked with food and board games and outdoor activities like baseball gloves and Frisbees. The area gave off a campground vibe. It reeked of normalcy—that is, if one didn't look south, to where the UN Peacekeepers kept their barracks, an assortment of military-grade trucks and even a tank parked there. This is where parents came to visit. Tours of the Academy itself were possible, but because of security concerns, they were rarely approved. Taylor sometimes wondered whether the administration was trying to protect the Academy's secrets from the parents or protect the fragile human parents from the volatile Garde housed there. Probably a little of both.

"I haven't told him anything," Taylor said to Nine. "What

would I say? That I got kidnapped by some psycho rich people, then rescued, and some of my friends almost died? That these same kidnappers got back in contact with me by hiding a letter in with the ones sent from my old school? That they want me back like I just finished a summer internship or something and I'm a top recruit? That I actually want to take them up on their offer, so that I can be like an undercover agent? That these Foundation monsters are probably watching him and might try to use him as leverage? No." Taylor took a breath. "Of course I didn't say anything."

"For the best." Nine grunted.

Taylor frowned. "I used to tell him everything. The first thing I ever hid from my dad was my Legacies, and that barely lasted a week." She shook her head. "It's weird. He can tell I'm holding something back."

Nine fiddled with the joints on his cybernetic hand. Taylor watched him out of the corner of her eye. She hadn't known Nine for long, but already Taylor recognized how he could get awkward and flustered whenever he tried to go into heart-to-heart mode.

"It can be tough when parents are involved," Nine said. "I mean—I wouldn't know, personally, but I can imagine. We don't have to do this part, not if you don't want to."

Taylor pushed a hand through her hair. "It'll be temporary," she said. "That's what I keep telling myself."

"Right," Nine said. "Your dad sounds like a cool dude. He'd probably be proud if he knew what you were doing."

"Proud and freaked out. Or miserable and lonely. Maybe all the above."

Taylor rubbed her forearm, feeling the skin where there should have been a scar. She'd had a minor surgery last week, performed by Lexa and Dr. Goode under the training center. She had healed the wound herself, but it still felt off.

"That feel okay?" Nine asked.

"Yeah. Just . . . weird, I guess."

Nine flexed his metal arm. "You'll get used to it."

Some movement on the road leading into the barracks drew Taylor's attention. It was beyond strange to see her dad's dented brown pickup truck rolling through a security checkpoint. The context was all wrong.

Taylor stood up, feeling a little dazed.

"I'll be over here if you need me to, uh, hop in and be all official or whatever," Nine said.

"I'm good, thanks," Taylor replied over her shoulder, crossing the grass to where her dad had parked.

There he was. Her dad looked a little road weary, his beard grown in, his hair messy, but he grinned when he saw Taylor. She ran the last few steps to him and he wrapped her in a hug, smoothed her hair down, and kissed her forehead. For a minute, Taylor felt like a little girl again.

Her dad held her out at arm's length. "Look at you. Wow."

"Come on, Dad," she said. "It hasn't been *that* long."

"I know, I know. But you've changed," he replied, studying her. "Can't quite say how, exactly. It's good, though. You look like . . . well, like a young lady I'd choose to protect the planet, I suppose."

"Oh, stop," Taylor said. She took her dad by the elbow. "You hungry? All these cabins have food. I could make you something."

Her dad took a deep breath and puffed out his chest. "Feels good to stretch my legs, actually. Air is nice out here. I've never been to California."

So they walked around the grounds. The Academy and the surrounding barracks and visitors' center were built on a former nature preserve, so there were plenty of woodsy trails for them to hike along.

She told him about her classes, her training of her powers at the hospital, and about her friends. All things that they'd covered before on her phone calls, back when they were more regular. In turn, he brought her up to speed on the dreadfully mundane lives of her cousins, on the TV shows they used to watch together, and on the condition of the farm.

"Those Harvesters really tore up the fields," he said. "Kind of ironic. They'd make terrible farmers." He shook his head. "The government was nice enough to clear away all the wreckage they left behind, but they still set me back some. Figure if I tighten my belt and subsist on microwave dinners for the winter, I should get through well enough."

"You're already hurting for money," Taylor mumbled, half in thought.

"Well, I wouldn't say I'm hurting. Just going to be a lean season—"

"No, Dad, it's okay. In fact, it's great."

Her dad raised an eyebrow. "I don't follow."

By then, the two of them had done a full circuit of a trail and returned to the main visitors' area. Nine was still hanging out by the picnic tables. He gave Taylor a discreet nod when she glanced in his direction—everything was all set.

Taylor took her dad by the elbow and led him towards one of the cabins.

"Come on, I'll explain in here," she said. "Where it's private."

"Don't seem any more private in here than out there," her dad observed once they were inside. The cabin was simple and cozy—a sofa and some chairs, a dining table, a selection of movies, none of which were rated higher than PG-13 or had anything to do with aliens. And, of course, there was a security camera in one corner. That's what her dad was focused on, his hands on his hips. The setup reminded Taylor of Einar's cabin in Iceland; perfectly comfortable and seemingly normal, but never unobserved.

"Yeah, those things are everywhere," Taylor said, looking at the camera, too. She covered her mouth as if she were yawning and whispered. "Just act normal for a second."

"Normal?" her dad replied. "I thought I *was* acting normal."

Taylor grimaced as her dad failed to follow her lead on the secretive whispering, but just then the red recording light on the security camera blinked twice. That was the signal.

She exhaled and turn to her dad. "Okay, we aren't being watched anymore."

Taylor's dad glanced from her, to the camera, and back. Taylor expected total bafflement, but instead she got her dad's bemused squint, the same one he used on a farmhand that tried to cut corners.

"So," he said, "now you're going to tell me what's going on with you, right?"

"You could tell, huh?"

"Of course I could tell. I'm your dad. You might be a Garde now with problems that I can't even begin to understand, but that doesn't mean I don't know when something's gnawing at you."

Taylor bit the inside of her cheek. "The thing is . . . there's only so much I can tell you. Um, for your own good."

"For my own good," he repeated, then lowered himself into one of the kitchen chairs. "Gosh, I better sit down for this. My daughter's gone and become a secret agent."

Taylor couldn't help but smile at that. *If he only knew.* The truth was, there was only so much Taylor *wanted* to tell her dad. It was probably better that he didn't know she'd been kidnapped, or that she was trying to return to those same kidnappers.

"There are some bad people outside the Academy, worse than the Harvesters, even . . . ," Taylor began slowly. She had rehearsed this speech earlier but was still carefully choosing her words. "They see people like me—Garde—as commodities. It's like, they want to get a monopoly on us and then charge high prices for our services. And they don't care who gets hurt in the process."

A deep frown set in across her dad's face. "Always comes down to money in this world, don't it? I imagine you'd be in high demand, being a healer and all. Some people see the miraculous and are like—hell, how can I turn a buck off this?"

"Yeah. Exactly," Taylor replied. "My professor, you saw him out there—"

"Number Nine. 'Course I saw him." Taylor raised an eyebrow, so her dad explained. "I've been doing my research on the people taking care of my daughter. Nine, he's the wild one."

"He's chilled out a lot," Taylor said with a shrug. "Anyway, he thinks these people are going to try to recruit me to their organization. He thinks they might even have spies in the Academy. We want one of their people to approach me so that we can expose them."

Her dad rubbed his jaw. "These people sound dangerous, Taylor."

"I know, but—"

"I'm sorry, you don't need to explain," her dad said, interrupting her. "I just broke a promise to myself."

"You what?"

"I promised myself that—no matter what you told me, because I knew it was going to be something—I promised myself that I wouldn't go on about how dangerous it might be. Your life is dangerous now. I saw that firsthand, when those nuts showed up on our doorstep. You'll always be my little girl, and so there's obviously a part of me that'd like nothing better than to drag you back to Turner County, government contracts be damned, lock you up on the farm, and keep you safe forever."

Taylor smiled sadly, "There's a part of me that'd like to go."

Her dad wagged a finger at her. "Maybe, but I don't think it's a very big part anymore. And that's okay. I hear it in your voice. You want to get these people."

"What they're doing is wrong, Dad," Taylor said, her voice steely. "It's disgusting."

"Well, I'd hate to be them, on the wrong side of my daughter with her mind made up. You just promise me that you and the other heroes are watching each other's backs."

"We're not heroes, Dad, but . . . yeah. I promise."

"Good," her dad said. "So, what do you need from me? How can I help?"

Taylor looked down at her feet, scuffing the wood floor. "I'm not sure you're going to like it. You can say no."

"Lay it on me."

"So the thing is, we need to give these people an in. A reason to approach me. Something they can try to bribe me with . . ."

Her dad tilted his head. "Aha. I see. Your poor dad subsisting on Hot Pockets is something these folks might use as leverage."

"Yeah," Taylor replied. "Well, it's a start, anyway . . ."

One week later in Turner County, South Dakota, two watchers waited for Brian Cook to drive his junker of a pickup truck down the country road. They were parked on the shoulder, in a nondescript wood-paneled station wagon. Nothing that would stand out. These two were pretty used to hiding in plain sight.

"There he is," said the guy in the passenger seat, pointing at Brian's passing truck.

"Right on time," his partner answered. She sat behind the steering wheel, her blond hair bundled under a thick woolen hat. If Mr. Cook noticed them there, waiting for him to leave his farm, he didn't acknowledge the fact. She waited until Cook's truck was out of sight, then opened her door. "Come on. Let's go on foot, just in case someone's watching."

Outside the car, the guy rubbed his hands together, breath misting in front of him. "Geez, could we maybe get a mission somewhere tropical next?"

She smirked at him. "Here," she said, holding out her hand. "You know the drill."

"Never get tired of this either."

As soon as he took her hand, she turned them both invisible.

Six and Sam trudged across frozen mud as they moved away from the highway, eventually crossing into Mr. Cook's fields. Five minutes later and the little house Taylor had grown up in came into view, along with the barn. They had it on good authority that the barn was empty of animals. Mr.

Cook had sold off his horses and pigs to make ends meet that winter.

"I have to say it," Sam declared. "This is a far cry from saving the world."

Six snorted. "No shit. But Nine says it'll help him with their Foundation problem. The guy's cool with it. He knows it's coming. Anything irreplaceable he was supposed to have gotten out of the house."

Sam shook his invisible head. "Just dark days, Six. One day you're defeating a hostile alien race bent on world domination and the next you're wrecking some poor schmuck's house. Shit. Do they even get tornadoes in winter?"

Six raised her free hand, and the sky over Mr. Cook's barn began to darken.

"They do now."

CHAPTER EIGHT

"WHAT ABOUT THIS?" KOPANO ASKED.

Kopano emerged from his room wearing one of the outfits that his dad had picked out for him back in Lagos, when they'd been flush with cash after Kopano first developed his telekinesis. During those days, when he was working security for his father's shady delivery service, his dad had told him he needed to look more stylish. So from the Udo Okeke small-time-criminal fashion collection came a black silk shirt tucked into pleated gray pants, the buttons of the shirt unbuttoned just enough to give a sense of Kopano's muscles.

Kopano spun in a 360 and spread out his arms.

"Looks good, right?" he asked hopefully. "Very cool."

Nigel, spread out on the couch in their suite's common room, let loose with a deflating cackle.

"I hate to break this to you, mate, but you look like the bouncer at the world's douchiest nightclub in that getup. Or, at best, like a bloody gangster."

Kopano stroked his chin. "You don't mean that as a compliment."

"No!"

Kopano frowned. He phased through his clothes except for his boxer shorts and let the outfit crumple to the ground, then kicked it into a pile with the other rejects.

"You're putting too much thought into this, brother," Nigel said.

"It has to be right!" Kopano replied. "My father once told me, um . . . well, it doesn't make much sense in English. And it's kinda vulgar. But basically, the male peacock—"

"Your dad picked out those clothes for you?" Nigel interrupted. When Kopano nodded glumly at him, he went on. "Then I think we can toss his ideas in the bin along with any other silk shirts ya might got lying about."

Kopano had gotten that advice once before. On his last day in Nigeria before taking off for the Academy, his mom had told him to leave all his father's "wisdom" in Africa. His dad was, in fact, an unrepentant hustler whose frequent swings of fortune always kept Kopano and his two brothers on the verge of poverty. His mom made things work. Or, as she would say, *God provided*. That was the thing about Kopano's mother—she was very religious. Kopano suspected that she harbored beliefs similar to those of the Harvesters—that her own son and his new friends were tainted by the devil.

He knew that she prayed for his Legacies to be "cured." She told him so in her infrequent letters.

"Don't know why you want my advice on this anyway," Nigel grumbled as he poked a finger through one of the many moth-eaten holes in his thrift-store Black Flag tank top. "I'm not exactly the foremost authority on how to dress to impress a bird, eh?"

Still thinking about his parents, Kopano replied, "Wisdom can come from unlikely sources, my friend." He clapped his hands and grinned. "You have great style. I always thought so, back when I first saw you in that vision. It was like—this dude here, he is out of a movie. No one can be that cool."

Nigel smirked. "What kinda movie?"

"You know, one of those British ones where everyone is a robber and talks fast and shoots each other."

"Yeah," Nigel replied, nodding. "Yeah, cool. I'll take it. But maybe you should stop thinking about movies and appearances and all that and just try to look normal. Taylor seems like she appreciates normal."

Kopano snapped his fingers. "See? What did I tell you? Good advice."

Kopano stepped through the wall and back into his room, once again rummaging through his closet. He pulled on a worn pair of blue jeans and a green waffle-knit sweater. It's what he would've worn if this was any other day and not Christmas Eve when he had something special planned. It seemed low effort but . . .

"Not bad," Nigel said when Kopano returned to the

common room. "At least you look like yourself. And like you aren't trying to impress anybody."

"But I *am* trying to impress her," Kopano replied.

Nigel closed his eyes and massaged his eyelids. "Oi, but you don't want her *to know* you're trying to impress her."

Kopano flopped down in a chair across from Nigel. "You know, if you'd just asked Ran for me—"

"Told you, I'm not into the wingman thing," Nigel replied. "I ask Ran to ask Taylor if she'd be interested if Kopano came courting, next thing, we're in one of those boring Jane Austen novels, eh? No. Not for me. I'm staying neutral in all this."

Kopano squinted at his friend. Back in Lagos, any one of Kopano's boys would've been happy to talk him up to a girl he liked. It was expected. Of course, Nigel was much, much different from his friends back home. This wasn't the first time Nigel had mentioned "remaining neutral." Kopano still didn't understand what exactly he meant. Who did Nigel have to stay neutral for? It's not like Kopano was in some kind of war.

Before Kopano could say anything more, the door to Caleb's room opened and he came out with a duffel bag tossed over one shoulder. He nodded to them both and set the bag down with a sigh. Caleb had been much more social since they'd all run off together and nearly gotten killed. Kopano had also noticed a sharp decline in the amount of behind-closed-doors conversations Caleb had with his various duplicates. Despite the newfound friendliness, Caleb always seemed to get quiet when Kopano would bring up his crush on Taylor. Kopano had heard that some Americans could be kind of prudish. He chalked it up to that.

And anyway, it struck Kopano that Caleb had a lot on his mind the last few weeks. He was, after all, one of the few students who was allowed to visit home for the holidays, even if just for a couple of days. The Fugitive Six were all still on probation for their escape from campus, so it must have been true what everyone said about Caleb—his uncle, the retired general who helped save the world, got him preferential treatment.

"Guess it's time for me to go," Caleb said with a forlorn look down at his bag.

"Are you excited?" Kopano asked with raised eyebrows, even though it was obvious Caleb was far from it. "When's the last time you saw your family?"

Caleb thought about it. "After the invasion, I guess, but before the Academy opened." He glanced at Nigel. "Back when they had us basically quarantined."

"Fun times, those," Nigel said dryly.

"Such a long time!" Kopano replied. "You must miss them."

Caleb thought that over for a second. "Actually, I'd kinda gotten used to them not being around. Easier to . . . I don't know. Not think about them?"

"Shit, my parentals haven't even sent me a holiday card," Nigel said. "And that's the way I prefer it."

"Are they bad people?" Kopano asked Caleb. He knew enough about Nigel's parents from the stories he told about them shuffling him off to boarding school and forgetting about him, but Caleb hardly talked about his family. The only thing Kopano really knew was that they were all in the military and very strict.

"No," Caleb answered quickly. "No, they're fine. They're just . . ." He shrugged. "It's hard to explain."

"I'm jealous," Kopano replied. "You get to go home and show your family what a tremendous Garde you've become. If I was you, I'd be strutting around Nebraska like I owned the place."

Caleb shook his head. "I'm not really a . . . strutter."

"You'll be fine, mate," Nigel said, sounding as sincere as he ever did. He stood up and awkwardly embraced Caleb, which seemed to surprise both of them. "Don't let 'em get to you. And don't bottle anything up. That's when the trouble starts, eh?"

"Yeah, it's only a couple of days," Caleb reminded himself. "Anyway, what're you guys going to do for the holiday break?"

"Four whole days without classes—ol' Professor Nine's so generous," Nigel replied. "Probably sleep a bunch. Maybe work on my guitar."

He said that last bit with a wink at Caleb, and the duplicator smiled back conspiratorially. Kopano knew the two of them were working on some music project upstairs in the empty suites, but he hadn't been asked to join, so he didn't stick his nose in.

"I am going to cook Christmas rice," Kopano declared.

"And, if I'm lucky, some romance."

Nigel clapped a hand over Kopano's face. "Never say that again."

Caleb swallowed, looking at them. "Oh, you hanging out with, uh, Taylor . . . ?"

Kopano nodded. "If everything goes as plan— Uh, Caleb?"

Caleb's face had gone literally blurry, like a transparent copy had been placed over him but not quite lined up. It was a duplicate trying to emerge from his body. Caleb squinted and, before the clone could pop fully loose, it evaporated like a ghost. Kopano and Nigel eyed him as he scratched sheepishly at the back of his neck.

"Nerves, I guess," Caleb explained. He glanced at the wall clock and picked up his bag. "I better get going. You know how security gets when you keep the helicopter waiting."

"Happy Christmas!" Kopano yelled, and wrapped Caleb up in a hug, slapping his back.

"Yeah," Caleb replied. "You, too."

◇ ◇ ◇

The week before, Kopano had been aghast when he'd first seen the dining hall's holiday menu. A boring turkey dinner? Basically the same turkey dinner they had served a month ago for American Thanksgiving? That wouldn't do at all.

"Where is the rice?" Kopano asked anyone who would listen. "How can they not serve Christmas rice?"

Most of the other students looked baffled when he complained about the rice, but Dr. Chen had taken an interest. Kopano was in her cultural relativity seminar that semester—the class was meant to help them understand the wide variety of UN communities they'd be assisting once they were full-fledged Earth Garde. Everyone needed to take it before graduating.

"This might be a good opportunity to learn about each other's cultures," she said. "I could probably arrange something with the kitchen staff . . ."

And she had. Over the last week, students were allowed to file ingredient requests and sign up for time in the kitchen, where they could then prepare a traditional dish from their homeland that would be shared by the other students on Christmas. Doing so was good for extra credit in Dr. Chen's class, assuming they also gave a short presentation on the food's significance.

"Psh, extra credit." Isabela had rolled her eyes when Kopano told her about the concept. "What does *that* matter? Like these silly grades will ever mean anything."

But not everyone was as cynical as Isabela. A handful of other students signed up for kitchen time, including some who weren't even in Dr. Chen's class.

Christmas Eve was Kopano's turn in the kitchen. He was happy to take one of the later slots, when things would be quiet and peaceful. Conveniently, after her staged altercation with Isabela, Kopano knew that Taylor would be just finishing up her shift cleaning the dining hall not long after he was to begin.

So Kopano worked slowly. In one pot he cooked a whole chicken seasoned with curry, thyme, and onions. Next to that, he fried up two purple slices of beef liver, which would get cubed up and added to the rice. The chewy bits of meat were always Kopano's favorite part of the dish, but some of the other students in class had made grossed-out faces when he mentioned liver.

"That kind of reaction," Dr. Chen explained, "is exactly why we have this class."

Still, Kopano wanted to get the liver part done before Taylor showed up. He didn't want to gross her out.

Kopano looked over his shoulder to where the gift he'd gotten for Taylor sat on a clean counter, far enough away to avoid catching any grease spatters. He swallowed back his nerves, worried again that she would think it was stupid— his romance adviser Nigel probably would've called it lame, which was why Kopano had made a point of not showing him.

While the liver cooked, Kopano let his eyes wander to the dishes his classmates had made. Most of them had gone with desserts. Simon, the French guy who could transfer his knowledge through objects, apparently had some secret pastry-chef skills. He'd made something called *la bûche de Noël*—it looked to Kopano like a giant Ho Ho surrounded by little mushrooms made of frosting. He started to pick a piece of frosting loose from the top but turned his hand transparent at the last second, resisting the urge. What would it look like if Taylor came in and found him scarfing down all these desserts?

Well, maybe they could just turn it into her latest act of rebellion.

Ever since this plan to infiltrate the Foundation kicked off, Kopano had been seeing less of Taylor. He knew that she needed to seem isolated, even from the other Fugitive Six, if they were going to convince the Foundation to approach her again. The shady organization had to think it was their idea, like they were rescuing Taylor from a life she hated. But that didn't make it easier for Kopano. He and Taylor had arrived at the Academy together, had always relied on each other—it was easy to forget that Taylor was just acting and to start to feel like they'd really drifted apart.

And what would happen if this plan actually worked? The Foundation would take Taylor and then . . . what? Kopano would be stuck back at the Academy, with nothing to do but hope things turned out okay. Professor Nine insisted they had agents in the field who could watch over Taylor, people he trusted, but that didn't make Kopano feel much better. It was a dangerous idea, one he probably wouldn't have gone along with if it hadn't been Taylor's plan to begin with.

Kopano was deep in thought, chopping onions and occasionally wiping his runny eyes on his shoulder sleeve, when a voice startled him.

"I always knew you were a big softie, but those are a *lot* of tears . . ."

Taylor stood in the doorway, watching him with a tired smile. She wore a plaid shirt with the sleeves rolled up and a tank top along with a formfitting pair of jeans. Her blond hair was held back by a bandanna. Even though she was pushing a bucket of dirty water with a mop, the sight of

Taylor made Kopano's mouth go dry. She looked beautiful even when she'd spent the last few hours cleaning up spilled food.

"It's the onions," he insisted with a defiant sniffle. "The onions. I swear."

"Uh-huh," Taylor replied. She used her telekinesis to send her mop and bucket into the adjacent supply closet, then wandered over to Kopano. "What kind of weird cookies are you making that have onions in them?"

"I'm not making cookies," Kopano answered with a dismissive wave of his knife. "I'm making Christmas rice."

"Oh. Everybody else made desserts." Taylor poked around one of the nearby shelves, stuck her hand under a piece of wax paper, and pulled out a chunk of baklava.

"You think just because now you're the Academy's resident bad girl you can raid the kitchen whenever you want and devour the hard work of your classmates, eh?"

Taylor chewed thoughtfully. "Yep. You want one?"

"Obviously."

Taylor reached back to the tray and pulled out another cookie, then floated it out in front of Kopano's face.

"You know," Taylor began with a crafty smile, "Isabela says you're one of my stalkers."

About to bite into the cookie, Kopano let out a sharp cough and had to turn his head away. He took a moment to compose himself while Taylor tried to stifle laughter. Whenever he was embarrassed, it was Kopano's strategy to bull forward with humor and bluster—he'd picked that up from his dad.

"Why would she say such a thing?" Kopano asked with hammed-up offense. He plucked the cookie out of the air and popped it into his mouth.

Taylor shrugged playfully. "I don't know. Because you have a habit of popping up? Like, after I made that scene in chemistry class and had to help Professor Burroughs inventory the supplies, you just happened to develop a sudden interest in obscure chemical compounds."

"That was for practice!" Kopano exclaimed. He waved his hand back and forth to demonstrate. "I wanted to see if there were any substances I couldn't pass through. Serious science stuff."

"Uh-huh," Taylor replied. "A likely story."

Kopano pretended to be sullen and went back to chopping his onions. That Isabela always had a way of saying whatever was on her mind . . . which was usually gossip, or else her many theories about what the other students were secretly feeling or thinking. Most of the time, though, she was right. She had certainly nailed Kopano. He *had* been arranging ways to bump into Taylor around campus.

He didn't care that Isabela had called him out. On the contrary. This was good news—it meant she and Taylor were talking about him. Taylor had noticed.

"We used to be able to hang out more," Kopano said. He brushed his chopped onions into a frying pan, where they began to sizzle. "I know why we can't as much these days. Because you are supposed to be a cynical and angry young lady. Chilling with me would be bad for your reputation.

All you would do is laugh and smile all the time and say things like 'Oh, Kopano, you are so funny and handsome.' This would of course blow your cover."

Taylor laughed and smiled, just as Kopano had predicted. "Of course," she replied, but her face soon clouded over. She glanced at the security camera on the kitchen's wall. "We have to be careful talking like this."

"I already told Lexa we'd be in here," Kopano said.

For cybersecurity reasons cooked up by Professor Nine, all the Academy's surveillance footage—and who accessed it—went through Lexa. That way, if Taylor slipped up or needed a break from playing the bad girl, she wouldn't be caught on camera. Kopano had made sure to tell Lexa not to record in the kitchen that night.

"But you're not a stalker," Taylor said dryly, her eyes warm.

"So maybe I have arranged to bump into you here and there," Kopano continued with an airy wave of his knife that ended with him chopping the stem off a pepper. "Is this stalking? I don't even know what this word means, but I think not."

"Oh, sure. Play dumb," Taylor said. She hopped onto a clear section of counter and sat there with her legs dangling. "I'm not complaining. Hiding out together beneath the training center isn't the same as actually hanging out. I've missed it."

Kopano flashed a grin. "I still take my pledge to you very seriously. I am dedicated to making your experience here as boring as possible."

Taylor snorted. "I think boring has pretty much gone out the window. Thanks for trying, though." She reached out and pinched Kopano's sleeve. "This sweater looks good on you."

For all his attempts at being smooth, he couldn't keep the dumb grin off his face.

"Huh? This? Just something old I tossed on."

CHAPTER NINE

TAYLOR HAD BUILT UP A TOLERANCE TO CHORES. It came from her old life, when she spent every day after school and most of her summers helping out around the farm. School, chores, homework, sleep. It was a rhythm that Taylor was used to. She could turn off her mind and just get stuff done.

When a student got in trouble at the Academy—and Taylor had made a point of getting in trouble a lot lately—the administration favored two kinds of punishment: extra training sessions with Professor Nine or community service around the campus. Both punishments boiled down to basically the same thing—a loss of free time. Taylor didn't mind that so much. All she did in her free time was worry, so better to have a bunch of dull tasks to take her mind off things.

Mopping floors on Christmas Eve, though? That was something that would happen to a desperate orphan in one of those sad British holiday stories. And yet, Taylor had been looking forward to it.

Normally, she didn't wear any of her nice outfits when she was going to be spending her off time scrubbing grime out of crevices. But, she'd had a feeling that Kopano would show up tonight. Or, maybe more than a feeling. A hope.

Sitting on the counter beside him, occasionally brushing her shoulder up against his—entirely by accident, of course—Taylor felt at ease. Like she could be herself. Not the old, nervous, homesick Taylor who had first come to the Academy, or the angry, revenge-minded Taylor who had emerged after the incident with the Foundation. With Kopano, she was in her sweet spot, perpetually. Kopano made her feel comfortable and hopeful, like they were always on the verge of some great adventure where things would work out perfectly.

"He's hot," Isabela had said to her earlier that day, in their suite, when Taylor mentioned she thought she might see Kopano that night. "You should hook up with him. A Christmas miracle!"

"God, Isabela, it's not always about hooking up," Taylor replied.

"Not always, no. But this time?" Isabela wiggled her eyebrows. "This time? Yes. So much yes."

"I don't know, I mean—I like him. We're friends. And he's, um—I mean, yeah, sure, objectively, he's an attractive guy. But I don't know if he even likes me that way and, if he did, I don't know if I'd want to mess with the friendship—"

"Oh, he likes you that way," Isabela said with a smirk. "Please. That you guys haven't done it yet is crazy. Everyone knows it's going to happen."

"Isabela!"

"What else is there to do around here? Besides plan our secret war against a bunch of rich assholes? Might as well have some fun."

"You've got a one-track mind," Taylor replied with a nervous laugh. She looked across the suite for help, where Ran was listening with a faint smile. The Japanese girl shrugged.

"I agree with Isabela," she said simply.

The memory made Taylor's cheeks warm, the flush luckily covered by the steamy kitchen. Kopano stood over the stove, shaking a heavy pan filled with fried rice. There was a light sheen of sweat on his forehead. Without thinking about it, Taylor grabbed a clean towel off the counter and lightly wiped his forehead.

"Ah, thank you," he said with that infectious grin of his. "You make a very good assistant chef."

"Happy to help," she replied, glancing down at his growing vat of fried rice. "With whatever this is . . ."

"Christmas rice!" Kopano declared again. "You think it's strange, eh? I should've maybe made desserts like all these others, but that's not how we do it in Nigeria."

"You don't have desserts there?"

Kopano stuck out his stomach and slapped his free hand

against it. "Of course we do. But the rice . . ." He tilted his head. "This story might be boring."

"No, tell me. I like hearing about your home."

Kopano beamed. "Before I was born, there was a revolution in my country. My mom and dad were very poor. Dirt poor, you'd say. I guess most people were back then. They would consider themselves lucky if they had a cup of rice to eat for dinner."

"Wow," Taylor replied. "That's terrible."

Kopano shrugged. "Terrible, maybe, but it turned into a cool thing, in a way. For Christmas, the people who could afford to would make big pots of rice like this one and invite their neighbors over to eat. It was a tradition in the village my mom was from that carried on even after the revolution was over."

Taylor eyed the pan of dark, chopped meat that Kopano was gradually stirring into the rice. "Is that liver?"

"Shh, it's the secret ingredient," Kopano replied, chuckling when Taylor wrinkled her nose. "Anyway, every Christmas my mom would cook this and invite all the neighbors in our apartment building over to have some. My dad didn't like it. He'd forgotten the lessons of the hard times and would always complain. *Why do I have to feed all these people, huh? These freeloaders.* But my mom did it anyway and, I think, my dad secretly enjoyed having all these visitors he could brag to about his wife's cooking. It was fun. I liked having a full house back then, everyone around."

"That's a nice tradition," Taylor said, but there was a

creeping sadness behind her smile. She folded her hands between her legs and looked down at them. "My dad and I . . . we didn't do big celebrations like that, didn't really invite anybody over. It was cool, though. He would buy all these frozen appetizers from the store—like, real unhealthy stuff that we didn't normally eat, and we'd just binge on them all day and watch movies in our pajamas. It was . . . it was kinda awesome, now that I think about it."

Kopano put a hand on her shoulder. "It will turn out okay, Taylor. I promise."

Taylor nodded. She wasn't so sure.

"It's hard to believe that place is gone now," Taylor said after a moment, swallowing. "Gone because of me, basically. I know my dad agreed to it and I know it's for a good cause but—" She shook her head. "He's staying with a cousin, sleeping on his futon. I hate to imagine that's what his Christmas is like."

Kopano put his hand on his heart. "You have my solemn promise that, when these Foundation people are brought to justice, I will return to South Dakota with you and we will rebuild. As you already know, I am very strong."

Taylor snorted and wiped the back of her hand across her eyes. "I'll hold you to that."

Kopano put a lid on his vat of rice and stepped back with a satisfied exhale. "This needs to simmer a bit. Come on, let's get some air."

Taylor hopped down from the counter and the two of them headed out of the kitchen. As they went, she noticed

Kopano sneakily grab a small package from a shelf by the door. He tried to hide it behind his back.

"Hey, what's that?"

Still hiding the package behind his broad back, Kopano turned around and walked backwards through the kitchen's swinging doors. He smiled sheepishly at Taylor.

"This? Um . . . it's a present."

"Kopano. What did you do?"

Taylor followed him into the student union. The lights were still on, but the place was completely deserted at this time of night. After the heat of the kitchen, the cool air was a relief. The strings of blinking lights were reflected in Kopano's eyes.

"Before you say anything, you should know it was just dumb luck. I pulled your name for Secret Santa."

Taylor advanced on him, eyes narrowing. "But I didn't sign up for Secret Santa. We all agreed it wouldn't make sense with my jerk attitude."

"Oh," Kopano replied. "Really? Hm. Then I must have written your name and put it in the hat, which, um . . . was not the hat everyone else put names in but one of Caleb's that I found in our suite. You know, I did think it was weird you were the only name in there, but I don't know how Secret Santa is supposed to work!"

"You are so full of it," Taylor replied with an incredulous laugh.

Kopano finally stopped with the dopey excuses and held out the little box to Taylor. "Happy Christmas," he said.

She took it, eyeing the slapdash wrapping job he'd done, the corners all wrinkled and uneven. Guys never knew how to wrap presents.

"I hope . . ." Now Kopano's face was suddenly serious. "I hope I didn't overstep or something."

Taylor held up the box and shook it. "Why? What is it?"

"Open it. I'll explain."

Taylor ripped away the sloppy wrapping paper and revealed the small box within. She glanced up at Kopano, who shrugged like he didn't already know what was inside. Taylor pulled off the lid.

Inside the box was a small chunk of wood, dark brown, the edges sanded smooth. "TC" was carved into the soft surface, the grooves worn and darkened with age. The chunk of wood was wedged into the open side of a seashell. At least, that's how it looked at first glance. Upon further examination Taylor noticed that the shell and the wood were melded together, the edges of the cedar at points seeming to grow right out of smooth shell. The whole thing was attached to a leather cord—a necklace.

Taylor picked up the amulet cautiously, almost afraid she would break it. As she ran her fingers over her initials, she felt bumps on the shell's reverse side. She turned it over and found a delicate pattern of azure stones—Loralite—the tiny shards embedded into the shell's light pink surface.

"Kopano . . . wow."

She blinked her eyes, mouth open slightly. She traced her thumb over the initials and the memory came back to her—the barn, a boring day in the summer a couple of years ago, and Taylor had secretly carved her mark into the wall. She'd felt guilty and stupid about it afterward—covered it up with bales of hay so her dad wouldn't notice—and, as far as she knew, he never had.

"How . . . ? I did this," Taylor said, dragging her thumbnail through the carving. "This is from home."

"Yes, um . . . so, I emailed your dad. I hope that's okay," Kopano replied, his nervousness unfeigned.

"You emailed my dad," Taylor replied in disbelief.

"Yes. He's very nice."

Taylor stared at him.

"It was after you hatched the plan with Nine to have his people, you know . . . destroy the place. I thought, if that was me, I would want a piece of what was left. I wrote to your dad and that is what he sent me."

"So he did know," Taylor said absently, looking down at the gift.

"The shell is from outside on the beach," Kopano continued. "I guess that's kind of obvious."

"It's like they're growing together," Taylor said, fingering the spot where smooth shell met rough wood.

"I used my Legacy to fuse them. Made the wood transparent, slid it into the shell, and released. Same thing with the Loralite."

Kopano turned the piece over so Taylor could examine the Loralite embedded in the shell, their fingers brushing as he did. The azure slivers were arranged in the shape of a

Loric glyph—Taylor only knew what they were because of a TV special she'd seen about Loric mysteries in the wake of the invasion.

"Where'd you get . . . ?"

"After our little adventure," Kopano said. "I may have pocketed some of the broken stones. Not enough to teleport, at least I don't think so. But still cool. I got Lexa's help with the symbol. It means 'home' in their language, but it can also mean 'here,' like where you are at any given moment. I don't know. It seemed fitting."

Taylor gave a small, disbelieving shake of her head. "Kopano, it's amazing. I love it."

He clapped his hands and blew out a relieved exhale. "I'm glad!"

Taylor pulled the necklace on over her head and fluffed her hair loose from the leather band. She turned it so the Loric symbol was facing out, liking how the rough wood felt against her skin, a reminder of home.

Kopano grinned. "Ah. Prettier than I'd even imagined."

"Ha, shut up." Taylor laughed, rolling her eyes. Her lips pursed suddenly as a thought occurred to her and her shoulders slumped a bit. "The thing is, Kopano, we all agreed we weren't doing presents, and it's not like there's somewhere for us to shop, anyway. Not that that stopped you from making this awesome gift, which—I'm not good at crafts, my art projects always got thrown in the garbage . . ." She realized she was rambling. "What I'm saying is that I'm sorry, but I didn't get you anything."

Kopano waved this away like he was offended at the very thought. "I didn't expect you to. The point of the holiday is giving, not receiving, yes?"

Taylor's gaze drifted away from Kopano as an idea hit her. More an urge than an idea, really. Her eyes darted across the many holiday decorations that the faculty had placed all around the student union. She knew it was here some-where . . . ah, there, right over the entrance, of course. She squinted and put her telekinesis to work.

"There is something I've wanted to give you for a while, though," she said, and gave her eyebrows a goofy pump so that Kopano would look up.

A piece of mistletoe hovered above them.

"What is it?" Kopano asked. "A plant?"

As usual, Taylor couldn't tell whether Kopano was joking or not. She didn't care. Without another word, she went up on her toes and kissed him. Maybe she'd surprised him at first, but he caught on quickly, returning the kiss, his hand on the small of her back. Taylor leaned against him, not wanting to stop, her fingers tickling the stubble on his jawline.

Taylor lost track of time, forgot about all the burdens and dangers she was facing, and could think of only Kopano's warm mouth.

When they finally pulled apart they were both out of breath, which made them laugh. Taylor reached out and held Kopano's hand.

"Merry Christmas," she said.

CHAPTER TEN

CALEB CRANE
THE CRANE RESIDENCE—OMAHA, NEBRASKA

CALEB SAT IN ONE OF THE STRAIGHT-BACKED living-room chairs and fed wrapping paper into the fireplace, watching cartoon snowmen curl into themselves as the little blaze consumed them. Presents were over. His gifts were stacked in a tidy pile next to him. He'd received the usual—socks and underwear, plain white T-shirts in a plastic package, a few solid color polo shirts, a good pair of blue jeans, and a pair of sturdy boots.

Every year, Caleb's dad made it very clear to Caleb's mother that the boys were to receive practical gifts that they could use. His dad was a sergeant at Offutt Air Force Base, where he was known as a stern disciplinarian. He brought that attitude home with him and didn't let up, even on holidays.

Thinking about it, Santa had always been a real drag in the Crane household.

Caleb's most exciting gift every year, if you could call it that, was whatever hardcover book of history his dad picked out for him. Without fail, it would be something that Charles Crane had read before, so that he could quiz the boys come January.

This year's selection was about the mysterious death of George Patton, written by some newscaster Caleb had seen on TV ranting red-faced about how dangerous Garde integration was for the future of the United States.

Caleb resisted the urge to toss the book in the fire.

Caleb's mom was in the kitchen, preparing dinner. His dad was in the den, watching a football game. And his brothers . . .

Well, they were sitting on the couch opposite Caleb, grinning like wolves.

Charles Jr.—or Charlie, as he was called around the house—was the oldest, six years Caleb's senior. Christopher was the middle son, only 18 months younger than Charlie. Caleb often wondered if things would've been different if his two older brothers hadn't been so close in age, if they'd all been spread out more, or if there had been a fourth brother, younger than Caleb, to even the odds—he wondered if they would've ganged up on him less if any of those things were true.

They all looked alike, a fact that Caleb couldn't help but find ironic. All the Crane boys possessed the same sandy-blond hair, square jaws, and ears a little too big for their heads. Charlie kept his hair buzzed short and proper, like their father. He was already something of a big shot at Offutt—an officer at only twenty-three—following in his father's footsteps. Chris kept his hair a little longer and Caleb got the sense that he'd trimmed it off his ears and shaved his sideburns fresh for this trip home, not wanting to invoke their dad's ire. Not that Chris would ever admit to that. He was at Omaha Community College, studying engineering, after he'd gotten the boot from the Air Force Academy last year. What he'd done to land in trouble was a big secret, but Caleb knew from a whispered conversation with his mom that Charles Sr. could've pulled some strings for Chris's benefit and kept him enlisted. His dad had refused. No special treatment for his boys. They screwed up, that was on them.

Caleb didn't feel sorry for Chris. His dad's rules—you fight your own battles—had caused him to get the shit kicked out of him by his older brothers on a weekly basis. No one ever stepped in for him.

"Can I ask you a question?"

That was Chris. Caleb must have been staring at him. Maybe Caleb was smirking a little bit, thinking about the misfortune that had befallen his brother. That was a mistake. It was always better to avoid eye contact in this house.

"What?" Caleb replied.

Chris took a swig from his bottle of beer. He'd gotten a bit of a potbelly since Caleb last saw him. Both his brothers were drinking, a small colony of bottles on the coffee table in front of them.

"Now that you're a big-shot mutant or whatever," Chris began, "can we still call you *Gay*leb?"

"You should never have called me that in the first place," Caleb replied quietly. "Actually, my roommate Nigel is gay."

Caleb wouldn't have been able to explain why he said that. He always did that kind of thing when he was younger and getting stared down by his brothers—volunteered information, overshared, gave them ammunition. In his sessions with Dr. Linda—before they found out she was an evil spy for the Foundation—she had suggested that Caleb's anxiety about his brothers was why he was so taciturn and repressed.

Charlie sucked his teeth at the mention of Nigel. "I'll never understand how these goddamn aliens picked who got superpowers."

"Legacies," Caleb corrected.

"Whatever." Charlie was much subtler than Chris when it came to insults; always had been.

"That's sweet," Chris butted in, leering at Caleb. "You and this kid make out all the time?"

"No. We don't make out," Caleb said flatly. "You're ignorant as shit."

Chris barked a laugh. "I'm ignorant? You hear that, dude?" He asked, nudging Charlie. "Little brother goes off to freak school in California and all of a sudden he talks like some liberal blogger. You going to lecture me about trigger warnings next?"

Before Caleb could reply, Charlie wrapped his arm around Chris and pulled him close, smiling slyly.

"Bro, do you remember the year of Santa Claws?" Charlie asked Chris in a stage whisper.

Chris clapped a hand over his face. "You mean the best Christmas ever? How could I forget that?"

Charlie grinned at Caleb. "You remember that?"

"Yeah," Caleb replied. "I remember."

Santa Claws. That was what the brothers considered to be one of their better pranks. It was Christmas Eve and Caleb had only managed to get to sleep after what felt like hours of tossing and turning, too excited about the morning to come. Chris had shaken him awake. Whispered in his ear, *"Wake up, Caleb, I think I hear Santa Claus."*

How had Caleb been so stupid? He shook his head at the memory. He was young and hadn't yet learned to be suspicious of everything his older brothers said and did.

"You were so damn excited . . . ," Chris laughed, recounting the story. "Kept trying to hold my hand and shit . . ."

Caleb remembered. He *was* excited. It was like they were on a secret mission. He was almost more thrilled that Chris had thought to include him than he was to see Santa Claus. They crept through the house, towards the living room where Caleb sat now. They could hear the rustle of wrapping paper and booted footfalls. Caleb peeked around the corner and had to clap a hand over his mouth to stifle a gasp. Santa was really there, his back to them as he rummaged through the presents, a red suit and curly white hair, just like in the storybooks.

"I shoved him around the corner," Chris said, wiping his eyes.

"And that's when I turned around . . . ," Charlie added.

Santa loomed over young Caleb. He's wasn't like the stories at all. Huge fangs filled his mouth and his face was smeared with blood. Instead of fingers, he had long claws that shone in the Christmas tree's blinking lights.

"Ho, ho, ho!" Santa had bellowed. "You're going to die!"

His brothers were cracking up now.

"Had all that fake blood and the vampire teeth left over from Halloween," Charlie explained. "Took us a while to tape all the steak knives to my fingers."

"Worth it," Chris said. "Totally worth it."

Young Caleb had shrieked and run upstairs, sobbing and hysterical when he launched himself into his parents' bed. That was, as it happened, how he learned that Santa wasn't real.

"You pissed your pants, too," Chris said.

"I was eight," replied Caleb.

"I think dad was madder about that than the prank," Charlie said with a smirk. "They'd just gotten you over the whole bed-wetting thing."

"How long did we get grounded for?" Chris asked, shaking his head.

"Oh man, so long."

"Always telling on us," Chris said to Caleb, taking a disapproving swig of beer.

"I thought there was a monster in the house," Caleb replied.

And what had been the aftermath of Santa Claws? For starters, Caleb had to endure a stern lecture about how neither Santa Claus nor monsters were real, and how he needed to develop some backbone. The older boys had gotten grounded for a month, which, of course, they viewed as Caleb's fault because he couldn't take a joke.

"You guys beat me up almost every day for like a month after that," Caleb said quietly.

"What else were we supposed to do?" Charlie asked innocently.

"It was boring being stuck in the house," Chris said with a chuckle.

"I'd like to see you try that now."

Caleb flinched and glanced over his shoulder. One of his duplicates had sprung loose. He stood behind Caleb with his arms crossed, glaring at the brothers.

Both Charlie and Chris had fallen silent. Their eyes were wide, Chris frozen with his beer bottle in front of his mouth. It occurred to Caleb that his brothers had never seen what he could do. The first duplicate had been an accident, but . . .

Caleb decided to go with it.

In a moment, there were six copies of Caleb, three on either side of his chair. They stood there cracking their knuckles or rolling their necks, like they were getting ready for a fight. Caleb sat back calmly, one eyebrow raised.

"Sucks to be outnumbered, doesn't it?" he asked.

Charlie swallowed with some difficulty. "Easy now, bro. We were just messing around."

At a mental command, each of the duplicates took one forceful step forward. Charlie yelped. Chris threw himself over the back of the couch.

Caleb laughed. He couldn't remember ever openly laughing at his brothers like that.

Of course, the victory was short-lived.

"What in the hell is this?"

Caleb's dad stood in the doorway, drawn away from his football game by the commotion. He looked from the gang of duplicates on one side of the room to his older boys cowering on the other. His thin lips curled in stern disgust, which he aimed directly at Caleb.

"Didn't think I'd have to make this clear, boy, but I don't want none of that alien shit going on in my house."

"Or what?" one of the duplicates asked.

His father's face turned red, all the way up through his buzz cut. He wasn't used to insubordination in any facet of life. He glared at the offending duplicate, then at Caleb.

"I know that *thing* didn't just sass me," Caleb's dad said icily. "In my own house."

Caleb stared at his dad, whose face just got redder and redder. His palms were sweaty. He knew that he should back down and defuse the situation by absorbing his duplicates. He'd probably already gone too far by using them to intimidate his brothers. Garde weren't supposed to use their Legacies against defenseless humans, even if they were total jerks.

But then—what could Caleb's dad actually do to him? Caleb didn't live here, didn't eat his food, didn't rely on him in any way. His dad didn't have any power over him. Caleb hadn't even wanted to come home in the first place, and tomorrow he'd be whisked right back to the Academy. Caleb was free of all this.

And yet, his father's glare made him feel small again.

"Please, Caleb, can we just listen to Dad? He looks so mad."

Caleb flinched. That mewling voice was his own. One of the duplicates had broken ranks with the others and was half doubled over like he might vomit from nervousness, wringing his hands together and staring pleadingly at Caleb.

It'd been months since Caleb had last allowed his feelings to overwhelm him and lost control of one of the clones. For a while Caleb had thought his duplicates had minds of their own—or at least that's what he tried to convince himself—but really they were like emotional release valves. Too much pressure in Caleb's head and one of them could act out.

Of course it would happen right after his big moment of triumph over his brothers. They were both smirking now, Chris snickering behind his hand even though he was still half hiding behind the couch. With every second that the duplicate fretted and whined, Caleb's dad looked less angry and more mystified.

His mom, meanwhile, cooked dinner in the kitchen, pretending nothing was going on. Like always.

The duplicate made a wet sucking noise, flapping its

lower lip like it was trying to keep itself from crying.

The embarrassment was too real. Caleb shot to his feet and absorbed the duplicates. Not making eye contact with any of them, he stormed out of the room. His father let him go. Too weirded out, probably.

"Did you see that?" he heard Charles ask Chris.

"He's a goddamn mental case," Chris replied. Caleb grabbed his coat and walked right out of the house.

He only made it as far as the porch.

It was freezing outside, no more than twenty degrees, a dusting of frost on everything. Caleb's fingers tingled and his cheeks stung. What was he doing? Running away from home? He'd already kind of accomplished that.

No. He was just getting some air. That was the manly thing to do. Cool down, let it blow over.

He sat down on the porch swing, the wooden slats freezing on the backs of his legs, the metal chains creaking at his weight. He stuffed his hands in his pockets and blew out a cloud of mist. He shivered.

This was miserable, but he'd stay out here all night if he had to. Skip dinner. Wait for everyone to go to bed. Get out of here in the morning.

That was a good plan.

A set of headlights lit up the quiet block. Caleb watched them come. They belonged to a black SUV, the kind with heavily tinted windows and armor plating down on the sides. A government vehicle for sure, which wasn't such an unusual sight being so close to the military base. He'd been driven from the airport in a car just like it, the UN Peacekeepers not breaking off until he was safely ensconced with his family. He glanced down the block; his bodyguards were still there, parked at a respectful distance to keep watch. He felt sympathy for the small detachment of Peacekeepers who had to spend the day sitting around a nothing block in Omaha. At least someone was having a worse Christmas than him.

To Caleb's surprise, the SUV pulled into his driveway. For a moment, he let himself hope that this was his ride to the airport and they'd come to collect him early.

Then, the SUV's back door opened and his uncle stepped out.

"Did I miss dinner?"

Retired General Clarence Lawson wore a fur-trimmed black parka that hung open, revealing a tacky Hawaiian shirt and khaki pants beneath. He rubbed his hands together, breathed into them, then hastily zipped up his coat. His silver buzz cut stood out in the night, accentuated by his leathery tan.

Uncle Clarence didn't come to Christmas in Omaha. Ever. Either he was too busy with work or, after he retired, he was too busy enjoying golf courses drenched in the Florida sun. He was Caleb's mom's older brother and, at other family events over the years, Caleb had occasionally perceived some tension between Clarence and his father. That was to be expected. They were both military men, but Caleb's dad's career had plateaued at sergeant, whereas Clarence was once the chairman of the Joint Chiefs of Staff. The highest-ranking officer in the country.

He was now something of an American hero. Uncle Clarence had been called out of retirement during the invasion to coordinate the resistance against the Mogadorians and was widely credited for unifying the world's many governments, not to mention the Loric, around a cohesive battle strategy.

At first, Caleb was surprised to see him there. But then it dawned on him that this was exactly why he'd gotten special dispensation to come home for Christmas. The general wanted to see him.

"You frozen to death?" General Lawson asked as he clomped up the steps onto the porch. "Or did you not hear me?"

Caleb blinked, then shrugged in response to his uncle's original question. "They might be eating. I don't know."

"Don't care if you're missing dinner, huh?" Clarence glanced towards the front door, frowning. "They up your ass already?"

Caleb shrugged again. His uncle was trying to be all jocular and friendly, but Caleb didn't buy it. The last time they'd seen each other had been at a military base on an island— Guantanamo, Nigel always theorized—where they put the Garde no one knew what to do with while the Academy was built. Things there hadn't been great.

Nonetheless, Clarence sat down on the swing next to Caleb.

"Going to make an old man sit out here and freeze? Okay. That's your prerogative." He reached inside his coat and pulled out a long metal case, producing a cigar from within. "You want one?"

"No thanks."

"Hmm. There was a time that would've been 'no thank you, sir.'"

Clarence was half joking with the criticism, but Caleb bristled. It was too close to something his dad would say. Caleb felt the sudden urge to release one of his duplicates and fought it back. Meanwhile, the general held a Zippo to his cigar, puffing obliviously until a thick cloud of fragrant smoke wafted up from the tip.

"How are things at the Academy?" Clarence asked as he settled in next to Caleb.

"Fine."

"Heard you got in a bit of trouble. Unauthorized departure from campus. Maybe some more serious violations of Garde protocol."

"Why did you bring me here?" Caleb asked sharply. When his uncle didn't answer right away, he pressed on. "You did bring me here, right? Pulled strings."

"I am your uncle, Caleb."

"I haven't heard from you in more than a year," Caleb replied. "You must want something."

The general's eyes narrowed. He tapped ash off his cigar.

"They've changed you at that place. Used to be you were loyal. Eager to please." Caleb opened his mouth to reply, but

Clarence raised his cigar to stop him. "Not saying it's a bad thing. It's good you're becoming your own man. I thought we understood each other but if you've got a problem with me—"

"You made us give away our Chimærae," Caleb blurted. "And I *helped* you. I can't believe I helped you do that. What was I thinking?"

"You were following an order, just like I was," Lawson replied quietly. "We didn't know what might happen with those creatures . . ."

Caleb looked his uncle in the eyes. "Are they dead? Or are they, like, getting poked and prodded in a laboratory somewhere?"

Lawson met his gaze steadily. "Honestly, son, I don't know. I could look into it for you."

"Don't do me any favors," Caleb replied, looking away.

Clarence silently puffed away on his cigar for a few cold seconds.

"I'll be straight with you," he said at last. "I got you this little vacation from the Academy so I could be the one to tell you. They're promoting you to Earth Garde."

Caleb's mouth fell open. "What?"

"I've still got friends in the organization; they gave me the heads-up. Prevailing wisdom after your skirmish with those Harvester folks is that you're ready for fieldwork. Not to mention, reports from the psychiatrist there have greatly improved."

Caleb's whole body felt numb, and not from the cold. "I'm . . . I'm leaving the Academy?"

"Should go through in the next week or so. You're going to be on a detachment with Melanie Jackson herself."

The prospect of working alongside the president's daughter did nothing to diminish the dread Caleb was feeling. They were doing important work at the Academy, planning against the Foundation. He couldn't leave. Not yet.

"I'm not . . . I'm not ready."

"Earth Garde seems to think otherwise." Clarence paused and leaned forward to make eye contact with Caleb. "Thing is, I'm also here to ask you for a favor."

"A favor."

"Like I said, I've still got colleagues involved with the Earth Garde program. Some of them have approached me about concerns they're having."

"What kind of concerns?"

Now his uncle got cagey. "Nothing they can put their finger on, exactly. Just oddities here and there. Strange allocations of resources. Preferential treatment. That sort of thing. You remember why they called me out of retirement in the first place? Back during the invasion?"

"Because the Mogs had corrupted too many people in the government," Caleb answered distractedly. "They needed someone they could trust."

"That's right," Clarence replied. "Authorities made a lot of arrests in the year after the invasion. But suppose . . . suppose they didn't catch them all, huh? Maybe there's still some MogPro people out there. What would they be doing now, do you think?"

"They'd be figuring out ways to exploit the new world," Caleb said. "To use the Garde to their advantage."

"Maybe so, maybe so." Lawson nodded. "You have any experience with organizations like that?"

Caleb looked at his uncle. How much did he know? Was he dropping hints that the Foundation could be tied to remnants of MogPro or was this all just a big coincidence? Caleb pictured the tidbits of research they'd gathered and theories they'd mulled over. Should he share that with his uncle? Clarence puffed innocently at his cigar, like the two boys were just out here chewing the fat in the freezing cold.

"No," Caleb said. "Haven't heard about anything like that. Just guessing."

Caleb stared down at his hands. For a moment, his fingers doubled—twenty of them, interlaced in his lap, shaking slightly. A duplicate trying to get loose to tell his uncle the truth. He caught himself just in time. He was agitated, conflicted—that was always when he lost control.

He took a deep breath. Steadied himself. Maybe his uncle had good intentions and was on the side of the Garde. But he'd taken away the Chimærae. He'd used Caleb in the past.

Caleb couldn't trust him. He could only trust his friends at the Academy. He forced himself to be of one mind on this.

The indecision lasted only a few seconds. If his uncle noticed anything awry, he didn't say anything. In fact, he changed the subject.

"You know who Wade Sydal is, Caleb?"

"The weapons manufacturer," Caleb replied. "He makes

all the gear the Peacekeepers will use on us if we ever get out of hand."

Lawson snorted. "I've seen what Garde can do. If you lot set your mind to do something, I don't think Sydal's trinkets will make much difference in the long run. That said, our country's investing a great deal in his Garde deterrents. He's an old friend of President Jackson, you know? Big campaign contributor."

Caleb recalled how the Harvesters were armed with anti-Garde technology, presumably supplied by the Foundation. He and his friends hadn't been able to figure out whether the gear was stolen or Sydal was double-dealing.

"You think he's one of them?" Caleb asked.

"One of whom?"

Caleb winced. He'd slipped up, forgotten he was supposed to be talking around the existence of the Foundation.

"One of your . . . I don't know," Caleb said, covering. "Conspirators? Mog sympathizers? You won't even say."

Clarence tapped ash off his cigar, chuckling. "Doubt it. I was just reading an article about him on the flight up. Interesting guy. Maybe you'll have a chance to meet him once you're in Earth Garde. I'd love to hear what you think."

"Uh, okay," Caleb said.

"You'll do great out there. But keep your eyes open," Clarence said, and patted Caleb on the knee. "If you see anything odd or even if something doesn't feel right, you know how to reach me."

"Yeah," Caleb replied. He was still coming to terms with

all this. He'd be leaving the Academy, just when he was finally settling in. "Okay."

And that was that. General Lawson stood up, wet the tips of his fingers, and pinched the end of his cigar. He shook some feeling into his feet.

"I'm going to go see what your mom's cooking," he said. "Don't freeze out here, son."

Caleb nodded and watched his uncle go inside. A shiver came over him and he huddled deeper into his coat, staring down the darkened street.

"You really can't go home again," he muttered to himself. "Or maybe the expression should be . . . you *shouldn't* go home again."

No one replied. For once, all the duplicates agreed with him.

CHAPTER ELEVEN

LUNCHTIME AND THE DINING HALL WAS BUSTLING with activity. Groups of students filed through the buffet line, filled their trays, and lounged around tables. Others scarfed down lunches and rushed off—some kids still hadn't finished their end-of-semester assignments and it was the last day to get those in. It was New Year's Eve.

Kopano smiled, enjoying all the activity. He picked up a corner of his turkey sandwich and leisurely bit into it. He didn't have anything to do today except wait for the night's festivities. On the second floor, volunteers were hanging streamers and cardboard *HAPPY NEW YEAR!* signs. That wouldn't take long with Maiken Megalos and her super-speed zipping around up there.

With Nigel and Caleb at an emergency band practice,

Ran in training, and Isabela who-knows-where, that meant Kopano was eating his lunch alone. He didn't mind. From his table, he had a clear view of Taylor serving food. Dining-hall duty was part of her punishment for decking Isabela. He thought she looked good, even in a hairnet.

Kopano spaced out, thinking about that kiss on Christmas Eve and wondering how he could arrange a repeat perfor-mance without blowing Taylor's cover. He didn't notice the chatter in the room die down. He probably would've missed the whole broadcast if Simon, sitting at a neighboring table, hadn't called his name.

"Kopano," Simon said, pointing up at the TV, "isn't that you?"

Someone had put on Wolf News. Kopano was familiar with the American network from his current-events class. They broadcast a lot of stories about lurking aliens and dan-gerous Garde. Everyone knew their coverage was slanted, so it wasn't a channel that typically got played in the student union. Yet, all eyes were on the TV now.

The screen was split. On the left was the host, Don Leary, a red-faced man in his late fifties, his majestic head of ink-black hair plugs swept back. On the right was some grainy cell phone video, the same clip repeating over and over.

"I repeat, this footage is not for the faint of heart," Leary gravely declared. "Even after the harrowing events of the Mogadorian invasion, it's still disconcerting to see these superpowered *things* in action. But what makes this even harder to watch is that these aren't extraterrestrial invaders being assaulted. These are American citizens. And the attackers? Not aliens either. Human beings. Ones supposedly being trained to 'protect us.'"

Kopano focused on the looped footage. It was dark and jumpy, filmed by someone hiding behind the back end of a car. Even so, Kopano recognized the location. It was the stretch of California highway where the Fugitive Six had fought the Harvesters.

In the video, the sky lit up. A tracer of red cut through the dark, descended, and exploded. Bodies flew up from the blast site, limp and lifeless. A motorcycle careened by, flipped end over end.

Another glow ignited down the road. The person filming zoomed in towards the source of the fireworks, revealing Ran with glowing objects in either hand. As the camera filmed, she hurled one of these bombs at a passing motorcyclist, knocking him off and sending his bike skittering.

The camera suddenly jolted. Someone had been viciously thrown against the car the cameraperson used for cover. The view zoomed out just in time to reveal Kopano punching a biker across the face with enough force to bend his body over backwards.

Kopano watched himself turn—empty-eyed, emotionless—and charge the camera. The video cut off there. Of course, the nice people at Wolf News immediately started it over. Leary spoke over the clip.

"Our sources have identified the two assailants in the video as students at the UN's Human Garde Academy in

California. Their names and countries of origin are being kept private because they're minors, but the footage speaks for itself. This is a heinous attack on American soil by two dangerous individuals drunk on their own power. It is exactly the kind of incident the government promised *wouldn't* happen as a result of the Academy. Do you feel safer with hundreds of these . . . these creatures running wild in our own backyard? I certainly don't . . ."

Kopano looked away, his eyes blurry with frustrated tears. He wiped his face on the back of his hand, hoping that no one else in the student union would notice.

Luckily, most of his peers were also watching the news broadcast. Or maybe that wasn't lucky at all. They were all seeing Kopano—literally out of his mind—viciously beat ordinary people.

The broadcast switched over to an interview with a leather-clad man in a neck brace. A Harvester. He claimed that they were just a group of bikers out for a peaceful ride when they were accosted by the Garde. The host treated him sympathetically, asking him softball questions. Kopano tuned it out, his ears ringing.

He stood up, harder than he'd meant to, and knocked over his chair. Everyone was looking at him now. Simon scooted his chair backwards, like he was afraid of Kopano.

Kopano's fists were clenched, a fact he didn't even realize until Taylor appeared at his side and squeezed her fingers through his.

"It's all a lie," she said, not caring that such a display

might jeopardize her rebellious reputation. She raised her voice a bit, so the other students could hear. "What they're saying isn't how it went down at all. Missionary bikers on a ride for Jesus? Give me a break! Look at these clips. How convenient that they edited out all the parts where they *shoot guns* at us."

Some nearby students murmured agreement. But a few also edged away from Kopano. And others whispered to each other behind their hands.

"Look at me," Kopano said, crestfallen. The news was rerunning the clip over and over. "I look like a monster."

Taylor squeezed his hand tighter. "That's not you," she replied. "Don't worry. This will get sorted out. Professor Nine will have your back."

When the news broke, Ran was in the training center with Nine. While most of the other students had left for lunch or free time, Ran wanted another run at the obstacle course. She wouldn't use her Legacies. Her new thing was to see how far she could make it relying only on her natural physical abilities.

Grinning, Nine had taken up the challenge beside her. They were both sweating, panting, and sore. As they ran across adjacent balance beams, a log attached to two steel chains swung down from the ceiling at them. Ran slid down on her knees, ducking beneath the battering ram. She just managed to keep steady on the beam by hooking her foot around the narrow railing. Nine, on the other hand, opted to leap over the log. Ran saw him come down, foot off-kilter, practically on the side of the balance beam—but he didn't slip, he stuck right there, and quickly readjusted.

"Cheating!" Ran scolded. "You're using your antigravity!"

Nine gritted his teeth. "It's reflex. I can't help it. I'm too good."

Ran rolled her eyes and continued on, leaping from the beam to a set of monkey bars with rungs that let loose an electric shock if she hung on too long. Out of the corner of her eye, she spotted a small commotion at the entrance. Dr. Goode and Greger Karlsson had just entered, the two of them hunched over a tablet as they speed-walked, looking like they were in the middle of an argument.

"Nine!" Dr. Goode called out. "You need to see this!"

The tone of Malcolm's voice caused Ran to hesitate just a moment too long. The bars sent a jolt into her palms and she dropped off them, gnashing her teeth. Nine was already down, walking over to Malcolm and Greger with his hands on his hips.

"What's up?" he asked. "I'm trying to get my sweat on."

Ran normally wasn't nosy, but something told her she should probably pay attention to this meeting. Maybe it was the way Greger looked at her—with a weird half smile like he knew something that she didn't. Curious, Ran followed Nine, peeking over his shoulder to get a look at the tablet.

They watched the same broadcast that Kopano and Taylor had seen in the student union, the one that millions of homes across the world were tuned into at that very moment. Other stations were starting to pick up the story too, not to mention the websites and blogs. Ran and Kopano were officially famous for attacking some allegedly saintly bikers.

Nine looked up from the video. "So what? This is bullshit. Call a press conference and tell them the truth."

"The truth?" Greger replied with a raised eyebrow. "That you allowed a half dozen students to escape and that they caused chaos? That is already out there."

"Yeah, yeah. I look like a dummy, Earth Garde reviews my performance, knows that they need me more than I need them, blah, blah blah—this blows over." Nine stared down his nose at Greger. "The truth I'm talking about is that my students were attacked by some psychos and a mind controller. That video paints them as criminals, but they were acting in self-defense."

"Ah, *that* truth," Greger replied, stroking his chin. "That is a bit more problematic. It would involve Earth Garde admitting that there are rogue Garde out there, ones we can't actually control. This incident getting out is already quite the PR nightmare. We don't need to add to it."

"PR nightmare," Malcolm repeated, pinching the bridge of his nose. "Makes me pine for the days of Mogadorian warships."

"What is going to happen to us?" Ran spoke up at last, all three of the administrators turning in her direction. "Kopano and me. What will happen?"

"That, Ms. Takeda, is a very good question," Greger replied.

"You're sure that we're ready for this?" Nigel asked.

Caleb looked up as he eased a bass guitar into its case. He didn't hear Nigel talk like that often, his voice devoid of its customary brashness. He couldn't help but smile.

"You're nervous," Caleb observed.

"Nah, mate," Nigel replied quickly. He sipped daintily at the cup of tea he'd microwaved for himself—good for the vocal cords, he claimed. "I just thought we agreed we weren't going out for this dumb monkey-show thing."

A pack of Caleb's clones made a racket at the back of the room, dismantling a drum set and transferring it onto a dolly. They were on one of the dormitory's uninhabited floors, in the room they'd converted into a makeshift rehearsal space. Caleb wouldn't necessarily have described their band as good. They'd only been practicing together for a month and Caleb didn't have any prior experience with the drums, the keyboard, or the bass guitar—all instruments he was expected to play.

He had been practicing, though. Well, his clones had been practicing. Caleb multitasked. He often found himself sending one of his duplicates up here to work with an instrument while Caleb himself remained stuck in a classroom or doing chores. It was a strain, but totally worth it.

They knew three songs, all of them pretty simple. Nigel had picked them out based on some metric he came up with—ease of learning versus badassness. None of them were longer than three minutes and all of them contained ample opportunities for Nigel to scream.

"It has to be tonight," Caleb said. "We aren't going to get another chance."

"What? How do you figure?"

Caleb sighed and snapped the clasps closed on the guitar case. He straightened up and looked at Nigel.

"I'm leaving," he said. "Getting sent to Earth Garde."

Nigel practically spit out a mouthful of tea. "Come again?"

"Uncle Clarence told me over Christmas," Caleb said. "Apparently, I'll be leaving in the next few days."

"You've been back for like a week," Nigel replied. "Why didn't you say anything?"

Caleb shrugged and bent down, pretending to dust off the guitar case.

"I don't know. I didn't want to make a big deal of it."

"You planned to just disappear into the night, then? Without telling any of us?" Nigel set down his tea and came closer, putting a hand on Caleb's shoulder. "I know we weren't always tight, but you're one of us. We care about you, brother."

"I know," Caleb replied. "I—"

The duplicates stopped what they were doing and swooped in, wrapping up both Nigel and Caleb in a group hug.

"Ugh, get a hold of yourselves," Nigel complained, laughing. When he could breathe again, his mouth screwed up in thought. "You know, you don't have to let them enlist you. We're onto something here. The work we're doing with Nine and the others seems like it's just as important as any Earth Garde mission. That twat Greger is always trying to promote Ran. She keeps refusing to use her powers so he doesn't."

Caleb shot a look at his duplicates, who had gone back to breaking down the drum kit.

"I don't know. Not using my Legacy . . ." Caleb scratched the back of his neck. "Probably wouldn't be healthy for me."

"Yeah, good point," Nigel admitted.

"Besides, my uncle, he was being pretty weird about stuff. I almost got the sense that he was feeling me out about the Foundation."

Nigel's eyebrows shot up. "Feeling you out like he wants to take them down too or like he's one of them?"

"Honestly, I don't know, but I don't think my uncle is the type to work with them. He's too . . . he's . . ."

"He's got too big a stick up his ass," Nigel said.

"Exactly. He danced around actually telling me anything. Probably worried about compromising top secret intel." Caleb shrugged. "So I didn't tell him anything either."

"Good lad."

"He mentioned Wade Sydal, though. Like I might get assigned to do something for him. And, since his name has popped up in our investigation, I figure maybe I should go along with it. See what I can find out and report back to you guys."

Nigel rubbed his pockmarked cheek in thought. "Better than sitting around here waiting for the Foundation to make a move," he said at last.

"Yeah," Caleb replied.

"But you've gotta tell the others," Nigel said.

"I will, I will," Caleb replied. He looked around at the duplicates, who were done with the packing and now stared blankly into space, awaiting further orders. "So. . . guess we've got a talent show to get to."

"Let's melt some faces, mates."

CHAPTER TWELVE

DUANPHEN
VANCOUVER, BRITISH COLUMBIA, CANADA

"THE LOOK ON HIS FACE. I'M NOT SURE IT WILL ever get old."

Duanphen let go of the guard she was holding as Einar spoke. She'd been grasping him by the throat, letting her electric current fry his synapses. He fell at her feet, barely breathing, curls of smoke rising up from his dark suit. He looked virtually identical to all the bodyguards she'd worked with in the past—burly and arrogant, easy for her to take out, even with a bad leg.

"The Foundation," Einar continued his musing. "They think their money will keep them safe. Like they can just buy and sell us without repercussions."

Duanphen gave the guard at her feet a swift kick for emphasis. "The guards aren't rich. They're only lackeys."

Einar stepped around another guard who had shot at them, his gun now bent into a pretzel shape around his broken hands, thanks to Einar's telekinesis.

"I don't mean these fools," Einar explained in that know-it-all way of his that Duanphen found mildly infuriating. "You're right, though. There's no real pleasure to be taken from dispatching some thugs for hire."

"I didn't say that." Duanphen sneered at the men crumpled at their feet. "A trainer of mine used to say: '*Choose a violent life, expect a violent end.*' Certain people—men, usually—think that rule doesn't apply to them. They are always surprised when . . ." She dragged a thumb across her throat for emphasis. "Is this the look you're talking about?"

"I suppose so," Einar replied, and he smiled at her. "That moment of reckoning. It's a beautiful thing. You're on the other side of it now, not like in Thailand. Did you see it? When he realized that actions have consequences?"

"Mostly," Duanphen said, "I saw his back as he ran away."

"He won't be able to run for long."

The two of them stood in the gated driveway of an enormous mansion. Since being recruited by the Foundation, Duanphen had seen plenty of opulent places like this, but never from this angle. In the past, she was always the one staring out, like the guards at her feet, watching for trouble. Now, she was the danger, the predator. Growing up where she did, a place like this seemed possible only in fairy tales. She gazed at the burbling stone fountain and the gleaming sports cars parked around it. She thought of the executive back in Thailand . . . all the executives, the well-heeled men who had waved money at her during her pit fights.

She liked this view. She enjoyed showing up on their doorstep.

According to Einar, the mansion belonged to a member of the Foundation. They had caught him as he was leaving—driven in a limousine, of course, probably on his way to a swanky New Year's Eve party. The limo's headlights were still on, even though the hood was caved in from where the Beast had smashed it apart with his bare hands. Duanphen limped over to the vehicle, reached past the unconscious driver, and turned it off.

Duanphen heard screaming and more gunshots from inside the mansion. The man they were after had fled that way along with some of his guards. The Beast had given chase while she and Einar finished up out here.

The Beast. That's how she thought of Einar's other associate, the quiet boy who always kept his hood up, who seemed almost impossibly powerful. The Beast had broken her shin when they first met a few weeks ago, when Duanphen had been stupid enough to try fighting him. She was still stuck in a splint, thanks to him, limping around, slower than she'd ever been in her life. Einar promised they would find her a healer soon—a Garde healer, not the shady Thai doctor he had initially hired to patch her up. For now, she had to grit her teeth through the pain and hobble.

She kept her distance from the Beast as much as possible.

"Shall we?" Einar asked, and extended his arm to Duanphen.

"Yes," she replied. She slipped her hand through the crook of Einar's elbow and let him support some of her weight. They strolled inside, crunching across shattered glass and a broken door, following the path of destruction.

The Beast was a lunatic, and for all his smart talk, Duanphen figured that Einar was as well. Still, she had to admit, she enjoyed what they were doing. Duanphen had been under someone's heel her entire life. It felt good to be the one doing the stomping.

"Tell me about this man," she said to Einar as they walked through a hallway lined with fine art. It was a collection that belonged in a museum, stuck in here to only be appreciated by one very rich asshole.

"His name is Montgomery Eubanks," Einar said. "He used to run a hedge fund, but now he mostly works as a movie producer. He does the same job as your friend back in Thailand."

"He wasn't my friend," Duanphen said sharply, her hand tightening on Einar's arm.

"Easy. Figure of speech," Einar replied. "He manages a small network of buyers, auctions off the merchandise that the Foundation has on offer. Supposed to be anonymous. Compartmentalized. The Foundation is structured so that no one knows everyone's identity. Small interlocking circles. They think it keeps them safe. But I know some names and every one of them I find . . . well, they aren't so hard to make talk, are they?"

"You've told me all this before," Duanphen replied. She brushed her fingers across a marble statue of a centaur shooting a bow and arrow. "Will this Montgomery know where we can find a healer?"

"I hope so," Einar replied. "We'll gain access to his tablet and see where the Foundation's healers are assigned. Then, we'll go liberate one, just like I liberated you."

"And if he doesn't have this information?"

"Well, to start with, we'll kill him and steal his money."

"We planned to do that anyway."

Einar smiled. "True."

From deeper in the mansion came a rending sound like steel being ripped in half, followed by a terrified shriek. The Beast must have found where Montgomery went to hide. Einar picked up his pace a bit and Duanphen had to grit her teeth to keep up.

They rounded a corner just as a pair of guards came charging down an adjacent stairwell. So, the Beast hadn't killed everyone in here. The two guards were well trained and fast. They raised their handguns and fired.

Duanphen was faster. With one telekinetic burst, she knocked their arms in the air so their bullets thudded harmlessly into the ceiling. Then, Einar took over.

"You hate each other," he said coldly. "You've hated each other for years. Why don't you finally do something about it?"

Duanphen could see the rage bubble up in the guards' faces—neck veins popped, eyes widened, teeth bared. Like mirror images, they turned and shot each other in the chest.

Einar barely glanced at the guards as they fell to the floor. He pulled on Duanphen's arm and they continued past the staircase.

"Come on," he said. "We don't want to leave Montgomery alone with our friend."

They followed the sounds of frightened whimpering and emerged into a cozy room that served as a library. Most of the books were on the floor now, one of the large shelves having been thrust aside so someone—Montgomery, obviously—could gain access to a panic room. Two feet of solid steel sealed by a heavy-duty magnetic lock. That had been the panic-room door, at least until the Beast got hold of it. He'd cleaved it in half like a tuna can. Duanphen swallowed, a wave of relief passing through her. She'd been lucky back in Thailand that all that monster did was break her leg.

The Beast sat hunched in a high-backed chair, breathing heavily. Their quarry, Montgomery Eubanks, was laid out at his feet, one of the Beast's boots on his neck so the man could just barely suck in air. Montgomery was handsome and polished in that way Duanphen had noticed a lot of rich men were, a result owed to subtle plastic surgeries and moisturizer. His tuxedo was all shredded and his head was bleeding, but he was alive. Alive and totally still, not moving a muscle, probably afraid that the Beast would crush his throat if he so much as flinched.

"Happy New Year, Monty!" Einar shouted. He gestured to the Beast. "It's okay. You can let him up."

The Beast slid his foot away and Montgomery sat up, coughing and rubbing his throat.

"You demented little brat," Montgomery said, glaring at Einar. "You know you'll never get away with this, don't you?"

Einar smirked at Duanphen. "They always say that."

"They're looking for you," Montgomery said. "Powerful people. You can't hide from them forever."

Einar stretched out his arms. "Who's hiding? Not me. Where are these powerful people?" He put his hand over his eyes as if to shield them from the sun, then pointed at the dead body of one of Montgomery's guards. "Is that one over there?"

"You're—"

With a snap of Einar's fingers, Montgomery fell silent. His eyes took on a glazed quality and his mouth, seconds ago twisted in anger, fell half-open so that Duanphen thought he might start drooling. Despite the cut on his forehead and his dire situation, the businessman suddenly had a look of stoned calm. That was Einar's doing.

"Enough small talk, I think," Einar said. "Montgomery, would you be so kind as to fetch your tablet for me? We're in need of a healer."

Montgomery got to his feet and stumbled into the panic room, picking his way delicately through the curled shreds of metal that used to be the door. He returned with his tablet, an exact replica of the one Duanphen's executive had carried, and handed it over to Einar.

"There are . . . there are no healers," Montgomery said, his voice slurring. "None available."

Einar raised an eyebrow as he flicked through the information on Montgomery's tablet. It was all there—Garde potentially up for auctions, contact information, bank accounts. Another small window into the Foundation that they could force their way through.

"Where are the healers?" Einar asked.

"Don't know . . . ," Montgomery answered, swaying on his feet like a hypnotism victim at a magic show. "Special assignment. Outside my . . . outside my knowledge. Heard rumors about Siberia."

"Siberia?" Einar cocked his head. "What's in Siberia?"

Montgomery shrugged his shoulders in a way Duanphen found utterly childish. She sighed and shifted on her feet, the bones in her leg grinding like uneven gears. She would have to live with this pain a little longer yet.

"There is one . . . ," Montgomery mumbled, leaning in to open a file on his tablet. "There is one potential. Sources say . . . recruitment . . . should be soon."

Einar looked down at the opened file and let loose a laugh. Duanphen had never heard a noise like that come out of him. Einar never sounded surprised about anything.

"Her?" Einar asked, his eyes shining. "The Foundation thinks they can recruit *her*? Again? Because it went *so* well the first time."

Montgomery nodded dumbly. "Reports are . . . reports are

she's disgruntled. Suss . . . susceptible."

Duanphen craned her neck to look at the screen. There was a blond girl pictured there, pretty if chubby-cheeked in that way Duanphen immediately associated with all Americans.

"You know her," she said to Einar.

"We've met," Einar replied. He rubbed the back of his head, fingering a knot of scar tissue. "She hit me with a shovel."

"She doesn't like you."

"In her defense, I was trying to kill her friends . . ."

Duanphen's eyes narrowed. "You said we don't kill our own kind."

"Not when we can avoid it, obviously. It was a complicated time. I was a bit out of my mind."

Duanphen tilted her head. Did this strange boy think he was in his right mind now? She wondered, not for the first time, what she had gotten herself into. Over Montgomery's shoulder, she could see the Beast sitting stone-still in his high-backed chair, somehow managing to loom over them without even standing up.

Perhaps detecting her unease, Einar put a hand on her shoulder. Duanphen knew that he could use his Legacy to *make* her trust him. She wouldn't even know it was happening. Einar could easily make her a loyal soldier, as empty-headed as Montgomery. But he hadn't. The skepticism she continued to nurture was evidence enough that he'd kept his word from their first meeting and not used his Legacy on her.

Instead, he talked. Always talked.

"I've changed," Einar said gently. "I used to believe the Foundation cared about me. It took Taylor here . . ." He looked down at the girl on the tablet. "It took her causing some trouble to open my eyes. When I made a mistake, I saw how expendable I was to the Foundation. At first, I was furious with her and her friends. I thought they ruined my life. I wanted to hurt them. But now I realize that anger was misplaced. I should've thanked Taylor and the others. She cut the gilded leash the Foundation had around my neck. Made me realize that we Garde can only rely on each other. And that we can't let anyone control us. Isn't that right, Monty?"

The rich man murmured agreement. Duanphen said nothing. Einar liked to talk about this new world he was creating, but so far it was only the three of them. Not exactly a revolution. Not yet. Even so, for the first time in her life, Duanphen felt truly free.

She liked it.

"If the Foundation spies are right and Taylor really is sick of the Academy . . ." Einar's thin lips compressed into a smile. He minimized the girl's picture. Then, he opened up a banking app and typed in an account number, passing the tablet back to Montgomery. "Be a good boy and transfer your liquid assets, eh, Montgomery? Be quick about it. Seems we've got to go do some recruiting of our own."

CHAPTER THIRTEEN

THE FUGITIVE SIX
THE HUMAN GARDE ACADEMY—POINT REYES, CALIFORNIA

KOPANO SAT ON THE COUCH IN TAYLOR'S DORM suite with his head in his hands. She sat next to him, watching him closely and occasionally reaching out to pat his back.

"I feel like I just want to hide," Kopano said.

"Psh!" Isabela answered with a wave of her hand. She sat on a chair opposite, air-drying her freshly painted fingernails. "Why should you hide? They should be giving you a medal and a movie deal for crushing those *punheteiros*."

"I didn't want to crush anyone," Kopano replied. He peeked out from between his fingers and looked over at Ran. She stood next to the window, quiet, watching as most of the student body gathered in the courtyard below. A makeshift stage had been set up there for the talent show, part of the festivities the administration had cooked up for New Year's Eve.

"We know you didn't," Taylor told him gently.

"They had it coming," Isabela insisted. "I say it's too bad you didn't crush more of them."

Kopano looked up at her. "You didn't see the video."

"Nope. I didn't see it happen in person either, because they had already shot me. You remember? If not for you and the others, I would probably be dead in a ditch or on a hook in a meat locker like that girl the Harvesters kidnapped. I feel nothing for them. You shouldn't either, you softie."

"What did Professor Nine and Malcolm say about it?" Taylor asked.

"They were mad, obviously," Ran replied. She looked at Kopano. "They will protect us. They promised."

"Where are your two boyfriends?" Isabela asked him with a smirk. "They should be here."

Kopano shrugged and started to say he didn't know, but Ran interrupted with a chin jerk in the direction of the courtyard.

"They're getting ready to perform," she said. "I see them down there."

Isabela snorted. "I thought Nigel said such a nonpaying gig would be beneath him."

Kopano stood up abruptly, wiped the back of his hand across his eyes and put on a resolute face.

"We must go," he said.

Taylor looked up at him. "Weren't you just talking about

hiding out for the rest of your life?"

"I'm over it," Kopano said.

Isabela shook her head and Taylor gave him a look—they both knew that wasn't true. For all his braggadocio, Kopano was probably the most sensitive one of them all. Or at least the most idealistic. That video of him hurting the Harvesters would gnaw at him.

Kopano caught their looks and shrugged. "Fine. I'm not over it. But there's nothing I can do about it now." He waved his hand dramatically. "And what kind of friend would I be if I missed the debut performance of Nigel and the Clones, huh?"

"A friend with eardrums," Isabela replied.

The four of them arrived on the lawn while Lisbette was still onstage. She used her Legacies to create towering ice sculptures of fairies and nymphs while doing interpretive dance to some tinkling new-age track. Most of the student body, along with many administrators, were already there, watching from picnic blankets and politely clapping whenever Lisbette pulled off a flourish.

"I hate this ballet crap," Isabela said a little too loudly. Some instructors turned around to give her a look. She ignored them. "There's no beat. No passion."

"You have to admit the sculptures are pretty," Ran replied, gazing up at the delicate glass-like wings that Lisbette crafted with deft motions of her fingertips.

"I admit nothing," Isabela said.

Taylor rubbed her arms. "She's making it cold out here."

Kopano interpreted that as a signal and happily put his arm around Taylor's shoulder. Isabela smiled at that and tried to catch Taylor's eye, but Taylor deliberately avoided her look. She'd been very cagey about whether Kopano and she were *a thing* now, ever since their kiss. Isabela could tell that Kopano at least thought they were.

Giving up on exchanging glances with Taylor, Isabela craned her neck to look around. "I wonder if anyone smuggled in some booze."

"Doubt it," Taylor said.

"I knew this would be too wholesome for me."

The New Year's Eve festivities were a campus-wide thing. There was the talent show stage out there in the courtyard, where they would later play some outdoor movies once the student entertainment ran out. There were board-game stations set up in the student union, where all-night breakfast was being served. Supposedly, Professor Nine had traveled to Mexico to personally procure a "butt-load" of primo fireworks. The students and faculty were all there, plus even some UN Peacekeepers who hadn't drawn guard duty. It reminded Taylor of the yearly lock-in her old school had done to raise money for whatever charity the seniors selected.

Everyone seemed to be having a good time. Not as good of a time as Isabela would've wanted, but still. A few people shot uneasy looks at Kopano and Ran—those came more from the administrators and soldiers than the other Garde, actually—but the Wolf News video failed to cast a major pall over events. Even Taylor let some of her carefully cultivated bad-girl persona slip for the night. She leaned into Kopano.

"I think everything's going to be fine," she told him.

"Really?" he replied.

"Just a feeling I've got." Taylor smiled. "First time I've had that feeling in a while, actually."

After Lisbette finished up with her ice sculptures, a team of duplicates hustled by her. They set to work plugging in guitars and assembling a drum kit.

Kopano rubbed his hands together. "Yes! Here we go!"

Nigel slapped Caleb on the shoulder. "You ready, mate?"

Through the eyes of his duplicates already onstage, Caleb could see the crowd. Altogether, there probably weren't more than one hundred people out there, but they were the one hundred people who he'd spent nearly every day around for the last year. Normally, it would be pretty embarrassing to flame out in front of them.

"If we bomb, I might not have to see most of these people again," Caleb replied, thinking about his looming departure from the Academy.

"That's the spirit," Nigel said. He grabbed a bottle of water and dumped the entire thing over his face and head, soaking through his white tank top. "Let's go!"

Nigel jogged out onto the stage and Caleb followed. Caleb, like all his duplicates, wore a black button-down shirt, dark slacks, and a red bow tie. Nigel, of course, had chosen the outfits. A round of applause that Caleb thought sounded skeptical greeted their arrival. Nigel swaggered right up to the mike stand where the lead guitar was propped and slung it on. Meanwhile, Caleb positioned himself behind the keyboard.

There weren't a lot of keys in the songs they'd chosen, but this spot afforded Caleb the best view of the stage and his duplicates. It helped him multitask the parts if he could oversee his clones rather than have to look through each one's eyes. There was a clone on bass and one on drums, plus one carrying a megaphone and dancing around, a role Nigel referred to as "hype man."

Caleb focused. Simultaneously, all the duplicates readied their instruments.

"We are Nigel and the Clones," Nigel growled. He looked down at the mike, then kicked the stand over and used his Legacy to amplify his voice. "And we're here to make you shit your britches!"

That was Caleb's cue. "One, two . . . ," he said into his mike. "Onetwothreefour!"

"I GET NERVOUS!" Nigel shrieked.

And they were off, beginning with a loud and jangly rendition of "I Get Nervous" by the Lost Sounds, followed by "Vertigo" by the Screamers, and closing with the Sweet's "Blockbuster." Nigel played his lead guitar like he was trying to choke it. He writhed across the edge of the stage, kicked wildly at the air, and punctuated every shouted lyric with an appropriately dramatic snarl. At one point during the set, Caleb was pretty sure Nigel lay down on his back and did some hip thrusts.

Caleb couldn't pay too much attention to Nigel during the performance. He was too busy making sure the duplicates stayed in time with each other, that the messy punk songs didn't get too incomprehensible. He felt like a conductor almost, flitting between his duplicates, putting the bass guitarist on autopilot so he could slow down the drummer, who had gone out of control. His own fingers stabbed at the keyboard almost without thought. He was in total control, yet it also felt to Caleb like an enormous act of letting go. He wondered, briefly, what his dad and brothers would think if they saw him up here.

Caleb wasn't the only one up there using his Legacy. Nigel pitched in too, although Caleb could never be sure how much his friend's sonic manipulation played into their band's sound. If one of the clones went off-key, Nigel bent their sound until Caleb could fix it. If one of them played too fast or too slow, Nigel lowered the volume on them until they got back in time.

Even though Nigel thought it would be more theatrical if the duplicates performed with stony stoicism, Caleb couldn't help but let his grin spread onto all of their faces.

It was a team effort. A masterpiece. It was the most in sync Caleb had felt in his entire life.

They rocked it.

When it was over, the crowd clapped politely. A lot of the instructors stuck fingers in their ears to make sure they could still hear, then blew out sighs of relief. The students made faces at each other, laughed, and mimed headbanging.

Isabela took her hands away from her ears. "Is it over?"

Taylor nodded. "They're done."

"Thank God," she said.

"You have to admire their . . . enthusiasm," Ran said diplomatically.

Taylor snickered, then glanced over at Kopano. He stood a few yards in front of the girls, both hands over his head in the shape of devil horns, bellowing for an encore.

"Well," she said. "At least they've got one groupie."

With the talent show over, most of the student body broke off into smaller groups, the same cliques that always tended to form up in the dining hall—tweebs, elemental Legacies, fans of the Smiths, the Academy's fledgling drama club, et cetera. They mingled, played board games, stuffed their faces or watched TV in the student union. They had the New Year's Eve countdown on. It was the first time that the ball would be dropping in the rebuilt Times Square. New York City still looked bombed-out and emptier than it used to, big gaps in the skyline, like the city had gotten punched in the mouth. But there were crowds and bands and noisemakers and the countdown—the process repeating twice until it was finally the West Coast's turn.

The Fugitive Six didn't hang out to watch. None of them would've been able to explain exactly why, but it felt weird for them to mingle with the rest of the student body. There was a strange sense after Nigel and the Clones' performance that this was a special night, a momentous night. The six of them all snuck down to the beach. They didn't even talk about doing it. They just went.

At some point, Isabela had slipped away and returned with two bottles of champagne and some beers filched from one of the faculty apartments. The popped cork on the first bottle sounded like a gunshot on the empty beach and for a second they all stared at each other, ducked low and stayed still like they were trying to hide, but no one came looking for them.

They passed the bottle around. They tossed smooth rocks into the cold waves, dancing away from the foamy tide. They ran up and down the beach, playing some game of tag that no one was really sure of the rules for.

Distantly, they could hear chanting from the student union. The countdown. They joined in, screaming numbers into the night.

Professor Nine timed his fireworks display to erupt with the New Year. It was as badass as he'd promised—chaotic blooms of red and gold, fizzy bolts of silver, yellow bursts that expanded into the shape of smiley faces. The sand under their toes became like a kaleidoscope.

Nigel tossed his arm around Ran's shoulder and kissed her wetly on the cheek. She scrunched up her face and laughed.

Taylor and Kopano kissed. A peck on the lips that lingered. Caleb's mouth fell open when he saw that. Nigel didn't have the heart to tell him about Kopano's success over

Christmas. Although Caleb's stomach did a loop, the warm feeling from the champagne softened the blow.

Maybe Isabela saw Caleb staring at Taylor and Kopano and that's why she flung her arms around his neck and planted a wet kiss on him, all tongue and heat. When it was over, Caleb stammered and Isabela held a finger in his face. "Don't get any ideas, weirdo. It's just New Year's."

She kissed all the others too after that, but none the way she'd kissed Caleb.

At some point, Nigel climbed up onto a sand dune and got everyone's attention. He held his beer bottle like a microphone.

"Well, since the lad is too shy to tell you lot himself, it's on me to announce that tonight's performance of Nigel and the Clones will likely be our last for a while." Nigel held the bottle out like he was making a toast. "Our friend Caleb here is off to Earth Garde. Ready to protect the world with his legion of basic white-bread meatheads. We're going to miss you, mate!"

Everyone was surprised, taken aback as a group because partying down on the beach had started to feel like it was a place they would never leave. Kopano hugged Caleb, patting him hard enough on the back to knock the wind out of him. Ran went over to him and held both of his hands, bowing to him in a very traditional Japanese way, made a little wobbly because Ran didn't have much of a head for champagne. Caleb watched Isabela dance through the waves with her dress hiked up to mid-thigh; she was smirking at him and he wondered if she knew he was thinking about kissing her again. These moments stretched out, the night a blur.

At one point, Taylor stood next to Caleb. Everyone else was down the beach. It was quiet.

"I'm sorry you're going," Taylor said, realizing it was true only as she spoke the words. "I wish we'd gotten to know each other better."

"Yeah," Caleb replied. "Sorry I was so weird at first."

"Don't be sorry." Taylor looked around. "I think we're all a little weird."

They didn't talk about the Foundation, or Einar, or any of the crap they'd been through. They just celebrated. Only Taylor had ever actually been to summer camp, but that's what it felt like. The end of summer camp.

Until Dr. Linda appeared.

Ran was the first to see the diminutive psychiatrist as she waddled up the beach with a flashlight held out in front of her. At first, Ran thought that maybe she was seeing things, so she pulled on Nigel's sleeve and pointed at Dr. Linda.

"Is she real?" Ran asked.

"What the shit . . . ?" Nigel replied quietly.

Dr. Linda paused when she saw their little group and let out a sigh of relief. She plucked a walkie-talkie off her belt and spoke into it.

"I found him down on the beach," Linda said. "It's okay."

The moment was surreal. The Garde stood in a loose semicircle, facing Dr. Linda, their good mood dashed, uncertain what would happen next. Some of them—like Nigel and

Taylor—had spent too much time staring at Linda's picture on the bulletin board in their secret lair under the training center. They were paranoid. Was this the night the Foundation made their move? What else could she be doing here? Others, like Isabela, had more grounded concerns. Were they going to get in trouble again? Technically, the beach wasn't off-limits.

Caleb discreetly kicked a spent champagne bottle behind a piece of driftwood.

Finally, Dr. Linda spoke. She didn't seem mad. Or villainous. She seemed . . . oddly somber.

"Nigel," she said. "We've been looking for you."

"Me?" Nigel replied, squinting at her. "Looking for me?"

"Yes. You need to come with me."

The Garde all tensed up, tightening their ranks around Nigel. Dr. Linda stared at them like she couldn't comprehend.

"The hell would I go anywhere with you, Linda?" Nigel replied.

But before Dr. Linda could reply, more flashlights appeared on the beach. There were a couple of Peacekeepers, Malcolm Goode, and Professor Nine in the lead. He bounded ahead of the others, almost as if he'd anticipated this particular crew of Garde might have an adverse reaction to being confronted by Dr. Linda.

"Nigel," Nine said breathlessly. "Damn, dude. We've been looking for you."

Now, seeing Nine acting weird, was the first time Nigel

actually felt worried. Ran put a hand on his shoulder.

"That's what she said," Nigel replied, waving a hand at Dr. Linda. He put on a cavalier smile. "What's the hubbub, then? People clamoring for an encore?"

"Nigel . . ." Nine frowned, he looked over his shoulder at the other administrators as if for help. When Dr. Linda opened her mouth to say something, Nine cut her off and plowed ahead. "There's no easy way to say this, buddy."

"Spit it out, Nine."

"Nigel, your dad died."

CHAPTER FOURTEEN

NIGEL BARNABY
LONDON, ENGLAND

NIGEL PUT HIS HAND ON THE WROUGHT-IRON GATE of the Saint John's Wood house but couldn't bring himself to push it open. Instead, he stood on the sidewalk in the damp English weather and pulled the collar of his coat tighter against a sudden chill.

This was the house where he grew up. Two stories of white brick with twice that many chimneys for the home's multiple fireplaces. It looked like a country manor plunked down in northern London, but then most of the houses around here looked that way. The buildings were tightly packed together—this was still the city, after all—but what one couldn't see from the sidewalk was the sprawling backyard that looked like a polo ground, lined with immaculate rows of oak trees to provide total privacy from the neighbors. From the sidewalk, people couldn't see the basement addition, the pool and billiards table, the home theater. From the sidewalk, they couldn't see the years of misery Nigel had spent there, thinking that things couldn't get worse.

Until they did.

Nigel was in no rush to get inside. He shifted his backpack around on his tired shoulders. His eyes were dry and heavy, his limbs felt fuzzy. He hadn't slept in . . . well, with the time difference, Nigel supposed that he technically hadn't slept since the day before yesterday. He felt a little bit like he was dreaming.

The block was quiet now. In the early morning, it usually was. Clean and tree-lined with no pedestrians.

There was a black limousine parked at the curb. He supposed that would be their transportation to the funeral. Behind that was parked an unassuming brown van, which, at that very moment, rolled down its window so the driver could call to Nigel.

"Everything okay?"

The driver's name was Ken Colton, an American, a UN Peacekeeper. He was in charge of the four-man detail assigned to accompany Nigel on his visit home. He had square features, salt-and-pepper hair, and reminded Nigel of a TV dad from some sitcom. Or maybe Nigel was just feeling sentimental. Nigel's hesitation to go inside had raised an alarm with the Peacekeepers, but Nigel waved them off.

"It's fine . . . ," he said. "Just bracing myself, y'know?"

Colton nodded like he understood, gave Nigel that tight-lipped sympathetic smile that he'd been seeing a lot of lately, and rolled the window back up.

With a sigh, Nigel pushed open the creaky gate and trudged towards his home.

"I vowed never to go back there," he had told Ran. "Those people are toxic. All of 'em. I'd like to forget they ever existed."

"I know," she replied softly.

"So you agree, then," Nigel concluded. "I shouldn't go. Tell Mum to piss off and be done with it, once and for all."

"I didn't say that."

This was early morning on New Year's Day. The two of them sat on a bench outside the student union, the campus quiet, everybody sleeping in or otherwise cozied up in the dorms. Nigel's mouth still felt sticky and tasted bitter, even after he'd brushed his teeth three times. He had thrown up that morning. Nigel told himself it was from the drinking, but he hadn't had that much. He tried to ignore the growing knot in his belly.

That old anxiety. Like he used to feel at his boarding school. Like he used to feel at home.

It hadn't started right away. When Dr. Linda and Nine interrupted their beach party to break the news, Nigel had basically felt numb. The whole night seemed surreal, like it was happening to someone else. For months, Nigel had barely thought about his dad and he assumed the reverse was true as well. Hearing about his death was like learning that the dictator of some distant despotic nation had died—all Nigel could think was *Oh, good.*

The mounting sense of dread hadn't really kicked in until Dr. Linda and Nine ushered him to a private room where his mom waited on the phone. Nigel had never known Bea Barnaby to tolerate being placed on hold, so she truly must have wanted to talk to him.

The conversation seemed like part of a dream now. A hazy memory. Nigel could remember only snatches of what his mom said. Her voice sounded brittle on the phone, tinny and far away.

"You must come home, love," she told him. "You absolutely must. I know it hasn't seemed like it of late, but we *are* a family. We need each other more than you know."

Nigel recounted those details to Ran later that morning. He was already packed. The Academy had lined up a helicopter to fly him off campus and then a private plane to whisk him off to London. They had a security detail arranged for him. Now that it was all sorted—now that he had time to think about it—Nigel didn't want to go.

"She didn't even sound sad on the phone, not really," Nigel told Ran. "More like desperate. Like I was the last caterer available on short notice. The funeral is sure to be a scene, all their colleagues and business partners and quote-unquote friends. Wouldn't look proper if I wasn't there."

Nigel paused. Ran waited, not pressing him.

"Dad actually told me once that they only had kids to keep up appearances," Nigel continued eventually. "Like they needed 'parenting' for a cocktail party conversation topic. In their circles, leaders of industry and all that—he said it looked *strange* not to have a family. *Wouldn't want people thinking we're queers, eh?* He said that to me. I think I was twelve."

Ran put her hand on Nigel's forearm. "I'm sorry," she said.

"Thing that eats me up the most is that he didn't live long enough for me to tell him what a shit dad and a wanker he was," Nigel replied. "Now I'm supposed to go over there and pretend he meant something to me."

"You do not have to pretend."

Nigel looked up at her, that familiar cockeyed grin taking shape. "You saying I should put all this in my eulogy?"

"No. I'm *definitely* not saying you should make a scene," Ran replied. "But you should look at this as a chance to find some closure. To pay your respects . . . or lack thereof. Let them see that you have become a great person in spite of them. Maybe there is a chance you can reconnect with your mom. If not, then you could put them behind you once and for all. But you will never know for sure if you don't go."

Nigel leaned his shoulder against Ran. "Been storing that up somewhere? Jesus. Most I've ever heard you speak all at once. You must be exhausted."

"Shut up," she replied.

When Nigel first set foot in the grand foyer of the Barnaby manor, no one noticed what a great person he had become. In fact, no one noticed him at all.

A swirling bustle of servants moved between the sitting room, the dining room, and the kitchen. They were in the midst of preparing for that afternoon's funeral—setting out covered trays of food, arranging place settings, some last-minute dusting and polishing. Nigel recognized some of the servants—his parents employed a small retinue of butlers, maids, and groundkeepers—and quickly determined that they were in charge of supervising the temporary help—the caterers, waiters, and valets. None of them noticed Nigel standing there dumb and mute.

A framed photograph of Nigel's father sat on an easel just inside the front door, surrounded on all sides by masses of wreathes and bouquets, the flowers growing with each passing second as a florist and her team added new arrangements. Nigel stared at the not-so-recent picture of his father; he looked dapper and serious. Nigel had to think where he'd seen that image before.

It was from his dad's company website. The photo he used to advertise financial services.

Nigel stepped carefully around the throngs of people, feeling like they were all engaged in a complicated dance that he dared not interrupt. At least until he spotted Willoughby, the family's longest-tenured servant. The man stood imperiously supervising a team of maids as they dusted the brasswork on the main staircase. Nigel touched his sleeve.

Willoughby turned with a raised eyebrow. "Yes?"

"Have you seen my mum, Willoughby?"

"And you are?"

"It's me. Nigel. Heir to all this aristocratic uselessness."

The older man squinted at Nigel for a long beat as if he couldn't make sense of what he was seeing. However, as soon as things clicked, Willoughby bowed deeply at the waist and became appropriately obsequious.

"Master Barnaby, my sincerest apologies. You have . . . changed." Willoughby took Nigel's hand in his gloved one, clasping firmly. "Might I add, heartfelt condolences on the passing of your father. He was a titan."

"He was a tit," replied Nigel briskly. "My mother, Willoughby. Where is she?"

"Lady Barnaby has already departed for the cemetery, I'm afraid. Busy with some last-minute arrangements, I'm sure. Your sister is here, though. I believe she and her husband are downstairs . . ."

After thanking Willoughby, Nigel skirted around the activity and took the elevator down to the basement. Immediately, the tang of salt water hit his nostrils, reminding him in a vague way of California. But, no matter how hard he wished it, Nigel wasn't back at the Academy. That was simply the smell of the belowground pool. The whole basement was cast in the water's shifting light, flashing aquamarine and gold.

Jessa, Nigel's sister, didn't look back at him when the elevator opened. She sat with her feet soaking, already attired for the day's festivities in an appropriately formal black dress. Her blond hair was tied back in simple ponytail. Jessa was eight years older than Nigel. Like him, Jessa had been sent off to boarding school when she turned twelve, so they barely shared any time in this house together. To Nigel, she often felt more like a friendly cousin than a sister.

"Hello, Jessa," Nigel called.

Her head snapped around immediately. "Nigel!" she practically shrieked. She hopped up and ran to him, wet feet slapping against the marble tile. Jessa hugged him and Nigel felt suddenly at home in a way that he wouldn't have thought possible.

"You're going to wrinkle your dress," he said, peeling free of his sister.

"Sorry, sorry," she replied. "I just—well, I wasn't sure you'd come."

"It's dad's funeral," Nigel said. "Thought I should put in an appearance."

Jessa rolled her eyes. "As if the old man did anything for you. For either of us. Went and died on one of his business trips. Mom tell you that?"

"She didn't tell me much."

"Heart attack in some third-world country while he was doing God knows what. Call girls and cocaine, probably."

Nigel stared at his sister. It had been more than a year

since he'd seen her and even then their last visit hadn't been for any substantial length of time—just the usual cold Christmas at Barnaby manor. For the first time, he realized that Jessa had eight more years of experience dealing with their parents than he did. No wonder she had married young and moved away from London.

"Hell, Jessa," Nigel replied with a shocked laugh. "I didn't realize I'd missed you."

Jessa pinched his cheek. "Good to see you, too. Like I said, I wasn't sure . . . if *I* didn't show, Mother would disinherit me; I'd never hear the end of it. But you? You had a ready-made excuse. *Important business. Can't get away. I'm a bloody alien now.*"

Nigel blew out a sigh. "Not an alien."

"You know what I mean." She took a step back from him. "Go on, then. Don't keep me in suspense. Let me see something."

It took Nigel a moment to realize what Jessa wanted. Then, he casually reached out with his telekinesis and levitated a nearby vase filled with multicolored sand. Jessa clapped, then waved her hands above and below the vase as if to check for strings.

"Marvelous. Simply marvelous," she said. "Owen? Did you see this?"

Nigel turned to see Owen, his brother-in-law, emerging from the nearby lounge where a muted soccer match played on the wide-screen television. Nigel had only met Owen a handful of times and he'd never failed to remind Nigel of a grown version of a Pepperpont boy. Nigel tried not to hold that against him. Owen was generically handsome, clean-shaven, chestnut hair immaculately combed, his black suit slim and perfectly tailored to his rugby player's frame. He was, in Nigel's experience, perpetually attached to his phone, always checking stock prices. Even now, he had to slip the device into his jacket pocket before he could give Nigel a firm handshake.

"Nice to see you again, Nigel," Owen said. He eyed the still-floating vase. "It's just like on the telly."

"Isn't it?" Jessa agreed. She put her hands on her hips. "So, lads, what should we do now?"

Nigel smiled; he could tell his sister was joking. But Owen looked flummoxed.

"We've got to get going, love," he said. "You know. The funeral?"

"Oh, right." Jessa tapped her forehead. "That."

Owen glanced from Nigel to Jessa. "He's supposed to change, isn't he?"

"Change?" Nigel asked.

"I think you look cool, brother," Jessa said, flicking one of the frayed strings on his hooded sweatshirt. "Like some conquering rock star returning home after a yearlong bender, but with superpowers."

"That's what I was going for."

"But mother dearest gave me strict instructions to outfit

you in the suit she left in your room. Better change or else she'll have them dig an extra grave, eh?"

Nigel didn't see his mother until the cemetery. She stood out, even at a distance, as Nigel made his way along the path between mausoleums, flanked by Jessa and Owen. She sat in the front row, right beside the empty pit where they'd be lowering his father's gold-detailed coffin. It was drizzling, so maybe Nigel's mom had just grabbed the closest garment at hand, but Nigel sort of figured the bright white raincoat his mom wore over her black mourning dress to be some kind of statement.

"My son, don't you look nice," Bea Barnaby said as Nigel took a seat beside her. The uncomfortable wooden chair was dry thanks to the row of umbrella-wielding well-wishers situated behind the family.

"Thanks," Nigel replied, even as he pulled uncomfortably at his shirt collar.

He wore the simple black suit, white dress shirt, and tie that his mom had left out for him. His discomfort at being dressed this way wasn't at all due to the clothes themselves— they fit perfectly, his mom somehow knowing his exact measurements. No self-respecting punk would wear this monkey suit. In a very small act of rebellion, Nigel had left his shirt's top button undone and tied a knot sloppy enough to earn demerits back at Pepperpont.

Surprisingly, his mother didn't seem to care. She slipped

a hand through the crook of his elbow and leaned against him. That was a pretty huge display of affection for the Barnaby family.

Bea looked good for a woman in her early fifties. She wore her blond hair in a jaw-length pageboy with a sharp side part. Her eyes were vivid blue and prone to dissecting looks. Bea's face was smooth, only a tasteful wrinkle here and there. Nigel was sure she'd had work done, but it was good work.

"You look tired," she said to him.

"Whirlwind twenty-four hours," Nigel said dryly. "Lost Dad and all."

Bea cleared her throat, as if getting ready for a prepared remark. "I know it might not have seemed like it, Nigel, but your father loved you very much—"

Nigel snorted. He felt his mother's steely gaze upon him but didn't dare meet her eyes. Ran was right. There was no point in making a scene, of making this any more miserable than it already had to be. Just get through it. Let his mother have her delusions.

He was surprised when she leaned close to him, her lips to his ear.

"Fuck it, then," Bea whispered. "The man was a bastard and we're better off rid of him. That's the bloody truth of it."

Nigel nearly burst out laughing. The crass admission from his mom was just so out of character. First Jessa, now her. Nigel had to admit to himself that maybe he'd built up just how terrible his family was. Maybe closure—or a new understanding of one another, like that two-faced Dr. Linda liked to say—was actually possible. He warmed to the feeling of his mom's hand on his arm.

"I want to hear everything," Bea said. "About your new life. Once all these dreadful formalities are over, we need to catch up."

"Yeah," Nigel replied. "That'll be good, mum."

Eventually, a priest showed up and said some words, read a few Bible verses. Nigel zoned out. He found himself doing that throughout the rest of the day. He was overtired, it was hard to focus, and a big part of his identity had been called into question. He'd always imagined himself as the great rebel, running off on his family, leaving all the bastards behind. But now, they didn't seem so cruel and distant. Instead, their lives seemed complicated and sad.

The funeral director handed out roses and everyone took a turn tossing one onto his father's coffin. Nigel tossed his rose. After him, his mom picked up a handful of damp dirt and sprinkled it on the casket. She made a dramatic show of looking for somewhere to brush off her hands.

They went back to the manor, a whole procession of cars, many of them operated by hired drivers. The house filled up. There were more people there than there had been at the actual funeral. Waiters escorted around trays of hors d'oeuvres. People Nigel could barely tell apart stuffed their faces while having grave conversations.

Nigel stood to the side with Bea and Jessa. They let the room come to them, as was appropriate and expected.

Handshake after handshake, sometimes paired with a squeeze of his upper arm. Dozens of dainty air-kisses to his cheek.

"Condolences, lad."

"Truly sorry about your father."

"He'll be missed."

And on and on. Nigel's neck was sore from all the nodding, his mouth dry from saying thank you over and over again. It was a bombardment of sympathy. As the afternoon went on, his collar and tie got looser and sloppier.

At some point, his mom handed him a glass containing a few fingers of Scotch, neat. "Look like you could use that," she said.

Nigel stared at her for a second, then shrugged and took an indelicate sip. The Scotch certainly didn't help him focus, but it did blur the edges of things, made it easier for him to force smiles.

His mom didn't have any problem with that. Bea was in her element. At some point, the reception turned into a networking event. She mingled, worked the room. There was a steady procession of men—usually the ones who hadn't showed up with wives, but not always—who kissed Bea's hand and professed their heartfelt sympathy. If she needed anything or, say, wanted to get a coffee and just talk, they were available.

"Can't tell why most of these people are here. Certainly not to honor our father," Jessa said to Nigel out of the corner of her mouth. "I'd say a good chunk showed up so they could hit on Mom, but then I also think there's a sizable crowd here to catch a glimpse of the Garde."

The back of Nigel's neck prickled. "Huh? Really?"

"Don't tell me you haven't noticed."

"Been kind of . . . in my own head."

"Up your own arse, you mean," Jessa said with a laugh. "Look at those two," she said, gesturing at an older couple across the room. "Right now they're saying how they thought you'd be taller and glowy-er."

Nigel pushed his fingers through his hair and found that he was sweating. Now that Jessa mentioned it, there were an awful lot of people staring at him. Waiting for him to do a trick, maybe.

"They did not . . ." Nigel paused. He saw black spots for a moment. "They did not say glowy-er."

"I'm an excellent lip reader; maybe that's *my* Legacy," Jessa replied, then narrowed her eyes at him. "Nigel? You all right?"

Nigel steadied himself on a nearby end table. It had all hit him like a ton of bricks. The sleepless trip to London, the jetlag, the Scotch.

"Think I might need to lie down," he mumbled.

His mom was at his side, her cool hands pressed against his cheek and forehead. When had she popped up? Nigel hadn't even noticed.

"Go on up and rest, love," she said gently. "You won't be

missing anything down here."

Nigel nodded and did as he was told. As he stumbled out of the sitting room, he got the odd sensation that everyone in there had turned to watch him go.

When he woke up, it was night and the house was quiet.

Nigel sat up in bed—his bed, the firm mattress with the wooden frame that he always banged his gangly knees against—drenched in sweat and with a splitting headache. He felt like he might be coming down with something.

Someone had placed a glass of ice water next to his bed. He drank greedily.

Even though this was his childhood room, it had never really felt like *his* space. The walls were covered in bookshelves filled with musty old editions of classics he'd never read. There was a globe in one corner and an antique train set in the other. The wallpaper was a snowy woodland print, all big-eyed owls and foxes darting around trees. No records. No posters for punk bands. Not even an anarchy symbol. This place wasn't him, it wasn't—

Wait. What was that smell?

Nigel sniffed the air. He could swear that he smelled gasoline.

He swung his feet out of bed, crossed the room on wobbly legs, and poked his head outside. The hallway was dark, but the smell of gas out there was stronger.

"Mom?" He called. "Jessa?"

The floorboards creaked. It sounded like something was being dragged around. The noise came from downstairs. There were lights on down there, a faint glow on the nearby staircase.

"Oi," Nigel said, rubbing his eyes. "I miss the funeral pyre?"

No answer.

Something wasn't right. Nigel regretted calling out now— like a dumb-ass in a horror movie. He crouched low into a fighting stance that Ran would approve of, ready to pounce if a threat came lurching out of the shadows. He crept to the top of the stairs.

There was someone lying on the floor down there. Was that . . . ?

Ken Colton. His Earth Garde escort. The man's eyes were open, staring straight up at the ceiling. Open and unblinking. Dead eyes.

The front door was open, the portrait of his father knocked aside. Two men in black body armor walked through, carrying the body of another Peacekeeper. Nigel didn't remember her name.

Their outfits were familiar. Just like the men Nigel had fought in Iceland. Blackstone mercenaries.

The armored men dropped the woman's body next to Colton and went back outside. One of them was whistling.

A third mercenary came around the corner carrying a red canister of gasoline. He dumped some of it on the

Peacekeeper's body, then moved on, splashing it on the curtains and on the picture of Mr. Barnaby. Nigel could see the gas now, glistening and pooling all over the hardwood floor.

"Nigel?"

It was his mom. She stood in her bedroom doorway, head tilted. Nigel motioned for her to be quiet, to stay back, but she came towards him anyway. Nigel took a step in her direction, trying to intercept her before the mercenary noticed her.

"Get back, Mum, there are bad men here," Nigel said, using his Legacy to direct his voice so only she could hear.

"You weren't supposed to wake up so soon, love."

"Huh?"

Before Nigel knew what was happening, his mom had stuck a syringe into the side of his neck. Nigel's eyes widened. He grasped at her, then flailed backwards. His limbs already felt heavy, his vision blurry. It was like a more intense version of how he'd felt after she gave him that drink before.

He looked into his mother's eyes and the truth hit him, piercing the fuzziness that was overtaking him.

An older British woman with blond hair. That's how Taylor described the lady at the Foundation who Einar reported to.

She'd even signed her letter *B.*

What were the bloody chances?

As Nigel reeled backwards, he spotted another mercenary. This one came out of his mother's room carrying her luggage.

"Well? Don't let him fall and hit his head, you daft bastard!"

At his mom's order, the mercenary dropped the luggage and looped his arms around Nigel's chest. He was too weak to fight. He tried to use his Legacies—to scream, to shove with his telekinesis—but he couldn't focus. All he wanted to do was sleep.

Bea gently stroked his cheek with the back of her hand.

"There, there," she said. "Sleep now. When you wake up, we'll have that chat."

CHAPTER FIFTEEN

KOPANO OKEKE
RAN TAKEDA
THE HUMAN GARDE ACADEMY—POINT REYES, CALIFORNIA

KOPANO HATED TO RUN.

That's not to say he didn't like to exercise. He enjoyed training; he loved games and competition. But running simply for the sake of running? What was the point of that?

Breathing hard, Kopano chugged past the four-mile marker on the dirt track that snaked around the Academy grounds. Only one more mile of this boredom to endure. It still disappointed Kopano that not all training at the Academy was cool Legacy-related activities. In fact, the good stuff only really took place under Nine's tutelage, while the vast majority of their exercise regimen was overseen by other faculty—strength coaches, boot camp sergeants, world-renowned personal trainers. Sadists, all of them, their shared goal to turn the young Garde into perfect athletic specimens.

Kopano wasn't supposed to use his Legacies on this five-mile run. But if he made his body a little lighter as his calves got sorer, who would know the difference?

Footsteps pounded behind him. Kopano glanced over his shoulder, saw Nic Lambert bounding along behind him. The Belgian kid was broader and taller than Kopano, more powerful, thanks to his enhanced-strength Legacy, and clearly the better runner. He'd started a full ten minutes behind Kopano.

"Come on, Kopano, pick it up!" Nic yelled in a way that was probably meant to be encouraging.

Kopano's brow furrowed, but he was too winded to form a reply, and then Nic was by him anyway. He couldn't wait to return to the dorms and commiserate with Nigel, who also hated these purposeless runs. The thought of venting to his friend actually got Kopano to pick up some speed.

Except, Kopano realized, there was no one back in his suite to complain to. His pace returned to its dogged norm as the disappointment set in. Caleb had been transferred to Earth Garde and Nigel was home mourning his father for at least a few more days.

It had dawned on Kopano three days ago, during that first night having the pod to himself, that he had never really been lonely before.

At first, the solitude had seemed like a cool novelty to Kopano. Back in Lagos, he shared a room with his little brothers. Personal space there was a foreign concept. Of course there were times when he could sneak off and be alone, but even then there was always a reassuring bustle of activity nearby, the voices of his parents or neighbors audible through the thin walls of their apartment. Even though he had his own room at the Academy, it was still pretty much the same deal. Either Nigel or Caleb (sometimes many Calebs) were in the common room and, if not, he could still sense them moving about in their own rooms.

The first night, Kopano had thrilled at sitting around in the common room wearing nothing but his boxers, singing along loudly to whatever came on the radio. But, that got boring quick, and the quiet of his pod started to feel unnatural.

He spent most of that night in Taylor's suite, lingering there late enough that Taylor could barely keep her eyes open. He only left when Isabela started mocking him about being too scared to stay in his own room by himself.

This wasn't an easy time for Kopano to be without his friends. The coverage about him and Ran was still playing around the clock on all the cable news networks. Apparently, there was nothing those journalists liked more than speculating what might happen next. Would the Garde be sent to jail for assault? Would they be deported to their home countries? Would there be another attack? The hypothetical questions were answered by experts whose fields ranged from international law to child psychology, and all their opinions were somehow considered to be breaking news.

Up ahead on the track, Kopano spotted Ran. He grimaced. She wasn't part of his endurance training seminar, which meant she was out here for the fun of it. He slowed his pace

so that he wouldn't catch up to her, then veered off the track
entirely and headed for the dorms. If his instructor noticed,
Kopano would just lie and say he'd gotten a cramp.

Ran was the reason Kopano hadn't spent every night
hanging out in Taylor's suite. He was avoiding her. He knew
it was stupid—Ran was just as much a victim as him—but
being around her reminded him of the whole Harvester
controversy. It's not like Ran tried to talk to him about the
incident—the girl didn't say much of anything, especially
without Nigel around to coax words out of her—but he knew
that she'd been hanging around the student union, watching
the news as much as possible, letting the demented coverage
of their misdeeds buffet her.

He wanted to forget about the whole thing, ignore it
until it went away. He couldn't understand why Ran was
so obsessed with watching the men on the news call her a
monster.

From the corner of her eye, Ran watched Kopano veer off the
track and head for the dorms. She had slowed her pace to
see if he would like to run with her, but wasn't offended that
he instead chose to run away. She didn't take it personally.
Their faces were often together these days, grainy screen-
grabs on television, newspapers, and blogs. Ran couldn't
blame Kopano for wanting some space.

Ran picked up speed, relishing the burning in her lungs.
Soon, Nic Lambert came into view. She passed him easily, a
faint smile on her lips as she felt the boy increase his pace in

a valiant attempt to keep up with her.

Ran had spent a lot of time on the track lately, exhausting herself on purpose, burning away the angry energy inside her that welled up whenever she watched Wolf News, which, lately, was often. If Kopano had asked why she watched so much of the channel's distorted coverage, she would've told him how it confirmed her own concerns about her Legacies. She'd sworn off her destructive powers for the same reasons the newscasters on Wolf News articulated—she was dangerous, unpredictable, deadly.

And yet, hearing herself described this way, knowing how the media had twisted the details of their encounter with the Harvesters beyond recognition—this all infuriated Ran. She couldn't reconcile those two feelings.

So she ran. And she kept watching.

Actually, it was about time for Don Leary to come on. He was the worst of all the Wolf News blowhards, which meant Ran never missed an episode. Ran left the track and headed for the student union, stretching out her back and legs as she went.

It was late afternoon, the sun just starting to dip low—that weird time when it was too early for dinner but too late for lunch. That meant the student union wouldn't be crowded. No one would compete with her for use of the TV.

As Ran approached, she noticed a group of Peacekeepers in jumpsuits milling around outside. They were a maintenance crew, engaged in breaking and pulling up tiles around the entrance and dumping the fragments into a nearby Dumpster. They had blocked off the student union's entrance with yellow caution tape. Ran stopped short and raised a questioning eyebrow at the nearest Peacekeeper.

"Mold," he explained with a shrug. "We'll be done before dinner."

"I see," Ran said, not letting her disappointment show. She started to turn away, but the Peacekeeper stopped her.

"You look like you could use something to eat," he said, noting Ran's sweaty appearance. He lifted up the yellow tape. "If you don't mind the noise, I think they left some cold sandwiches out from lunch."

Ran bowed her head and smiled. "Thank you."

"Sure," he replied. "Gotta keep our best and brightest fueled up, eh?"

She ducked under the caution tape and entered the student union, deserted except for the sweating Peacekeepers, immediately making a beeline not for the sandwiches but for the remote.

Kopano stopped outside his dorm room and listened, hoping to hear the abrasive chords of one of Nigel's punk bands. No such luck. Only silence waited for Kopano. He sighed and loosened his molecules, passing through the door like a ghost.

"Another night alone in my underwear," Kopano declared to the empty room.

"Um, maybe you could hold off on that?"

Kopano practically jumped out of his skin at the sound

of a woman's voice. He turned and found a smiling Peace-keeper standing in the doorway to Caleb's room. She was in her thirties, with short brown hair and freckles, and wore the blue-and-white jumpsuit of a cadet, the ones they some-times sent onto campus to do jobs that didn't fall under the Garde's comprehensive chore list—usually maintenance stuff. From her accent, Kopano could tell she was American.

"Didn't mean to scare you," she said, stepping aside so that Kopano could see past her. There was a second Peace-keeper, a male, in Caleb's old room, this one pulling the sheets off the bed and loading them into a large hamper.

"You didn't scare me," Kopano said, and puffed out his chest. "Okay, maybe a little," he added and the Peacekeeper chuckled. "What are you doing in there?"

"Got to get the room ready for the next occupant. All kinds of stuff we have to do," she replied. The woman waved a handheld Geiger counter at Kopano. "Would you believe we have to test the mattress for radiation?"

"Seriously? But that's got nothing to do with Caleb's power."

"Yeah, we know that. Still, it's one of the regulations." She rolled her eyes. "We should be out of your hair in thirty minutes or so."

"No rush," Kopano said. He actually felt grateful for the company. "Will there be a new roommate coming soon?"

The Peacekeeper shrugged. "No idea." She snapped her fingers as if remembering something. "Oh, hey, we found this in the closet. Think your friend left it behind."

She held up a gray canister. It looked like hair spray without a label. Kopano squinted and walked forward for a closer look.

"What is it?"

"We are going on five days since we here at Wolf News first broke the story of two Garde going on a rogue rampage across California," proclaimed Don Leary, the red-faced goon whose abrasive manner of speech Ran had somehow grown inured to since she became a voracious viewer of his channel. "And what has the response been from Earth Garde?"

Leary paused for rhetorical emphasis and Ran found herself hesitating with a square piece of tuna salad sandwich poised just in front of her mouth. A statement from Earth Garde appeared on the screen next to Leary's head. He proceeded to read it out loud, inflecting some of the words with sarcastic emphasis.

"We at Earth Garde are *aware* of the *incident* in California. We are currently conducting an *internal investigation* into the matter and are confident that the Human Garde Academy and Earth Garde complies with the *UN standards* in the Garde Declaration."

Leary shook his head in disgust. His words echoed around the virtually empty student union. Ran sat right under the mounted big-screen television, legs crisscrossed, half-eaten sandwich in her lap. She used to sit like this back home when she was a kid, right in front of the TV, letting her favorite anime engulf her. Wolf News wasn't nearly as entertaining, but she still couldn't look away.

"What are the bureaucrats at Earth Garde really saying here?" Leary asked his viewers. "They're saying that we here—*in America*—basically don't have any rights. Attacked on our own soil by superpowered foreigners, and this is a matter not for the California state police, not the FBI, not the NSA—*for the UN*. The United Nations, folks. Are you kidding me? Who put them in charge?"

Ran sensed movement behind her. She glanced over her shoulder and saw that a couple of Peacekeepers from outside had come in to rummage through a toolbox, although she caught them surreptitiously peeking at her and the TV. She wondered what the soldiers thought of this whole mess. After all, she and Kopano weren't the only ones getting dragged by Leary. The Peacekeepers were getting it bad as well. She turned her attention back to the news.

"Ms. Takeda."

Ran's shoulders tensed. Now there was a voice even more unwelcome than the broadcaster.

Greger, dressed as usual in one of his expensive suits, stepped between the Peacekeepers as he entered the student union and approached.

"You shouldn't watch this ill-informed buffoon," he said, waving at Leary. "He's too one-sided."

Ran wasn't in the mood for another one of Greger's slimy

recruitment speeches. She wrapped what was left of her sandwich back in its plastic and stood up.

"I was just going," she said.

"Ah, I see," Greger replied. "Well, have a nice rest. We'll talk soon."

"A nice—?"

Ran felt a pinch. She twisted her head. Something was sticking out of her neck. She groped for her throat and yanked out a tranquilizer dart.

"What ith thisss . . . ?"

Her mouth was already numb. As her vision dimmed, Ran noticed that the Peacekeepers by the door had found what they were looking for in their toolbox. Tranquilizer guns with suppressors. One of them had shot her.

Ran stumbled. Greger caught her under the arms and supported her weight.

"I know you don't trust me," he said. "But this is for your own good."

"What is that?" Kopano asked. "Cologne or something?"

The Peacekeeper shrugged again, her smile unwaveringly pleasant. As soon as Kopano got close, she pressed down a button on the top of the canister. With a pressurized hiss, the bottle sprayed an odorless mist right in Kopano's face. He laughed in surprise at the sudden numbing sensation.

"Weird," Kopano muttered. "I don't think . . . that's . . . Caleb's . . ."

He fell on his face, knocked out.

The two Peacekeepers picked him up and dumped him in the hamper, covering his body with the old sheets from Caleb's bed.

CHAPTER SIXTEEN

TAYLOR COOK
THE HUMAN GARDE ACADEMY—POINT REYES, CALIFORNIA

"WHAT DO YOU MEAN YOU DON'T KNOW WHERE THEY are?" Taylor shouted.

Nine ground his teeth together as he paced back and forth. "Relocated for their own protection. That's all Earth Garde told me. After they already took them." He pressed his knuckles into his metal palm. "Greger didn't even have the balls to tell me in person."

Their words echoed off the walls of the service area beneath the training center. Their hidden lair seemed so much bigger now that two-thirds of the Fugitive Six were gone. Taylor stood next to the bulletin board covered in their intel about the Foundation. All that digging seemed pointless now and the room, once a safe place for Taylor and her friends, felt cold and empty.

"They took them," Taylor said, still in disbelief. "Snatched them up just like the Foundation would have."

"I don't know if that's a fair comparison," Malcolm said. He stood in the middle of the room, between Nine and Taylor, his hands out and open, perpetually ready to calm someone down. "We don't actually know the full story here. It's possible Earth Garde got wind of some threat and took them into custody for their own protection."

"I thought the Academy and Earth Garde were the same thing," Isabela said. She sat at the table, looking more cool and collected than the others. Her nails clicked repeatedly against the laminate surface, the only sign she was feeling any anxiety about what was going on. Taylor envied her friend for being so in control.

"Our responsibility here is to train and take care of young Garde," Malcolm replied. "Once you're promoted to Earth Garde, the UN is in charge until your five-year service period is over. Ultimately, they call the shots, especially considering how this incident with the Harvesters happened *outside* the Academy."

A chill crept up Taylor's spine. Wasn't this exactly what Einar had described to her back in Iceland—that Earth Garde was just a bigger, more public version of the Foundation? She bit the inside of her cheek.

Nine snorted. "Oh, bullshit, Malcolm. If there was some threat from this dumb-ass scandal, there's nowhere safer than here."

"I don't disagree with you," Malcolm replied. "I'm just explaining the way the laws—"

"How do you figure?" Taylor interrupted, staring at Nine.

"What?"

"How do you figure they'd be safer here?" She asked. "You couldn't keep them safe from these Earth Garde people, couldn't keep us safe from those Harvesters and the Foundation in the first place. How would you keep them safe from whatever comes next?"

Nine stopped pacing and glared at her. "Are you doing your little bad-girl routine right now? Because I am not into it. And blaming me for you guys running off and stepping in shit, I mean, wow, that's rich."

"I'm not blaming you for that," Taylor replied. "I'm blaming you for being crap at your job."

Nine locked eyes with Taylor for a tense couple of seconds, no one else in the room saying a word. Then, he turned pointedly away and looked at Lexa, her fingers bouncing seamlessly across the two keyboards. Her eyes were slightly red-rimmed from a recent lack of blinking.

"Tell me you've got something," Nine said.

"When we hacked Greger's account, I left open a back door into Earth Garde's network," she replied. "If there's something here about where they took Ran and Kopano, I'll find it."

Malcolm cleared his throat, peering uncomfortably over the top of his spectacles. "I have to ask . . . to what end?"

"What do you mean?" Nine replied. "So we can bust them out, obviously."

"Bust them out," Malcolm repeated. He put his hand on Nine's shoulder. "You're thinking like it's the old days, Nine. These aren't Mogadorians who have captured the students. Their lives aren't in danger."

"You don't know that," Taylor butted in. "And anyway, even if they are safe with Earth Garde, they still shouldn't be under arrest or detained or whatever. The whole scandal is bullshit. We had every right to defend ourselves against those Harvesters."

Malcolm turned to her. "Earth Garde are our allies. People we've trained and fought alongside work for them. They're good people. If this is what they think is best . . ."

"Then why are they acting like snakes?" Isabela asked, her voice calmer than Taylor's but no less sharp. "Why do this behind your backs?"

"I don't agree with their methods and I wish we were kept more in the loop," Malcolm conceded. "But, I imagine Greger knew that, if he was up front about Earth Garde's decision, he would encounter . . . resistance."

"I would've tried to stop them," Nine grumbled.

"And what kind of damage would that have led to?" Malcolm asked. "No. I think our research down here has made us all a bit paranoid. We can trust Earth Garde. I truly believe that."

"The only people I trust are either in this room," Taylor

said, "or somewhere they shouldn't be."

Before Malcolm could respond, Lexa made a noise. Her breath caught in her throat, eyes widening. Whatever information she'd hacked into, it wasn't good news. Nine was immediately beside her, reading over her shoulder, his mouth moving as he went.

"You better look at this," she said to Malcolm.

Taylor and Isabela exchanged a look. While the administrators were all huddled on one side of the table, Taylor and Isabela were being kept in the dark as usual.

"Secrets don't make friends," Isabela said with an annoyed toss of her hair.

Malcolm had gone a shade paler from whatever he read. "I think . . . I think we better adjourn this meeting for now so we can discuss some, ah, administrative matters."

"Oh, hell with that," Taylor replied.

With her telekinesis, Taylor took hold of Lexa's laptop and levitated it out of reach before the Loric woman could grab it. Nine stepped back—the computer almost hit him in the chin—but made no effort to stop Taylor.

"Hey!" Lexa shouted as she shot up from the table. "That is *not* okay!"

"Let them see it," Nine said grimly. "They deserve to know."

Taylor turned the laptop in the air so she could read the screen, Isabela coming over to stand next to her. Lexa had accessed a report filed to Earth Garde's top secret security database.

INCIDENT REPORT 0010319

. . . developing . . .

Earth Garde Central contacted by SIS agents in London responding to a fire in the Saint John's Wood neighborhood where a detachment of Peacekeepers was deployed. A home registered to Reginald Barnaby, deceased father of Earth Garde asset #003-NB was burned to the ground. Preliminary investigation by local authorities indicates arson.

Bodies of Peacekeeper detachment recovered on scene. All operatives KIA. Autopsies suggest fatalities occurred prior to fire. Involvement of foreign government and/or terrorist organization suspected. Investigation in process.

Whereabouts of #003-NB and mother remain unknown. #003-NB sister and brother-in-law were staying at a nearby hotel and have been detained until investigation concludes. Media blackout protocol in place with assistance from SIS and local authorities. Minimizing dissemination of sensitive information is a priority.

. . . developing . . .

As she finished reading, Taylor forgot to maintain her telekinetic grip on the laptop. It would've fallen to the floor if Nine hadn't snagged it with his own telekinesis and returned it to the table in front of Lexa.

"They . . . they got Nigel," Taylor said, covering her mouth with her hand. "Jesus. What the hell is going on?"

"He's not dead," Isabela replied, her voice cracking a little. "The report said they couldn't find him, right?"

"Yes," Malcolm quickly jumped in. "Those Peacekeepers that went with him, however . . ."

"They're keeping this stuff from us," Nine said, and he resumed his pacing. "Someone burned down Nigel's house three days ago and took him and no one's told us. Greger's people came in here and grabbed two of my students . . ."

"And don't forget Caleb," Isabela said. "You think that is a coincidence, hm? That he would be transferred out just now?"

"Let's not get paranoid," Malcolm said. "We need to keep our heads."

"You keep *your* head, old man," Isabela snapped. "You're not the one in danger."

Malcolm pursed his lips and turned to Nine, again using that fatherly tone to try calming him down. "We will figure this out, Nine," he said.

Taylor understood that Malcolm was only trying to protect them and to abide by the rules—she imagined her father would've taken a very similar tact. Still, that didn't make her any less angry. Her friends were being picked off one by one by sinister forces and the people tasked with protecting them were basically sitting on their hands. She strode forward and put herself in Nine's path.

"What are you going to do about this?" she asked hotly.

Nine flexed the fingers on his cybernetic arm, looking down at Taylor. His eye twitched as he tried to keep his emotions in check.

"We'll start making inquiries," Malcolm said. "We'll talk with our allies."

"You'll sit around," Taylor said. "And wait for them to come for the rest of us."

"We have an entire student body to think about," Malcolm piped in again. "Taylor, please believe us when we say that we'll do everything we can to help Nigel, Ran, and Kopano. I'm—I'm as angry about this as the rest of you. But we can't do something that would endanger what we've built here."

"Malcolm's right," Lexa said. "We need to play it smart."

Taylor ignored the others, still looking up at Nine. He was the one with Legacies. He'd been chased across the world, fought for his life, battled the Mogadorians. Only he could understand what Taylor was feeling—the need to do *something, anything.*

Nine's shoulders slumped. He looked away from Taylor.

"They're right," he said quietly. "We have to think about the bigger picture here. There's a right way to attack these problems . . ."

Taylor snorted and started to turn away, but Nine grabbed her hand.

"Believe me, I'd love to rush out of here and start punching things until this was all straightened out," Nine said quietly. "But life doesn't work that way anymore. Not for me."

"We aren't actually going to listen to those *peidão*, are we?"

"No. Of course not."

Taylor and Isabela moved briskly away from the training center on the path back to the dorms. The night was cold enough to make Isabela dramatically chatter her teeth and rub her arms. The campus was deserted, the rest of the student body happily asleep, ignorant to all the forces that would exploit their Legacies if given half the chance. Taylor envied them.

"Good," Isabela said. "Because, the way I see it, you owe every one of us a rescue. Time to pay up."

Taylor snorted and shook her head. She was glad to have Isabela at her side, her own confidence bolstered by the Brazilian's brashness.

"Should I sneak us out of here?" Isabela asked. "Even the added security is no match for my skills. We could be on our way to the nearest secret Earth Garde facility in no time."

"That's the thing about secret facilities, though," Taylor replied. "They're secret. What happened to Ran and Kopano is totally screwed up, but at least we know they're still in the Earth Garde system somewhere. Safe. I'm more worried about Nigel. That fire . . ."

"Smells like the Foundation, yes?"

"Yeah."

Isabela shook her head vigorously. "Professor Nine—*pah*. I can't believe him. He hulks around all badass but when it comes down to it, when Nigel is taken and people murdered he's like, *Oh, sorry, we must listen to the dorks and stay here.* All those boring nights planning and when something finally happens, they puss out. Hey, where are we going?"

Taylor had turned off the path that would lead them back to the dorms, instead leading Isabela towards the cul-de-sac of small cabins where the on-site faculty lived.

"Nine's not totally neutered yet," Taylor replied. She held up an access card with the faculty emblem on it, the kind that would unlock any door in the Academy. "He slipped me this."

"Aha. Good boy."

"Way I see it, we've only got one lead to the Foundation. I know we've spent the last couple of months trying to set her up, to get her to recruit me, but . . . the situation has changed."

"Dr. Linda," Isabela said quietly, a predatory smile spreading across her face. "You want to confront her."

"I'm going to wake her up and get answers out of her," Taylor answered darkly. "One way or another."

The two of them slipped between cabins, the windows all dark, everyone asleep. They closed in on the one where Dr. Linda lived. She had a few flowerpots on her doorstep and a peace sign pinwheel that turned lazily in the night air. Not exactly the lair of a blackhearted spy. *That's what makes her so dangerous*, Taylor reminded herself.

"You are thinking of beating answers out of her, yes?" Isabela whispered, reading her mind. "Torture, maybe?"

Taylor frowned. "If that's what I have to do . . ."

"I think . . . ," Isabela replied, smirking now. "I think I know a better way."

CHAPTER SEVENTEEN

CALEB CRANE
SYDNEY, AUSTRALIA

ON THE OTHER SIDE OF THE WORLD, A TEAM OF Calebs hefted a steel beam onto their shoulders and marched forward. The duplicates were sweating, their light blue Earth Garde T-shirts stuck to their backs. Caleb wiped his face, sweating too—he wasn't sure if the clones were perspiring because he was, or because they actually had sweat glands of their own. He tried not to ponder weird questions like that anymore. He cringed as the thought called to mind that time in class when he suggested harvesting organs from his duplicates.

Still couldn't believe he said that one out loud.

The clones were a silent centipede, carrying the girder down the rocky slope of the construction site and stacking it with the others. Caleb was in control. There were no stragglers mouthing off, voicing Caleb's private thoughts. They all moved as one.

Ever since the trip home for Christmas, Caleb had felt more relaxed, more centered. Nigel would have been proud of him, Caleb thought. *Bloody zen-like,* Caleb could imagine him saying. He hoped his friend was all right.

He also hoped that feeling would last.

Caleb stood on the edge of the pit, supervising his duplicates from there. His muscles ached, but not from lifting anything. It was the dull throb that happened whenever he had a lot of duplicates active for a protracted period of time. They'd been out here all afternoon, Caleb and the others doing the work of a whole construction crew all on their own.

He stood on the edge of what used to be the Sydney Opera House. Caleb had seen pictures of the place, the overlapping concrete shells that looked like shark mouths popping out of the ocean. It had been a cool place, at least until a Mogadorian warship turned it into a crater.

And now they were here to rebuild. That was Caleb's first assignment as a member of Earth Garde—to travel the world and help areas still recovering from the Mog invasion.

Caleb turned to look out over the water, smiling as a cool breeze prickled his skin with mist. Uncle Clarence had warned him to keep an eye out for anything suspicious while on assignment, but there wasn't any of that here.

They were doing good work. Helping actual people.

"Uh, excuse me," piped up a voice at Caleb's elbow. "Are

you . . . the one in control?"

Caleb turned to find a short, middle-aged man at his side, a laminate badge around his neck identifying him as press. Five vans full of them had shown up an hour ago, there for a preplanned photo op and to write some positive coverage about Earth Garde's humanitarian efforts. None of them had paid much attention to Caleb until now.

"In control of . . . ?" Caleb asked.

"Them," the reporter said, motioning at the mass of clones currently carrying another steel beam into the pit.

"Yeah," Caleb said. He smiled and extended a hand. "I'm Caleb Crane, sir. Duplicator. What can I do for you?"

"Yeah, uh, nice to meet you." The reporter quickly shook his hand. "Would you mind getting your duplicates out of the way for a bit? They're visually confusing and a little, um, creepy."

"Oh," Caleb replied. "Yeah. Sorry."

Caleb tried not to take the request personally. He already knew that he wasn't the main attraction here. That honor belonged to Melanie Jackson, the blond-haired and blue-eyed daughter of President Jackson who had shepherded the United States through the Mogadorian invasion. Through the eyes of his duplicates, Caleb saw her in the center of the construction site, flowing hair pulled back by a bandanna, wearing a cutoff T-shirt that showed off her tan arms. She carried a broken chunk of pipe on her shoulder—part of the works they were clearing out—the five-hundred-pound burden held with an impossible ease as she casually chatted with reporters.

To Caleb, Melanie seemed nearly as alien as the Mogadorians. She was a celebrity. The face of Earth Garde. Always so cool and self-possessed. She even sweated in the perfect amount. With the press around, she was smiling and gregarious, but at the hotel they were staying in, she mostly kept to herself. Caleb was pretty sure she had already forgotten his name.

Caleb sent a mental instruction to his duplicates to set down the steel beam they were lugging around and clear out of Melanie's background. Maybe he was distracted or maybe the reporter's request annoyed him more than he realized. Either way, instead of gently laying down the beam, his clones simply dropped it on the stack.

The resulting noise was sharp and loud, like a massive hammer being struck. Pretty much everyone around the construction site flinched.

Melanie did more than that. She flung the section of pipe off her shoulder and lunged for cover behind a pile of debris. It was as if she'd come under attack.

Everything suddenly felt slow motion to Caleb. The section of pipe fell towards a pair of slow-moving reporters, big enough to crush them. They shielded their faces and shouted.

The pipe stopped. Suspended in midair. Telekinesis, but not Caleb's. And definitely not Melanie's.

"Got it!" Daniela Morales cried with a daring smile. "Just a little teamwork demonstration for you guys."

Daniela. Caleb had been relieved to see her on his first day, even if the last time they ran into each other she'd been turning his feet to stone. He was even more relieved to see her now. She'd been down in the pit using her stone-vision to shore up a salvageable section of foundation, another background sidekick for Melanie. But, a more useful one than Caleb. With her telekinesis, she set the pipe down in a nearby scrap heap. Danger averted, Daniela was quick to take a flamboyant bow for the camera, eliciting relieved laughter from the reporters and a smattering of applause. She made it look like the entire incident was intentional.

Caleb blew out a relieved sigh.

A Peacekeeper-assigned press secretary was soon on the scene, telling the reporters that Melanie and the other Garde were tired and that it was time to call it a day. Melanie, no longer hiding behind the rubble, waved shakily to her audience as she was escorted away by a half dozen armed Peacekeepers. Daniela dusted off her hands and climbed up the rocky slope to where Caleb awkwardly stood around. None of the lingering reporters paid them any attention.

Even though she was the same age as Caleb, he felt like she was older—Daniela acted like she'd seen it all. Well, she once battled a fifty-foot-tall Mogadorian monster specifically engineered to kill Garde so, Caleb supposed, in a way she had. Daniela was one of the first Human Garde to make contact with the Loric. She had fought alongside John Smith in the battle of New York City. There were stories that she'd even saved his life. Because of her friendship with John and experience in the field—even if that experience was really only a couple of crazy days—Daniela had been allowed to skip the Academy and go directly to Earth Garde.

As she approached, Daniela worked a finger in and out of her ear and smiled playfully at Caleb.

"Busted my eardrum with that shit, man," she complained. "Your clones got butterfingers."

"Sorry," Caleb replied, rubbing the back of his neck. "I got distracted."

"I'm messing with you. Relax."

They stood next to each other on the edge of the site. On the other side of the pit, Melanie and her entourage had already made it to where the armored cars were parked. They drove away, leaving a handful of Peacekeepers and a couple of cars behind for Caleb and Daniela.

"I didn't mean to scare her," Caleb said quietly.

Daniela snorted. "Not your fault. Girl is jumpy as hell. Last week she about punched a hole through some poor guy's chest because he happened to be standing close by when a car backfired."

"Seriously?"

"Yep. They won't be putting that shit in any of the press releases, though."

The two of them started around the edge of construction site, taking their time.

"Why is she like that?" Caleb asked, looking around. "I know I've only been here a couple of days, but this doesn't seem like a very stressful job."

Daniela tucked a stray braid behind her ear, her face turning somber. "They didn't tell you what happened last year?"

Caleb shook his head.

"She was doing relief work in the Philippines. Some crazies attacked her. Kidnapped the kid she was working with, even. Some Italian. A healer."

Vincent Iabruzzi. Caleb knew the name and the incident from the information the Fugitive Six had gathered on the Foundation. Taylor had met the guy when she was in Abu Dhabi. Caleb didn't know that Melanie was present the day that Vincent was taken.

"Are they looking for him?" he asked. "Or, I mean, did they find him?"

Daniela lowered her voice, even though there was no one around. "They try to keep the nasty stuff from us because Melanie's all sensitive, but one of the Peacekeepers told me they found his body in the jungle. Had to identify the poor kid from dental records. I guess the Peacekeepers rounded up the crazies that did it. Some cult that thought they could steal his quote-unquote magic powers."

"Wow," Caleb said. "When did they find him?"

"A few weeks after he got taken," Daniela replied. "Don't say anything to Melanie. She's still holding out hope and Earth Garde wants to keep her happy."

A few weeks. Caleb shook his head. The timeline didn't make sense. Taylor met Vincent in the United Arab Emirates well after that. The body must have been a fake planted by the Foundation and the cult used as scapegoats just like the Harvesters had been.

"All we've done is help, yet some people already hate our kind," Daniela continued, misreading Caleb's solemn face. "You know all about that, huh?"

Daniela gave him a meaningful look, probably thinking about Caleb's run-in with the Harvesters. She had been there for that battle, but how much did she know about who was really behind it, who had set that conflict in motion? Did Daniela know about the Foundation? Even though Caleb felt like he could trust Daniela, he kept his mouth shut.

"Yeah," Caleb replied. "It's messed up."

"Uh-huh. Anyway, in case you haven't realized it yet, we aren't just here to help build stuff and stand in the background of pictures."

"We aren't?"

"Jetlag making you slow?" She elbowed him playfully. "We're here to keep an eye on Ms. Earth Garde. In case something else goes down. Strong as she is, she never hit the Academy. She never ran for her life during a Mog ambush. She's not hard like us, and the higher-ups know it. But she's marketable as shit and makes people feel safe. They know that, too."

"So we're like bodyguards?" Caleb stared at Daniela. "They . . . they told you all this?"

"I'm not stupid. I pieced things together. I mean, obviously they also want us here because we've got useful Legacies for the Repair Civilization World Tour. But we're also here to keep Melanie safe. Maybe stop her from flying off the handle, when possible."

"Dang," Caleb said. "I feel even worse now about dropping that beam."

Daniela patted Caleb on the shoulder as they reached the cars. "It's not a bad gig, being her sidekick. We get to help a lot of people, travel the world. You ever think you'd get to go to Australia?"

"No way," Caleb said, smiling now, relieved that they were moving on to less heavy subjects.

"Yeah, me neither. I'd never even been to Staten Island before all this"—she let her eyes flash silver, the telltale sign of her activating her Legacy—"went down."

"Well, I've still never been to New York," Caleb replied.

"Don't worry. You will. That's the other good thing about this detail," Daniela continued. "Princess Melanie needs a lot of vacations. Pretty much any time she wants. And we get to go along, since we're basically the only friends she's allowed to have."

Caleb's brows wrinkled at that. Melanie hadn't seemed very friendly to him so far. She acted like he and Daniela weren't even there. He'd thought socializing at the Academy had been difficult to wrap his head around, but this was a whole other level of complicated.

A Peacekeeper saluted them and opened the back door of an SUV. Caleb saluted back, then climbed in after Daniela. She was still talking.

"After Sydney, I heard we're heading back to the States.

Some rich friend of Melanie's family offered to host us at his beach house. It's in Florida, which—" Daniela made a face. "Definite downgrade over Australia. Still, should be a chill time."

Caleb sat back and the let the air-conditioning wash over him. His skin was hot from being in the sun all day, his atoms quaking from spending so much time using his duplicates.

"What rich guy?" Caleb thought to ask, opening one eye to look at Daniela.

"Think Melanie said his name is Sydal. Wade Sydal."

CHAPTER EIGHTEEN

TAYLOR COOK
THE HUMAN GARDE ACADEMY—POINT REYES, CALIFORNIA

DR. LINDA SLEPT CURLED UP ON HER SIDE. THE floorboards creaked under Taylor's feet as she approached the woman's bed. The psychiatrist stirred. Taylor made no effort to hide her footfalls. As Dr. Linda blinked awake, Taylor clapped a hand over the woman's mouth, gentle but firm.

"Please don't scream," Taylor said. "I need your help."

Taylor made her eyes wide, the whites shining in the near darkness of Linda's bedroom. She forced her hand to tremble, knowing that Linda would be able to feel the tremor. She wanted to seem desperate and cornered. After weeks of perfecting her badass act, Taylor wasn't totally sure she could pull this off.

Linda's hands were still pinned under the sheet. Taylor had checked the room quickly before waking her up. She didn't find any weapons—just novels, scented candles, and collections of crossword puzzles. There was also the tablet computer that all the faculty carried, the one connected to the Academy's systems. Linda would be able to summon security with that. Even so, Taylor had left it on her nightstand within reach.

It was important that Linda feel like she was in control.

If there was a momentary flare of panic at being woken up by Taylor looming over her, Linda had tamped it down. Her eyes now regarded Taylor with the customary calmness, like they were in session. She nodded her agreement. She would be quiet.

Taylor took her hand away and stepped back. Linda sat up in bed but didn't reach for her tablet. No one would ever consider the therapist an intimidating presence, and in her oversized flannel pajamas, her graying hair all wild and uncombed, Taylor could only think of how fragile she looked. Hard to believe this woman could be her enemy.

"Taylor . . . ," Dr. Linda said quietly. "This is highly inappropriate."

"I know, I know . . ." Taylor paced back and forth in front of Linda's bed and pushed her hands through her hair. The woman watched her, gaze steady. Taylor hoped she wasn't overdoing it. "I didn't know where else to turn, what to do . . . *they took Kopano and Ran.*"

It wasn't hard to work emotion into her voice. Stealing her friends away, taking Kopano just when they were starting to get closer—Taylor wasn't sure she could forgive Earth

Garde for that. *Use it*, Isabela had told her outside Dr. Linda's house. *Make her believe.*

"Yes. I received a memo about that," Linda replied measuredly. "I believe they're calling it protective custody. It's for their own good—"

"This is already protective custody!" Taylor snapped. "We're already prisoners! And this just shows . . . just shows that Earth Garde will do whatever they want with us. They don't actually care. We're just . . . weapons."

"Now, Taylor, I understand you're upset . . ."

Taylor put her hands over her face. "I should've listened to the Foundation. They were right about everything."

Linda was quiet. Taylor peeked at her through her fingers. Her mouth was quirked to the side, eyes narrowed as she studied Taylor.

"Why did you come here?" Linda asked. Her voice betrayed nothing.

"I didn't know where else to go," Taylor said shakily. She took a deep breath to make it seem like she was trying to get a grip. If this was going to work, Linda needed to believe this next part. "I went to confront Nine about what happened to my friends. Outside his office, I heard him and Dr. Goode talking. They're going to send me away, too, to whatever Earth Garde prison they shipped the others. They're afraid the Foundation will try to take me again and don't want to endanger the other students. They talked about how safe I'd be there because the security is impenetrable. Because I'm a healer, they said, I'm too valuable to lose. They don't care—they don't care what I want!"

"Hmm," was all Dr. Linda said in response. She picked up her tablet and turned it on, but to Taylor's relief she didn't call security. Instead, it looked like she was scrolling through her messages.

"I know . . . I know I've been a pain lately." Taylor pressed on with her begging. "I know I've made it seem like I don't want to be here. But I'd rather stay here than be in some Earth Garde prison for the rest of my life! Please, can you tell them? Tell them I'll be good?"

"Calm down," Linda replied. "I'm looking at your file. There's nothing here about you being transferred."

"I swear, I—"

Taylor jumped theatrically as someone pounded loudly on Linda's door. Right on time.

Linda's eyebrows shot up and she got out of bed. Taylor intercepted her before she could go far, clinging desperately to her arms.

"It's them!" she whispered. "Please! Please don't tell them I'm here!"

"It's okay," Linda said. "Stay here."

Taylor let her go and watched, peeking around the corner of Linda's bedroom door, as the psychiatrist straightened her pajamas and went to answer the knock. She cracked the front door open just enough to see Nine standing there, leaning against the frame, smiling smugly.

"'Sup, Linda," Nine said. "I wake you?"

Linda feigned a yawn. "Yes, but it's okay. What's wrong?"

"Taylor Cook isn't in her dorm," Nine said. "Earth Garde decided to transfer her out with the others after all. We think she might have caught wind and run off again. Trying to keep this on the down low right now. Not going to look good for me if I let the same dumb-ass bounce out of here twice. But . . . any ideas where she might have gone?"

Linda hesitated. The moment of truth. Taylor had laid the groundwork with her story and now Isabela—in the guise of Nine—made it seem real. If Linda was truly spying for the Foundation and if they really wanted Taylor back, then Linda would have to act.

"Let me get dressed," Linda told Nine. "I'll meet you at the administration building."

"Hurry up, okay? Or it's going to be my ass—"

Linda shut the door in his face. She turned to face Taylor.

"We have to move quickly," she said.

"What—?" Taylor still playing dumb. "What are we going to do?"

Linda said nothing as she crouched down in her living room. She pushed aside a throw rug and pried up a loose floorboard. Linda reached into the gap and produced a satellite phone. Her finger hesitated over the buttons as she looked at Taylor.

"I can get you to the Foundation," Linda said. "If you're sure that's what you want."

Taylor was taken aback. There was something about Linda's voice—she sounded conflicted, like she didn't want Taylor to make this choice.

"Seriously?" Taylor asked. "You're—"

"Yes," Linda said quickly. "Should I make the call?"

Taylor nodded, doing her best to sound sincere. "Yes! Thank God! What they're offering—it's definitely better than here. They're right about Earth Garde. About everything."

"Hm," Linda said noncommittally. Then, she dialed a preprogrammed number on the satellite phone. Someone answered on the first ring. "I have an emergency," Linda said.

A pause. Taylor could hear a man's voice. He sounded curt and displeased.

"I know," Linda replied. "I know. But they are transferring Cook out tonight." A pause. "Somewhere more secure than here. I don't know." Another pause. "No. My cover is intact. Only Cook knows now." Pause. "Yes, she's here with me." A sharp response from the man on the phone, enough to make Linda flinch. "I can meet you tonight, yes. Let me write it down." Linda grabbed one of her crossword puzzles and scratched down an address in the margin. "Okay," Linda said meekly, then hung up the satellite phone.

The psychiatrist took a shaky breath, then returned the phone to its hiding place under the floorboards. Taylor took a step towards her.

"Is everything okay?"

"I have to go," Linda replied. "You stay here. The Foundation will send someone to get you."

"Who?"

"I don't know. We aren't allowed to cross paths. They'll get you out."

There was someone else. Another Foundation mole. Someone capable of sneaking her off campus. She'd half expected Linda to smuggle her out in the trunk of her car. This complicated things.

Linda disappeared into her room to get changed. She came back a few moments later, Taylor still standing there dumbfounded—although not all of it was feigned this time. Linda grabbed her car keys and the piece of paper she'd written the address on. Then, she came to stand before Taylor.

"Why . . . ?" Taylor asked. "Why didn't you tell me you worked for them?"

"I'm sure you can guess the answer to that," Linda replied. She put her hand gently on Taylor's shoulder. "I shouldn't tell you this. It's . . . it's too late to change anything. But you need to be careful with these Foundation people, Taylor. Maybe they can offer you a better life than Earth Garde. Maybe that's true. But they are dangerous."

Taylor hadn't expected this. "I . . . I know."

Dr. Linda kept speaking, looking through Taylor as she did. Taylor got the feeling that Linda had never said these words out loud before.

"Two months after I was offered the job with Earth Garde, my sister became ill. A brain tumor. A man from the Foundation contacted me, said they could heal her if I would report to them about the students here. I . . ." Linda looked down, blinking. "I knew it wasn't ethical. But my sister has three kids. I don't have any of my own, you see . . . but I imagined my nieces and nephews growing up without their mother and . . ."

Linda trailed off. A cold feeling came over Taylor. In the weeks since the Fugitive Six realized Dr. Linda was the mole, they had built her up into a treacherous villain. But she wasn't that at all. She was just another victim of the Foundation.

Before too much sympathy developed, Taylor remembered her role. She still needed Dr. Linda to think she believed in the Foundation's philosophy.

"They healed her, right?" she asked. "They kept good on their promise?"

"Yes. They sent someone like you." Linda squeezed her arm. "But my part of the agreement, well . . . that appears to never end. A deal made with these people—I hesitate to use the metaphor—but it is like selling your soul. I hope you know what you're getting into."

"I . . . I'll be fine," Taylor replied, but Dr. Linda had already turned away. Without another word, she walked out the front door, leaving Taylor alone in her little home.

Stay here. Stay here and wait for someone. But who? And how long? Linda had told the man on the phone that she would be transferred out that night. That meant the Foundation would be acting quickly.

Taylor's first move was to uncover the loose floorboard and grab Linda's satellite phone. There was only one number programmed in there. She set the phone on the coffee table, in plain view. Maybe Isabela would come in here and grab it, show it to Nine and Lexa so they could trace the number.

Isabela. She'd done her part, pretending to be Nine. She was supposed to be hiding outside, keeping watch. What would she make of Dr. Linda leaving the house? Taylor went to one of the windows to try to signal Isabela, let her know that everything was going to plan. Well, sort of. How would she communicate that a second Foundation spy was on the way? If they spotted Isabela, the whole game might be given away.

Taylor approached one of the windows. A cool breeze blew in, stirring up some of Dr. Linda's papers. She peeked outside, but couldn't see Isabela in the darkness.

"Taylor."

She spun around at the sound of a boy's voice behind her. Miki stood in the middle of Dr. Linda's living room, his diminutive form dressed in a tank top and basketball shorts like he'd just rolled out of bed. He looked tired and Taylor thought she glimpsed uncertainty in his dark eyes.

"Miki," Taylor said, trying not to sound too surprised. "You're . . . ?"

"Yeah," he said quickly. "I'm supposed to get you out of here."

"How . . . ?"

How did you get in here? How long have you been work-ing for the Foundation? How did they recruit you? How is a tweeb supposed to help me escape from the Academy? These questions caused a traffic jam in Taylor's brain, so she ended up standing there staring dumbly at Miki.

"Better if we don't talk here," he said. He stepped forward and offered Taylor his hand. "Grab on."

"Grab on?" Taylor tentatively took his hand. "Miki, what do you *do*?"

"I turn into wind."

"What?"

"It's going to feel weird at first," Miki replied. "Try not to panic."

Taylor tried to ask a follow-up question, but her mouth was gone. Her whole body was gone. She was weightless, disoriented and dizzy. Her vision expanded —she could see all of Dr. Linda's room at once, a complete 360. She twisted and rose, spun and circulated. If she'd still had a stomach, she probably would've thrown up.

She could still feel Miki. He was holding her, even though neither of them had hands anymore. They were intertwined. This whole thing was disconcertingly intimate.

Then they started to move and Taylor forgot about all of that. They squeezed out through Dr. Linda's window, dipped low, and then gusted out across the Academy. Soon, they were high and soaring. A leaf got caught up with them; it felt weird and prickly. The experience reminded Taylor of riding in her dad's truck when she'd hang her arm out the window and let it ride the wind.

She only panicked a little bit, when she realized that she couldn't breathe. She didn't need to breathe, though. She *was* air. Still, not having those functions we take for granted, not really having a body—it messed with her mind.

And then they were on the beach, twenty miles north of the Academy. It was dark and she was human again, on her hands and knees, gasping for breath and trying not to throw up from the dizziness. She spit in the sand, panting.

"You okay?" Miki asked. He stood a few feet away, looking windblown but mostly unruffled.

"God, a little warning would've been nice."

"I did warn you."

"A little more warning."

"Sorry," Miki replied. "I know it's tough to get used to. And I don't get to practice very often, since I'm not allowed to show the instructors."

Taylor sat in the sand catching her breath and looked up at him, trying to get a read. He caught her watching and frowned.

"So how did you play Dr. Linda?" he asked.

Taylor's hands tensed. "What do you mean?"

"I know she buys into that act you've been doing since you guys got back," Miki replied. "But . . . I'm the wind, you know? I've been through every air duct in the Academy. I saw your guys' dope underground hideout."

Taylor swallowed. She got up slowly and squared up with Miki. He was a master at telekinesis and could probably carry her out to sea and drop her with his weird wind Legacy. But if she had to fight, she would.

"Easy," he said, holding up his hands. "I haven't told

anyone. And I won't. The Foundation's got something on me, but I'm not on their side."

Taylor stared at him, incredulous. "If you knew about us, if you aren't against them—why didn't you tell us? We could help you. You could help us."

Miki gazed out at the ocean. "Obviously I don't trust them, but tonight's the first time they actually asked me to do something. Called me on a cell phone they smuggled in for me, told me it was urgent I helped you escape. I figured your plan had finally worked."

"That doesn't answer my question."

Miki shrugged. "I didn't want to approach you guys until . . . well, until I was sure you could actually stop them. No offense."

Taylor pursed her lips. "Some offense taken."

Out on the ocean, a small boat's light broke the inky darkness. It blinked three times, went dark for a few seconds, then blinked three more times.

"That's your ride," Miki said.

Taylor shook her head silently. About thirty minutes had gone by since she first broke into Dr. Linda's house. The Foundation had arranged this extraction in less time than it took to cook a pizza.

Miki held out his hand. "I'll fly you out there, if you're up for it."

"Better than swimming," Taylor replied, trying to recapture some of the badass energy that had gotten her this far. It wasn't easy—this was really happening. She was returning to the Foundation. She nervously took Miki's hand.

"Seriously, good luck," he told her. "I hope you take these bastards down."

Whatever response Taylor might have made, it was swallowed up in the wind.

CHAPTER NINETEEN

ISABELA SILVA
THE HUMAN GARDE ACADEMY—POINT REYES, CALIFORNIA

ISABELA SILVA DID NOT THINK OF HERSELF AS A hero. Hell no.

She knew some of her friends thought of themselves that way. Kopano, Taylor, and Nigel for sure. Ran, probably, even if she was too much of a wannabe pacifist to say so. Caleb, well, he probably didn't know what to think about himself, that was his whole deal. Anyway, although they didn't admit it, she knew that her friends thought of themselves as the second coming of the Loric Garde. They were a small group fighting against a powerful enemy in a secret conflict, their lives and potentially the fate of humanity on the line. Professor Nine, the big idiot, he encouraged this thinking with his secret hideout and special training.

Isabela couldn't give a shit. The Foundation were bad

people, sure. The Harvesters were about the worst pieces of human garbage she'd ever met. And given enough time and less supervision, Isabela was certain more of her fellow Garde would turn rotten like that Einar guy.

Point being, Isabela knew the world was full of bad people. It was never *not* going to be full of bad people. Her friends thought they could make a difference and that was cute, but Isabela knew it would never happen. There would always be a next battle, a next bad guy.

So, if she was so cynical, why was she hiding in the bushes alongside Dr. Linda's house, keeping a lookout?

For starters, it was less boring than sitting in her room doing homework.

But also, for the same reason she'd kept hanging around the rest of the Fugitive Six, even though their last adventure got her shot. They were her friends. Isabela might have been a cynic, but she was also loyal.

In the shadows outside Linda's house, Isabela let her mask slip. She touched the leathery ripples of her burn-scarred cheek. They'd seen this face, her true face—and they didn't judge. They accepted her.

So, she would accept their silly hero fantasies and help them not get themselves killed. At least it made life exciting.

Movement. Someone was leaving Dr. Linda's. Isabela cut short her reverie, rolled her eyes at her own self-reflection, and quickly shape-shifted back into her unscarred form.

It was the psychiatrist herself. Alone. Isabela scowled. Had their plan worked? Dr. Linda walked down the path that led out of the faculty village, towards the administration building. Linda had told Isabela—when she was in the guise of Nine—that she would go there to help search for Taylor.

She couldn't let Linda go talk to the real Nine, not until Taylor had made contact with the Foundation. But Taylor was still inside. Was she supposed to wait there or . . . ?

"*Merda*," Isabela grumbled. They should've worked this out better.

Isabela ducked out of her hiding spot and decided to follow Dr. Linda. She jogged between cottages, running parallel to Linda, getting ahead of her. She didn't want to get noticed by any of the security cameras. She picked a shadowy spot between two cottages and waited for Linda to catch up.

"Dr. Linda," Isabela hissed. "*Boa noite.*"

The little woman practically jumped out of her skin. Isabela hid her smirk. They'd been hard on her tonight, breaking into her house and then sneaking up on her. She had it coming.

"Isabela," Linda kept her voice down, inching off the path to come closer. She played it cool. "It's after curfew. Why are you up?"

"Where's Taylor?" Isabela replied bluntly. "Are you going to help her escape?"

Isabela knew how to play this game of lies. Their original story was that Earth Garde was sending Taylor away. It made sense that Isabela would know about that, but she didn't let on that she knew Linda was part of the Foundation.

"I . . ." Linda glanced back towards her house, not sure how much she should say. "It's taken care of."

"What does that mean?"

A sudden breeze blew in between them. Something on Dr. Linda jingled. The woman was holding her car keys. So, she wasn't going to see Nine after all. She was fleeing.

"Taylor will be fine," Dr. Linda replied, trying to find her authoritative voice. "I had . . . a friend of mine is getting her off campus."

"What friend? You don't have any friends."

Dr. Linda pinched the bridge of her nose. "Please, Isabela. Go back to your room. Forget we had this conversation."

Isabela craned her neck back towards Linda's cabin. Was there someone else there? Someone who would get Taylor out? Another Foundation lackey?

"Who is your friend?" Isabela asked. "What if I want to go too? Will they take me?"

"Isabela, no. Enough," Linda replied firmly. "Go back to your room or I'll call security."

"No, you won't."

They stared at each other. Linda's gaze didn't seem so penetrating out here in the night. Isabela made sure to keep her knowing smile on, even as her mind raced. Should she let Linda go? What happened to Taylor? Who was coming to get her and how would they get off campus?

"Isabela, you need to answer me honestly." Isabela noticed the therapist's voice shaking, not with anger but with fear. "I remember how you won those silly Wargames. Was that . . .

was that you before? Pretending to be Nine?"

As gifted a liar as Isabela was, Dr. Linda was still a woman who read people's emotions for a living. Just the slightest hesitation from Isabela gave Linda her answer.

"Oh no," she said, and took a sharp step forward. "Do the two of you know what you've done? The danger you're toying with?"

Before Isabela could respond, a flashlight beam swept across the nearby path. A single Peacekeeper strolled along there, doing one of the checks that had become routine since the Fugitive Six last snuck off campus.

Isabela grabbed Linda by the arm and pulled her back the way she'd come, through the shadows. Linda came willingly—she didn't want to be caught out here any more than Isabela did. They made it to her doorstep just ahead of the Peacekeeper's flashlight and Isabela used the access card from Nine to let them in. Linda was breathing hard; Isabela hoped that she wasn't having a heart attack.

"Taylor?" Isabela called out as she closed the door behind her and shoved Linda onto the couch.

No response. Her friend was gone. Somehow, the Foundation had whisked her away in the space of a few minutes.

She rounded on Dr. Linda. "Where did they take her?"

"I don't know. I don't even know *how* they took her." Linda looked bewildered and exhausted, her frizzy hair a mess. "What are you two trying to accomplish?"

Isabela snapped her fingers in Linda's face. "I ask questions, not you." She glared at Linda until the woman gave a meek nod. "Where were you going just now?"

"Thanks to your ruse, I was going to meet Nine—"

Isabela's nostrils flared. "No point in lying, *estúpido*. Everyone knows you are a Foundation spy. They've known for weeks, only keeping you around to see what you might give away. Soon you will be arrested."

"I—the Foundation made—"

Isabela took a menacing step forward. "Where were you going?"

"To meet with—I suppose you would call him my handler. I don't know his name. He's who I give the information to. He likely wants to know what happened here tonight."

"Where were you to meet him?"

Linda handed Isabela an address scratched onto a torn corner of a crossword puzzle. Isabela wiggled her fingers.

"Car keys, too."

There were other ways to infiltrate the Foundation besides letting them recruit you. Isabela wasn't about to let Taylor go on this mission all by herself.

Fifteen minutes later, Isabela drove Dr. Linda's hybrid hatchback through the faculty parking lot towards the Peacekeeper checkpoint at the Academy's exit. Besides the car keys and the address, Isabela had also swiped Linda's ID card and satellite phone. She left the psychiatrist gagged and tied up on her bed. By the time anyone found her, Isabela would be long gone.

She looked at herself in the rearview mirror. Her skin wrinkled and pale, her hair a bushy gray rat's nest.

"I am a smart lady," Isabela said, mimicking Dr. Linda's pretentious way of enunciating. "Tell me about your earliest memory. That is enough for today. Freud. Zoloft. Nocturnal emission."

Good enough, she decided.

Isabela pulled up to the gate. A Peacekeeper emerged from the booth, stern and middle-aged, not one of the ones Isabela had encountered in her previous forays off campus.

"ID," he said flatly.

Isabela handed him Linda's ID and he swiped it through a card reader. She waited, tapping her foot anxiously against the floor. The Peacekeeper turned the tablet around so the screen faced her, an image of an eye there overlaid with a blue graph matrix.

"Retinal scan," he said.

"Ah, yes," Isabela replied. That was new. Her heartbeat picked up. Did her shape-shifting accurately copy that level of detail? She'd never thought to find out.

"Can't sleep again, huh?" The Peacekeeper said conversationally as her eye was scanned.

So Linda had made late-night excursions from the Academy before. What would she say?

"If the crosswords do not work, I find long drives soothe the overactive mind," Isabela said as properly as she could manage.

"More of a sudoku guy myself," the Peacekeeper replied.

His tablet beeped. Not a good beep. It was the kind of sound a computer made when an error popped up.

"Inexact match," the Peacekeeper said with a sigh.

"Maybe I blinked," Isabela replied.

"Thing can be tricky," he said, handing back her ID. "Whatever. Could have you here until sunup waiting for the tech to work."

He reached for a button behind him and opened up the gate. Isabela gave him a warm smile, then drove through. Never underestimate the power of a middle-aged white woman to escape scrutiny.

Isabela drove into the night. She put the address she'd taken from Dr. Linda into the car's GPS. Then, she found a dance music station on the car radio and rolled down the windows. Yes, this was a potentially dangerous situation and yes, she was currently disguised as an old woman with a very crappy car—that didn't mean she couldn't exert a little style as she cruised south on the mostly abandoned coastal highways south of the Academy.

It didn't hit her until the wind blew through her hair how much she had missed these excursions off campus and the freedom that came with them. She used to do this all the time before the administration got wise, sometimes by herself and sometimes with her former boy toy Lofton, stealing an identity and a car, then driving south to San Francisco to party for a night.

This was serious, Isabela reminded herself.

Still, now that she knew how the Academy's "upgraded" security protocols worked, she would have to sneak out more often.

The address Dr. Linda had was for a surf shop in Sausalito. The quaint shoreline town was quiet as Isabela drove through its hillsides, hardly any other cars on the road. In the distance, through a thin sheet of fog, Isabela could see the inviting glow of the Golden Gate Bridge. She'd been here before but never stopped, breezing through on her way to San Francisco. It was only an hour south of the Academy. So the Foundation thought they could set up that close without trouble.

The dinky surf shop was in a strip mall close to the shore, sandwiched between an organic juice bar and a skate park. The parking lot was empty. Isabela pulled in and waited, turning the station to some dull classical crap before she did. She tried to look as uptight and nervous as possible, just in case Linda's Foundation contact was already here and watching from nearby.

She didn't have to wait long. A bloodred muscle car soon prowled into the lot, its engine like a jungle cat. Even if it hadn't been dark, the car's windows were tinted, so Isabela had no way of discerning who was inside.

"Nice car," she murmured as the Camaro pulled alongside Linda's crappy ride.

Isabela sat behind the wheel and waited, not sure what the protocol was for her psychiatrist's clandestine meetings with members of an international conspiracy.

After about a minute of stalemate, the passenger door to the other car was shoved open by the driver. An invitation.

Isabela got out and shuffled to the Camaro, doing her best

to look stooped and nervous.

"Linda, you know I don't like to be kept waiting," a man chided as Isabela climbed awkwardly into the bucket seat. "You come to me. I don't go to you."

The Camaro driver was in his thirties, dark-haired and stubbly, with thick lashes that made it look like he was wearing eyeliner and a face just a bit too angular to be actually handsome, although he probably would've argued that point. Isabela knew his type. He reminded her of a certain drug dealer back in Rio who used to haunt the clubs and hit on underage girls. He wore an expensive leather jacket. His car smelled like coconut air freshener and cigarettes.

"Sorry," Isabela said quietly. "Difficult night."

The man snorted. "Oh, was it *difficult* for you? You call me up in a panic, tell me we need to get the Cook girl out tonight and then—what did you do? Did you pull strings and call in favors to make that happen? Was that you? Or was it me?"

"You," Isabela replied.

"Right. And, lucky for you, that operation was successful. So, congratulations. You finally did something halfway useful."

After weeks of planning, Taylor was in. Isabela suppressed a smile.

"I have to ask, Linda—"

The man half turned so he was facing Isabela directly, angling his head so she was forced to look in his eyes.

"Were you compromised? You said on the phone—Cook

knows you're working for us. Does anyone else? How big a mess did you make there tonight?"

Isabela pretended to consider his question. "I was careful."

"It's okay," the man said in a way meant to sound soothing but that Isabela could tell meant it definitely would *not* be okay. "If you messed up, we can protect you."

"Oh, really? Will you spirit me away? Will you make me therapist of all the children you've stolen?"

The driver looked at her funny. "Don't get mouthy, Linda."

"What happens if I'm found out, hmm?" She pointed at a bulge in the man's jacket that was clearly a concealed weapon. "That? You dump me in a ditch somewhere?"

"I—"

"And what happens if *you're* compromised, *cabrão*?"

Isabela waited a split second to see the alarm dawn on the man's face. She loved that moment. Then, with her telekinesis, she looped his seat belt around his neck and pulled tight.

"Gah—!" The driver clawed at his neck with one hand and reached for his gun with the other. Isabela's hand shot out, grabbed his thumb and twisted until she heard a pop.

Howling and spitting, the man groped to get his door open. Isabela relaxed her stranglehold with the seat belt enough so he could push the door open.

Before he was halfway out, Isabela yanked the door closed with her telekinesis. His head went through the window. He slumped there, head and one shoulder out the window, seat belt still looped around his neck, broken glass stuck in his face. Unconscious.

Now, Isabela moved quickly. Taking out this fool was one thing, but she didn't want to get spotted by the local authorities or some random bystanders. That would make a mess.

She shape-shifted back to her preferred form, lifted both of her feet and kicked the guy out of his car. She exited right behind him, pulling him along towards Dr. Linda's vehicle. Moments later, the Foundation idiot was laid out in Linda's trunk, tied up with ripped shreds of his leather jacket. Isabela riffled through his pockets.

In his wallet, she found an ID for Alejandro Regerio. His real name or an alias? Isabela had no way of knowing. He had a local address, at least, so that would be her next lead. He also carried three hundred dollars cash, a pair of credit cards, a condom, and a half dozen punch cards to local taco trucks.

"Mr. Foundation," Isabela murmured. "You are so basic."

She took his gun and attached the holster to her own chest. It was a nice one—chrome plated and polished, with an ivory grip. Fancy firearm hadn't helped him much. She also took his cell phone, which looked like a burner.

Isabela peered down at Alejandro, trying to get a good idea of his face. She'd messed him up pretty bad. In the end, she needed to consult his ID to make sure she got the details of his features correct.

When Isabela slammed the hood closed on Dr. Linda's

car, she did so as Alejandro Regerio. Foundation fixer.

That was easy. She wondered how far up the ranks she could climb like this.

Busting Alejandro's window had been an oversight. True, it had been totally badass and felt great, but now Isabela had to dust all the broken glass off the seat, and she couldn't roll up the window.

Hopefully, he had another ride stored back at his pad. He seemed like the type.

Isabela navigated towards the address on Alejandro's ID. It wasn't far, only about thirty minutes up into the hills, according to the GPS. She drove like she imagined Alejandro would, slouched, her elbow jutting out the window, shifting gears with exaggerated force like she was in a street-racing movie. Getting into character. She'd only met the man for a few minutes, but she had a pretty good grip on how he talked and acted.

Before ascending into the hills, Isabela picked up Dr. Linda's satellite phone. She dialed the number she'd been forced to memorize—the one they'd all been forced to memorize after their last excursion off campus. Nine's cell phone.

"Who's this?" he asked gruffly after the third ring.

"Is that how you answer your phone?" Isabela replied, her normal voice issuing from Alejandro's mouth.

"Isabela?" he exclaimed, then made an effort to lower his voice. "Where are you?"

"Off campus. But you knew we'd do that, didn't you? Bad boy, giving Taylor your key card."

"I don't know what you're talking about."

"Mm-hmm. I left a little present for you in the trunk of Linda's car." She gave him the address of the surf shop, unable to keep the smile out of her voice. "No one will notice he's missing. Because he's not."

"What did you do?" Nine asked quietly. "This isn't the plan we discussed . . ."

She snorted. "What plan? That went bye-bye with Ran, Kopano, and Nigel. I'm in. Taylor's in. For infiltration class I think we should get As, yes?"

"We made arrangements for Taylor," Nine said. "We have ways of keeping her safe."

"I can handle my own protection. You know this."

Isabela could hear Nine grinding his teeth, but when he spoke again she could hear something else in his voice—pride, maybe a little respect. The big doofus loved charging into battle. Of course he approved of Isabela's play.

"Isabela, seriously, if things get dangerous—"

"Don't worry," she cut him off. "Escaping unpleasant situations comes very easy to me."

With that, she hung up the phone. That was enough talk.

Isabela cruised into the hills, whipping over the winding roads at a breakneck pace. Her plan was simple. She would find this guy's house and go through his shit. She'd dig up whatever she could about the Foundation and send it back to the Academy. Then, she would find Alejandro's supervisor or boss or whatever, and do the same thing to that person that she had just done to Alejandro. Rinse and repeat, until there was no more Foundation to worry about.

It was a solid plan, she thought.

However, it did not account for a large man in a hooded sweatshirt walking into the road right in front of her.

He was like an apparition, emerging from the trees on the side of the road without warning. Isabela shouted and cranked the wheel to the left, slamming on the brake. The back of the Camaro lifted and jerked, fishtailing, as she swerved.

It happened too fast. She hit the guy at thirty miles per hour.

The impact was like she'd driven into a telephone pole. The front of the car buckled around the hooded figure's body. Isabela was thrown forward. Her airbag deployed, but she still smashed her face, could immediately feel warm blood creeping down from her eyebrow and the bridge of her nose.

Black smoke curled up from the engine. Isabela's eyes were filled with tears, but she blinked them back. Her head was swimming—a concussion, for sure. She felt her grip on Alejandro's appearance slipping and tried to focus.

Through the cracked windshield, she saw the hooded figure struggling to free himself from the car. He was wedged in there pretty good. He was also alive. How was that possible? What the hell had she just hit?

Isabela didn't wait around to find out. She scrambled out of the car and staggered desperately towards the trees, trying to put some distance between her and the attacker.

"Running will only make it worse, Alejandro."

Isabela wiped blood out of her eyes. There was a boy on the side of the road. He was smartly dressed, his hair parted from the side, and spoke with a faint European accent. She'd never met him before, but she knew him immediately.

"Don't look so surprised," Einar said. "Surely your bosses told you I might pay a visit."

"*Merda, merda, merda*," Isabela spat and kept running. She knew that to listen to this boy was death. He would control her and—

As she reached the trees, someone grabbed her by the throat. A third attacker. Female, skinny and tall, Asian. An electric pulse ripped through Isabela, her whole body convulsing. The girl's touch was like a lightning bolt.

Isabela fell and, as she did, she lost control. She was Alejandro when the girl touched her, but Isabela when she hit the ground. Not her preferred form of Isabela either. Her embarrassing, hideously scarred true shape.

Isabela tried to rally, tried to use her telekinesis, shapeshift, something—but the voltage combined with the head injuries were too much. She was already starting to fade when the three attackers gathered around her.

"Well," Einar declared. "Isn't this a surprise?"

CHAPTER TWENTY

KOPANO OKEKE
UNDISCLOSED LOCATION

"KOPANO!"

His head hurt. His eyelids were too heavy to open, limbs sluggish and numb. All Kopano wanted to do was go back to sleep.

"Kopano! Are you in there?"

Someone was shouting his name. A girl's voice. Sounded like trouble.

"Can you hear me?"

With a groan, Kopano managed to open his eyes. He stared up at a single uncovered fluorescent light flickering in a water-stained ceiling that he didn't recognize. His head felt clogged, like when he'd come down with a flu back home and his mom would force him to drink cough syrup. Where was he? What happened to him? He tried to remember.

A nice Peacekeeper in his room. She found some of Caleb's old cologne or something? Sprayed it in his face?

"I hear you moving in there! Say something if it's you."

Kopano rubbed his eyes and worked some moisture into his mouth.

"Ran . . . ?" he asked, uncertain; her voice was coming through muffled. "Ran? Is that you?"

"Yes! Can you move?"

Kopano decided he couldn't answer right away. He sat up on a firm cot and swung his legs over the edge. His bare feet touched cold concrete. He looked down at himself—a dull gray jumpsuit with no identifying marks, no zippers, no buttons, all Velcro. He was in a small room with nothing but his cot, a sink and toilet, and one empty shelf. The door—through which Ran's voice was coming—was thick metal.

It all dawned on Kopano fast. He felt sick to his stomach.

"Holy shit, Ran. Are we in prison?"

She didn't answer. "Can you move?" she asked instead, her voice taut.

Kopano got up unsteadily. He cringed at a sharp pain in his temple. He reached up and touched a bandage there, heavy gauze and medical tape, a sharp throb beneath. Had he hit his head?

"I . . . I can move," he said.

"Then stand back from the door."

The door began to glow. Kopano recognized the dark crimson of Ran's explosive energy. He yanked up the mattress and used it as a shield, wedging himself in the far corner between the sink and the slab of concrete that held up the bed.

The explosion came seconds later, a burst of kinetic energy and tearing metal that made Kopano's head ring all the more. The door to his cell rocketed backwards and smashed through his toilet, water and chunks of plaster spilling across the floor.

Ran padded into the room. She wore the same prisoner outfit as Kopano and had a similar bandage on her right temple. She had her sleeves rolled up and the knuckles of her right hand dripped blood. Kopano got the sense that she'd been in a fight.

The situation might have been dangerous and disorienting, but that didn't stop Kopano from striding forward and sweeping Ran up in a hug. The brief terror of finding himself in prison was greatly diminished by her presence.

"I'm so happy to see you," he said.

Ran gently brushed free of him. "No time for that. There are guards." She squeezed his arm quickly. "I am happy to see you, too."

"What the hell is this place?"

"I don't know," Ran said. "But I do not intend to stay and find out."

Kopano followed Ran out into the hall. Dimly lit and dingy, its old concrete walls sweated with moisture. There were other cells like the one that Kopano had come out of, their doors left ajar to show that they were empty. Kopano looked to the right. He could tell that was the direction Ran came from because of the smoking husk of another cell door, this one blown outward, a security camera that dangled broken from the wall, and the bodies of three guards in body armor and helmets.

"Are they dead?" Kopano asked quietly.

"Unconscious," Ran answered.

He frowned at the path of destruction. "Our first reaction to waking up in a place like this is to start hitting people and blowing things up," he said. "Maybe we do belong here."

"That was my first reaction, not yours," Ran said coolly. "You do not have to come with me. But, we do not know if our captors are friends or enemies. Kidnapping and imprisoning us without any process would suggest to me they are the latter. But you do what you will, Kopano."

"Okay, okay," Kopano said, holding up his hands. "I'm with you. Just . . . let's not hurt anyone too bad, at least until we know what's going on."

"I won't hurt anyone who doesn't try to hurt me," Ran said. She picked up a chunk of shattered porcelain and charged it with her Legacy.

They crept down the hall in the opposite direction of Ran's former cell. They went around two corners, encountering nothing else but more security cameras. Ran promptly ripped them out of the walls with her telekinesis.

"Where is everyone?" Kopano asked.

"They will come," Ran replied. "Those others had weapons like you faced during the Wargames. Shock collars and chaff grenades to disrupt telekinesis. Be ready."

They turned another corner and there was finally a break from the monotony of empty cells. Ahead, two thick double doors appeared to lead to a different section of the prison.

Between the Garde and the doors were a half dozen guards. They all wore heavy black body armor and helmets with face shields, a dim glow emanating from within suggesting they were using HUDs—heads-up displays that would assist with aiming, plus grant them night vision and heat vision. Two of them were armed with plastic riot shields, two with the crossbow-shaped Inhibitors that Kopano remembered from the Wargames, and two with long metallic sticks that resembled cattle prods. They were organized in a tight group and had clearly trained for exactly this kind of combat.

But they didn't stand a chance.

Kopano's first move was to try yanking their shields away with his telekinesis. All the guards were tethered to their weapons, though, thick cords connecting their armaments directly to their body armor. Kopano's grab for their shields knocked the guards off-balance a bit, but it didn't disarm them or break their formation.

Ran took a different approach. She tossed her charged chunk of toilet at the guards. They were prepared for that, the shield bearers knocked the explosive down and pinned it to the floor. When it exploded, the force sent them flying hard into the hallway walls, but they had managed to spare the rest of the group.

One of the back-row guards tossed a grenade at their feet. It released a puff of glittering chaff and then emitted a pulsing burst of blinding light, all this creating a highly disorienting strobe effect. That was their best method for disrupting telekinesis.

The guards fired their Inhibitors. Auto-locking collars attached to tensile cords that discharged crippling amounts of electricity, the projectiles programmed to seek the heat of the carotid artery. Kopano had been struck by one of these collars before. Not an experience he was looking to repeat.

With the chaff and the strobe, it all happened too fast for him and Ran to deploy their telekinesis. Still, Kopano was ready. He grabbed Ran's arm and turned them both intangible. The collars sailed right through their ghostly necks, Kopano guided Ran to the side of the cords, then turned them solid again.

Before the guards could reel their collars back in, Ran screamed and charged.

She leaped into the air and hit one of them in the neck with a jump-kick, pinning him against the wall by grabbing hold of his partner and staying suspended between them. Her foot on the throat of one guard, she held the other by his Inhibitor and began charging his weapon, the crimson glow cutting through the strobe effect.

The guards with cattle prods came forward and Ran was out of limbs to fight them off with. Kopano moved to intercept. He phased through Ran and her two guards, then hardened his molecules in time to punch the nearest guard in the helmet, shattering the mask over his face and putting him down. The second one jabbed at Kopano's abdomen with his cattle prod. He turned transparent again, let the guard stumble through him, then turned solid to grab him by the back of the head and slammed him face-first into the nearest wall.

Two down. But now the guards with the shields were starting to get back up.

As they did, the guard with the charged Inhibitor panicked and released his weapon, hitting a button inside his glove that disconnected it from his tether. Ran rolled to the floor, releasing the guard who she'd been pinning with her foot to let him gasp for breath, and slung the charged Inhibitor at the guards with shields.

This time, they were too slow. They took the brunt of the explosion and were flung back down the hall, their shields hanging limp from their armor tethers.

Four down.

The guard nearest Ran snatched up one of the cattle prods and charged her before she could regain her feet. Kopano intercepted him, his diamond-hard elbow crunching through the guard's mask in a single blow.

Seeing his colleagues decimated, the last guard tried to retreat. With her telekinesis, Ran looped one of the shield cords around his ankles so that he fell on his face. As he struggled to get back up, Kopano bounded over and put him down with a precise blow to the back of the head.

Ran stomped down on the grenade, cutting off the annoying strobe effect. Then, she looked at Kopano and wiped sweat off her forehead. He grinned.

"Practice makes perfect," he said.

"Come on," she replied. "Let's keep going."

They moved quickly towards the end of the hall. The double doors were sealed by a set of bars and a heavy-duty hydraulic contraption, but that couldn't stop Kopano. He led the way, reaching behind him to grab Ran's hand, going transparent while they were still in motion and passing right through the doors.

Kopano expected more hallways and more guards. Instead, their narrow confines opened into a large room with a vaulted ceiling. A bank of monitors dominated one wall, some of them tuned to static, thanks to all the cameras Ran had broken on the way in. There weren't any guards, just one solitary woman seated at a conference table. Although she had a weathered look about her—auburn hair streaked with gray, scars on the side of her face—Kopano thought the woman to be in her forties. She raised an eyebrow at them and he felt almost embarrassed for bursting in on her.

"Let me start by saying that I don't condone the way Greger brought you two in," the woman spoke calmly, like they'd already been having a conversation. "I figured there would be some resentment on your part. That's why I arranged for a little exercise out in the hall." She waved back the way they had come. "Get that aggression out. Thank you for not hurting any of the guards too badly."

"I know you," Ran said quietly. "You were at Patience Creek."

Patience Creek. Kopano had heard the place mentioned in

hushed whispers. It was the secret military base from where the Garde and humanity waged their resistance against the Mogadorian invaders. A massacre happened there when the Mogs infiltrated the place. Ran, Nigel, and Caleb had survived—others weren't so lucky.

"Yes, hello, Ran, Kopano," the woman said, inclining her head to each of them individually. "I'm Karen Walker."

"Hi," Kopano replied, feeling more than a little bewildered.

"You are an FBI agent," Ran said flatly. "We are not Americans. We do not answer to you."

"I *was* an FBI agent," Walker corrected. "And I'm sorry about this next part; it's going to be unpleasant. But I'm supposed to demonstrate who is in control. Let's continue this conversation in about thirty minutes."

Walker hit a button on her cell phone—it was just sitting there innocuously, on the table—like she was checking a text. Instantly, before Kopano could respond or do anything whatsoever, a white-hot light exploded behind his eyes. His whole body convulsed and he toppled over. Unconscious.

So much for escaping.

CHAPTER TWENTY-ONE

ISABELA SILVA
SOMEWHERE IN WESTERN CANADA

SOMEONE WAS TOUCHING HER.

That was the first thing she became aware of. A sweaty hand gripped her wrist, almost like someone was taking her pulse. But that wasn't it; there was something more happening in that touch. She felt an odd sensation, a tickle—it reminded her of this dumb game she used to play with her sister where they'd prick each other with their fingernails and then pull an imaginary thread up from the skin. It felt like that.

It all came back to Isabela in a rush. She'd been attacked by that psycho Einar and a couple of unidentified minions. She kept her eyes closed, trying to get a feel for her surroundings. She was on a bed of some kind, not a comfortable one, probably a cot. Wherever they'd taken her, it stunk—like body odor, fast food, and gasoline. Or maybe that was just the guy touching her.

Seriously, someone was touching her. And laughing quietly, like an amused child.

Isabela knew that the right move would be to play possum. Wait for this creep to go away before she opened her eyes.

But he was *touching* her.

She opened her eyes. A large young man stood over her, gripping her wrist in his meaty paw. He was chunky and pale, his head shaved, his eyes glistening with tears. By the size of him, Isabela figured this was the guy that she'd crashed into. He wore a sweat suit and a weird headband— or wait, that wasn't a headband, it was an eye patch that he'd flipped up. What kind of weirdo brute was she dealing with?

The hand that wasn't holding on to Isabela gripped a hand mirror, which he'd just been peering into. He looked down when Isabela stirred, but didn't seem alarmed or particularly menacing. In fact, he looked almost giddy.

"I . . . I didn't think it would work," he stammered. "It's, uh, your skin—"

Her skin. *Merda*, she'd almost forgotten. He'd seen her true form and even though that didn't seem to matter much, considering she was among killers and crazies, Isabela still didn't hesitate to shape-shift into her preferred shape—skin perfect and restored, beautiful again.

When she shape-shifted, the guy's skin shimmered. For a moment he became tan like Isabela, before fading back to his creamy whiteness. He giggled. Actually, giggled.

"It's amazing!" he babbled. "You're amazing, I'm—I'm *whole* again."

Enough of this madness. Time to bail.

"Get off me!" Isabela shouted.

The guy's grip was tight, but not tight enough to hold Isabela. Especially not when she kicked him in the chest while simultaneously shoving him with her telekinesis. He staggered backwards against the metal wall of the tiny, featureless room.

The transformation was immediate. As soon as he lost contact with Isabela, the guy changed. One of his eyes turned into a ghastly hollow. Some weight melted off him—he was still big, but now his body sagged. Worst of all was his skin. He was covered in patches of blackened, dead flesh, like a patchwork of tumors. Isabela couldn't help but scream.

"Stop! I don't want to hurt you—!"

"Stay away, you freak!"

And then, she bolted.

Isabela sprinted out the only door, leaving behind the cot and fleeing into a deserted hallway. Dim lighting, steel walls, narrow, dusty. She darted by a panel covered in glowing symbols in a language she couldn't understand but that looked like something in Dr. Goode's lab. Where was she? Didn't matter. She needed to find people. She knew the stories—Garde were always being kidnapped and brought to top secret facilities, and top secret facilities were staffed with prison guards and science dorks. If she could find some, she could blend in, steal an identity, and get clear of this mess.

She hurdled over a pile of blankets and dirty laundry—was that where someone slept? What the hell was this place? It didn't exactly seem populated. Was this some abandoned complex where these weirdos were squatting?

Find a door. Get outside. Disappear.

Footsteps echoed behind her, the freak shouting at her. "There's nowhere to go!"

If there was nowhere to go, then why was he chasing her? Idiot. That meant there *was* somewhere to go.

Isabela turned a corner, sprinting down another claustrophobic hallway. There was a door up ahead. Heavy-duty, bolted in place with thick bars that would normally require two people to lift—an emergency exit. She ran towards it, using her telekinesis to rip away the constraints as she went.

"Don't—!"

She shoved against the door as hard as she could with her telekinesis. It flew outward.

Night. Sky. Rushing air.

They were flying. She was on some kind of aircraft.

"Oh, fuck me," Isabela had time to say before the freezing wind sucked her outside.

And then she was falling.

Spinning and out of control, the wind buffeting her. Above, she caught a glimpse of the vessel—silver and bug-like and soon out of sight—now nothing to see but the ground below. Darkness, treetops, snow. She couldn't even die looking at some pretty lights.

She screamed, because what else could she do?

"Got you."

An arm around her waist, gripping her tight. Floating. *She was floating.*

The monster had her. He could fly. He'd saved her. And, apparently, he had also grabbed the emergency exit door that she had knocked loose—it floated nearby, held by his telekinesis. But that meant . . .

"You're Garde," she said, breathless from the screaming and the wind.

"I am Number Five," he replied.

"Merda."

CHAPTER TWENTY-TWO

KOPANO OKEKE
TOP SECRET WATCHTOWER FACILITY—LOCATION UNKNOWN

KOPANO CAME AWAKE SLOWLY. HIS EARS RANG AND his head pounded, a vague coppery taste bitter on his tongue. When he opened his eyes he expected to find himself back in his cell, but he was still on the cold floor of the control room. Karen Walker still sat at the table as before, although now she was reading a newspaper.

"How . . . what . . . ?" he mumbled, unable to form a coherent thought as he propped himself up on his elbows. Next to him, Ran moaned. She too had been taken down.

"Good, you're awake," Walker said, folding up her newspaper.

"What did you do to us?"

She tapped the side of her head where Kopano's and Ran's bandages were. "An Inhibitor chip has been surgically implanted into your skulls," she said matter-of-factly. "If I hit the panic button on my phone, a temporarily debilitating shock will be administered to your nervous system. If—"

Kopano was still rubbing the side of his head in disbelief when Ran reached out with her telekinesis and yanked the phone away from Walker. She was on the floor, half leaning against the wall, yet even in that compromised position her glare was pure murder.

"Let us out of here," Ran growled.

The device in her hand let out a series of shrill beeps. Walker cringed sympathetically.

"I wish you'd have let me finish talking," she said.

Another explosion of white light. This time, Kopano managed to howl before he passed out.

Thirty minutes went by. When Kopano woke up again he was still on the floor, but his head felt even worse than before, like it had been wedged in a vise and then dropped to the bottom of the ocean. Ran was next to him, awake first this time, dark circles around her eyes. Walker had her phone back.

"As I was trying to say," Walker continued patiently, "the Inhibitors will also issue a shock if the controller ever leaves my immediate radius. There's also an electric fence setting where they will shock you for going too far away from me. I'd rather not have to use that one, but will if you run. My controller here is not unique, there are others. Destroying it will get you nowhere."

This was not what Kopano had pictured when he dreamed

of being in Earth Garde. He sniffed loudly, then covered his face with his hands so this evil woman couldn't see how close to tears he was.

"You're torturing us," he murmured.

"No, I was against this part," Walker replied. Kopano was surprised at the tenderness in her voice. "Now that you understand your situation, I hope to never use the Inhibitors again. Really."

"So long as we do what you say," Ran said darkly.

Walker met Ran's gaze briefly, then looked away. "No. You have an option. If you decide you'd rather not work with me, you can return to your cell. You'll be taken care of until such a time that Earth Garde decides you're no longer dangerous."

"Dangerous?" Kopano exclaimed. "How are *we* dangerous?"

"To humans. To your classmates. To the public image of Earth Garde. Take your pick." Walker pointed out the door. "That's the choice. A detainment of indeterminate length or you work for me and Operation Watchtower."

Ran simply glowered, but Kopano took the bait. "What's— what's that?"

"Watchtower is a joint venture among a number of the world's covert intelligence agencies—the CIA, Mossad, MI6, others—that operates on a need-to-know basis within Earth Garde. You would be among our first recruits."

"This is not a recruitment," Ran said. "This is coercion."

Kopano shot her a look. Obviously their situation beyond sucked—he didn't even want to think about how someone had drilled a microchip into his head—but there was no way he would go back in that cell. Not when this spy lady was offering them a way out.

"Why us?" he asked, his voice hitching higher than he would've liked. "What did we do wrong? Is this because of the Harvesters?"

"You didn't do anything wrong," Walker replied, softening her voice. "Your reports from the Academy are all glowing. I know it might not seem like it, but being selected for Watchtower shows the confidence that Earth Garde has in you. As for the Harvesters, everyone that matters knows that what happened was a matter of self-defense."

"Then why don't they say something?" Kopano asked, his eyes widening. "Defend us. The news, they call us monsters . . ."

"Unfortunately, taking a public stand would require Earth Garde to admit certain uncomfortable truths. I hate to say it, but image matters with you people. The Academy's reputation is already tarnished by your actions—justified or not. The whole Earth Garde program would take a hit if the public knew you were out there fighting a rogue Garde mind controller. It would be chaos."

Ran and Kopano exchanged a look.

"You know about him," Ran stated.

"Then . . . do you know about his bosses?" Kopano asked.

"We don't think he has a boss anymore," Walker replied. "You've seen the way the public has reacted to the footage of you two. Imagine the terror if they knew there were threats out there beyond Earth Garde's control. We can't afford for the world to lose faith in Earth Garde."

Kopano nodded slowly in reluctant agreement, but Ran spoke up again, her voice sharp.

"What about *our* faith in Earth Garde? Does what we think not matter?"

"I know this hasn't been the best introduction, Ran, but what we're doing here is for your own good. This way, Earth Garde can tell the world that you've been disciplined and transferred somewhere secure. And, in the meantime, you can do good work for Watchtower, an organization that prefers its operatives stay out of the public eye. Once you complete your first mission, show my bosses that you're not a risk to world security, I'll get those Inhibitors out of you."

"What's the missi—?" Kopano asked.

"No," Ran interrupted. "I have been very clear with Greger. I will not let my Legacy be militarized. I choose the cell."

Kopano stared at her. "Ran, you don't mean it!"

"I thought you might be a hard sell," Walker said. She hit a button on her phone and Kopano cringed, expecting a shock. Instead, the security monitors all switched over to a grainy photograph of a young man that made Kopano wince yet again. "But this mission is truly for the greater good, Ran. We are going to bring him to justice. Make sure he never hurts anyone again."

Einar. On every screen.

"Does that change your mind?" Walker asked.

CHAPTER TWENTY-THREE

ISABELA SILVA
SOMEWHERE OVER BRITISH COLUMBIA, CANADA

NUMBER FIVE. THE ONE ALL THE OTHER LORIC hated. Isabela had heard the stories about him. He betrayed his own people to the Mogadorians, then changed his mind and tried to fight with the good guys once the invasion started. She'd watched YouTube videos of his fight with Professor Nine, the two of them brawling through the heart of New York City like a pair of superpowered moron jocks.

Five was supposed to be dead. That's what Nine had told everyone, anyway. But he clearly wasn't dead. He was just severely messed up.

Isabela tried not to let any fear or awe show as Five flung her back onboard their little aircraft. Isabela recognized the vessel, too. It was a Skimmer. One of the smaller ships piloted by the Mogadorians. Where had Einar gotten ahold of that? How had he hooked up with Number Five?

Thanks to Isabela's escape attempt, the wind still rushed around them. She clutched a nearby railing so she wouldn't get sucked out again. Meanwhile, Five wedged the Skimmer's door back into place using a combination of telekinesis and brute strength. When he was finished, the door rattled like crazy but at least it kept the wind out.

"That was stupid," Five said, rounding on Isabela. She had a hard time looking him in the face but managed to stand her ground.

"You were groping me," Isabela replied.

"I was *not* groping you," Five snarled. "I saved your life."

Isabela tossed her hair theatrically. "My friend Taylor got rescued by John Smith," she said. "She gets John Smith and I get the ugly one."

Five's mouth tightened. "You aren't so pretty yourself."

To that, Isabela had no comeback.

An impressively tall girl poked her shaved head out of an adjoining room, eyeing both Five and Isabela with skepticism. That was the one who'd shocked her back in California.

"What happened?" she asked.

"She tried to escape," Five grunted.

"Does this pervert touch *you* when you sleep?" Isabela asked.

The girl raised an eyebrow, then looked at Five for clarification. "You were supposed to be watching her."

"I *was* watching her!" Five shouted. A short temper on that one, Isabela realized. He grabbed Isabela by the arm roughly enough that she'd have bruises. "Go back to sleep, Duanphen, before I break your other goddamn leg."

Duanphen gazed evenly at Five, holding her ground for long enough that she wouldn't look like a total pushover. But Isabela could see it—she was afraid. Five was not someone to take lightly.

"You are okay?" Duanphen asked Isabela, pointedly ignoring Five.

"No, I'm not okay, you silly bitch," Isabela answered. "You nearly killed me and now I've been kidnapped."

"Mm," Duanphen replied, simply. "Sorry about that. We thought you were someone else."

With that, Duanphen turned and limped back into her room.

Breathing heavily through his nose in a way that made the air whistle, Five dragged Isabela down the hallway. She soon realized how small the ship was. No more than three rooms with bare cots and tables, all of them cluttered with junk—food wrappers, dirty plates, clothes, and weapons. A lot of weapons, everything from traditional guns to Mogadorian blasters to some of the high-tech Sydal Corp stuff Isabela had seen the Peacekeepers use during their training exercises.

And then there was the massive pile of money spread out in banded stacks on a vacant cot. Some of that had been blown over, presumably when Isabela broke the door.

So they were living on this ship, they were heavily armed, and they were rich as hell.

They reached the cockpit—a glittering panel of instruments, a windshield with a complicated display, and two bucket seats. Einar sat in one of them, one leg propped up on the console, steering laconically.

"She's awake," Five announced.

"I figured," Einar replied. He hit a couple of buttons on the console, turning on some kind of autopilot, and stood up. Einar looked more put together than his companions, his preppy clothes clean and his hair meticulously gelled to one side. "Hello, Isabela. My name is—"

"I know who you are, *pinto*," Isabela interrupted. "You're the mind controller."

"That's not technically accurate."

Isabela tried to jerk away from Five, to get closer to Einar. "Are you controlling this sack of shit right now?"

Five's grip tightened. "No one controls me."

"I don't want to manipulate you," Einar said, his hands open. He drew nearer. "I won't use my Legacies against you, Isabela. Not unless you force me—"

He was close enough. Isabela lunged forward and kicked Einar between the legs.

"*Coma merda!* That is for Nige—!"

There was a brief moment of pure satisfaction as Einar doubled over and fell to his knees, simultaneously gasping and retching. But then, Five slammed Isabela up against a wall, knocking the wind out of her. Isabela's feet were lifted off the ground, Five's forearm pressed into her throat. She tried to jab at his pressure points, but his skin was suddenly made completely of metal and she only succeeded in jamming her fingers. There were gulfs in his metal carapace, though—the dark patches of skin that looked like tumors remained unchanged. Even gasping for breath, Isabela couldn't bring herself to touch them.

"Five . . . ," Einar wheezed. "That's enough. You'll hurt her."

"She runs her mouth worse than Nine!" Five yelled back, his breath hot against Isabela's face.

Isabela started to see spots in her vision. She pried uselessly at Five's metal fingers. With a roar, he let her go. Isabela slid down the wall and, above her, Five punched the wall where her head used to be. *Wham, wham, wham*—like a hammer striking an anvil.

"Put me out," Five snarled at Einar. "I don't want to feel like this."

Einar didn't say anything, didn't do anything that Isabela could see, but a moment later Five swayed on his feet. Isabela breathed raggedly, staring up at the imposing Loric. The bloodlust—so vivid in his remaining eye a moment ago— had seeped out of him.

"I'm . . . I'm sorry," Five said. "I lose my temper sometimes."

Isabela could only cough in response. Five's eye was half-lidded and spacy, like he'd been tranquilized. Before she could do anything, the big bastard sank to the floor beside Isabela. He ended up with his head in her lap and Isabela was too horrified by the whole scene to stop him.

"If anything should prove my newfound restraint . . ." Einar paused to cough and wipe tears from his eyes, looking at Isabela across the narrow space. "It's that I'm willing to let what you just did go."

"You tried to kill my friends," Isabela replied, her voice raspy.

"I regret that," Einar replied. "I wasn't in my right mind. But, in my defense, your 'friend' Nigel is probably a spy for the Foundation."

Isabela snorted. "What?"

"His mother, Bea, is one of them," Einar continued. "One of the important ones."

"Bullshit."

"His father, too. I can show you proof when I'm able to walk again."

"Nigel's dad just died. There was a fire at his house after the funeral. Him and his mom are missing."

"Ah, well, the fire is probably Bea's way of trying to throw me off her scent. I had nothing to do with that," Einar replied, holding her gaze. "As for Mr. Barnaby? Well. They *wanted* a war with me."

Isabela's mouth fell open. Had this crazy bastard just admitted to killing Nigel's father? Was she supposed to let that go? Part of her wanted to lunge at him again, even though she knew it would likely be futile.

"What were *you* doing posing as Alejandro?" Einar asked before Isabela could gather her thoughts.

"What were *you* doing trying to kill him?" Isabela countered.

"Duanphen, the third member of our revolution, she has an injured leg—"

"Boo-hoo," Isabela interrupted. "My whole body hurts from that car crash, thanks to you assholes. So what?"

"We'd learned that the Foundation planned to acquire your friend Taylor again," Einar continued over her. "Alejandro was in charge of that effort. We thought that he could be . . . *convinced* . . . to get us close to Taylor."

Isabela snorted. "You think she would help you? She hates you. We all hate you."

"I know Taylor wouldn't let someone suffer," Einar said. "The Foundation's reports said she was fed up with the Academy. If she was so desperate to return to the Foundation, I thought she should know there was a third option. Us."

"You idiot," Isabela said, with a disbelieving laugh. "We were infiltrating the Foundation. Not to just—just randomly kill them, but to bring them to justice."

Einar smiled at her indulgently. "Come on, Isabela. I've read your psyche profile. You're no crusader. These people are too powerful. You know there won't be justice for them unless we bring it to them."

Isabela shifted uncomfortably, and not just because Five was practically snoring in her lap. She was used to being the one reading people and didn't much care to be on the opposite side.

"There's no *we*," Isabela replied sharply. "Now. Are we done talking? Can you drop me off somewhere?"

"Back at your Academy, maybe?" Einar replied. "Where you're trained to use your powers for the greater good, so long as the greater good lines up with the agenda of whoever is in charge?"

"Better than this shithole spaceship," Isabela countered.

"These are humble beginnings," Einar replied.

Isabela started to reply but let out a shriek instead. Five had grabbed her hand. So violent just moments ago, now he was like a child. Isabela felt a tickle on her palm and Five's skin again changed to pale pink, the black splotches gone. Einar did a double take at the sight of his restored bodyguard.

Five chuckled. "Look at me, Einar. Whole again."

"This is a freak show," Isabela said. She didn't try to pull her hand away, not wanting to upset the insane Loric.

"He can take on the qualities of anything he touches," Einar told Isabela. "When he touches you, he must be able to tap into the shape-shifting qualities of your skin. Usually, he can't transform those dark scars of his. They were caused by some toxic Mogadorian chemical and—"

"Seriously," Isabela replied. "I don't care."

"You should. He's from a different planet, but he's one of us. A Garde. An outsider."

"I'm not—"

"And surely you can sympathize with someone wanting to restore themselves to a better state," Einar said, staring meaningfully at Isabela's unblemished skin.

She glared at him. Of course, Einar kept on talking.

"Five was the first person I sought out when the Foundation cut me loose," he said, speaking quietly so as not to disturb the spaced-out Loric. "Of course they had a file on him. A rogue Garde with flexible morals who isn't participating in the Earth Garde initiative? They always planned to recruit him. But I got there first."

"And mind controlled him," Isabela said flatly.

"Only when he asks me to," Einar replied. "He has demons. Anger, guilt, self-loathing. I can make him content. I can give him peace. He's trying to do better. We both are."

Isabela gazed down at Five. She felt the tiniest kernel of sympathy, though it was crushed by a metric ton of revulsion.

"Seems like therapy and smoking pot would be simpler," she said.

Einar smirked. "He was hidden away on an island, unaware of what has been going on in the world. I told him about Earth Garde and the Foundation. How the other Loric do so little to help us, merely delaying the inevitable battle with humanity, letting the powerless majority subjugate us in the meantime. I told him what the Foundation is after . . ."

"What *are* they after?"

"Something the Mogadorians were working on. Technology that could even the playing field with their biggest adversary. Us. Unlike those other coddled Academy kids, the six of you who broke out—you've seen it. What the world is like outside Professor Nine's protection. Where we're heading."

A chill went down Isabela's spine. She told herself that Einar was probably tweaking her emotions, making her receptive to his ominous stories. But at the same time, there was an intensity to the way he talked that pulled her in.

"I know how we look," Einar continued. She watched fractures form in his calm and calculated mask—genuine passion seeping through. "Like we're insane, right? But that's what happens when they force you to live on the fringes. You're observant—I'm sure you saw the money room when Five brought you here. We've already acquired over three million dollars from the Foundation. We're going to build something. A place where we can be free. Where we don't have to answer to anyone. How does that sound, Isabela?"

"It sounds good," Isabela admitted. "If only you weren't the one saying it."

Einar nodded, a hint of a smile on his lips. She'd conceded that his ideas sounded good and he must've viewed that as a small victory. Isabela thought about kicking him in the balls again.

"I appreciate that I'll have to earn your trust," Einar said. "Tell me, when you infiltrated the Foundation, did Taylor go, too? Is that how you got to Alejandro? By letting her be recruited?"

Isabela hesitated, not sure what she should tell him.

"I'll take that as a yes," Einar replied. "That's good. A

brave plan. I'm honestly sorry we ruined it. Do you think she'll be all right, without you watching out for her?"

Isabela gritted her teeth. She could already tell where this was going.

"Isabela," Einar said. "I believe we can help each other."

CHAPTER TWENTY-FOUR

NIGEL BARNABY
ENGELBERG, SWITZERLAND

ON THE FIRST DAY, NIGEL WOKE UP WITH A SCREAM.

There was a nurse standing over him, checking his blood pressure. Young and pretty, German-looking, her face quickly turning to a mask of horror as the decibels flying from his mouth shattered her eardrums. She stumbled backwards into a corner, covering her ears and cowering.

"Where the fuck am I?" he asked, getting out of bed and ripping off the Velcro sleeve she'd attached to his arm.

She couldn't hear him. Or maybe she couldn't understand English. Either way, she just crouched there and cried.

"Goddamn it," Nigel muttered, looking around. He discovered he was wearing a set of baggy flannel pajamas. The indignities never ceased.

He was in a posh bedroom—wood-paneled, an oriental

throw rug, a king-size bed behind him with silk sheets and lots of pillows. He felt well rested, despite being drugged. Whatever sedative his mom had used on him hadn't left him with any hangover.

Bloody hell. His own mother had drugged him. She'd had goons—those Blackstone guys he fought back in Iceland. Didn't take a rocket scientist to figure out whose side she was on. She'd killed the Peacekeepers who were supposed to watch over him and then . . . what? Set fire to his home?

Nigel pinched the bridge of his nose. He looked at the nurse again.

"You always think maybe your parents are a little evil, right?" he asked her, even though she stared at him uncomprehending. "But you never expect them to go full Hitler on you, eh?"

He wanted to seem cavalier and unruffled by this sudden change in fortune because he suspected that he was being watched. There was a small camera mounted in one corner of the room. There was also a TV on the wall opposite the bed—could be a camera in there, too. Underneath the façade, though, Nigel felt like he might be sick. His own mother was some kind of evil Foundation bitch. The day of the funeral, they'd actually been getting along. For the first time since he was small enough to sit in her lap, Nigel had actually *liked* Bea Barnaby.

The room reminded him of where they'd been keeping Taylor in Iceland. There was no handle on his side of the door and he got the feeling that no amount of telekinetic force would dislodge the slab of reinforced wood from its frame. He figured that the windows were probably equally impenetrable, but he at least wanted to get a look at what was outside.

Through glass that appeared to be six inches thick, Nigel looked out at a quaint European village. He was on the fourth floor of what was probably the tallest building in this snowy hamlet. Down below, groups of people equipped for skiing moved towards the great silver mountainside at the village edge.

"The Alps," Nigel said. "Never been to the Alps."

Nigel took a deep breath. One of his favorite training activities was exploding wineglasses with high-decibel shrieks. What did Dr. Goode say? That every object on Earth had a frequency that caused it to vibrate and—if he could hit the right note—he could theoretically shatter anything? Well, maybe not *anything*. Nigel didn't know. He hadn't paid a ton of attention to the science part. He just liked breaking stuff.

He screamed, funneling the sound towards the window so he wouldn't further injure the poor nurse. He went as high and shrill as possible and, once, he thought the window started to vibrate. But, when he finally ran out of breath, his throat scratchy and raw, the glass was still intact. Probably wasn't glass at all, but that blastproof plastic they used all over the Academy. His mom would be prepared.

"Oh well, had to try," he said with a cough. He went to the nurse and crouched over her. "Oi, sweetheart, how do you get out of here? There a key card or something? A secret knock?"

She stared at him blankly, her lower lip quivering. Nigel's ear prickled at a brief burst of static behind him. The TV had come on.

"My dear, please don't assault the help. It's uncouth."

His mother was on the screen. Bea Barnaby looked well rested, a steaming mug of tea cupped in her hands. She wore a woolly sweater and her reading glasses. She looked straight ahead at Nigel, proving his theory that there was a camera in the TV.

"Cheers, Mum," Nigel replied, playing it cool. "Where are you?"

"I'm right downstairs," she answered.

"Ah. Can I come down to see ya?"

She smiled. "I don't know if that'd be a good idea yet. I don't think you'll behave."

Nigel smiled back, all teeth, trying to keep control of his temper. It wouldn't do to snap. Not yet. He needed to get some more information first and it seemed clear that his mother wanted to talk.

"Jessa down there with you?" He'd last seen his sister after the funeral—before he was drugged, before his mother killed his bodyguards and presumably burned their bodies. Was she alive? Was she in on this?

"She's back in London," his mom answered. "I sent her off to a hotel with her clod husband. Going to be a traumatic few days for her, I suppose. Losing her whole family. But I thought it best if we left her out of this."

"Losing her whole family . . ."

"Papers should have it in a day or two. We burned alive. Least that's what it'll look like. Your friends at Earth Garde will see through that." She shrugged. "They won't be able to do anything about it, though."

"You're a murderer," Nigel said, thinking now of the Peacemakers. "Sit there drinking your tea and you're a murderer."

"It's not murder when you're at war, dear," his mom said flippantly. "And make no mistake, a war is what's happening. A great battle for control of you and people like you."

Nigel stepped aside so his mom could see where the nurse still crouched in the corner of the room.

"You want her back, you're going to have to open the door," he said. "Let me out, Mum. I'll join you for tea."

"Her? We don't care about her," his mom replied. A man in black body armor passed behind her. So she had mercenaries down there, too. "In fact, she was only meant to check your vitals. She wasn't supposed to find out what you are. We'll have to deal with her now."

Nigel remembered the little girl they'd found at the cabin in Iceland, the one the Foundation had threatened to kill in order to keep Taylor in line. His skin crawled—that his own mother could be capable of something like that. How had he come from a person like that?

"You're sick," Nigel said, unable to keep his voice from shaking with disgust. He'd wanted to keep his cavalier attitude intact, but now a woman's life was at stake. "You know that, right?"

"Individuals have the luxury of cloaking themselves in righteousness when it comes to innocent lives," Bea said.

"You quoting the fascist handbook now?"

She ignored him. "Larger entities—governments, religions, corporations—they must weigh the greater good against the survival of the innocent. You'll come to understand that, dear."

"Ah, so that's what this is? Indoctrination into the family business?"

His mother smiled, like she was proud of his perception. "I simply want us to have an open and honest conversation. I want you to see how the world works."

Nigel pointed at the nurse again. "You do anything to her, I swear, that'll be the end of it. I'll find a way out of here. Failing that, I'll fuckin' off myself. You want a nice chat with sonny boy, stop killing people."

"Fine. I agree. She won't be harmed," Bea said this flippantly, like whether or not one ordered a murder was the equivalent of looking at a dessert menu. "We'll talk again tomorrow."

"What—"

Hss. A vent in the ceiling that Nigel had failed to notice opened up, emitting a rush of air. Some kind of gas. He tried to squeeze the slats shut with his telekinesis, but too late. The stuff acted quickly. He stumbled backwards and only barely managed to land lengthwise on the bed.

"Nigel Barnaby. You have no idea how happy I am to see you."

In the haze brought on by the gas, Nigel remembered Iceland. That's what Einar had said right before he took control of Nigel's emotions, brought him back to those Pepperpont days, made him walk out on the ice. Einar had looked up at one of the cameras.

"I hope you're watching," he'd said.

The psycho knew. He'd been taunting Nigel's mother.

After that, the death collar had mysteriously detached from the Icelandic girl, and Taylor had been allowed to return to the Academy. She'd received a bloody thank-you note.

All because she'd saved Nigel.

On the second day, when Nigel woke up, the nurse was gone. But, there were other additions to his room.

The first thing Nigel noticed was that a record player had been placed next to his bed. An expensive one, glossy wood to give it that old-timey feel but with a totally digital display. A stack of records had also been arranged on the shelf beneath his nightstand. He expected the kind of stodgy crap that his parents might be into, jazz or whatever. Instead, he found a wide variety of his favorites—from the Clash all the way up to Pissed Jeans. Someone had done their research.

Attached to the record player was a short note in his mom's elegant cursive. *The walls are soundproof. No need to be considerate.*

So after yesterday's demonstration of dominance, this was the soft touch. Butter him up. Show him that life with the Foundation wasn't so bad. They had tried the same thing with Taylor.

Also on the nightstand was a copy of the *Guardian*. The paper was folded to one of the interior sections, where Nigel immediately recognized a black-and-white photograph of the charred remnants of his family's London home. Nigel skimmed the article—*grieving family, wealthy philanthropists, accidental blaze, surviving daughter unavailable for comment*—no mention of their names, Earth Garde, or any details that seemed indicative of foul play. It was as if his mother had written the article herself. He tossed the newspaper aside.

Across the room, a desk had been added and, on top of that, a tray of breakfast food. Pancakes and sausage, fruit, doughnuts, a carafe of juice and a kettle of tea. Nigel's stomach growled. When was the last time he'd eaten? He had to remind himself that his mother was surely watching or else he would've lunged right for the food. He casually poured himself some tea and sipped.

On the table, there was a remote control for the TV. He turned it on, half expecting Bea's face to pop up. Instead, the screen filled with icons—pretty much every streaming video service one could ask for.

Nigel looked up at the camera watching over him. "All the comforts don't mean this isn't a prison," he said.

There was no response.

At first he thought he might resist and be Gandhi-like in his abstention, but Nigel was too hungry and too bored. He spent the day stuffing his face and listening to music.

He let himself smile and look content.

He knew his mother was watching. Let her go ahead and think it was this easy to break him down.

They'd wanted to get someone inside the Foundation. Here was their opportunity.

On the third day of his captivity, a strange glow woke Nigel in the middle of the night. He rolled over in bed and found his TV on. Bea was on-screen, a half-empty wineglass clutched in one hand, a nearly empty bottle visible in the foreground.

"Ah," she said. "You're awake."

"I am now," Nigel grunted. He worked himself up onto his elbows. "Were you watching me sleep?"

"Used to do that when you were a little boy," Bea responded.

Was she drunk? Was this part of her manipulation? Nigel didn't know what to think. He stayed quiet, waiting for her to speak.

"Your father's greatest love was money," his mom said wistfully. "Money or Asian call girls. One of the two."

Nigel raised an eyebrow. "Okay."

"Don't get me wrong, I liked the money, too," Bea continued. "But I also wanted to make the world a better place. I truly believed in what he told us."

"What who told you?"

"Setrákus Ra."

Nigel sat up straighter, eyes wide. His mom had just casually mentioned the leader of the Mogadorians, the tyrant who had driven the Loric to extinction and then, when that wasn't good enough, invaded the Earth.

"You picked a real wanker for a role model, Mum."

"He promised us a world without sickness or hunger," she continued like she didn't hear him. "All we had to do was make ready for his arrival."

"You were MogPro," Nigel said quietly. "You were bloody MogPro."

"Many of us in the Foundation were." She sipped her wine. "We learned the error of our ways, believe me. No one wanted to follow Setrákus Ra once we learned what he really was. The US did a thorough job of exterminating our American counterparts, but once the invasion was over, we here in Europe slipped through the cracks. Some of us formed the Foundation as a way to deal with our changing world."

"Out with one evil organization, in with another," Nigel replied.

"We've since expanded, blossoming into a better network than MogPro ever was. With Setrákus Ra, it was all lofty promises to pave the way for tyranny. Not with us. Thanks to our carefully cultivated relationships with your kind, we can actually deliver results. Miracles, even. We're in more countries than Earth Garde now. We turn a profit."

"Carefully cultivated relationships," Nigel repeated with a snort. "Why are you telling me all this?"

She raised her glass to him. "I don't know, darling. I suppose it's like you said. The family business."

It would be too easy if Nigel just said, "Sure, great, I'm in," and tried to join up with the Foundation. His mom would see through that. No, if she was going to believe he'd been won over, he needed to live up to his stubborn reputation.

So, Nigel made a wanking motion. "You really think I'm going to buy into this? A little drunken chat, some mild imprisonment, and we're on the same team? Piss off."

"Setrákus Ra told us the history of the Loric and why he overthrew them," Bea continued. "How those with Legacies reigned over those without, a council of elders composed of the planet's nine most powerful Garde. Did you know that's how their society worked? Like something out of Nietzsche."

Nigel could guess what the Mogadorian tyrant probably told his mother. The old bastard wrote an entire book of propaganda. But, on the day he first got his Legacies, Nigel had been sucked into a vision of Lorien's past, just like all the first generation of Human Garde. He'd seen firsthand the truth of Setrákus Ra's motivations. He wasn't a liberator; he was petty and power-hungry.

"Setrákus Ra was a liar," Nigel said simply.

"Perhaps. But then, history is written by the winners," Bea countered. "True or not, there are lessons to be learned from what happened on Lorien."

"Like?"

"Like how your Academy is destined to fall apart. It

was formed during a time of unprecedented goodwill, the world's nations bound together after confronting a common enemy." She drained the last of her wine and poured herself another. "That goodwill's all dried up now. Training teenagers to serve some nebulous global entity? Please. Countries will abandon Earth Garde—it's already happening—and hoard their Garde like nuclear weapons."

Nigel grimaced. What his mother said appealed to his cynical side, the anarchist side, the part of him that had lived through Pepperpont and that assumed all people were basically shit. But then he thought of Kopano and Ran, the heroic ones, how hard they tried to do good in the world. He thought about how he himself had run away from a bad situation—one caused by his parents, as it happened—to go fight an alien invasion.

"You're wrong," he replied, wishing he sounded more certain. "People are better than you give them credit for."

She smiled, almost like she was proud that her offspring was capable of such optimistic thought. Her teeth were stained with wine.

"And then what will happen," Bea continued, "is war. A war between those with powers and those without. The end result being either the extinction of Legacies—a great loss to humanity—or the subjugation of the nonpowered, which, well . . . not so rosy either way, is it? We in the Foundation believe we can head off these eventualities but, unfortunately, the first battles are already being fought and soon it will be too late to reverse course."

Nigel squinted at the screen. "What first battles? What are you on about?"

"One of yours has already broken the Garde Declaration. He's killed humans in cold blood. Colleagues of mine in the Foundation, their security, anyone who gets in his way."

A cold feeling took hold of Nigel. He sensed where this conversation was going.

"He killed your father," Bea continued. "He almost killed you."

Nigel gritted his teeth. "Einar."

A shadow crossed Bea's face, as if the boy's very name frightened her. She nodded once.

"He'll come for me, eventually," she said simply. "The security I have here won't be enough to stop him."

Nigel looked away. He said nothing.

"Will you let me die, Nigel? Your own mother?"

Nigel didn't sleep that night. Bea's words rattled around in his brain.

His parents were bad people. MogPro rejects, bloodthirsty capitalists, murderers. When Nigel was a boy, his father had sent him away as soon as his presence had become inconvenient. After Nigel fled Pepperpont, the old man had never even tried seeking him out. Too busy with the Foundation, probably. He didn't love the bastard.

So why did he feel the cold yearning for revenge?

Well, he told himself, *Einar did try to drown me.* He owed him for that.

Now, his mother only wanted him around to save herself. Or did she still have some repressed maternal affection? She'd been happy to have him saved in Iceland. She'd been watching him sleep . . .

Could he let Einar kill her?

And his mother was probably right. Einar's going around slaughtering Foundation people—bad as they were—could set off a war. The psycho would ruin all their lives.

Nigel wanted to scream. So, he did. After all, the walls were soundproof.

That morning, his fourth day in captivity, the door to his room slid open.

His mom stood there, hair a bit tousled, cheeks puffy from last night's drinking. There was no team of mercenaries behind her—she was alone, fragile. Nigel could've easily pushed her aside with his telekinesis and made his escape. She must have known that, but she opened the door anyway.

Bea said nothing. She clasped her hands and waited. It was on him.

"All right," Nigel said, deciding right then what he would do. "I'll help you."

CHAPTER TWENTY-FIVE

CALEB CRANE
MELBOURNE, FLORIDA

CALEB'S SHOULDERS WERE STARTING TO BURN. With a groan, he rolled over on the blanket and reached for his T-shirt. He pulled it onto his sunbaked torso.

"Ow," he said.

"Man, I told you to reapply," Daniela scolded. She grabbed the tube of sunscreen and tossed it into Caleb's lap. "Pale ass is gonna look like a lobster out here."

"Yeah," he replied, blowing out a sigh. "Yeah, you told me."

It was a cloudless day, unseasonably warm, the white-capped waves sending salty spray up on a lazy breeze. The sand shimmered here, the beach pristine, without any other people in sight. Next to Caleb, Daniela reclined on her elbows, her lean body clad in a white bikini, sweat dimpling her abdomen. Caleb should've been enjoying the hell out of this.

So why wasn't he?

A private beach, all to themselves on Florida's Space Coast—so called because it was where NASA and any number of defense contractors, including Sydal Corp, were headquartered. Maybe it was their host that bothered him. Maybe that's what kept Caleb from completely turning off his mind and enjoying this unearned vacation.

But Mr. Sydal—Wade, he insisted they call him *Wade*— had been nothing but nice to them. They stayed in guest rooms in his sprawling beachside mansion. He fed the visiting Garde lavish meals cooked by his personal chef, showed off his multitude of engineering projects, and let them use the beach and his infinity pool. Massages and tennis lessons were also on offer, although Caleb hadn't partaken in either. It'd been almost a week of that pampering and Mr. Sydal— *Wade*—asked for nothing in return.

Sydal spent most of his time in his technology-filled basement workshop. The gadgets and gizmos in there would've made Dr. Goode jealous, Caleb thought. Sometimes, he took meetings at the navy base in the area. He had his own paid security detail.

This was a cream-puff detail. There was no reason for Caleb to feel so on edge.

And yet, he couldn't shake that feeling.

Caleb thought about calling his uncle. But what would he tell Uncle Clarence? That Melanie Jackson was a huge wimp who needed a "break" from Earth Garde life after a week of photo ops and some light construction work? She'd been protected from the worst of the invasion by her president father, had never gone to the Academy, and was basically coddled at Earth Garde. Did she really need a vacation from her vacation?

Maybe that wasn't the most charitable assessment of Melanie, but it didn't help Caleb's opinion that she mostly ignored him and Daniela, preferring instead to spend her free time video-chatting with people from her old life—prep school classmates, senators' kids, future leaders of the free world.

No. Lawson wouldn't care about that. That was kid stuff.

What did his uncle want him to uncover?

A crab scuttled past their blanket, black eyes like twin periscopes swiveling around. The little guys were called ghost crabs. Caleb had first spotted them scampering across the sand a few days ago. Bored and tired of swimming, he'd spent a solid hour reading about them online.

"Check it out," Caleb said, pointing the gold-tinted crustacean out to Daniela. "Those guys change their colors to blend in with the sand. Pretty cool, huh?"

Daniela tipped down her paperback—some lurid romance novel she'd picked up at the airport—so she could regard Caleb.

"You could learn something from them," she said.

"What's that supposed to mean?"

As they watched, the crab buried itself back in the sand,

only its pair of elongated eyes visible.

"It means you could try going with the flow a bit," Daniela replied. "I see you over there, wheels turning and shit. You've been sulking around since we got here."

"I'm not sulking," Caleb responded sulkily. "Don't you just think . . . I don't know? Like this is weird?"

"Man, we saved the world from an alien invasion," Daniela replied, her braids shaking back and forth as she laughed. "I mean, the Loric did most of it, but we were there, too. They should be giving us free vacations for the rest of our lives. Be like the crab, man. Chill."

"I think they blend in like that to avoid predators."

"You see any predators out here, Caleb?"

Caleb turned his head to look back at the beach house.

"I don't know."

People were starting to gather on the house's back deck. Caleb could see Wade there. The man was supposedly in his fifties, but his baby face and angular black goatee made him look younger. He wore his hair long like a surfer, not a strand of gray in there—just like his beard. In another bout of boredom, Caleb had watched some of Mr. Sydal's TED talks from before the invasion, where he lectured on the possibility of achieving immortality—physical or digital. It all went over Caleb's head, but just by looking at him and listening to him talk, Caleb could tell the guy wanted desperately to stay young forever.

Sydal was surrounded by the usual horde of assistants and interns. All of them were young and attractive, fresh out of Ivy League schools. They mingled with the more professionally dressed research-and-development reps from various engineering and military concerns, everyone gathered to watch the day's launch from the comfort of Sydal's estate.

Caleb could pick out the military brass from the crowd by their haircuts and rigid postures. For a second, he swore he saw his dad up there. Too much sun.

In the middle of it all, of course, was Melanie. Even at a distance, she looked especially vibrant. Her blond hair flowed loose around her head, the wind plucking at her tennis skirt and blouse. Sydal kept a fatherly arm around her shoulders, introducing her to his various guests. Just like on their missions with Earth Garde, Melanie held herself apart from Caleb and Daniela, so much so that he was always surprised to see how easily she turned on the social charms.

Waiters circulated through the crowd on the deck with hors d'oeuvres and cocktails. Caleb and Daniela had been invited to Sydal's little party but had opted to watch the launch from the beach instead.

"Crazy that guys like him are still interested in space travel," Caleb said to Daniela. "Especially when we know there's nothing really out there. All the aliens are trying to come here."

"You're just full of deep thoughts today."

"Thanks."

A loud chant started on the deck. A countdown from ten. Caleb tipped his sunglasses down to watch the vessel take off. The sleek, silver-plated ship rose up from its launchpad down the beach and cut soundlessly through the perfect blue sky. The aircraft was disc-shaped, like the cliché idea of a flying saucer. Sydal probably thought that was clever. A crimson glow came from the wannabe UFO's underbelly. It looked like it was on fire, but those were actually the thrusters.

That was repurposed Mogadorian technology. The military had recovered tons of Skimmers after the invasion and Sydal had been selected as one of the developers to work on reverse engineering it. Today was a big day for Wade and Sydal Corp: they were the first company to get a prototype flight-ready. In an effort to distance his work from the hostile aliens that provided its foundation, Sydal had christened the ship the *Shepard-1*, named for the first American to make it into space.

The *Shepard-1* swooped around, propelled by its thrusters, stable and under control. It did a loop-the-loop, much to the delight of Sydal's guests. Then, the ship went vertical, rising higher and higher, until it was just a silver speck. Caleb lost sight of it. The plan was for the *Shepard-1* to reach the exosphere. The crowd on the deck fell silent, huddled around Wade and his tablet that displayed the craft's diagnostics.

"Hope it doesn't blow up," Daniela remarked.

Moments later, a cheer went up from the deck. The *Shepard-1* had reached the edge of Earth's atmosphere. Soon, the ship came back into sight, drifting gracefully back down and onto its launchpad.

Everyone applauded. A complete success.

"Cool," Daniela said dryly, barely looking up from her book. "Nice to see we humans have got spaceships now. And it's nice that thing didn't shoot at us, huh?"

Caleb glanced back at the deck where Sydal was getting bombarded with back-patting and handshakes.

"Don't you get the feeling that this Sydal guy thinks everything that came from the war—the tech, the blasters, the warships, even us with our Legacies—it's all just toys for him to play with?"

Daniela shrugged. "What do you want from a nerd like that? He probably reverse engineered a Rubik's Cube when he was a toddler. And I'm pretty sure Dr. Goode does the same stuff."

"It's different," Caleb replied. "Malcolm is trying to help us."

"I'm going to go take a nap," Daniela said. She closed her book, stood up, and gathered her towel. "Try to chill out, okay, Caleb? No one here is out to get you."

Caleb did not chill out.

A few minutes after Daniela left, Caleb stood up and headed back to the mansion. The gathering on the deck was now a full-fledged cocktail party, none of the guests eager to leave behind Sydal's hospitality. No one paid Caleb any attention as he skirted around the side of the house and entered through a side door.

During the tour when they first got there, Wade had briefly taken his Garde guests by his workshop. It was on the first floor, right across the hall from the gym. Sydal had laughed sheepishly about his "geek sanctuary," told Caleb and the others that they'd find his projects boring, and instead guided them into the fitness center where he had elliptical machines hooked up to VR.

Caleb had wanted to poke around the workshop ever since. What better time than now, when everyone else was distracted at the *Shepard-1* reception?

Sydal didn't even keep the room locked. The workshop got plenty of light from its floor-to-ceiling windows, a view of the beach visible beyond. The space was immaculately organized, tools and gears and circuit boards all in their proper places. A half dozen drones of various sizes sat dormant on a workbench. On a nearby easel were a stack of hand-drawn schematics.

Caleb put his hands on his hips. This wasn't exactly an evil lair. It sort of reminded him of Dr. Goode's laboratory, although way less chaotic. What had he really been expecting to find?

A familiar shape on the topmost schematic caught his eye. With a curious frown, Caleb approached the easel.

The technical sketch looked at first like a thumbtack combined with a microchip. Caleb recognized the device as the same one they pulled out of that girl Rabiya's temple when they rescued her from the Harvesters. An Inhibitor. There were handwritten notes in the margins of the sketch, the tidy writing presumably Sydal's. *Easily removed; difficult to attach; painful.*

Caleb flipped to the next page. A human skull was sketched there in perfect detail. One of the Inhibitor chips was drawn directly attached to the bone, its little prong penetrating 3.4 millimeters—the exact measurement was scribbled right there, along with a bunch of other calculations that Caleb couldn't make sense of. There were more notes. *Highest possible voltage? How much = too much? Prone to short-circuit.*

Grimacing as he imagined having one of those things stuck directly into his head, Caleb went to the next sketch. This one wasn't nearly as technical as the ones that preceded it. A freehand version of da Vinci's *Vitruvian Man* was jotted on the paper in pencil, squiggles of blue highlighter running through the limbs, coalescing in the chest and head. Columns of impenetrable equations spread out from the figure, some of them running up against the edge of the paper.

Written across the page: *Source of Loric energy? Can it be detected? Neutralized?*

Caleb wished he had a cell phone or a camera. He wondered what Dr. Goode would make of these designs.

"What are you doing in here?"

Caleb jumped at the sound of a woman's voice. It was Lucinda, one of the Sydal's many college-aged interns. She was pretty, in her early twenties, with hair the color of nutmeg, a smattering of freckles, and sharp green eyes. She was dressed professionally, a neat skirt and a high-collared blouse. She had a stack of paperwork under her arm. Caleb swallowed.

"Uh . . . ," he replied, not sure what to say. "I was just—"

"Those are all out of date," Wade Sydal said airily, waving at the sketches as he entered the room behind Lucinda. He smiled at Caleb as he set down his tablet, the one that had been monitoring *Sherpard-1*. "Sometimes when I can't sleep, I doodle. Please don't judge my work based on those."

"I wasn't. I mean, I—" Caleb's eyes cast about desperately, looking for an excuse for him to be in here. He settled on the bench full of robotics. "I was curious about the drones."

"You're a nervous guy, Caleb. I've noticed that about you," Sydal said, coming over to stand before him. He jerked his thumb in Lucinda's direction and lowered his voice. "All my assistants are trained to keep an eye out for intellectual piracy, but don't let her intimidate you. I'm sure we've got nothing to fear from a member of Earth Garde. Right, Lucinda?"

"Right," Lucinda replied, barely even looking at Caleb anymore. She was on her phone, answering emails.

"Piracy, uh, no, I was just, uh—" Caleb took a deep breath. Infiltration wasn't really his strong suit, apparently. "I was just bored, I guess."

"Hey, *mi casa es su casa*," Sydal replied. His eyes lit up and he considered Caleb anew. "I'm a little busy right now with the whole groundbreaking spaceflight thing—"

"Oh, yeah, congratulations," Caleb said hurriedly.

"Thanks," Sydal replied. "But hey, next time you're bored, I'd love to take a look at those Legacies of yours. Maybe run a few tests. See what we can figure out. Duplication pretty much defies all known physics, right? I live for that stuff."

"Oh, um . . ."

Caleb let his gaze slide to Sydal's sketches. The man seemed intent on figuring out how the Loric ticked and how to stop them. Should Caleb really submit to some kind of tests? He couldn't think of a polite way to say no and, as the awkwardness between him and grinning Wade stretched on, he felt one of his duplicates nearly pop out from the anxiety. Caleb took a breath, steadied himself, and nodded in a way he hoped was casual.

"Yeah, sure," Caleb said. "Cool."

"Cool!" Sydal repeated, slapping Caleb on the shoulder. "Lucinda, get something with my young friend here on the calendar." Just like that, Sydal was leaving the room again, returning to his cocktail party. He shouted over his shoulder. "The people in this house are going to change human existence! What a time to be alive!"

CHAPTER TWENTY-SIX

TAYLOR COOK
BAYAN-ÖLGII PROVINCE, MONGOLIA

"YOU KNOW, I WAS LED TO BELIEVE THAT LIFE with the Foundation didn't suck," Taylor said, trying and failing to keep her teeth from chattering. "There wasn't anything in the brochures about freezing my ass off in Russia."

"Mongolia," the woman on the video chat corrected.

"Whatever," Taylor replied. She burrowed deeper into her parka, clutching the tablet with numb fingers despite a pair of thick wool gloves. "It's negative thirty degrees here."

"I sincerely apologize for rushing you into your first assignment," the woman said. She was the middle-aged lady with the chopped blond hair who Taylor had caught a brief glimpse of talking to Einar back in Iceland. Her name was Bea, allegedly. There was something vaguely familiar about her, but Taylor couldn't quite put her finger on it. Seeing the cozy fire and steaming mug of tea at Bea's location did little to improve Taylor's mood. "Normally, we let our recruits enjoy the lifestyle the Foundation provides before asking them to fulfill a task, but you were needed urgently."

"Needed," Taylor repeated. "I don't even know what I'm doing here."

"Healing. That's all we'll ever ask you to do, Taylor. Save lives, make them better."

Always the same Foundation propaganda, Taylor thought. The lady was like a broken record.

"Would you mind taking me through the events that led you to leave the Academy?" Bea asked. "In your own words."

Taylor raised an eyebrow. "I already told your people everything."

"Indulge me."

So Taylor went through it all again. It helped that she didn't have to lie. She told Bea how Earth Garde had taken Ran and Kopano, arrested them without charges for crimes that were actually self-defense. She talked about how Nigel had disappeared in London and how Earth Garde was keeping that information from them. She said she didn't trust the administration to keep her safe or look out for her best interests.

"Thank you, Taylor. Very enlightening," Bea said when Taylor was finished. She glanced over her shoulder—someone else was in the room with her, listening in—and flashed a self-satisfied smile in their direction. "We'll be in touch soon."

The connection went dead. Immediately, the soldier standing watch over Taylor reached out and took the tablet away from her. They were even more strict here than at the Academy about communication with the outside world. That shouldn't have surprised her—she was part of an international conspiracy now.

Taylor touched her forearm surreptitiously. Her key to getting out of this and hopefully bringing down the Foundation was hidden there. They'd done a full body scan on her the day after she left the Academy, but hadn't found it. Just like Malcolm Goode had said, what she was carrying wouldn't set off any alarms; it couldn't be detected. Not until it was activated, at least.

And for that, she would need to gain access to a phone.

A week had gone by since Miki spirited her away from the Academy. He had dropped her on a boat where a couple of mercenaries disguised as fisherman were waiting. They'd been very polite about tranquilizing her.

She'd woken up on a private airplane beside a redheaded woman with a faint Russian accent. She never introduced herself, but she was kind and deferential to Taylor. Even though the woman was just some Foundation go-between, Taylor tried to memorize her face. The Russian carried one of the tablet computers that Taylor soon learned most of the important Foundation people had—password protected and coded to their fingerprints, so it wouldn't be an easy thing to hack. The steward fed Taylor truffle french fries while the redhead asked her questions.

"The Foundation will provide you with a private residence. Where would you like that to be?"

"Somewhere warm and tropical," Taylor answered. "Would a private island be too much to ask for?"

The woman smirked. "We have more private islands than we know what to do with. I see in your file that your father is a farmer in South Dakota. It's possible that we could slip him out of America . . ."

"No," Taylor replied quickly. "He won't want to come. But . . . could you help him? In other ways?"

The woman nodded. "Some investments will be placed in his name. Of course, I probably don't need to remind you that all of this is contingent on your continued cooperation."

"Of course," Taylor said, detecting the implicit threat in the woman's words and smiling like she didn't mind. "Where are we going, anyway?"

"Ukraine," the woman replied.

That was the first hint Taylor got that her private island would be a while in coming.

From the tiny airfield in Ukraine, a helicopter had flown her here, five days ago, to the freezing edge of the middle of nowhere. The ride in had been one of the most harrowing experiences of Taylor's life, the chopper buffeted back and forth by savage winds, snow flurries limiting visibility.

They'd made it. And she'd been cold ever since.

Wordlessly, her soldier chaperone led her out of the tent and the small radius of its struggling space heater. He was dark-eyed and bearded, maybe Middle Eastern, armed with an AK-47 assault rifle. Taylor had given up trying to communicate with any of the hundred soldiers stationed here. Even if they spoke English—which often wasn't the case—they were under strict instructions not to talk to her. They were a hodgepodge of nationalities, probably mercenaries, like the Blackstone guys she'd encountered in Iceland. Only the executive officer—the XO, as he was called, a lean, blond-haired South African in his early fifties—ever spoke to her, and that was usually to give her an order.

Outside, the cold hit Taylor immediately, but at least the snow had stopped. She pulled her balaclava down to protect her face and then followed the soldier back to her tent. The mercenary encampment looked like something out of a sci-fi movie, like they'd colonized an alien world. Twenty tents stood in a grid, a convoy of ATVs and jeeps parked around them, some concrete barriers erected at the edge of camp to cut the wind. Beyond that, there was nothing but hilly plains covered in pure white snow, with the occasional patch of brown scrub grass poking through. The sky today was big and blue, reminding her a bit of South Dakota.

"Weather reports say we got three days without any snow," said a guard posted in front of the XO's tent, his voice muffled by his own ski mask.

"You know what that means," his companion muttered. "They'll have us out there doing night work."

"Ah, Christ," the first one replied. "You're right."

"Least it means we might get out of here quicker."

Just because the guards weren't speaking to her didn't

mean that Taylor had stopped listening. She still didn't know what they were up to out here, what the Foundation was after. Every day, half the detachment drove out somewhere over the western rise, not returning until sunset. That's when Taylor did her healing, when the men came back fatigued and sullen and with ailments they weren't allowed to explain.

She'd been looking for a chance to poke around ever since she'd gotten here. A night shift might be exactly the opportunity she'd been waiting for. It was hard enough to tell anyone apart during the days, with all the face masks and winter clothing. Under cover of darkness Taylor thought she might have an even better chance to slip in with the soldiers unnoticed.

Her silent escort brought Taylor back to her tent at the center of camp, where he nodded to the guard posted outside and left. Taylor glanced at the man standing watch and felt a pang of sympathy—even his eyes, the only part of him she could see, looked cold. Taylor had wondered aloud on her first day in Mongolia why she was being guarded like a prisoner. Weren't they all on the same team? The XO had assured her that it was for her own protection. His people were disciplined, yes, but some had been on the frozen wasteland for months.

"You understand," he'd said. "Pretty teenagers bring trouble with them."

Taylor's skin had crawled then and she hadn't asked any questions about her chaperones since. She would need to give them the slip tonight, though, if she wanted to see what the mercenaries were up to out here.

"Oh my God, close the damn flap before we all catch pneumonia!"

Lost in thought as she entered her tent, Taylor was slow to seal out the elements and thus earned a sharp rebuke from Jiao. Taylor had first met the slim Chinese healer in Saudi Arabia, where she'd been domineering, fashionable, and almost killed by Einar. Jiao didn't seem so chic and intimidating now, perpetually stuck in the same frumpy winter gear as Taylor. She hated this assignment and made sure to keep the others as miserable as she was.

"Calm down," Taylor replied, rubbing her hands together. "If you catch pneumonia, we'll just heal you."

Their tent was far from the glamorous lifestyle that the Foundation promised its recruits. Three cots, a card table, a hot plate, and a stockpile of blankets and thermal underwear. The XO assured Taylor that they had one of the best-working space heaters in the company, although that did little to chase away the perpetual chill.

"Gin," Jiao declared, ignoring Taylor's response to slap her cards on the table. "I win again, Meat Boy."

"It's Meatball," Vincent corrected. "And please don't call me that."

"Which?"

"Either."

Dark-haired and pudgy, Vincent was the final part of the healer trio assigned to Mongolia. Unlike Jiao and Taylor, the

Italian boy hadn't joined the Foundation willingly. He had been trained at the Academy and promoted to Earth Garde before getting kidnapped by the Foundation last year and pressed into service. Now, he seemed perpetually on the verge of tears and always jumpy, although that could've been the shivering. Taylor had been looking for an opportunity to talk with him one-on-one, but Jiao or one of the guards was always around.

Vincent fumbled the cards, trying to shuffle them. "Play again?" he asked.

"No," Jiao replied, standing up from the table and stretching. "We'll have to work soon and I'm tired of beating you." She turned to Taylor. "You talked to Bea? She say how long we'll be stuck out here?"

"No," Taylor replied, not bothering to hide her own disappointment. "She wouldn't give me a straight answer."

"Typical," Jiao said. "You must be questioning your decision to come back to us."

"A few more weeks of this and maybe I will," Taylor said, glancing at Vincent. "But the Academy was terrible, too. You have no idea."

Vincent said nothing and simply looked away from Taylor, fiddling with his deck of cards. She thought maybe he would defend the Academy, but Vincent was probably too broken for that. Maybe he'd come to like the Foundation lifestyle—they could promise a lot, that much Taylor knew. They could also blackmail and extort. Taylor wasn't sure whether Vincent was a sellout or a coward. Neither would be particularly useful to her.

"Well, for what it's worth, this is the worst assignment they've ever sent me on," Jiao said.

Taylor wondered how committed Jiao was to the Foundation's work. These little conversations helped her probe deeper into her companions, but they weren't revealing anything that would truly bring down the Foundation.

"Worse than when Einar got you shot and threw you through a window?" Taylor asked.

Jiao smirked and flexed her knee, remembering the fight back in the UAE. "Please, that was nothing," she said. "I healed those wounds in ten minutes and spent the night dancing with one of the prince's handsome bodyguards."

Taylor rolled her eyes. Before anything else could be said, they heard the rumble of trucks returning to camp. The mercenary convoy had returned. Jiao breathed a sigh out through her nose, the air turning to mist. Vincent stood up, put away his cards, and paced nervously.

"Here we go," Taylor said.

The soldiers came in three at a time, one for each healer. They set down their rifles at the entrance, then stripped off balaclavas and gloves and whatever other pieces of body armor were in the way of their injuries. And they were *always* injured. Or maybe damaged was the more accurate way to put it. Regardless, by Taylor's count, fifty went out each day and, without fail, fifty returned. A whole unit in need of healing.

Soon, the tent smelled like body odor and cigarettes.

Vincent did his work in timid silence, but Jiao kept on a running monologue in Chinese, barking sharply at any soldier that tracked snow or mud into their tent. The tent was usually quiet except for Jiao's ravings; the soldiers didn't talk to the Garde and they rarely talked to each other.

Taylor's first patient was a muscular Asian man who stared deferentially at the ground while she grasped his hands, healing the beginning of frostbite on his fingers. He had some deep cuts on his knee and shin—it looked like he'd fallen. She healed those, too. Then, she pressed her hands against the sides of his neck and healed the sickness.

On their first day in Mongolia, Taylor had discerned that it wasn't just bumps and bruises that the Foundation wanted them to heal. It was the sickness, present in everyone who returned from the mysterious expedition site. Taylor had trained in hospitals while at the Academy—she'd encountered the flu and strep throat, cancer and a random case of smallpox, even the Arab prince's late-stage leukemia that had taken four of them to heal. None of those maladies felt like this sickness.

It was as if a darkness were growing in the soldiers. Taylor could sense tendrils of it when she used her Legacy. She could swear that the illness fought back against her.

Every day, she cleansed the soldiers' bodies of the sickness. And the next day, they came back.

By her fourth soldier, Taylor wasn't cold anymore. Sweat shone on her forehead.

A dislocated shoulder. More frostbite. Cuts and scrapes.

And always the sickness.

What was out there that was infecting these men? What did the Foundation want with it?

Taylor needed to find out.

"Hey, um, Taylor . . . ?" Vincent spoke up, already sounding exhausted. "Could you help me out over here? This guy's real bad."

"Sure, one second," Taylor replied, finishing up with her own patient before stepping over to Vincent.

Taylor cringed when she saw the man standing in front of Vincent. He'd stripped down to his pants, pale skin nearly blue from the cold. His right side was entirely covered in dark burns, the skin cooked and blackened. Spreading out from that grievous wound were discolored black veins. He stood resolute, teeth gritted, like he wasn't in an incredible amount of pain.

"Kid bloody tells me it's *bad*," the soldier said, speaking out of turn in a thick Scottish accent. "What kinda bedside manner's that, eh?"

"S-s-sorry," stammered Vincent.

"How did this happen to you?" Taylor asked as she pressed her hands to the Scotsman's burns, letting her healing energy slowly restore the skin. Next to her, she felt Vincent beating back the sickness—it *was* stronger in this guy than any of hers had been. She could actually see the black veins in his chest recede while they worked.

"Finally some goddamn action, that's how it happened," the soldier said.

"Shut up, MacLaughlan," chided one of the other soldiers. "You know the rules."

"What?" MacLaughlan exclaimed innocently, eyeing Taylor as she tended to him. "The pretty American lass wants to hear some war stories, who am I to deny her?"

Just then, the XO poked his head into the tent, a steely glare aimed in MacLaughlan's direction.

"MacLaughlan!" The XO shouted, sounding good-natured in the same way Professor Nine did right before he ordered you to run laps around the campus. "Did I hear you volunteering to do a double?"

MacLaughlan gritted his teeth. "Aye, boss," he said, deadpan. "Can't wait to get back out there."

"Great!" The XO looked at Taylor. "That's enough healing, then, my dear. He'll be back in here tomorrow morning."

Taylor and Vincent both stepped back from MacLaughlan, his burns only half-healed, the black veins still creeping up his rib cage.

"Sorry," Taylor murmured.

"No worries," MacLaughlan replied with a wink. "I'll rub some ice on it. Plenty of that, eh?"

The rest of that day's healing passed without incident. Afterward, they were brought what amounted to a feast on the dreary tundra—stale pumpernickel bread, canned oranges, a tasteless hard cheese, and sausage from a mystery animal. Of course, they all wolfed it down, even if Jiao did so while holding her nose. Healing that many people was exhausting work and left them all starving. Taylor felt the exhaustion creeping in, the emptiness inside her from too much healing, the tingling in her fingers from overusing her Legacy. It was the same as every day since she'd been here—wake up, freeze, heal, eat, sleep.

She needed to break that pattern tonight. If only she could stay awake.

After dinner, Vincent yawned and stumbled to his cot. "Man, I can't believe we have to do that again tomorrow morning."

"Whatever gets us out of here quicker," Jiao replied. She snorted. "Don't know what you're whining about, anyway. Taylor and I do way more work than you."

Taylor made no comment, although it was true. Vincent definitely didn't have the same abilities that she and Jiao had. Or, at least, he wasn't pushing himself as hard. Maybe he'd been promoted too quickly from the Academy. Or maybe this was Vincent's small act of rebellion against the Foundation. Taylor didn't know.

The days were short in western Mongolia and night came on quickly. All three Garde were soon snuggled into their heavy-duty sleeping bags—Taylor had been assured by the XO that they were the same kind used by climbers when they summited Everest. They all shifted in unison, grumbling as they tried to get comfortable on their rock-hard cots. The healers didn't talk to each other and Taylor found herself missing the camaraderie of the Academy.

Taylor wormed her hand up her sweater and clutched the amulet Kopano had made for her, relieved that the

Foundation people hadn't taken it away. She wondered where Kopano was at that moment. She hoped he and the others were okay.

The rest of the camp was still alive—the mercenaries talked loudly in a variety of languages, eating and drinking, cleaning their guns, playing cards. The wind howled. Taylor tried to keep her eyes open, waiting for a sign that the soldiers were going out on their night mission.

She snapped awake at the sound of revving engines and one mercenary yelling at another to get his ass in gear. *Damn it.* She'd dozed off. The soldiers were already moving out. She would need to get going quickly if she wanted to slip into their midst.

Taylor glanced in Jiao and Vincent's direction. They were both sleeping, Vincent even snoring gently. The soldiers outside were noisy as hell, but after a nonstop healing session, the Garde could probably sleep through the apocalypse. Taylor's whole body ached from the cold and the exertion as she pushed herself to get out of bed.

She couldn't just keep sitting around and doing the Foundation's bidding. She needed to do something. Find out what they were up to out here at the ass-end of nowhere.

Taylor crept towards the entrance of their tent and slowly undid the zipper enough to peek through. As usual, there was a guard posted-up right outside, but he was too distracted by the convoy of mercenaries leaving to notice her.

Still, she would need a distraction to get by him.

With her telekinesis, Taylor reached out and began

unmooring the metal pylons from the tent nearest to hers. When they were loose enough, she waited for a strong gust of wind—those were never long in coming out here—and then gave the tent as firm a telekinetic shove as she could muster.

The shelter went flying, exposing a half dozen soldiers sleeping within. Immediately, they started shouting and scrambling, flinging themselves out of bed to grab their flying tent. Just as Taylor hoped, the soldier watching the Gardes' tent left his posting to go help.

Taylor slipped into the night. She pulled her balaclava over her face and tried to puff herself up, walking like a man. No one paid her any attention. She speed-walked towards the headlights of the departing convoy.

Of course, Taylor knew this was dangerous. Maybe a little crazy, like something Isabela might do. "*Act confident,*" Isabela had told her once, "*and you can bullshit your way through any situation.*" She leaned on that wisdom now. She also reasoned that no matter what she did out here, short of revealing herself as a spy, the Foundation wouldn't let anything happen to her. She was too valuable.

Men all around her were climbing into trucks and driving into the night. Steeling herself, Taylor picked a random SUV and climbed into the backseat.

She cringed immediately. The SUV she'd chosen was empty except for the driver, who was giving her a weird look in the rearview mirror. And the driver was MacLaughlan.

"The hell ya sittin' back there for?" he asked her. "I don't got cooties."

Taylor made a noncommittal grunting sound and slouched. Maybe he'd think she was one of the mercenaries who didn't speak English, tired and grumpy from having to do night work.

"I know the feeling," MacLaughlan replied with a snort. It had worked! He started to put the truck in gear, but then paused and looked at Taylor again.

"You forget something, ya git?"

She stared blankly at him. He patted the M16 attached to a rack along the truck's middle.

"Your weapon, dingus, where's your weapon?"

Taylor winced. It hadn't even occurred to her to steal one of the rifles.

She didn't know what to say and now MacLaughlan was really looking at her.

"Take your hat off," he ordered.

Swallowing, Taylor did as she was told. MacLaughlan's eyes lit up immediately.

"Ah, the curious gal," he said, amused. He twisted around in his seat to eyeball her, wincing thanks to the burns that Taylor hadn't finished healing. "You think this is a trip to the mall or something?"

"I want to see why I'm out here freezing my ass off," Taylor replied honestly, trying to sound self-assured. "Take me with you and I'll finish healing you."

MacLaughlan stared at her for a moment. Then, he shrugged and awkwardly unbuckled his body armor so that Taylor could reach her hands inside.

"Fuck it," he said. "XO finds out, you tricked me with some alien magic, yeah?"

"Yeah."

MacLaughlan put the truck in drive and followed the line of vehicles out into the darkness of the plains. Taylor leaned forward and pressed her hands against his side, healing him while he drove.

"This reminds me of the time I stole my dad's car to dog it with Betty Garretty," MacLaughlan said with a laugh.

Taylor recoiled a bit. "Don't get any ideas," she warned. "I could throw you through that windshield in a heartbeat."

"Ah, don't flatter yourself, little miss," MacLaughlan snorted. "I got a wife and kids at home and you're all'a twelve years old."

They drove in silence after that. Eventually, Taylor finished healing MacLaughlan and leaned back in her seat, peering out the window. It was pure darkness out there. The convoy drove in a straight line, headlights illuminating only the truck in front of them and what seemed like endless snow and ice. They were traveling uphill, cresting the western rise, going no more than twenty miles per hour as they rumbled across the slippery terrain.

"What's out there?" Taylor asked, growing impatient after thirty minutes spent driving in a straight line.

MacLaughlan smirked. "Better you see it yourself. Almost there."

Indeed, Taylor saw lights up ahead. Not lights from a town, but flood lamps mounted on towering girders, like at a construction site. A crane came into view and some kind of heavy-duty drill that reminded Taylor of an oil derrick. Still, she couldn't see what all that equipment was for, not until they reached the top of the rise and started heading downhill.

Taylor leaned forward in her seat, eyes wide.

"It's a warship," she said.

The wreckage of one of the vast Mogadorian warships was spread out across the snowy valley. Even half-destroyed, the city-block-size ship was ominous. Clearly, where it hadn't been blown apart, it had been scavenged, chunks missing here and there, other sections dissected. It looked to Taylor like the skeleton of a giant metal locust.

"Aye," MacLaughlan replied. "And the thing leaks like a son of a bi—"

Before he could finish, a streak of red energy cut through the darkness and sizzled into the passenger side of the truck in front of them. MacLaughlan slammed on the brakes, narrowly avoiding the other truck as it skidded out of control.

"Hell!" MacLaughlan shouted. He pulled on a pair of night-vision goggles and grabbed for his rifle. "I thought we killed all these bloody vermin earlier."

Taylor stared out her window. "You mean . . . ?"

"Nasty bastards are out there, freezing their alien balls off," MacLaughlan answered. "Stragglers come through every once in a while, probably mad we're going through their stuff, ya know? Only a few of 'em. Nothing we can't . . ."

MacLaughlan trailed off as he looked through the goggles.

The entire convoy had stopped, mercenaries taking cover behind their trucks, assuming defensive positions.

"Bit . . . bit more than a handful," MacLaughlan breathed. He shoved Taylor. "Get yer ass down!"

Even as he did, the night lit up crimson. A hundred streaks of blaster fire sizzled across the plain, bombarding the convoy from both sides. The windows of their truck shattered and Taylor felt a blistering sensation on her cheek, smelled her hair burning. MacLaughlan let out a cry and was suddenly silent.

They were under attack.

There were Mogadorians on the tundra.

CHAPTER TWENTY-SEVEN

KOPANO OKEKE
ABU DHABI, THE UNITED ARAB EMIRATES

A CUPCAKE INSIDE A BOX COVERED IN BARBED wire. That's all it was. Simple as that.

Kopano stared at himself in the dusty mirror. His face was dappled with sweat and not just from the dry heat of the Persian Gulf. The café bathroom was tiny, dimly lit, and smelled like hookah smoke. He wiped a smudge off the mirror with his shirtsleeve, as if being able to see himself clearly would make this easier.

"Okay," he told himself. "Just like the cupcake, cupcake. No big deal."

The barbed-wire box and the tasty treat inside had been one of Professor Nine's favorite training games when they first learned Kopano could spread his molecules as well as harden them. It required him to keep part of his arm transparent while his solid hand reached for the cupcake.

"*Rest assured,*" Dr. Goode told him once, "*while it'll take time to master your Legacy, it is part of your biology now. Your body won't let you hurt yourself. It won't let you solidify your arm when it's sharing the same quantum space with the box in the same way that your lungs won't let you hold your breath forever.*"

Kopano really, really wanted to believe that.

He leaned close to the mirror and peered at the tiny wound on his temple. The bandage had come off a couple of days ago, leaving behind a glued-shut incision the same size as his little fingernail. The scab would probably come off in a couple of days and leave behind a barely noticeable scar. But, obviously, it wasn't the cut that concerned Kopano; it was what was underneath.

The chip. The one that gave Agent Walker and her people control.

Kopano pressed his index finger against the side of his head, turned the digit transparent, and then slowly, cautiously pushed his finger into his cranium.

There was a strange, fizzy sensation at the side of his head. He started to see spots and immediately yanked his finger out.

He waited a moment, hands braced on the sides of the sink, to see if he would have an aneurysm or something. There was a mild throb around his incision, maybe the beginning of a headache, but nothing Kopano couldn't handle.

"You're okay," he reassured his reflection. "You can do this. Just like the cupcake."

"What took you so long?" Agent Walker asked when Kopano emerged from the café. She leaned against their rented town car, aviator sunglasses glinting in the late afternoon sun.

"Sorry," Kopano replied. He rubbed his belly. "I got used to American food where they don't use any spices."

Walker made a face. "Ah. Condolences. You want to drive?"

Without waiting for a response, she tossed Kopano the car keys. They climbed into the air-conditioned sedan where Ran waited, stoic and silent in the backseat. She hadn't said much at all since they'd been "recruited" to Operation Watchtower, not even when she and Kopano were alone. Occasionally, he caught her staring daggers at Walker. Ran resented this whole thing and, since Kopano had more willingly gone along with the arrangement, she probably resented him, too.

Behind the wheel, Kopano eased them out into Abu Dhabi's stop-and-go traffic. He smiled, but caught himself before Ran or Walker saw. Abu Dhabi wasn't nearly as crowded and the glittering skyscrapers were mostly new and ostentatious compared to Lagos' gilded chaos, yet this place still reminded him of home. Maybe it was all the bad drivers— sports cars weaving through traffic at breakneck speeds, their operators paying more attention to their phones than the roads. Big men, probably, on important business. Kopano gripped the wheel and got into the flow. He glanced over at Walker, wondering what his father would think of him now, driving around this secret agent lady, on a mission.

Walker, as it happened, was in the middle of thumbing through crime-scene photos. Kopano caught sight of a man's body smashed on a sidewalk, dark blood and broken glass all around him, and gagged.

"Ugh, what are you looking at?"

"These?" Walker asked innocently. "Photographs of Einar's victims."

Kopano shook his head, suddenly hot despite the air-conditioning. He pulled at his collar and loosened his tie. He was dressed like a salesman—dress shirt, tie, slacks. The women both wore white tunics, khakis, and headscarves. Walker also wore a light brown jacket to conceal her sidearm.

"Put them away," Kopano said, waving his head. "You already know what happened to them. Now it's just morbid."

"Reminds me what kind of monster we're dealing with," Walker said. "Also, think it might be motivation to get our friend the sheikh to work with us." She held up one of the photos—a squadron of men in body armor, ripped practically limb from limb—so that Ran could see it. "What do you think of that plan, Ran?"

With a quickness that surprised Walker, Ran slapped the photo away. "Get that out of my face."

"I need you motivated, too," Walker said, sliding the

pictures back into their envelope. "That's all."

Kopano cleared his throat. He had decided that if Ran was going to be the malcontent, he would try to be the diplomatic one, maybe get on Walker's good side. She didn't seem like such a bad lady, kidnapping and chip implantation aside. She *was* letting him drive, after all.

"You really think those pictures will . . . motivate the sheikh to help us?" Kopano asked, giving Walker a chance to explain her plan and act all in charge. He found that adults liked that.

"They would motivate me," Walker replied. "Knowing there was a psycho Garde out there killing people? That he knows where I live? That I could be next on his list?" Walker shrugged. "Maybe we'll get lucky and catch Einar in the middle of trying to murder the guy."

"You have a strange definition of luck," Kopano said.

"Anyway, it's the best lead we've got. We haven't been able to pin down the identities of many of Einar's former . . . employers. Only got this one because his daughter—Rabiya, right?—got taken by the Harvesters. She told them who her father was while she was trying to talk them out of killing her."

Staring out the back window, Ran spoke without looking at Walker. "While we are here, you should arrest the sheikh. He works with the Foundation."

Kopano watched Walker out of the corner of his eye. She had a way of changing the subject whenever the Foundation came up. She even avoided saying its name when discussing

Einar's victims, even though membership was what they all had in common.

"One thing at a time," Walker said simply.

Kopano tapped his hands happily on the wheel. "Then that means you *will* arrest them, eventually."

"I've got no jurisdiction to arrest anyone or—hell—even be in this country," Walker replied. "Point is, the world is more complicated than you two make it out to be."

Ran fell silent again. They had left the city behind, trading the grid of tall buildings for a highway that cut through the desert. Even this highway seemed opulent to Kopano, with its equidistant palm trees and patches of soothing emerald green grass.

"I think my dad would love it here," he said. "He used to tell me about the world being complicated too, Agent Walker. It's how he explained ripping people off."

Walker stared at him for a moment, then turned to look out her own window. Kopano drove them on in silence.

Led by the GPS, Kopano steered them off the highway and onto a private road. The pavement glittered—Kopano swore it was laced with gold flakes. No one said a word until the palace came into view, the building rising out of the desert like something from a fairy tale, all sandstone columns and parapets, a parking lot out front cluttered with luxury cars shaded by groves of olive trees. Kopano shook his head— the audaciousness and splendor were like nothing he'd ever seen. Even his dad couldn't have imagined this place in his wildest dreams.

"Someone actually lives here?" Kopano asked.

"Crazy, isn't it?" Walker replied.

As the grandeur of the palace wore off, Kopano noticed the guards. There were dozens of them, some posted outside the front door, others on the roof and its walkways. They all wore white thobes and carried huge machine guns.

Kopano swallowed. "They know we're coming, right?"

"They know," Walker said flatly. "Operation Watchtower arranged to free up some of the sheikh's questionable international assets in exchange for fifteen minutes."

Ran leaned forward to peer up at the many guards. "Are you sure about this?" she asked. "We were not exactly kind to Rabiya when we last met. They may hold a grudge."

"Not kind to her?" Walker asked. "Way I heard it, you saved her from getting burned to death by a bunch of religious yahoos."

"Yeah," Kopano said. "But then we forced her to teleport us . . ."

"And she got home safe, eventually," Walker countered. "We're here trying to catch the guy who got her into all that mess. They'll cooperate."

"If you say so," Ran said.

The three of them got out of the car. Immediately, Kopano sensed eyes upon them. Eyes and guns, all the guards shifting or stopping in their patrols, angling their bodies towards them. Kopano let Walker take the lead, the woman walking confidently towards the palace's double-door entrance, but he put himself between the gunmen and Ran, making sure that his skin was hardened.

"That's far enough." A guard stepped out from the shade of a tree and held up his hand. Unlike the others, his thobe was black and he wore a golden pin on his lapel—a boss of some kind. He approached the trio with his rifle ready but low.

"I'm Karen Walker. We have an appointment with the sheikh."

"*You* have an appointment," the guard said. He gestured at Kopano and Ran. "These two may not enter. Their kind cause nothing but trouble."

Kopano frowned at that. Ran stared dead-eyed at the guard. Walker looked over her shoulder.

"Stay here," she told them.

"What if you get in trouble?" Kopano asked.

"I'll be fine," Walker said.

Kopano and Ran exchanged a look, but what could they do? If something happened to Walker in there—if she was killed—they'd be shocked into unconsciousness and probably soon be dead themselves. That was a lot of trust to place in someone.

"Be careful," Ran said coldly.

The guard led Walker into the palace, leaving Ran and Kopano alone with the dozens of steely-eyed guards. Kopano shifted uncomfortably.

"This sucks," he said. "I wanted to see inside."

There was movement up on the wall. Among the dour guards and their identical thobes, Kopano spotted a flash of color. There was a girl up there in a golden hijab and a leopard-print dress. Kopano couldn't be sure at this distance, but he guessed it was Rabiya. He raised a hand to awkwardly wave. She peered down at him and Ran for a moment, then disappeared back into the palace.

"Everyone's so friendly," Kopano said.

Ran frowned at him. Then, she licked her thumb and rubbed at a spot on his collar.

"You have something on you," she said. "Is this . . . blood?"

"Damn, good thing Walker didn't notice," Kopano said with relief.

He reached into his pants pocket, moving cautiously in case any of their hawkeyed guards thought he was reaching for a weapon, and flashed Ran the bloodstained microchip that he'd pulled out of his head.

"What . . . ?" Ran said.

"I got it out," Kopano said. "The chip."

Ran's eyes lit up. She moved in closer to Kopano, speaking quietly.

"How did you do it?"

Kopano demonstrated passing the fingers of one hand through the palm of his other hand and wiggled his eyebrows.

"I don't know what I should do with it now," he said, pocketing the chip again. "Smash it, maybe, or . . . ?"

"No!" Ran hissed. "They might notice it has been disabled. Keep it on you at all times."

"Okay, right," Kopano said. "Smart."

Ran tilted her head and flipped her hair back so her scar was in view. "Can you do mine?"

"I, uh . . ." Kopano swallowed. "I don't know. Doing myself was one thing but what if—I could touch your brain on accident or I don't know what else. It's a big risk."

"A risk I am willing to take to get this thing out of me."

"Okay, but maybe I don't want to risk accidentally lobotomizing my friend."

Ran frowned at him. Kopano frowned back.

Before anything else could be said, there was a small commotion at the palace gates. Rabiya emerged from within, flanked by guards who struggled to match her purposeful stride. Kopano and Ran both tensed up as she approached.

"I know you," Rabiya said by way of introduction. "You two are from the Academy, yes?"

Kopano looked at Ran. She regarded Rabiya with her typically stubborn silence, so Kopano shrugged and took the lead.

"Sort of," Kopano replied. "Yeah."

"And now you are here with an American agent to hunt Einar?"

"It's kind of a secret mission," Kopano said.

"Good enough," Rabiya said. She looked at the retinue of guards that continually inched closer. "Step back," she snapped at them. "Or you will incur my father's wrath."

Looking uneasy, the guards eased back a bit. One of them spoke into a walkie-talkie, probably notifying the sheikh that his daughter had come into the open.

"We must speak quickly," Rabiya said, urgent eyes locking first with Kopano and then with Ran. "And then you will need to make a very quick decision. Understood?"

"Not really," Kopano said.

Rabiya extended her hand and a torrent of cobalt blue energy funneled forth. Where her energy hit the driveway a glowing Loralite stone began to grow, making a noise like boots crunching over broken glass.

"My father will not help you find Einar," Rabiya spoke briskly, her eyes on Kopano and Ran as the stone grew. "After your fight with him in Iceland, Einar used me to teleport into a Foundation facility and steal a Mogadorian spacecraft. Then, he let me return here. He promised not to hurt my family during his little jihad. My father knows this. He will not risk upsetting Einar or the Foundation by informing."

"Please, sheikha," interrupted one of the guards. "You must go back inside. This is not appropriate."

The guard tried to take Rabiya by the elbow. In response, she shoved him with her telekinesis and sent him flying into the side of a nearby Porsche, the glass of the driver-side window shattering from the impact. Nervous and fidgeting with their weapons, the rest of the guards took a number of paces back.

"Why are you telling us this?" Kopano asked. Next to him, Ran picked up a handful of loose gravel, prepared to charge them with her Legacy if matters deteriorated further.

"Since my brother was cured," Rabiya continued as if she hadn't just assaulted one of her own guards, "my father wishes to wash his hands of matters related to the Garde. The beating I endured by the Harvesters shamed him. He claims our powers are against God. He will not let me practice. I have heard him on the phone discussing a surgery to implant an Inhibitor in me."

Kopano instinctively touched his own temple. "So, you want us to what . . . ?"

"I will help you find Einar. I know where he will strike next," Rabiya said. "In exchange, I want you to take me to the Academy. I wish to enroll there. You must decide now. My father's men will try to stop us."

She was right. Catching the drift of their conversation, the guards had started to creep closer, their weapons at the ready. The one with the walkie-talkie was speaking fast, probably relaying the situation to his boss in the black thobe.

"Stop this madness, sheikha!" One of the guards implored. "You father, he is coming . . ."

The Loralite stone was finished. Rabiya stepped forward. "Well?"

"Uh, the thing is . . . ," Kopano began, glancing nervously between Rabiya and her armed protectors. "We can't really speak for—"

"Yes," Ran interrupted. "We agree."

"Good," Rabiya replied. "Hold hands."

Kopano, flustered, let Ran grab his hand. Rabiya then took hold of Ran.

"We cannot leave without Walker," Ran said.

"Fine," Rabiya replied. "We'll get her."

A pair of guards lunged at them, but too late. Rabiya brushed her fingers against the stone and the world dropped out from under Kopano. He remembered this feeling from teleporting back and forth to Iceland, but that didn't mean he was used to it. He was swallowed up by the azure Loric glow, turned head over heels.

And then, in the space of a breath, he was somewhere else. A courtyard, to be precise, inside the palace. They'd emerged from a second, smaller chunk of Loralite hidden within a grove of palm trees.

"Look," Ran said. "You got to see inside after all."

Kopano, dizzy, barked a surprised laugh. It wasn't often that Ran made a joke.

He didn't have time to take in the vast courtyard's bubbling fountains and sculptures. Dead ahead Kopano spotted the guard in the black thobe dragging Walker across the courtyard by the hair. She'd been roughed up a little and disarmed, but her scowl was still in place. They were joined by two more guards and an imposing older man with a huge beard and a very expensive suit. Kopano took him to be Rabiya's father—the sheikh. He was in the middle of berating Walker as their group hustled towards the palace entrance.

"What corruption is this?" The sheikh bellowed in Walker's face. "Have you come to take my daughter, is that it?"

"Agh—what?" Walker replied, clearly clueless. "I don't know what you're talking about!"

Rabiya adjusted her headscarves. "Shall we rescue your babysitter, then?"

The three Garde stepped into view with Kopano leading the way. One of the sheikh's guards, startled by their sudden appearance, raised his rifle and squeezed off a single shot.

Kopano flinched as the bullet bounced off his hardened shoulder. It hurt, but on the same level as getting punched in the arm. He gritted his teeth and put on his scariest face.

He needn't have bothered. The sheikh lunged at the guard and slapped him to the ground. "My daughter is with them, you fool!"

In the commotion, Ran reached out with her telekinesis and yanked Walker away from the guards, not at all concerned with handling her gently. Kopano grabbed her out of the air, smiling at the look of utter bafflement on her face.

"What have you done?" Walker asked through her teeth.

Rabiya waved at the sheikh. "I am going to America, father! Don't try to get me back! Inshallah!"

She grabbed Ran's hand and in turn Ran put her hand on Kopano's shoulder. The sheikh and his men rushed towards them, but they wouldn't make it in time.

"We can't take her," Walker yelled. "We don't have the authority!"

"Then stop us," Ran replied.

There was nothing Walker could do.

Rabiya reached behind her, touched the Loralite stone, and they were gone.

CHAPTER TWENTY-EIGHT

TAYLOR COOK
BAYAN-ÖLGII PROVINCE, MONGOLIA

MACLAUGHLAN WAS DEAD.

Taylor tried to heal the man, holding him by the sides of what was left of his head. But there was no spark, nothing for her Legacy to rekindle. Gone. His face was a mess of burns from the Mogadorian blasters. There were places on his shoulders where his body armor had melted into his skin.

Taylor gagged. She'd been around sickness and seen death before, had watched Einar force the sheikh's guards to kill each other back in Dubai. This was worse, somehow. She'd at least known MacLaughlan a little, had been talking to him like five seconds ago. Was that really all it took to erase someone from the world? It almost seemed too easy.

Still ducked down in the backseat, Taylor saw a tongue of

flame burst out from under the hood of their truck. No time to ponder existential questions now, no time to freak out.

She needed to move.

But something had caught her eye when MacLaughlan was shot. Something had fallen off his belt as he shoved Taylor down. The urge to flee was strong, but Taylor fought it. She groped around on the floor of the truck, fingers scraping over broken glass, until she hit upon something hard and plastic.

A satellite phone. Hurriedly, she tucked the object into her parka.

Black smoke was filling the inside of her truck. Outside, she could hear shouting, gunfire, and explosions. A full-fledged battle.

She had no choice but to go towards it.

With her telekinesis, Taylor knocked the battered back door off its hinges and leaped out into the freezing night. She kept low, blaster beams sizzling through the air from both sides. It was an ambush. The Mogadorians had come at the Foundation's convoy from the east and west.

Mogadorians. Freaking Mogadorians. Taylor couldn't believe it. She'd seen the alien creatures on TV—pale and sunken eyed, tattoos on their scalps, hideous creatures that looked like they belonged in subterranean caverns. They'd failed in their invasion of Earth and been mostly eradicated or imprisoned, but Taylor had heard the rumors about pockets of them still at large, thriving in the world's more lawless places, avoiding the reach of Earth Garde.

Apparently, western Mongolia was one of those places. The pieces clicked together for Taylor, despite the panic. The Foundation had come here to procure something from the fallen warship. The Mogadorians had discovered them and not responded politely.

She could see them out there at the edges of the flood-lights' radiance, their pale faces and dark armor illuminated in bursts by their glowing blasters. A mercenary taking cover behind an overturned Humvee sprayed bullets at a pack of the aliens and Taylor watched as they exploded into clouds of dust. Unreal.

A blaster beam struck the burning truck she'd climbed out of. Taylor scrambled for cover and bumped right into a soldier doing the same.

"Shoot back, asshole!" The mercenary screamed in her face. He didn't recognize her, but quickly registered that she was unarmed. "Idiot! Where's your weapon?"

Taylor's heart beat savagely against her breastbone. Adrenaline flowed through her. They'd tried to prepare her for fights like this at the Academy, but training rooms and obstacle courses didn't get across the blood, mud, and madness. She was in over her head, but that didn't matter. She was Garde. And why were Garde put on Earth?

To kill Mogadorians.

"Here's my weapon," Taylor said to the soldier.

With her telekinesis, Taylor hefted a door that had gotten blown off one of the trucks and sent it careening into the

Mogadorian line. She was pretty sure that she sheared one of them clean in half.

"Ho-ly shit," said the soldier. He grabbed his walkie-talkie and shouted into it. "It's one of the assets! XO! It's one of the assets!"

Taylor didn't see the XO anywhere, couldn't really make out any individuals. It was chaos. The Mogs returned fire and she ran, pushing her way behind a group of mercenaries taking cover beneath the base of a flood light. When a Mog stepped into view, she used her telekinesis to rip his blaster away.

A mercenary collapsed beside her and Taylor immediately smelled burned skin. He'd been shot in the shoulder, the Mog blaster searing through his armor. Taylor crouched down and pressed her hands against his chest, healing him. The soldier stared at her wide-eyed, then brushed her off, reoriented his rifle, and returned fire on the Mogs.

"A thank-you would be nice," Taylor said, her words drowned out by gunfire.

Someone grabbed her by the shoulder. Taylor reacted by spinning around and elbowing the person in the face. The XO ducked just in time, narrowly avoiding getting his nose broken.

"The hell are you doing out here, Cook?" he screamed.

A howling Mogadorian charged into view. These things were practically suicidal. As he leveled his blaster, Taylor jerked on it with her telekinesis, causing him to discharge the weapon right under his own chin.

She tried not to think about how she'd learned that trick from Einar.

"I'm helping you not die," she responded to the XO.

He smirked at that. Taylor noticed that his mouth was bloody and that there was a sizable cut over his eyebrow. She reached out to touch him but he slapped her hand away.

"Don't waste your energy," he said. "Focus on the ones that need it."

Taylor started to turn from him, but then came a piercing shriek of metal. The steel beam holding up the floodlight above them had taken too much fire. It teetered and started to fall, a half ton of metal and spotlights collapsing right into their midst.

"Go!" screamed the XO. "Take cover inside the ship!"

CHAPTER TWENTY-NINE

DUANPHEN
A NICE RESTAURANT—SOMEWHERE IN THE UNITED STATES

DUANPHEN HAD SEEN RESTAURANTS LIKE THIS before, but only from the outside, while she waited with the executive's limo, scowling at anyone who got too close. Places like this, with its candlelight, white tablecloths, and clinking wineglasses—they weren't for people like her. They were for the wealthy, the powerful. Standing in the restaurant's dimly lit vestibule, Duanphen felt the same rising nerves as she used to before a fight.

"Why do you look like you're going to barf?" Isabela asked her.

Duanphen looked down at the Brazilian girl, who had settled comfortably onto one of the posh leather couches in the waiting area. "I feel out of place," she said.

"Psh." Isabela dismissed this with a wave of her hand.

"This spot isn't even that cool. And we are *definitely* the hottest people here."

Both of them wore new dresses—Isabela's a low-cut red one, Duanphen a more modest black sheath. They had gone shopping just that afternoon, spending some of the Foundation's money on appropriate attire. Duanphen had been relieved when Isabela offered—no, more like insisted—to pick out clothes for her.

Duanphen was glad they had kidnapped Isabela and happier still that the girl had agreed to Einar's plan and stuck around. Einar was very serious all the time, always preaching about how they couldn't trust humanity. It got exhausting. And The Beast—or, Number Five, as Duanphen reminded herself to call him—wasn't exactly friendly. Having someone normal in their group made Duanphen feel less insane for joining Einar's cause.

"Ladies? Shall we?" Einar said, as he returned from talking with the maître d'. "A table for three just happened to open up."

"What did you do?" Isabela asked, standing up. "Mess with his brain?"

"Why would I waste my energy on something so trivial?" Einar replied. He flashed the thick wad of bills he carried in his suit pocket. "The world's oldest form of mind control worked just fine."

Einar was polished as always. He hadn't needed to buy a new suit for the occasion, but he did anyway. He held his arm out to Isabela. She laughed at him.

"What do you think this is, some creepy date?" Isabela asked. "Ugh. Do you have a boner right now?"

"I—no," Einar replied. "You aren't even my type. I was just being gentlemanly."

Isabela breezed past him with a snort, following the host into the dining room. Einar followed, Duanphen smiling quietly as she came last. Those two were bickering nonstop, with Isabela usually the victor. Duanphen knew the girl got under Einar's skin, but no matter how infuriating the exchange, Einar never did anything. He could've controlled Isabela's emotions and made her docile, assaulted her with his telekinesis, or sicced Five on her. Instead, he showed restraint.

It was one thing to talk about not using your Legacies against other Garde. It was another to actually live by those rules and self-police. Thanks to Isabela constantly needling him, Duanphen had actually grown to trust Einar more.

The host led them to a booth near the front window, twinkling city lights visible beyond the glass. Duanphen sensed eyes on them. Surely, the other diners must have been wondering how these three teenagers could afford to get a table here. She ran a hand over the stubble atop her head. It was strange to be on this side of the glass.

"Ah, now this is more like it," Einar said, settling in across from the girls. "This is how all our kind should be living."

Isabela's eyes flicked around the room. "It's nice to be off that smelly-ass ship of yours, but aren't you worried about being seen?"

Einar waved this objection away. "They won't expect us to be here. It's fine."

"The Foundation will come back at you for what you've done," Duanphen pointed out. "They'll come back at *us*."

"Of course. But not tonight. And anyway, they've got nothing in their arsenal capable of stopping us. Or *him*."

Einar pointed towards the ceiling. Five was up there, in the air, keeping watch from the sky above the restaurant. He hadn't seemed offended that he wasn't invited to dinner. His broken skin would've been too conspicuous and Isabela was far from willing to hold his hand during the entire meal.

"He'll be hungry, probably," Duanphen said.

"Do you see the way he scarfs down that fast food?" Isabela asked. "He is *always* hungry."

"We'll get him some takeout," Einar said.

They studied their menus. The meals were complicated and none of them had prices. When their skeptical look-ing waiting arrived, Einar ordered himself a lobster. Isabela asked for a medium-rare filet mignon.

"Just a salad, please," Duanphen said. "Dressing on the side."

Isabela stared at her once the waiter was gone. "I need to teach you how to spend other people's money."

Einar cleared his throat. "Where were you during the invasion, Duanphen?"

She blinked at him. The question had come out of nowhere.

"Bangkok," she said.

"Did you have your Legacies already?"

"No. They did not come until later."

Einar turned to Isabela. "What about you?"

"None of your business," Isabela said, her lips pressed together. "Now, is this the part where I ask where *you* were and you get to the point of this random conversation?"

Einar breathed out through his nose. "Do you remember how Setrákus Ra went on TV and demanded that Earth's governments turn over all Human Garde to him?"

Isabela shrugged. "Yeah, I guess."

"My father was an investment banker. My mother was an international lawyer. Normal people, I thought. When Setrákus Ra made that request, they tried to tie me up." The candlelight flickered in Einar's eyes as he looked out the window. "They were part of a group called MogPro. You know what that means?"

Duanphen shook her head.

"Idiot humans who supported the Mogs," Isabela said. "This makes sense. Your parents *would* be assholes."

Einar frowned at that but continued on. "My own parents were going to turn me over to some alien monster simply because he ordered them to. I was weaker then, didn't have much control of my Legacies, but I fought . . ."

"Did you kill them?" Duanphen asked.

"No, I . . ." Einar drummed his fingers on the table. "I used my Legacy to turn them against each other. My mother hit my father in the head with a sculpture. He hasn't woken up. She is in prison."

"Are we all going to share our tragic backstories now?" Isabela asked, although Duanphen noticed there was less venom in her voice than before. "Is this supposed to be bonding?"

Einar shrugged. "Maybe. I want you to trust me, Isabela. I thought it might help if you knew where I came from."

Isabela leaned back and crossed her arms, considering this. Maybe Einar was telling this story for Isabela's benefit, but Duanphen was curious, too.

"What happened then?" she asked. "How did the Foundation find you?"

"During the invasion, there were other members of Mog-Pro like my parents started rounding up Human Garde on Setrákus Ra's behalf," Einar replied. "But then, the Mogadorians lost. MogPro failed. Many of them were running scared. However, MogPro knew the identities of some Human Garde. One woman had the idea to snatch these Garde up, to hoard us before Earth Garde could be formed, to use us for profit. That woman was Bea Barnaby."

"You're wrong about Nigel, by the way," Isabela snapped. "He didn't have a clue his parents were involved in that."

Duanphen had heard this Nigel boy brought up before. The son of the executive. She had heard the story about how Einar almost killed him. She watched him closely now, saw the shadow in his eyes. Shame.

"I believe you," Einar said. "I was so angry. I wanted to hurt him to hurt Bea. I assumed he was a spy. That was foolish of me. After all, I was ignorant of my parents' evil deeds until they tried to kill me. Why should Nigel be any different? The two of us are a lot alike, really."

Isabela snorted. "No, you aren't."

"Well, we have a lot in common," Einar said. "The Barnabys took me in. They helped me train my Legacies. Granted, the way they used me—taking me to board meetings, negotiations, auctions, and having me manipulate the outcomes—it was always for their benefit. But they made me think they really cared. Bea, especially. I was alone in this world and she felt . . . she felt like a mother."

Their waiter arrived with a basket of bread and some olive oil. During his speech, Einar's eyes had filled with water. He took a moment to blot at his face with his napkin. Isabela scrutinized him. Duanphen watched them both, taking it all in.

"I can't tell if you're full of shit or not," Isabela said, tearing loose a chunk of bread. "*Lagrimas de cocodrilo.*"

"I'm being honest," Einar said, recovering smoothly. "After months with her, I think Bea realized how powerful I was becoming. That I was too dangerous to keep close. She started sending me on more fieldwork. Keeping her distance. I began to realize how disposable I was. In the end, our Legacies will always make us a threat to them. The humans. That's why the Foundation exists. That's why the Academy exists."

"You act like they're the same thing," Isabela said.

"Not the same thing, but part of the same system." Einar leaned forward, lowering his voice. "Your Academy is guarded by Peacekeepers armed with anti-Garde technology. Those weapons are manufactured by Sydal Corp, a company whose owner has a standing arrangement with the Foundation. Sydal develops his weapons using alien materials he buys from the Foundation. He tests them on Garde that the Foundation rents him. And then, he turns around and sells those weapons to both the Foundation and Earth Garde. Everyone benefits except for us."

"You know everything," Isabela said with a snort. "But the Academy is not in on this conspiracy."

"Ignorance doesn't make them less complicit."

"You want to talk about complicit, *cabrão*?"

Duanphen interjected before the argument could go any further. She thought it best if they avoided making a scene in this fancy restaurant and she was also genuinely curious.

"What is it like?" she asked. "Your Academy?"

"Uh, good, I guess," Isabela said, swallowing. The question had caught her off guard. "Boring. They try to teach us stuff. Treat us like kids. Really dangerous kids." She glanced in Einar's direction and scowled. "Whatever. I'm not in love with the place, but there are some good people there who actually want to help us Garde. And we don't really have . . ."

She trailed off, staring down at the crumbs on her plate. Duanphen cocked her head, waiting for more.

"A choice," Einar said, finishing Isabela's thought. "Is that what you were going to say? That you don't really have a choice?"

Isabela glared at him. "So what if I was?"

"What if there was another option?" Einar asked. "One where you were free? Where you didn't need to do the bidding of some organization?"

Isabela let out a huff of breath, then turned to look at Duanphen. "You buy into all this?"

Duanphen fingered her crystal water glass, considering her words.

"When I first got my Legacies, I tried to use them to help myself. When I was discovered, I was put to work. First, for Bangkok gangsters. Later, for the Foundation. Not until Einar found me did I really feel in control. Instead, we must learn to rely on each other."

Einar folded his hands in front of him and flashed a satisfied smile. Isabela's eyes narrowed and she studied Duanphen's face, perhaps looking for signs that she was being controlled. But these emotions were Duanphen's own. She couldn't remember the last time she had spoken so much or so plainly. It felt good.

Their meals came. The three of them ate in silence, all of them considering what had been said before. Only when they were nearly finished did Einar nod his head in the direction of the restaurant's bar.

"She's here," he said to Isabela.

Isabela feigned a stretch, peering in the direction Einar had indicated. "Yeah. I see her."

"We'll follow your lead on this one," Einar said to Isabela.

"Tell us what you want us to do."

They hadn't come to this fancy restaurant only to eat dinner.

Who would travel all the way to Florida just for that?

CHAPTER THIRTY

TAYLOR COOK
BAYAN-ÖLGII PROVINCE, MONGOLIA

NEVER IN TAYLOR'S GRIMMEST NIGHTMARES WOULD she have imagined a scenario where she'd be running towards a Mogadorian warship.

And yet, here she was.

Blaster fire burned the air around her. Taylor was pulled along with the pack of mercenaries towards the cover of the warship. She hated the Mogs more than anything in that moment. Hated them for making her fight alongside the Foundation.

A streak of energy took the legs out from beneath one of her escorts and he fell screaming in the snow. Taylor tried to go back for him, but the XO had a tight grip on her arm and shoved her ahead. Looking over her shoulder, she saw two Mogs descend on the soldier as he tried to find his feet.

These ones didn't have blasters—they had swords. Serrated, silver, nasty things—they plunged the weapons into the soldier and then started stripping him of his gear.

The XO hit Taylor in the chest with something. A pistol. His secondary weapon.

"You know how to use that?" he asked.

"I've seen movies," she replied.

They took cover in what used to be the warship's docking bay, hiding behind smashed Mogadorian Skimmers that had already been stripped for parts. The mercenaries were efficient, setting up a perimeter and providing cover fire for their comrades who were still exposed. Taylor joined in, squeezing off bullets into the darkness, not sure if she was hitting any Mogadorians. When her clip was empty, she used her telekinesis, twisting Mog weapons away and flinging them into the night.

A stray blast shaved a panel off the Skimmer Taylor was hiding behind. It came down right on her head. She was lucky—a glancing blow, but she was still cut. New warmth seeped into her hair, which was already frozen with sweat, blood trickling down into one of her eyes. She fell onto her butt, more stunned than anything.

The XO spotted her immediately. "Asset is hurt! Get her the hell inside!"

"Stop," Taylor mumbled as another mercenary grabbed her under the arms and dragged her aboard the warship proper. "I'm fine. I'll heal it."

The soldier didn't listen. He dumped her inside the

warship, leaving her next to a pile of canisters and broken gears.

Taylor stumbled to her feet. She touched the cut on her head and let her Legacy do its work, cringing at the cold nugget of emptiness that formed within her whenever she used her healing on herself. A little woozy from the knock on the skull, she nonetheless started back towards the sounds of fighting.

A noise stopped her in her tracks. Was that a girl's voice? It definitely was. Taylor couldn't quite make out the words, but that was definitely someone calling out.

It was coming from deeper inside the warship.

Did the Foundation have a prisoner here?

With a glance back at the battle, Taylor followed the sound of the voice through the hulking ship's skeletal remains. Her path was illuminated in patches by the glow of the floodlights shining through the cracks in the ship's roof. She picked her way across debris—broken Mog blasters, torn radiation suits, empty packs of cigarettes.

As she got closer, Taylor realized the voice was speaking a language she didn't understand. In fact, it wasn't one she'd heard before—at least not until that night. The harsh and sharp syllables were Mogadorian.

Taylor got low, wary now that she'd stumbled into a trap.

She relaxed as she rounded a corner and entered a vast corridor. At the far end was a blinking communication array, somehow undamaged during the ship crash. The voice emanated from there. Whether it was a live broadcast or a recording, Taylor couldn't tell.

As Taylor listened, the Mogadorian girl switched from her guttural language to fluid English.

"This is Vontezza Aoh-Atet, trueborn daughter of the dead General Aoh-Atet, and current commander of the Mogadorian warship *Osiris*." The Mog did everything in her power to sound formal and lofty, but Taylor could tell that she was young despite her big titles. "We remain in our defensive position behind the Earth's moon as we have for the last four hundred days. Our supplies begin to run low. If there is any section of the fleet still receiving, please respond to our transmission."

Taylor raised an eyebrow. She'd heard about this. During the invasion, the Garde had briefly convinced the Mogadorian fleet that Setrákus Ra was dead. All hell had broken loose—some warships held strong while others fought against each other, their commanders vying for the role of Beloved Leader. One ship had even retreated into space. Apparently, that warship was still hanging around up there with this young-sounding Vontezza in control.

"If John Smith or any of the other Loric are listening," Vontezza continued, "I wish to meet with you under the flag of peace. What is left of the Mogadorian people have no stomach for further war . . ."

Based on the Mogs attacking the mercenaries outside, Taylor didn't think that was necessarily true.

Vontezza's message began once again in Mogadorian. A recording, then. Taylor took a step towards the console and her foot squelched down into something warm and sticky.

At first glance, it looked like the floor of the room was covered in a massive oil slick. But the stuff worming around on Taylor's foot wasn't oil—it was thicker and gummier. She took a hurried step back, worried the ooze would eat through her footwear.

She noticed the vats, then. Huge tanks lined up against the walls, all of them broken open. The black gunk had flowed forth from them. Squinting, Taylor thought she could make out pale shapes floating in the dark bog. Were those half-formed Mogadorian bodies?

Taylor had no doubt this was what the Foundation was out here collecting. The stuff looked exactly like the sickness she'd seen under the soldiers' skin.

Some toxic creation of the Mogadorians. What did the Foundation want with that?

"They're falling back!" Taylor heard a soldier shout. The sound of gunfire was waning. The battle was won.

She didn't have long to do what she needed to do.

Of the fifty men who left for the night shift, only thirty-one made it back to camp. It could have been less. Taylor, exhausted now, eyes sunken and heavy, still managed to heal a few dire cases on the way back.

The look on Jiao's face when Taylor appeared in their tent, joining the soldiers as they came for healing was price-less. Taylor must've looked crazy—haggard, with dried blood smeared on one side of her face, her blond hair tinted crimson. She could tell that Jiao wanted to ask her questions but didn't dare. The XO hovered nearby, not letting Taylor out of his sight.

Vincent didn't say anything either. He didn't meet Taylor's gaze. He paid attention only to the wounded soldiers who stepped up in front of him.

Taylor took off her boots and made Jiao examine her feet. None of the black oil had crept in.

"She's clean," Jiao reported to the XO. She waved her hand at Taylor's messed-up appearance and bone-weary posture. "Nothing I can do about the rest. She needs sleep."

"Not yet," the XO replied, gently taking Taylor by the arm.

The XO led her out. Some of the men gave her appreciative nods as she passed. Because she'd saved their lives? Or were they simply acknowledging that she'd fought alongside them?

Taylor ended up alone in the XO's tent. He let her sit on his cot, propped up against some pillows. Her whole body ached. She struggled to keep her eyes open as the XO paced back and forth. He accessed a tablet and placed a video call.

Bea. Her hair was pinned up and she wore a drab nightgown. They'd woken her up.

"What is it?"

"We had an incident," the XO reported.

He went through the details of the Mogadorian ambush, the number of casualties, and the damage to the site. He explained that Taylor had been out there with the men. Taylor kept her eyes on Bea, saw a hot glimmer of rage appear in the twist of her lips—she was mad at the XO. His negligence had endangered one of her most valuable assets.

When the XO finished his summary of events, Bea regarded Taylor. Her face was a mask now, calm and collected.

"Are you all right, darling?" she asked.

Taylor nodded.

"How did you end up out there?"

"One of the soldiers . . . MacLaughlan . . ." Taylor allowed her voice to be shaky. It would make the lies more convincing. "I hadn't finished healing him before because he was out of line. The XO was there, he saw. He came to our tent . . . he took me. Made me heal him on the way to the warship site. Then . . . I don't know. I don't know what else he planned to do."

She felt a little guilty besmirching MacLaughlan's memory, but he was dead. He wouldn't mind.

"This soldier? Where is he?" Bea asked the XO coldly.

"Dead in the ambush, ma'am."

"Good." Bea took a cleansing breath. "Can the excavation continue?"

"I'll need some reinforcements, ma'am," the XO responded. "Lost some men tonight. And I'm not sure how many more of those things are out there."

"Hmm." Bea pursed her lips. "The samples you've gathered so far already have a buyer and I can't tolerate a delay.

Select a few trusted men and bring what you've gathered to my location. The rest can stay until reinforcements are available."

Taylor let loose a small moan and shuddered. It wasn't entirely disingenuous. The thought of any more time in Mongolia seemed like a nightmare.

"And bring Ms. Cook along," Bea added sympathetically. "I think she's seen enough action for one tour."

Before, back on the Mogadorian warship, Taylor took MacLaughlan's satellite phone out of her coat. She breathed a sigh of relief that it hadn't been damaged in all the fighting.

She punched in a number. A number that she'd memorized a couple of months ago, when this plan was first hatched. A number for a cell phone that Professor Nine promised would get answered at any time, day or night.

Ring. Ring.

"Where's the asset?" someone shouted. "Where did you put her?"

They were looking for her. The battle had ended.

"Come on, come on," Taylor murmured, edging back into the shadows.

Ring. Ring.

"Find her!" the XO yelled.

Ring. Ri—

"Hello?" a young man answered.

"It's me," Taylor said, tears springing into her eyes. "I don't have long. Please, hurry."

"Put the phone up to your arm."

Taylor did as she was told, putting the phone against her forearm, right where there would've been a recent surgery scar. That is, if Taylor hadn't healed the wound herself.

She could still hear the guy's voice on the phone, though it took on a different quality now. Tinny and robotic.

"Activate!" he said.

That's what it sounded like when Sam Goode used his Legacy to talk to machines.

"Did it work?" Taylor asked, putting the phone back to her ear.

"Yes!" Sam said. "We see you."

The Foundation's scans hadn't discovered Taylor's locator chip because it hadn't been active yet.

Now it was.

A flashlight beam swept down Taylor's corridor. She pitched the phone into the Mogadorian ooze without saying good-bye and stumbled in the direction of the searching soldiers.

"I'm here!" she called. "I'm here!"

CHAPTER THIRTY-ONE

CALEB CRANE
MELBOURNE, FLORIDA

CALEB WOKE UP AT DAWN AND GOT DRESSED AS quietly as possible. While the rest of Sydal's mansion slept, he crept outside and started to jog down the beach. The cold spray from the ocean tickled his skin. He kept up a steady pace until he was clear of Sydal's property. Once he made it onto the public beach, he started to come across other early-morning joggers. They nodded and smiled at him like he was a normal person.

He found his way to a beachside juice bar. With a few bucks from his Earth Garde living stipend, Caleb bought himself a peanut-butter-and-banana smoothie. Drink in hand, sweat damp on his back, he settled into a chair on the store's porch, which looked out over the ocean. Occasionally, Caleb glanced down at his watch.

He was supposed to meet Wade Sydal that morning at nine so the inventor could run some tests on him.

It was ten before he finished his smoothie.

"Oops," Caleb said.

He didn't make his way back to the beach house until a couple of hours later, when he was sure that Sydal had to have gone into his office. He was right. The place was pretty much deserted.

Caleb found Daniela out by the pool, soaking her feet while she finished the last few pages of her novel. She tipped her sunglasses down to look at him.

"Yo, everybody was looking for you," she said.

"I went for a jog and lost track of time," Caleb said, the lie practiced.

"Uh-huh," Daniela replied. "Wade was all disappointed you didn't go to the office with him, but Melanie volunteered instead. I guess she's going to lift a bunch of shit while Sydal measures the energy stored up in her muscles."

"Great," Caleb said, plopping down next to Daniela and sticking his feet into the pool.

"Honestly?" She lowered her voice a little. "I don't really want that dude running tests on me either. I made some chunks of stone for him to analyze. He seemed cool with that."

"It's weird, right?" Caleb said, relieved that Daniela was on his side. "It's like he wants to figure out how Legacies work so he can cut us out of the process."

Daniela held up her hand. "Okay, whoa. I just don't want

him poking me and ogling me like he does his assistants. I'm not going in on a whole conspiracy thing with you."

Caleb and Daniela both turned as the screen door behind them snapped open. Lucinda, the Sydal assistant who had caught Caleb in the workshop the other day, stood there with a raised eyebrow.

"Aha," she said. "There you are, Mr. Crane."

Lucinda wore a pencil skirt and a blouse that she'd tied off to show a little midriff. Caleb hadn't realized the word "sashay" was in his vocabulary until he watched Lucinda approach them.

Lucinda stopped in front of them, her hip cocked to one side, and smirked. She eyed Caleb for a moment before speaking.

"Mr. Sydal was very disappointed you missed your appointment this morning," Lucinda said.

"Um, yeah," Caleb said, swallowing. "I went out for a run and lost track of time. Tell him I'm sorry."

"You can tell him yourself, at dinner," Lucinda said. "You'll be there, right? Or are you planning to disappear again?"

"No," Caleb said. "I'll be around."

"Good," Lucinda replied. She started toying with the knot on her shirt while she spoke, which Caleb found incredibly distracting. "Mr. Sydal would also like to know if you guys are okay with steak for dinner?"

"Uh," Caleb replied. "What?"

Daniela snickered. "Yeah, that's cool. Thanks."

Lucinda smiled at Caleb, then swayed her way back into the house. Daniela elbowed him.

"I think she was flirting with you, man."

"Seriously? No way."

Daniela patted Caleb's shoulder. "Accept that we're super-powered rock stars."

There had been guests at dinner every night since the Garde had arrive in Florida—officers from Sydal's company, representatives from NASA and the military, rich friends—but tonight's crowd was relatively small. It was just Sydal's entourage and the Garde. Sydal sat at the head of the long table on the sunporch, a fire-pit crackling nearby, the smell of grilled meat heavy in the air. He was flanked by four of his assistants—two guys and two girls, one of them Lucinda—the ones that were currently staying at the beach house to jot down Sydal's thoughts and see to his needs whenever they popped up. Was Sydal hooking up with one of his assistants? Caleb and Daniela had discussed that and come to no conclusions. He was affectionate with all of them, perhaps inappropriately so. Maybe that explained why Sydal's lawyer, a frumpy older man fresh from the golf course, was also present.

The spread was delicious, even if Caleb didn't want to admit it. Juicy steak, corn on the cob that was somehow fresh despite not being in season, potato wedges, a bunch of different salads—all served and bussed by Sydal's jovial live-in waitstaff. Someone was always nearby to top off Sydal's wineglass.

To Caleb's relief, Sydal spent most of dinner deep in conversation with his lawyer, the assistants taking notes. Meanwhile, Melanie sat across from the Garde, looking bored. Eventually, she forced herself to make conversation.

"What'd you guys do today?"

"Chilled by the pool," Daniela said.

"Nothing," Caleb said.

Melanie sighed. "Cool. I hung out at Wade's office all day because *someone* no-showed, but he didn't even have time to experiment on me."

"Tragic," Daniela said.

"He's going to give me a spaceship to apologize," Melanie replied. Caleb wasn't sure if she was joking or not.

"Sorry I missed our appointment," Caleb mumbled to Sydal when the CEO caught his eye.

"Caleb, my man, no worries," Sydal replied. "Like Melanie said, today was actually really busy for me. We got some offers on the *Shepard-One*. Seems like we're going to up our production schedule."

His lawyer, done eating and now busy with a tablet computer, slid the device in Sydal's direction.

"We've already got patent license offers from Northrop and Lockheed," the lawyer told Sydal, his voice low but not low enough to avoid Caleb's ears. "The navy and air force both want to know if you see any applications for ICBMs."

Sydal smiled. "Lots. Obviously. The propulsion system would scale perfectly. The range would be basically limitless."

Caleb shook his head and shoved another forkful of steak into his mouth. They were talking about intercontinental ballistic missiles. Of course the military would be interested in that. He imagined his dad and his brothers back at the base, discussing the farthest distance they could kill from.

"Also," the lawyer continued in Sydal's ear. "We heard back from our contacts in Europe. They're ready to sell. But the deal is happening in Switzerland and it has been requested that you come in person within the next twenty-four hours."

Sydal stroked his chin. "Switzerland, eh? I could do some skiing, I sup—"

"Excuse me, but why would you want to put your technology on something meant to kill people?"

The table fell silent and everyone turned their attention to Caleb. He raised his eyebrows and swallowed an uncomfortably large bite of steak.

The duplicate that now stood behind Caleb's chair didn't have anything in his mouth. He fixed Sydal with a churlish sneer—it half reminded Caleb of Nigel, in that moment—like a student challenging a teacher.

Sydal's lawyer looked uncomfortable but at the sight of the duplicate the man himself grinned.

"Finally! A demonstration! It's as cool as advertised!" Sydal clapped his hands. He looked from Caleb to the duplicate and back. "I'm not sure which one of you I should even look at. Amazing! To answer your question, the primary purpose of missiles is to act as a deterrent not to, you know, actually kill anyone. But that's not what's important right now. Seriously, buddy, Caleb, we have *got* to run those tests. Like, I want to go back to the office *tonight*." Sydal, mind working perhaps as fast as his mouth, glanced at Lucinda. "You see this? That's matter creation right there. Imagine the implications if we could crack that. Got one potato? Boom. Now you've got twenty. No more famine."

"If I'm a potato," declared the duplicate, "then you're a death merchant."

That drew some murmurs from the rest of the diners. Caleb chanced a glance up from his plate and saw that the assistants were all giving him dirty looks. All of them except for smirking Lucinda.

Daniela put a hand on Caleb's forearm. "Damn, dude, chill."

Again, Sydal didn't seem to take exception. He was unflappable.

"Death merchant," he said. "That's a good one. Would look cool on a business card. But no, Caleb, I don't think of myself that way. I'm an entrepreneur, a philanthropist, an inventor. I like to say that I've got my fingers on the pulse of the future—"

The duplicate put his hand on Caleb's shoulders. "We were attacked by weapons *you* made. Shock collars, grenades, all kinds of shit. And not just at practice in school.

These were hillbilly Bible-thumpers shooting at us. You *made* that happen."

"I'm sorry that happened to you, but—"

"Wade is just trying to keep the world safe," Melanie interrupted, glaring at Caleb. "In case one of us loses control of our powers or something. Like what's happening right now."

Caleb had been taking a backseat to the duplicate's rant—he'd already lost control and caused a scene, might as well let it play out—but Melanie's sharp voice brought him back to himself. In an instant, he had absorbed the duplicate and was peering down at the scraps on his plate, cheeks flushed red.

"I'm—uh, I'm sorry," he mumbled.

Daniela patted his back, trying to defuse the situation. "Too much sun for this guy."

"It's all good," Sydal said. His smile had never faltered. "Passionate discussion is the backbone of intellectual progress, son. I heard what you said and I'm definitely going to think about it, I promise you."

Sydal dusted off his hands like the matter was closed. Caleb felt immense relief—he even liked Sydal a little bit for how easily he'd let Caleb off the hook. Melanie was still glaring at him, of course, but he could live with that.

"I have some bad news, by the way," Sydal began. "An investment of mine is finally bearing fruit and I need to go to Switzerland to inspect the results. I know you guys were planning to stay for a few more days, but I'm afraid I have to cut this visit short."

Melanie glowered at Caleb, like this was all his fault. He

sank deeper into his chair, avoiding eye contact.

"Well," Daniela said. "It was fun while it lasted."

After dinner, Sydal and his gang of assistants retired to his home theater to watch an advance screening of a new space opera that was set to be released in a couple of months. Sydal had been the technical consultant. Melanie and Daniela joined them, but Caleb decided it was best if he kept his distance.

He sighed. It was just like those first months at the Academy. He was the weirdo again.

Caleb wandered around the massive house. He soaked his feet in the pool for a bit, but January in Florida could be chilly, so eventually he went inside. He drifted by the screening room—he could hear Sydal crack some joke at which all the assistants laughed.

With a frown, he wandered to his room. Tomorrow, he promised himself, he would do like Daniela said. Blend in. Be like the crab. Be normal.

"You're right to be suspicious of him."

Caleb turned at the sound of Lucinda's voice. She stepped out of the shadowy hallway that led down to Sydal's workshop. She had a backpack slung over her shoulder, stuffed full of what, Caleb couldn't tell. She had a mischievous twinkle in her eye, like she'd just been up to something and was challenging Caleb to call her on it.

"Uh, who?" That was the most articulate response Caleb could manage.

"Sydal, dummy," Lucinda replied, smirking at him in a way Caleb found oddly familiar. "He talks and talks and talks—yes? Only evil men talk so much."

"Are you . . . ?" Caleb glanced over his shoulder to make sure they were alone. "Are you sure you should be talking about your boss that way?"

"That handsy little toad is not my boss. I have no boss." Lucinda stepped closer. "He has a deal with the Foundation, you know. That's what he's going to Switzerland for. To pick up some alien thingy they've got for him. You need to find a way to go with him, Caleb."

"How do you—?"

As Lucinda drew near, her features changed. Her hair turned dark, her eyes sharp and knowing, her skin a flawless tan.

Isabela.

"Hello, handsome," she said, and kissed his cheek. "I've come to destroy the bad guys. Are you going to help or what?"

CHAPTER THIRTY-TWO

THE FUGITIVE SIX
ENGELBERG, SWITZERLAND, AND POINTS IN BETWEEN

NIGEL'S IPOD BLASTED THE CLASH AS HE PUSHED his shopping cart through the aisles of the grocery store. He bopped his head along with the music, happy to be out from under his mother's watchful eye, if only for a little while. He'd been cooped up in this little town for weeks now, a prisoner of sorts, though he had free reign to do anything he wanted in the sleepy, windswept hamlet. Mostly, that limited his choices to browsing at the bookstore, gazing at the Alps, or aimlessly wandering the streets with his headphones warming his ears.

There were Blackstone mercenaries stationed throughout the town, keeping an eye on him. Still, he could've given them the slip if he really wanted.

His mom had bet that he would stay. And she was right.

Something was going to happen here. He wanted to see how it played out.

Chips, a sausage, cookies, and a couple boxes of the most marshmallow-filled cereal he could find. These things Nigel dumped into his cart.

It was all so utterly mundane. In fact, after those first few days, his entire visit with Bea had been that way. Most of the time, when she wasn't video-chatting with one of her evil comrades, the two of them just chilled out. They played cards, watched movies, ate frozen pizzas.

His mom wasn't so bad, if you could forget she was a megalomaniacal killer.

There were times when she conducted Foundation business in front of him, trying to make him feel like a part of it. He'd seen Taylor on video chat. So she'd finally managed to infiltrate after all their setting up. Some proper secret agent shit, that.

He wondered about the story she told Bea. Ran and Kopano, abducted by Earth Garde as punishment for the tiff with the Harvesters. Was that true? A cover story?

Clearly, Bea thought knowing that would sway him to her side. She thought she could wear him down during this protracted vacation.

It wouldn't work. He would stop Einar from killing her. Couldn't very well let that prick win, could he?

And once that was done, he would bring his mother and all her cronies to justice.

His cart full, Nigel wheeled his way to the checkout

counter. There, he dumped all the groceries on the conveyor belt and bagged them himself. He did a rough tally of how much he'd taken, then took some of his mom's money out of his wallet and stuck it alongside the unattended cash register.

There wasn't another soul in the grocery store. In fact, most of Engelberg had been evacuated due to a phony avalanche warning. He still wasn't sure how old Bea had pulled that one off.

The only people left in town were Nigel, his mom, and a dozen Blackstone mercenaries.

Whatever was going down, it was happening soon.

Taylor snapped awake as their chartered plane hit some turbulence over Romania. She wiped the back of her hand across her mouth. She'd been drooling.

The exhaustion was real. She'd seen herself in the bathroom mirror a couple of hours ago. There were dark circles around her eyes and she swore she could see some strands of gray in her hair. She'd really pushed herself that night at the warship and was still recovering.

It'd been worth it, though. She was getting close. Close to the center of the Foundation.

She was carrying a beacon right to them.

There were dark clouds outside her window. She sat up in her seat, blinking groggily. The XO sat directly across from her, an amused smile on his freckled face.

"Was starting to think you could sleep through anything,"

he said. "Been bumpy for the last hour."

As if on cue, the plane vibrated once again. Taylor's stomach did a loop, but she kept her face stoic. She flashed the XO a cocky grin.

"Little turbulence is nothing after you've fought Mogadorians."

He laughed. "You're a piece of work, Cook."

She really was. God, how had it been less than a year since she first developed her Legacies? What would the Taylor of last winter think of Taylor now? She'd been a farm girl with a simple life that made her happy. Now? She was on a plane flying across Europe with a mercenary captain.

Life came at you fast.

"Speaking of those things, I've got a question for you," Taylor said. Now that she was fully awake, it was time to get back to pumping the XO for information. "When I was hiding inside the warship, I heard a voice . . ."

The XO snorted. "Oh, you heard *her*, eh? Our nutty Mog lost in outer space."

"What's the deal with her?"

"She's always making those broadcasts," the XO said. "Doesn't seem like anyone much cares, so long as she stays behind the moon."

The XO shifted in his seat and his suitcase banged against his knee. He winced and readjusted himself. The reinforced-steel briefcase was radiation-proofed, but even so Taylor could tell the XO was uncomfortable having it handcuffed to his wrist. Inside were a dozen vials of the viscous

Mogadorian ooze, ready for delivery.

Taylor nodded at the briefcase. "Doesn't that stuff freak you out?"

The XO eyed her. "A job is a job."

"Yeah, sure," she said. "But that crap is like poison and you're just . . . carrying it around."

"Kid, has anyone ever told you that it isn't your place to ask questions?"

Taylor rolled her eyes. "Sure. I get that a lot."

"Yeah, well, it's not *my* place either. Young people think that they're the only ones getting bossed around, living in the dark. Shit, that's adult life, too, unless you're further up the food chain than me." He patted the briefcase. "So, we take this where it's going. That's our lot. But hell yeah, Cook, I'll be happy when this thing is off me."

"Won't be long now," Taylor said.

Nigel's mom waited for him outside the grocery store. She stubbed out a cigarette when he emerged and smiled at him. Smoking and drinking—she'd been doing that a fair bit these last few days. For all her calm demeanor, Bea was nervous about this plan of hers.

She peeked into one of his bags. "Nigel, my goodness, this is all junk. I told you we have guests coming."

"What? You expect me to roll out the red carpet for a sociopath with a fifty percent success rate offing Barnabys?"

Bea pinched his cheek, her fingers cold despite the

unseasonable warmth at the base of the mountain.

"My dear, we're expecting more guests than just Einar."

Caleb rubbed his eyes, thinking back on that late-night call made on a cell phone provided by Isabela.

"Uncle Clarence?"

"Jesus, Caleb, it's the middle of the goddamn night."

"Wade Sydal is going to Switzerland."

"You called me at three a.m. to tell me that?"

"I . . . I can't tell you more for . . . for operational security reasons. But you have to make him take us with him. Say he needs Earth Garde protection or something. Pull some strings."

"Caleb, that's one big goddamn ask."

"It's important," Caleb had said. *"And if you ever want me to trust you, really trust you—this will be a good start."*

He'd barely slept after that. And now? Now, Caleb sat on a padded bench at the back of the *Shepard-1*, as far away from the others as he could get. He chewed his thumbnail and tried mentally to get his armpits to stop sweating.

"How great is this?" Sydal shouted from the front of the circular passenger compartment, his face pressed to the window glass that went all the way around the space, affording lucky passengers a 360-degree view of blue sky and ocean. "I'm so, so glad you guys could experience this with me!"

Of course Sydal had chosen to take his flying saucer to Switzerland.

Sydal extended his arms, showing off for the group gathered in the ship's lounge. That included Daniela and Melanie, and a trio of Sydal's stern-faced personal security guards. None of his assistants had been brought along. Maybe he felt like he couldn't trust them after what went down that morning—Lucinda, apparently disappearing with a bunch of files stolen from Sydal's workshop. And then the call from Earth Garde informing Sydal that there were credible threats being made against his life. Because of his close ties with the military, the trio of Garde had been assigned to him as bodyguards. Vacation was over.

Uncle Clarence had pulled it off.

"You guys feel that steadiness?" Sydal asked, not seeming the least bit bothered by his recent betrayal or the looming death threats. "It's like flying on a cloud. And check out that ocean view—amazing! Tell me this isn't going to change the future of air travel."

"It's so, so cool," Melanie replied, not even looking away from her window.

Caleb glanced out his own window and his stomach turned over, but not from the heights or the ocean whipping by below. He couldn't get what Isabela had told him last night out of his head. She'd been in a hurry to make her escape as Lucinda, but she'd found time to tell Caleb about Sydal's dealings with the Foundation.

How had she come by this information? How long had she been Lucinda? How was she even out from the Academy? Where were the others?

"Better you don't know yet," she told him. *"You won't like it, Boy Scout."*

As if that information wasn't weighing on him enough, Isabela had told him there was danger coming.

"We are going to bring him down," she had said. *"Him and these Foundation dogs. You must promise to stay out of our way. You must trust me, Caleb. We must be loyal to each other."*

Caleb felt sick. He also felt an agitated duplicate starting to pop out. He focused on keeping his feelings buried.

One of Sydal's guards stepped over to the beaming magnate. Caleb leaned forward to hear what was said.

"Our team in Florida apprehended Lucinda," the guard reported to Sydal.

"Oh, wonderful," Sydal replied, making no effort to keep their conversation private. "Tell our people to prosecute as harshly as possible."

"Thing is," the guard continued, "she was tied up in her apartment. Claimed that someone jumped her a couple of days ago. None of the stolen property was recovered . . ."

"Well." For the first time, Caleb saw a glimmer of annoyance on Sydal's smooth face. "That's certainly curious."

Caleb missed the rest of the conversation as Daniela sidled up next to him.

"Yo, quiet guy," she said. "Everything okay?"

Caleb itched around his collar. "Yeah, I'm just . . . feeling off."

"If you're still brooding about dinner last night, you

should stop. No one even remembers you going off on Sydal," she said with a grin. "Or maybe you're down because hot-ass Lucinda ended up being a cat burglar or something?"

"I . . ." Caleb touched Daniela's arm and lowered his voice. "I just have a bad feeling about this."

"You're nothing but bad feelings, man. You . . ." Daniela trailed off, noticing the seriousness on Caleb's face. "You know something, C?"

"Just . . . stay on your toes, okay?"

"Are you aware that this tiny landlocked nation is one of the world's wealthiest and most stable, with one of the highest standards of living?"

Nigel responded with a bored groan. The two of them walked through the abandoned village, heading towards the mountains. Nigel was still lugging the groceries and now regretted getting that extra tub of pretzels. His hands were cold and tired.

But then . . . there was no one around. So, he used his telekinesis to carry the bags and stuffed his hands into his coat pockets. The display of power didn't even register with Bea.

"Do you know how Switzerland came to that status?"

"I'm sure you're about to tell me, Mum."

"Nazi gold," Bea continued. "The Swiss remained neutral during the war and the Nazis needed a place to hide the ill-gotten gains they'd looted from their victims. The Swiss banks were happy to oblige and, when the Third Reich collapsed, the Swiss just happened to be holding all their profits. They were rich."

"What're you telling me this for?"

"There are fortunes to be made from chaos," Bea said. "The carefully neutral survive unscathed and prosper."

"Oh, right, so you're the bloody Swiss in this metaphor. Because you seem more like—"

"Yes, I'm a Nazi," Bea interrupted sarcastically. "Please. Don't be so predictable in your insults, dear."

Nigel fumed silently as they reached a large clearing near the base of the Alps. There were stone benches there and a marble fountain frozen solid for the winter. To the north was a large cabin—the Welcome Center for those skiing the Alps—its windows dark and abandoned. Attached to the cabin was a cable car that connected to the mountainous peak.

Bea did a full 360, gazing around the field.

"We'll do it here," she declared. Bea grabbed a walkie-talkie from her hip and spoke into it, waving her hand back and forth. "Do you see me, Captain?"

"We see you," a man's voice crackled over the walkie. "Setting up now."

Silva, Isabela. São Paulo, Brazil. Shape-shifter.
Silva exhibits excellent control of her Legacy and adequate telekinesis. She displays tremendous situational intelligence that would recommend her for all manner of espionage activity. However, Silva suffered severe burns prior to becoming Garde and thus is constantly shape-shifting to

maintain her appearance. She exhibits textbook narcissism and a disregard for authority verging on the pathological. Earth Garde has assessed her as a potential RTH and we are inclined to agree. Contact is not recommended.

"Pah!" Isabela spat, and tossed the tablet through her open door and out into the Skimmer's hallway. "Pathological, my ass! Bastards!"

Her rage was barely contained by the narrow supply closet that she'd declared her sleeping quarters. There wasn't a lot of private space aboard the Skimmer, so she'd dumped the crap that was in here and moved in a sleeping bag. She'd enjoyed her few days posing as Lucinda. The woman had a very comfortable bed.

Isabela's hands shook. She touched her cheek—smooth, unblemished. They knew about her. The tablet had belonged to one of the Foundation people Einar killed. She'd been scrolling through it, nosing through their files. And oh, were there files. Every Garde that was enrolled in the Academy and some that weren't—the Foundation knew about them.

They knew about her.

"Please don't go hurling around our evidence," Einar said, appearing in the hall outside Isabela's closet. He picked up the tablet and dusted it off. "We may actually need this."

Isabela sniffed haughtily to show her disregard, but also to hide the frustrated tears in her eyes.

"They wrote . . . bad things about me," she said.

"I know. I read it."

She glared at him.

"You should read my dossier when you have a chance," Einar said. "If you thought *yours* was bad . . ."

"They called me a—what was it? An *RTH*."

"Risk to humanity," Einar said. "They call me that, too."

Isabela's eyebrows shot up. "But . . . you are a killer! Why should I be lumped in with you?"

Einar shrugged. "They think they can predict our futures," he said.

Isabela considered this. "You should prove them wrong."

"What do you mean by that?"

"Stop acting like an angry child. Stop killing. Bring them to justice. There are good people at Earth Garde. They will help."

Einar pursed his delicate lips. "You just want to save Nigel's mother. I understand. He's your friend. But trust me, she is not worth saving."

"You read our files, yes? Then you know that the Garde at the Academy *like* Nigel. He was a hero during the invasion. You want to unite the Garde? Prove you are not a shitty little villain? Well, you need to stop killing people's moms and dads."

"You're oversimplifying things," Einar muttered, but he was listening. He was looking at Isabela the same way that Caleb had last night. Waiting for an answer.

"I have a plan," Isabela declared. "For when we get there. A fate worse than death for these Foundation bastards."

"What's worse than death?"

Isabela touched her smooth cheek and, for a moment, let her appearance waver. Einar's eyes widened as he caught a glimpse of her scars.

"For these people?" Isabela smiled. "Being seen for who they truly are."

From his vantage point, Nigel could see a dozen or so Blackstone mercenaries moving about on the rooftops at the edge of town. They'd have an unobstructed line of sight down to the clearing where he and his mom stood. He was sure there were others, too, who weren't visible to him. Maybe in the cabin, maybe up on the cable car.

"You sure you've got enough men?"

"One sniper would be enough for Einar," Bea said. "His Legacies are only effective at close range. I'll have every angle covered."

"You thought of everything," Nigel said dryly.

"Darling, when I plan an ambush, I *plan* an ambush."

"Might not even show up."

"He'll show up," Bea replied. "I made sure to leave ample bread crumbs for him to follow."

Nigel squinted. It looked like one of the mercs was carrying a rocket launcher. He whistled.

"Is that a bazooka up there? Christ, Mum. Going to blow us all up?"

"My dear, it's always best to be prepared for the unexpected."

"Do you know what you've done?" Agent Walker shouted. "We're talking international incident here!"

"You said our mission is to find Einar," Ran replied coldly. "She will help us do that."

"We've kidnapped the daughter of a sheikh from a nation that doesn't participate in Earth Garde," Walker responded. "Do you have any idea how illegal that is?"

Ran tapped her temple. "Is *this* legal?"

"You didn't kidnap me," Rabiya added. "I came willingly."

Walker and Ran didn't acknowledge her, too deep in their own argument. Kopano sighed and put his hand on Rabiya's shoulder.

"They're always fighting," he said. "In the meantime, best to just enjoy the view."

They stood on a mossy cliff overlooking a gorge filled with overgrown jungle. Fog rolled across the valley below and, through the misty gaps, Kopano saw the remains of an ancient village. Stone temples and houses, all built into the mountain walls. Next to him, a Loralite stone jutted out of the ground.

"Where have you brought us, exactly?" he asked Rabiya.

"Machu Picchu, in Peru," she replied, hugging herself. "No one has discovered this Loralite growth yet, so it's free from the usual checkpoints and security guards. I come here sometimes to think."

Kopano glanced over at her. She was hard to get a read on, but he thought he saw loneliness in her eyes.

"You can just teleport all over the world and see such

amazing things," Kopano said with a grin. "What a Legacy! I'm jealous."

"Yes, it's great until someone is trying to kill you."

"You can just teleport away!"

"It's not always so easy."

Kopano took a deep breath and extended his arms, letting the breeze blow across his chest. "At the Academy, they will teach you ways to defend yourself. You'll love it."

Rabiya glanced back at Walker and Ran. "Will they let me stay? If they send me back to my father after what I did . . ."

"Things will work out," Kopano assured her, although he wasn't so certain of that any more. He fingered the Inhibitor chip in his pocket, the one that he'd pulled out of his own head. What reason did he have to be positive when everything lately had sucked so hard?

He thought of Taylor, back at the Academy, probably worried sick about him. He'd made a promise to her, too, about keeping her safe and making life boring. Now he wasn't around to keep it. He thought about kissing her, about how their relationship was just getting started. Now, it was Kopano who had loneliness in his eyes.

Agent Walker snapped her fingers at Rabiya and Kopano as they both stared wistfully across Machu Picchu's crumbled architecture. Apparently, she and Ran had finished their latest argument.

"All right, since we're in this mess and we can't hide in Peru forever, we might as well know," Walker resignedly addressed Rabiya. "Where is Einar?"

"Switzerland," she replied. "Or, at least, he will be there."

"Why Switzerland?"

"There's a meeting happening there between one of the Foundation heads and one of their biggest customers. He won't be able to resist."

"And you know this how?"

"The woman from the Foundation approached my father about acquiring my services for the meeting. Apparently she wanted a quick getaway." Rabiya had held Walker's gaze throughout the mini interrogation, but now she looked away. "He denied her, but I heard the details. The meeting is soon."

Walker ran a hand through her hair. "Jesus. So this is all just a hunch of yours?"

"No," Rabiya replied sharply. "The Foundation woman in question is Bea Barnaby. She recruited Einar. He won't be able to resist attacking her."

"But he might not even know about this meeting," Walker groaned.

Ran stepped in close to Rabiya. "Did you say Barnaby?"

"Yes," Rabiya replied. "I think you know her son."

Kopano's stomach dropped. There really wasn't much reason for optimism in this world. None at all.

"How close can you get us?" Ran asked.

Rabiya draped her hand against the Loralite growth.

"Close."

CHAPTER THIRTY-THREE

TAYLOR COOK
ENGELBERG, SWITZERLAND

"WHERE ARE ALL THE PEOPLE?"

Taylor, the XO, and six other Blackstone mercenaries walked purposefully through the deserted streets of the Swiss hamlet. It was a quaint little spot at the base of the mountains. In her past life, Taylor would've loved to visit a place like this. Now, she saw shadows moving in every abandoned window.

"Boss lady had them evacuated," the XO replied. "Safer that way."

"So you're expecting trouble?"

He gave Taylor a look. "Cook, not a day goes by I'm not expecting trouble."

Taylor had to admit it was a stupid question, but she was nervous. The XO and his men had geared up when they arrived. They all wore body armor now and heat-vision goggles on their foreheads. All their weapons were tethered to their armor by titanium alloy cords, so their guns couldn't be ripped away by telekinesis. Taylor also noticed that some of them had adopted Mogadorian energy blasters recovered from the warship raid. A telekinetic could knock a bullet off course, but not redirect an energy beam.

That meant they were expecting trouble from Garde. But who?

The sun was going down. The snow on the mountains was tinted pink and dark purple, the clouds in the sky a wispy ripple. Taylor's breath misted in the cool air, but this was nothing compared with the temperatures in Mongolia.

A nice night. Too nice for a fight.

They rounded the corner and approached a clearing near the mountains. Taylor spotted two people up ahead, not military by the look of them. Civilians. The woman, with her close-cropped blond hair and her long winter overcoat, Taylor recognized immediately as Bea.

But the guy next to her made Taylor gasp and stop in her tracks, causing one of the mercenaries to bump into her with a grumble.

Nigel.

Taylor forced her feet to plod forward, her mind racing. The last time she'd seen Nigel had been on New Year's Day. He'd gone to London to bury his father and never returned. His shady disappearance had propelled Taylor to this point and now . . .

The resemblance clicked into place. Bea and Nigel. Mother and son.

Jesus Christ. If Nigel was Foundation, that would mean her cover was completely blown and she was walking right into a trap.

No. He couldn't be. Not Nigel. That wouldn't be punk rock at all.

But Miki had said they had ways. Ways of manipulating you. Turning you.

His own mom.

The distance between them was closing. He stared at her. Bea smiled warmly. Taylor didn't know what to say, how to play this situation. If only they had a minute alone so she could feel this out.

Hell with it, Taylor thought. *Be natural. Be yourself.*

Being herself meant rushing the last few steps up to Nigel and hugging him.

"Oh my God, Nigel! You're okay! They told us . . . well, they didn't tell us anything," she gushed. "We thought you could be . . ."

He didn't hug her back. Instead, Nigel extricated his gangly limbs from under Taylor's arms and took her by the shoulders, holding her at arm's length.

"Oi," he said with a sneer. "Getting the stink of sellout all over me."

"Oh, do calm down, dear," Bea said. "Not everyone can be as hopelessly righteous and naïve as you."

"Been bitching about how unhappy you were for months,"

Nigel said to Taylor, ignoring his mom. "But I never thought you'd actually go through with this shit and join these craps."

Taylor had to stifle a smile. He was playing along. She felt a weight lift from her shoulders. She'd forgotten what it was like to have an ally. It took some effort to cock her head defensively and raise her voice.

"You never understood how much was wrong with that place," she said sharply. "Do you know what happened to Ran and Kopano, huh?"

Nigel turned away as if he couldn't stand the sight of Taylor.

"Now, now," Bea said, clapping her hands twice. "There will be plenty of time to smooth out these squabbles later. For now, we must present a unified front. Our guests are arriving."

Taylor and Nigel both looked to the sky as a silver vessel sliced through the clouds and descended. The thing looked like a giant Frisbee. No. More like a B-movie flying saucer.

"The shit is this, then?" Nigel asked. "The martians invading?"

"That," Bea replied, "would be Mr. Wade Sydal."

Taylor knew the name. The weapons manufacturer and inventor. The one who designed the gear the Harvesters had used against them. She glanced at Nigel. His face was screwed up and he chewed his bottom lip. He was confused. So, his mom hadn't filled him in on every detail.

"You're selling him the stuff we brought from Siberia," Taylor stated to Bea.

"Indeed," she replied.

They formed up around Bea as Sydal's saucer landed across the clearing. Nigel and Taylor stood on either side of her, the XO next to Taylor, his men fanned out in a loose half circle behind them.

An entrance ramp extended from the saucer and a trio of dark-suited security guards filed down the ramp. They didn't look nearly as fearsome as the Blackstone mercenaries—they were lacking body armor, blasters, and a great deal of facial scarring. They looked warily at Bea's gang, but eventually called the all clear back into the ship.

Moments later, a boyish man with jet-black hair and a wide smile sauntered down the ramp. He extended his arms in cheerful greeting as he crossed the grass.

"Bea, you old hellcat, what a dramatic location you've chosen for . . ."

Taylor didn't hear the rest of his words. She was too distracted by the three people who made their way out of Sydal's saucer.

Melanie Jackson, Taylor had never met but she knew from all the magazine covers and YouTube videos. She was the face of Earth Garde.

Daniela Morales, Taylor had encountered briefly before. She was one of the first to develop Legacies. One of the only ones to fight alongside John Smith.

And Caleb Crane. Her friend. Her fellow fugitive. He looked as shocked to see Taylor and Nigel as they were to see him.

"Christ, one reunion after another," Nigel muttered.

The two groups stood on opposite sides of the clearing, not getting too close. Caleb awkwardly raised a hand and waved. Nigel gave him a too-cool up-nod. Taylor just stared.

Of course, the adults were talking. They *loved* talking.

"Is that my acquisition your man has there?" Sydal asked, gesturing at the XO.

"It is," Bea replied. She took a smartphone out of her coat and checked the screen. "Haven't seen the transfer clear yet, Wade."

Sydal took out his own phone and pressed a button. "There. A whole metric butt-ton of moola was just transferred to your daughter's trust account, like you asked."

That caused Nigel to give his mom a look. Bea checked her screen and, satisfied with what she saw, gestured for the XO to bring Sydal the case.

As the XO marched across the field, Sydal took a closer look at Bea's group. His forehead creased in consternation when he noticed Taylor and Nigel. Maybe she was mistaken, but Taylor thought he recognized them.

"Bea, light of my life . . ." Sydal said, his voice tense despite the levity. "Are those Garde I see at your side?"

Bea glanced at Nigel and Taylor, as if just noticing them. "Why, yes," she said. "Only two, I'm afraid. Couldn't acquire my third in time. You've got quite the entourage yourself."

"These three are lawfully assigned to me by Earth Garde," Sydal responded, a note of righteousness in his voice. "Yours . . . forgive me, Bea, but you aren't authorized to have them, as far as I know."

Taylor hated this. She hated these two talking about the Garde like they were *things*, like they were accessories. Yet, through her annoyance, she also sensed something important playing out. If Sydal dealt with the Foundation, then he already knew they had Garde at their disposal. But Bea had put him in the same space as them, with witnesses. She'd implicated him and now he was trying to play it off.

"My son and his friend are here of their own free will," Bea replied, her haughty tone goading. "Are you going to go tattle on me, Wade?"

Sydal's face twisted like he had a bad taste in his mouth. He snatched the reinforced briefcase containing the Mogadorian ooze away from the XO and handed it off to Melanie. Poor girl. She looked more confused than anyone and now she was stuck handling something truly toxic.

"As a law-abiding citizen, it's my obligation to report you," Sydal said. "This was very stupid of you, Bea. Very, very stupid. Our whole relationship . . ." He paused, as if trying to rein himself in from saying more. "Our whole relationship is based on *discretion*. You're ruining something gre—"

Case delivered, the XO had started his way back to Bea's group. The soldiers looking on weren't very tense. They probably interpreted this whole thing the same way Taylor did—as a pair of rich assholes showing who could piss the highest.

That's why none of them reacted initially at the sudden whoosh through the air.

Just like that, the XO was flattened by a giant mass. He lay on his back, writhing, one of his legs twisted, his arm bent awkwardly over his head.

At first, Taylor thought that a rock had fallen off the mountain and struck him.

But then the rock stood up.

The XO's attacker wore a baggy hooded sweatshirt that did little to hide his hideousness. His skin was an abnormal patchwork—mostly, it looked to be the consistency of gleaming steel, but then there were islands of cancerous black that reminded Taylor of the puddle of ooze she'd stepped in. The guy had only one eye and he swung it back and forth to take in both Sydal's group and Bea's.

Nigel took a half step back. "Five," he breathed.

"Anyone who shoots," Five shouted, "gets their head ripped off."

CHAPTER THIRTY-FOUR

CALEB CRANE
ENGELBERG, SWITZERLAND

SECONDS AFTER FIVE LANDED ON ONE OF BEA Barnaby's mercenaries and flattened him like a pancake, a Mogadorian Skimmer began its descent from above. The ship looked nothing like the sleek disk Sydal had built using its technology. This vessel appeared to have been through a war and was barely holding together—scorch marks on its sides, pieces hanging loose where they shouldn't, a visible crack in the windshield.

As spaceships went, it was a junker.

"You know who that is, right?" Daniela whispered to Caleb.

"Yeah, of course," he replied, trying to simultaneously watch the Skimmer descend and keep an eye on Five.

Unreal. This had to be the *we* Isabela had been referring

to. What the hell had she gotten herself into?

"I don't," Melanie hissed at them. "Who is he?"

"Five," Daniela replied.

"The *Loric*?" Melanie snorted. "Shut up. He's dead."

"He isn't dead," Caleb said. "Obviously."

Melanie held up the suitcase she'd gotten from Sydal like a shield. "Oh my God."

Sydal himself clearly wasn't used to surprises like this. Or, for that matter, threats about decapitation. He stomped his foot and screamed across the field at Bea.

"What is the meaning of this, Barnaby?" One of Sydal's guards touched his arm to keep him from advancing any further towards Five. Despite the Loric's threat, Caleb noticed that all of Sydal's men had their guns at the ready, tense, prepared to fire at the slightest provocation. The mercenaries on the other side had the exact same posture.

Across the field, Bea held up her hands like the picture of innocence.

"I'm as surprised as you are, Wade," she replied. "Young man, what is—?" She started to address Five, until he whipped his head in her direction.

"Shut up!" he snapped. "All of you!"

The Skimmer landed and a rickety entrance ramp began to unfurl from its side. Everyone turned to watch as three people exited the ship. The first was a girl Caleb didn't recognize. She was tall and thin, her head shaved, and even at this distance, he could see electricity crackling across her fists and arms.

Caleb recognized the next guy down the ramp. He'd only seen Einar briefly, back during their fight with the Harvesters on the highway. Caleb remembered him as slick and showy, wearing his fancy suit and carrying around an attaché case. He'd seemed so remarkably in control. Yet now, while Einar definitely gave off a certain arrogance that Caleb found immediately grating and he was still dressed well, there were hairs out of place and his suit was noticeably wrinkled. His eyes were tired. He looked, Caleb realized, like a guy who had been living inside a broken-down spaceship.

Following Einar out of the ship was Isabela. She held a cell phone in front of her and it quickly became apparent that she was recording video. Caleb's heart sank even more. As if it wasn't bad enough seeing Taylor and Nigel over there with the Foundation—and Nigel's mom, apparently—now here was Isabela backing Einar. He didn't know whose side he was supposed to take in this situation.

But . . . you know what? That didn't seem to matter. In fact, Caleb suddenly felt pretty chill about the whole standoff. Everyone else seemed to agree because they were all stepping back and lowering their guns.

Einar raised his arms and smiled.

"Hello, everyone," he began. "In case you hadn't guessed, I'm helping you all stay calm."

Caleb smiled and nodded. Yep. It was working. He felt great.

"For those of you who don't know me, my name is Einar."

He bowed in Sydal's direction. Then, he looked over at Nigel, the Brit wearing the same dopey grin as all the rest of them, despite being faced with the guy who once nearly killed him. "For those that I've met before, I'm truly sorry if I made a bad first impression. I'm learning."

Einar spoke laconically, giving off the impression of control. But Caleb saw a vein pulsing on the side of his head. Manipulating the emotions of this many people was a strain, even for a Garde as powerful as Einar.

"Let's play a game," Einar said. "If you are part of a vast criminal conspiracy to exploit and control Garde, please raise your hand."

Sydal's hand went up enthusiastically. So did Bea Barnaby's. All the guards and mercenaries also raised their hands. It was a combination of Einar compelling honesty and his two helpers simply using their telekinesis to jerk arms into the air. After a few seconds, only the Garde were left with their hands down.

"All of these people have ties to an organization called the Foundation. If you've heard of them, you are probably under their sway." Caleb realized that Einar wasn't speaking so much to the crowd as to Isabela's camera. "The Foundation even have their hands in Earth Garde, the so-called Human Garde Academy, and virtually every powerful organization on this planet. They think they can control us. Exploit us. Profit off us or kill us."

Einar paused for a breath.

"I am living proof that they cannot," he continued. "If you are watching this video and you are Garde, if you are trapped at Earth Garde's mockery of a training center, if you are a prisoner of the Foundation—I will find you. I will save you. I will *liberate* you."

Isabela got right into Einar's face, capturing the challenging curl of his upper lip.

"And if you are part of the Foundation or one of their lackeys, know that justice is coming." He snarled. "The Loric gave us these powers and abandoned us. Forced us to fend for ourselves . . ."

Caleb glanced at Five. He took no exception to this comment, his eye continuously sweeping the area for any sign of trouble.

"This is how we do it," Einar continued. "By banding together. By not abiding by any law they pass to control us. We will *not* be their pawns. They will *not* be our masters." He pointed first at Sydal, then at Bea. "Beyond their confession here, we have evidence showing how these two human leeches—Wade Sydal and Bea Barnaby—have committed multiple crimes against Garde. By the time you see this, copies of that evidence will have been uploaded. We will hold both of them in our custody until such a time that the governments of the world choose to uphold justice for Garde and pro—"

A shot went off. Not from anyone in the clearing, but from one of the rooftops at the edge of town. Einar and Isabela both flinched.

The bullet hovered inches from Einar's eye. Caught by Five's telekinesis.

For a moment, staring at the bullet, Einar looked like he might throw up. Then, he swatted it out of the air and jerked his chin towards the rooftops.

"Five, deal with that, please. Don't be gentle."

Wordlessly, Five took off, flying in a blur towards whatever poor bastards were posted on the roofs. Soon, the sound of fruitless gunfire and screams reached Caleb's ears.

Einar wiped some sweat off his forehead, despite the cold.

"Well, I don't plan to suffer the fate of every revolutionary just yet," he muttered. "Duanphen," he said to the tall girl. "Go get Mrs. Barnaby. I'm afraid my restraint won't hold if I have to do it. I'll tend to Sydal."

Through the mellow haze of Legacy-induced calm, Caleb watched Einar and Isabela approach their group. No one moved. Daniela and Melanie both slumped like they were drugged. Sydal's guards, too.

Everything is fine, Caleb told himself. *It's all good. Let it happen.*

But another part of him fought. Railed against Einar's control. *This wasn't right. He needed to do something.*

A duplicate popped out from Caleb. Just like it had happened a hundred times before, whenever Caleb lost control of his emotions, whenever he tried to suppress a strong feeling.

Except this duplicate was calm. Just like Einar wanted.

Caleb was not.

"I can't let you do this," he said, stepping forward to block

Einar's path towards Sydal.

Einar's eyes widened, then narrowed. He focused on Caleb.

A deeper sense of calm washed over him. A drugged sleepiness.

No. Let one of his other selves feel that.

Caleb created a duplicate that sat down immediately and began sucking his thumb. His own head was clear.

"What . . . ?" Einar stopped in his tracks.

"You said you could keep them calm," Isabela snapped, staring at Caleb.

"I am," Einar replied. "He's . . . doing something."

"I agree with a lot of what you said," Caleb said diplomatically. "Things are messed up. But this isn't the way."

"Caleb, this is what we wanted!" Isabela said. "Isn't this what we spent all that time planning? We're bringing them down! We can be free of all their bullshit . . ."

"No," Caleb said. "You're starting a war. You're teaming up with a psycho who tried to kill our friend."

Einar's expression darkened. "Enough," he growled. "There's no time for this."

A wave of fear washed over Caleb. He made another duplicate to take on that emotion. The clone ran screaming back towards town. Caleb himself took another lurching step towards Einar, but now felt telekinetic pressure against his chest. Einar was pushing him back.

"Stop fighting me, Crane," Einar spat, sweat now soaking the front of his shirt. "This is the way."

Caleb took another step and howled. One of his fingers had been bent back, twisted by Einar's telekinesis.

Isabela slapped Einar across the face. "You said you wouldn't hurt anyone!"

"He's forcing me," Einar snapped.

That was all the distraction Caleb needed. He closed the distance. And then there were three of him.

All angry.

"This is for trying to kill Nigel!" The Calebs shouted in stereo.

All of them punched Einar in the face.

He went down, the calm shattered.

And all hell broke loose.

CHAPTER THIRTY-FIVE

HOW THE WAR BEGINS
ENGELBERG, SWITZERLAND

LATER ON, MOST PEOPLE WILL POINT TO THE MAYhem in California as the start of the war between the Garde and humanity.

They're wrong.

It really started in Engelberg.

"Ma'am, we can't let you and your . . . kids up there," the soldier said, with a skeptical glance into the car. "There's an avalanche advisory. Whole town has been evacuated."

Agent Walker fumed. She sat behind the wheel of the SUV they had hurriedly rented in Zurich, fresh after teleporting in. Well, not so fresh. The Loralite stone was located in a small cave adjacent to the Rhine Falls—another rock outcropping unknown to the world except to Rabiya. Ran wondered how much Loralite there was blossoming ever upward from the earth.

They'd gotten soaked by freezing spray on the hike from the waterfalls to Zurich and their clothes were still stiff, despite running the heat nonstop for the ninety-minute drive south to Engelberg. That whole episode had earned Rabiya a cussing out from Walker. Ran enjoyed that; she liked seeing the older woman miserable.

Of course, Kopano had called the waterfall "refreshing." Always so positive. It made Ran grind her teeth, except when his cheer also annoyed Walker.

It struck Ran that Walker thought this whole Rabiya thing was just a wild-goose chase, that the girl was simply using them to get away from her controlling father. Ran wasn't entirely convinced of the girl's intentions either. But she certainly didn't mind seeing Walker made to sweat a little.

When they hit the roadblock heading to Engelberg, though, that's when Walker started to believe. What kind of public-safety patrol wore body armor?

"By whose authority are you keeping us from passing?" Walker asked the guy manning the barricade.

He squinted at her. "Lady, by whose authority are you asking me questions? Get outta here."

"Why does he sound American?" Kopano, sitting in the passenger seat, murmured so only the people in the car could hear.

"These men are Blackstone," Rabiya whispered. "We must get through them if you want to get to Einar."

The guards suddenly jerked away from their car. There were loud noises coming from up the road. Ran knew that sound.

Gunfire.

"Seriously, lady," the guard said, turning back to Walker even as he unbuckled a buzzing walkie-talkie from his belt. "Turn around before something bad happens to you."

"Okay, okay," Walker said meekly. She rolled up her window and put the car in reverse. "Ran?"

"Yes?"

"I'm going to need you to blow up that barricade."

Ran picked up a stone from a small pile that she'd collected at the waterfall. She charged it with her Legacy, the crimson glow lighting the interior of the car and reflecting in her eyes.

"As you wish."

Nigel's first reaction when Einar's artificial calm broke was to cackle. The bloody ponce. Delivering his addled revolutionary speech into a cell phone camera like some John Smith knockoff and then he goes and gets his lights turned out by Caleb.

It was the most wonderful thing Nigel had ever seen.

There wasn't enough time to savor the moment. Einar's henchwoman—he'd called her Duanphen—was nearly back to their busted-ass ship, dragging Bea by her arm.

"Oi, world's least-chill Buddhist!" Nigel shouted, his words carrying sharply into Duanphen's ears so that her shoulders bunched and she flinched. "Bring back my evil mother!"

Duanphen spun to face him. Nigel lashed out with his telekinesis, mustering as much force as he could. He shoved her to the ground and Bea with her.

He saved their lives. Because that's when the cross fire started.

Sydal's men shot first, covering their boss's retreat into his idiotic flying saucer. A pair of bullets struck the mercenary nearest to Nigel, thudding into his body armor and knocking him off his feet. Too close.

The mercenaries fired back, their blasters sending sizzling bolts of energy towards Sydal's men. One dropped, his black suit scorched through. The rest were protected by a sudden flash of silver light that manifested a waist-high wall of rock. That would be Daniela, using her Legacy.

With the advantage of cover, Sydal's men returned fire and sent the Blackstone mercenaries scrambling for the nearby fountain. Nigel felt something like a beesting on his shoulder and glanced down. He'd been grazed.

Taylor tackled him to the ground. Only seconds had passed since he knocked down Duanphen and Bea, but that seemed like an eternity when guns were blazing.

"This is a damn shit show," he said to Taylor.

"I've been in way too many shoot-outs lately," Taylor replied. "What do we do?"

Nigel glanced across the field. Duanphen and Bea were still down. The Garde had her head perked up, waiting for a break in the shooting to move. Bea lay there cowering with her hands over her head.

He sighed. "Gotta save my bloody mum. She's probably Satan herself, but I can't let these muppets take her."

"You don't need to explain," Taylor replied. "I'll take down the shooters."

"You get that tracker in your arm working?"

"Yeah," Taylor replied. "Help is on the way, hopefully."

"Good on ya," Nigel said. He squeezed her arm. "Right, then. Don't die, love."

"You neither."

As the shooting started, Isabela grabbed Caleb around the neck and pulled him off the unconscious Einar. They fell backwards and Isabela wrapped her legs around Caleb's torso, squeezing him tight. She was choking him.

"Look what you did, *babaca*!" she yelled. "We *had* them. We *had* them!"

Caleb's duplicates reached down and pried Isabela's arm out from under his chin. Then, a dagger of blaster fire created a hole in one of their chests, the clone vanishing into thin air. Caleb and Isabela both ended up scrambling for cover behind Daniela's newly formed wall. Isabela used her telekinesis to pull Einar's limp body with them.

"I can't believe you're on his side," Caleb said to her.

"I'm not! I mean—" Isabela punched the ground. "I don't know!"

"You were just choking me."

"I'm sorry," Isabela replied. She reached out and touched Caleb's cheek. "I thought you were going to kill him."

"I'm not the killer," Caleb snapped. "He's—he almost murdered Nigel."

"He thought Nigel worked for the Foundation," Isabela replied. "You don't know how deep their corruption goes. That little slug you're here protecting, he doesn't care about us, Caleb. At least Einar, at least he's one of *us*—"

Caleb looked around. Their wall was getting pelted by blaster fire by the Blackstone mercenaries, but it was holding. Sydal's guards were returning fire. Melanie crouched nearby still holding that briefcase, her eyes panicked. Daniela was next to her.

Sydal was gone. He had fled back into the ship.

"We can't let them kill each other," Caleb said.

"Why not?" Isabela replied.

Before Caleb could respond, a loud roar pierced the air.

Five was back.

He landed feetfirst on one of Sydal's guards, crunching him up against Daniela's wall. The burly Loric looked down, saw that Einar was beat-up and unconscious, and his face curled. Two blaster beams fired by the mercenaries struck Five in the chest but did nothing except leave scorch marks on his steel-plated skin.

The last of Sydal's guards tried to get his gun pointed at Five, but was far too slow. Five used his telekinesis to bend the gun into a pretzel around the man's hand, then punched him with enough force to knock three of his teeth out.

Five looked at Isabela.

"Where's Sydal?"

She pointed inside the saucer.

"Good." He pointed at Einar. "Watch him."

Five stalked towards the entrance ramp.

Three Calebs stood in his way.

Taylor scrambled on her belly from her exposed position to where the rest of the mercenaries were taking cover. While these guys were obviously used to being under fire, they had less experience operating without a commanding officer. Taylor thought the XO was still alive after Five landed on him, but he was in no shape to lead.

"Jesus Christ!" one of them shouted. "Someone secure the asset!"

One of the soldiers leaped out of cover, firing wildly at Sydal's guards, and then grabbed Taylor by her coat and hustled them both behind the fountain. Bullets whizzed by overhead, chipping away at the granite basin. A few of them returned fire while the others bickered.

"We need to get the XO! Check if he's still alive!"

"No! He would want us to protect Barnaby. If she gets taken . . ."

"Hell with her, I'm not fighting that goddamn Lori—"

With her telekinesis, Taylor pulled the trigger on one of the blasters, firing it into the legs of the men shooting at Sydal's guards. They screamed and collapsed as their body armor melted into their knees.

Taylor felt a pang of guilt. She'd fought alongside these guys, maybe even saved their lives before.

But they were on the wrong side.

"What the hell?" One of the standing mercenaries shouted at the one who'd done the shooting. The shooter stared down at his weapon, looking completely baffled. Before he could respond, the first soldier smashed him across the face with the butt of his rifle.

Another, standing nearby, stared at Taylor. He pointed.

"Wait! It's her! It's her!"

Taylor telekinetically yanked his weapon away as far as she could with the tether, pulled it taut, and used it to clothesline the nearest soldier.

The last one standing lunged at her. Taylor had to resort to more physical tactics. She kicked him in the groin, then swept out his legs. A move that Isabela had taught her. Before he hit the ground, Taylor telekinetically grabbed his rifle and smashed it into his face.

"You—you're supposed to be on our side," one of the wounded mercenaries mumbled.

Before they could regain any footing, Taylor focused on their weapons and bent the barrels down so they weren't usable.

"Stay down," she said. "And maybe I'll heal you when this is over."

Five plodded forward, two of Caleb's duplicates clinging to his legs. He stomped down on one, crushing its head and causing it to vanish. He snarled and picked up the other one just as Daniela unleashed a torrent of stone-vision in his direction. Five used the clone as a shield, then slung the chunk of rock back in Daniela's direction.

"Get out of my way," he growled.

"I can't do that," Caleb responded. He stood on the ramp to Sydal's saucer, the last line of defense.

Five moved closer. In response, Caleb unleashed a trio of new duplicates to tangle him up. Five yanked at him with his telekinesis; Caleb pushed back and remained unmoved. He was drenched with sweat from the exertion of churning out the copies. Five dispatched them easily.

"You think that man cowering in there would protect *you*?" Five yelled as he smashed his steel-plated fist down on a Caleb's head.

Caleb kept his mouth shut. Focused.

He knew the answer to Five's question was no, just like he knew that Five would eventually break through the duplicates and reach him. But still, he had to fight.

Behind them, against the wall, Isabela was trying to wake up Einar. Caleb couldn't wrap his head around that girl's motivations. He wasn't sure she even knew herself.

Five broke a duplicate over his knee. Caleb replaced it.

To his left, Daniela got woozily back to her feet. She was bleeding from a cut on her forehead. Five had clipped her with the rock he'd thrown at her. Melanie was there to help her up.

"Daniela," she said, eyes wide, this whole thing too

surreal for her. She'd done nothing but take cover since the fighting started. "You're bleeding."

Daniela slapped her across the face. Hard.

"Bitch, you have superstrength!" Daniela shouted at Melanie. "Help us *fight* him!"

Caleb heard a clanking noise behind him, but didn't have time to react before the ramp was pulled out from under him. He fell to the ground and rolled as the entryway was retracted back into Sydal's saucer. The magnate had sealed himself up in there.

And he'd caused Caleb to land right at Five's feet.

Five pulled him up with his telekinesis before Caleb could stop him, and he grabbed him around the throat. Caleb's team of duplicates tried to pull him free to no avail.

"You should've listened," Five said almost sadly before clubbing Caleb across the face with his metal hand.

Caleb saw a flash of light and tasted blood. He lost control of his duplicates and fell face-first to the ground, his jawbone snapped in two places.

With the shooting stopped, Nigel was free to run full speed at the girl dragging away his mother. She was nearly to their ramshackle Skimmer. Duanphen's stride was purposeful, her grip tight on Bea's upper arm.

His intention was to take her by surprise. He aimed his shoulder for the space between her shoulder blades, an old-fashioned rugby tackle.

But Duanphen had worked security for years. She knew

when a threat was bearing down on her.

At the last second, she ducked and let Nigel stumble by her. She reached out and brushed her fingers against his neck, sending a mild electric charge through him.

"Gah!" Nigel yelped, arching his back. He put himself between Duanphen and the ship. "What've you got? Legacies of an eel?"

"Mm," Duanphen replied, stone-faced. She shoved Nigel's mother to the ground and took up her Muay Thai stance. "I am not here to fight you."

"Then don't," Nigel replied. "But I can't let you take my mom."

"I know your mother. I knew your father," Duanphen said. "Perhaps better than you do, I think."

"You a therapist, too?"

"They are not worth fighting for," Duanphen said. "Let justice be done."

Nigel took in a huge breath of air, readying a scream.

That's when Sydal's ship lifted off.

Einar came awake slowly. His face hurt. It felt like his nose was broken, his lip split, and one of his eyes was swollen half-shut. He'd never been beaten up before.

"Unacceptable," he said, the word coming out garbled.

The first thing he noticed was Caleb, sprawled out in the grass just a few yards from him. Like Einar, Caleb's face was a bloody mess. Einar couldn't exactly remember the last few minutes, but maybe he'd done that in some kind of adrenaline surge. Given back to Caleb a beating just as hearty as the one he'd endured.

No. Unlikely.

Isabela knelt over Caleb, stroking his hair, shielding him from the battle still going on. Einar's head swam. He needed to rejoin the fray, but couldn't focus yet. For the moment, he watched, playing possum.

There was Five. He must've been the one to take down Caleb.

A good friend, that one.

A shadow fell across Einar. Sydal's ship was taking off, the saucer wobbling into the air with a burst of thruster power.

Damn it. They'd failed.

Five didn't give up easily. He roared in frustration as the ship lifted off, and attempted to fly after it, but a beam of silver energy crackled forth and hit his feet. In the blink of an eye, Five was connected to the ground by a stalagmite of stone, courtesy of Daniela.

So Earth Garde was still in the fight. Not good.

Five bellowed—half floating and half suspended by Daniela's rock. He was forced to double over and pound away at the craggy snare, trying to break his legs free.

That's when Melanie sprang into action. Of course Einar had noticed the so-called face of Earth Garde when his squad first showed up. As expected, she shrank away from actual conflict. And yet, there she was, charging towards Five with a scream. She swung the briefcase that Sydal had collected from Barnaby like a wrestler would wield a steel chair.

Melanie might not have been much of a fighter, but she was strong. Really strong. And apparently motivated. Even with his metal-plated skin, the blow sent Five's head jerking hard backwards. The reinforced case broke open from the impact, spilling some strange vials onto the ground. Five slumped, hanging from Daniela's stone growth by his ankles. He groaned, not quite unconscious, but close.

Melanie reared back for another swing, but stopped before connecting. She turned around slowly. She had been so focused on psyching herself up to attack Five that she'd completely missed the fact that Sydal was leaving without her.

"Wade? Wade—wait!" As Einar watched, Melanie's face crumpled in a mixture of shock and dejection. "Where— where is he going?" She put both of her hands in her hair, pulling it, and looked imploringly at an equally surprised Daniela. "He's—he's just *leaving* us?"

Einar snorted. Their plan might've failed, but at least he got to see the figurehead of Earth Garde realize just how little humanity cared about her

Isabela looked in his direction, realizing that he was awake. She opened her mouth as if to say something, then closed it. She didn't alert the others that he was conscious.

She was giving him a chance to retreat. Einar intended to take it.

Einar stumbled unsteadily to his feet. He looked at Five, still trapped in rock, only semi-awake. There was nothing

Einar could do for him. He needed to save himself.

With Daniela and Melanie still distracted by Sydal's departure, he scrambled towards his Skimmer.

Duanphen was too fast for Nigel. As he was about to scream at her, she lunged forward and clamped a hand tightly over his mouth.

"Please don't," she said. "My ears are still ringing from the last time."

She hooked her arm through his, bending it at the elbow. Nigel grunted in pain, felt the electric tickle of her palm against his lips.

Nigel's eyes darted around. His mom was on her hands and knees, breathing hard. No help there.

But here was Taylor, running across the battlefield towards them. Duanphen hadn't seen her yet.

Suddenly, Taylor flipped up in the air and came crashing down on her shoulder. It was like someone had chopped her legs right out from under her.

Einar. Great.

The Icelandic psycho staggered towards them. Blood coated the lower half of his face, the skin above pale, making him look like a zombie.

"Duanphen!" he shouted. "Get Mrs. Barnaby and let's—"

He was cut off by a high-pitched whistle.

A missile. Its smoky tail leaving a trail that led back to the cable car.

Nigel knew his mom had posted someone up there.

Someone with a bloody rocket.

They all stopped to watch the impending destruction.

It wasn't heading for their battlefield, though.

The rocket made a fiery red-and-orange blossom when it struck Sydal's saucer. The silver disk teetered, wobbled back and forth, black smoke snaking up from its engine. Then, with a burst of crimson light from the thrusters, a second explosion split the craft in two, the glittering chunks crashing down into the Alps.

"We . . . ," Einar breathed. "We are going to be blamed for this."

Nigel turned to look at his mother in horror. This was her plan.

She had arranged to make this deal with Sydal—a powerful man, a public figure, a supposed ally of Earth Garde.

And at the same time, she'd been dropping breadcrumbs for Einar, luring him here.

She had engineered this whole confrontation to kill Sydal. But why?

What had she said before?

There were fortunes to be made through chaos.

Bea wasn't on the ground anymore. She wasn't cowering. In fact, while all the others had been distracted by the missile strike, she had drawn a small pistol from inside her coat.

The pistol she used to shoot Einar in the throat.

CHAPTER THIRTY-SIX

THE BATTLE OF ENGELBERG
ENGELBERG, SWITZERLAND

NIGEL COULDN'T EXPLAIN WHY HE DID IT. HE hated Einar. The bastard had dredged up some of the worst memories of his life, used them to make Nigel feel weak and helpless, nearly killed him.

But Nigel's family had been making him feel weak and helpless all his life.

As Bea pulled the trigger a second time, Nigel used his telekinesis to rip her gun away.

Einar groped at his throat, his eyebrows raised in surprise. Blood poured in a fountain down his shirtfront. He opened his mouth to speak and a bubble of dark crimson came out.

He clamped a hand over the wound and fell down.

"Am I . . . ?" he managed to say. "Am I dying?"

Even at this distance, Isabela could feel the heat rolling off the wreckage of Sydal's spacecraft. One of those Blackstone mercenaries must have shot it down. What kind of game was Nigel's mother playing?

She didn't have time to think about that. Melanie was wailing at the sight of the explosion, Daniela was trying to console her and Caleb was breathing laboriously through his smashed face.

But that wasn't what drew Isabela's attention.

Although still suspended by Daniela's rocky protrusion, Five had shaken off the effects of Melanie's vicious blow to his head. His breathing now came in quick rasps that reminded Isabela of a bull penned up before release. As she watched, a bit of froth fell from his lips.

Five dangled directly above the contents of Sydal's brief-case.

"This . . . ," Five spoke through his teeth. "This is what they're selling? This? *THIS?*"

In a blur of motion, Five pulled himself up and bashed his way free of Daniela's stone bond. Floating now, he let out a roar and plummeted straight down at Daniela. She barely had time to turn around before Five was on her, hitting her in the sternum with both fists. He slammed her to the ground with enough force that Isabela heard the girl's ribs break.

"Daniela!" Melanie shouted. There were tears on her cheeks, but she still managed to lunge at Five.

Five took to the air, floating over Melanie's outstretched

arms. As she stumbled past, he spun and slammed his knees into her back, running her towards Daniela's wall of stone. Melanie had time to scream before Five slammed her head first into the rock and she went limp.

Breathing raggedly, Five floated above them all. He grabbed the vials of black goop that had set him off—Isabela noticed how the empty obsidian color matched the splotches of dead skin on Five's body. The vials spun around him, under his control. He glared down at Isabela, fire in his single eye.

"This stuff is evil," he snarled. "Pure evil."

"Okay," Isabela replied, holding up both hands. "Now relax."

"They should die for this," Five replied. Isabela followed his eye—it was wide enough that she could see the white— as Five scanned the field and located Nigel's mom. "Starting with her."

Before Isabela could try to talk him down, Five flew towards the others.

After Nigel ripped his mother's gun away, Duanphen acted quickly while Nigel was still trying to figure out what to do. She charged Bea and struck her under the chin with a flying knee. The older woman screamed and fell onto her back. Nigel noticed Duanphen wince when she landed—one of her legs was injured.

Instinctively, Nigel grabbed Duanphen around the waist and tried to drag her away from Bea. She shucked him off, though, grabbing his wrist and twisting until he flipped onto the ground. She let a brief jolt flow into him, then released him.

"You still defend this woman?" Duanphen asked. "Even after you've seen what she's capable of?"

"She's—she's my mom, for shit's sake," Nigel said. "Just stop fighting and I promise she'll pay for—"

"She will pay now," Duanphen replied.

Of course, Nigel had a feeling that Duanphen wasn't going to just stand down. That's why he focused on the sound of flames crackling behind her from where Sydal's ship had gone down. He amplified the noise so it sounded like a wall of fire was rushing towards her back. Duanphen flinched and turned, and that's when Nigel kicked her in her bad knee.

Before she could recover, Nigel grabbed a nearby stone with his telekinesis and smacked Duanphen across the face. He stood up, rubbing his wrist where she'd twisted it.

"Now, let's take a deep breath and—"

Five swooped down and grabbed Nigel by the throat. His grip was literally iron, his fingers digging into the side of Nigel's neck. Five lifted him up, floating them above the scene. Nigel couldn't get a breath in to scream.

Five saw Einar then. He was still clutching his throat, clinging to life, but there was an impossible amount of blood pouring over his fingers.

"He wouldn't want me to kill you," Five said to Nigel, his voice shaky with rage. "But you are a traitor to your own kind. Working with the Foundation. You deserve this."

His grip tightened. Nigel couldn't get a word out. He saw spots.

And then, a chunk of blue stone the size of a refrigerator struck Five. The impact sent him cartwheeling through the air and knocked Nigel free. He hit the ground next to the mysterious mass of Loralite, hacking and gasping for breath.

The stone had come from the direction of the road. Only telekinesis could propel something that large that fast. He squinted in that direction and was able to make out a few vague shapes and another glint of azure light. Who had saved him?

And could they please do it again?

Nigel rolled over and saw that Five had righted himself in the air and now loomed over him. Instead of pressing the attack, he stared confusedly at the Loralite.

In a flash of light, two figures burst forth from the stone. Nigel's eyes filled with tears at the sight of them.

Ran and Kopano.

They put themselves between Nigel and Five, Ran's fists glowing with stored energy.

"You stay the hell away from him," Ran snarled.

By that time, the Blackstone mercenaries that Taylor had taken out were beginning to stir. With all their weapons broken and dismantled and many of them hurt, there was no way they were going back into the fray. Not with so many Garde running around. They intended to beat a hasty retreat.

Until Karen Walker pointed her gun at them.

"All you bastards back on your bellies," she said. "No one moves until this is sorted out."

The mercenaries could have rushed Walker, maybe taken her, but some of them noted the teenager wearing a hijab at Walker's side. No way that she wasn't another Garde. They did as Walker said.

Not worth it.

From their vantage point near the edge of the clearing, Walker and Rabiya had a clear view of the carnage. Bodies both dead and injured, discarded weapons of human and alien origin, a broken-down Skimmer, a random wall of stone, a burning spaceship—and just a few Garde left standing.

"Shouldn't we help them?" Rabiya asked.

"I know that guy out there," Walker replied. "That's Number Five. If Ran and Kopano can't stop him, our best chance is to just hope he doesn't notice us."

Kopano recognized the monstrous one-eyed guy with steel-plated skin as Number Five. How many times had he watched that video of Five battling Professor Nine in New York City? It was literally the coolest thing Kopano had ever seen.

Oh man. He was about to fight a full-fledged Loric.

Why were they fighting? What the hell had gone down here?

Kopano didn't know. He didn't care. Five was going after Nigel. That made him an enemy.

With an unhinged scream, Five charged at them—flying,

not on foot. Kopano and Ran spread out, trying to flank him. Ran launched two charged projectiles in Five's direction, but he grabbed them with his telekinesis and redirected them at Kopano.

The two stones exploded right in front of Kopano's face. He tightened his molecules so there wasn't any pain, but the flash of light momentarily disoriented him.

"Kopano!" Ran shouted. "Ghost!"

Just as his vision cleared, Kopano saw Five flying right for him. Thanks to Ran, he was able to go transparent and avoid catching two of Five's metal-plated fists to his chest. Hopefully, that would put Five off balance enough for them to counterattack.

Except Five kept going. Kopano wasn't even his target.

It was the woman behind him. Kopano had barely registered her. Middle-aged, blond, a bloody nose. She'd just gotten back to her feet when Five loomed over her.

"Mom!" Nigel shouted.

Mom? Oh, damn.

"I brought this back for you!" Five snarled down at Nigel's mom.

Then, he smashed a vial of black ooze across her face.

The trampled snow was cold against Taylor's cheek. What had she been doing? Running towards something. But then she'd flipped up in the air, landed on her head, and . . .

It felt so, so good to rest after these last few days.

"Taylor! Taylor! Oh, you lazy shit, get up! Get up!"

Hands on her shoulders, shaking her. She blinked her eyes open and dazedly looked up.

"Isabela . . . ," she said. "Hey."

Her roommate slapped Taylor sharply on the cheek and the sting was enough to wake her up. She could still hear fighting, shouting, screaming.

So the battle hadn't ended without her.

"He'll kill them," Isabela said quickly. "He's crazy!"

Taylor scrambled to sit up. She looked across the field, saw Five soaring down to punch someone across the face.

Not someone. Kopano. Oh my God. Kopano and Ran.

"I have to help . . . ," Taylor said, getting to her feet, intent to do whatever she could against the mad Loric.

"You have to heal him!" Isabela said, pointing towards where the snow was dark from an expanding pool of blood. "He can calm Five down!"

Taylor swallowed hard when she saw who Isabela was pointing at.

Einar.

Bea screamed and collapsed, clutching at her face. The black ooze seemed to be writhing of its own volition, worming its way into the tiny cuts caused when Five smashed the vial.

Ran grabbed Five with her telekinesis and yanked him away from Bea. He spun to face her, breathing hard, eyes wide. She recognized the look in his eyes.

Bloodlust.

He flew towards her, but she pushed at him with her

telekinesis. Ran put up a wall of pure force. Five had to struggle to gain even an inch in her direction. She watched veins pop to life on his forehead, sweat beading on his face. He was coming.

Ran couldn't hold him alone.

She didn't have to.

A few yards away, Kopano pressed on Five with his own telekinesis. Nigel joined in, too. Together, the three of them had Five trapped in a box of telekinetic pressure. His every muscle was flexed and straining as he tried to move, flares of his own telekinesis causing the dirt and snow around his feet to churn.

Nigel took his eyes off Five for a moment, glancing at his mom, who was sitting on the ground, wiping that muck off her face and trembling. Gritting his teeth, he put a little extra force behind his telekinesis, hoping to break a few ribs.

Five still fought. Ran felt him pushing back against all of them, straining to be free. Out of the corner of her eye, she sensed movement. Taylor and Isabela. Doing something.

"What . . . ?" Kopano panted. "What do we do with him?"

"Hold him," Ran said, through gritted teeth. "Until—"

An arm looped around Ran's neck from behind, snuck under her chin, and cut off her air.

"Hell!" Nigel shouted, seeing Duanphen too late. "Ran! Watch out!"

Ran's whole body arched as Duanphen sent electricity coursing through her.

Without Ran, Nigel and Kopano couldn't maintain their grip on Five. He burst free and launched himself towards Nigel.

Taylor knelt over Einar. There was so much blood. The hole in the side of his neck was dark, the bullet having gone straight through. Einar's eyes were glassy and empty. He stared up at the sky, unseeing.

She hesitated. Would it be so bad if he were dead? He was so pale. Taylor wasn't sure there was even a spark left in him to rekindle.

Isabela touched Taylor's shoulder. "Try," she said. "We'll need him."

"Can't believe I'm doing this," Taylor muttered.

She placed her hand on Einar's neck. His skin was deathly cold already.

Still, Taylor let her healing energy flow.

A strange memory returned to Ran as Duanphen's electricity crackled through her.

She'd lost control of her Legacy once in Dr. Chen's seminar. Accidentally, she had charged her desk to explode and then been forced to suck the concussive energy back in. That was the same technique she'd used to shock Nigel back to life in Iceland. Moving volatile energy from place to place, sparking molecules to life. Absorption, release, destruction.

She felt pain as Duanphen's voltage streamed into

416

her—pins and needles in her every nerve, spasms, blood in her mouth.

But she could take it, Ran realized. She could let the energy fill her.

"What . . . ?" Duanphen murmured in Ran's ear, her grip loosening. "What are you doing?"

Ran didn't exactly know. It was instinct. Duanphen's shocking touch no longer hurt. Ran was feeding off it, soaking up the energy, letting it gather inside her.

Duanphen broke away from Ran and stumbled backwards. Ripples of currents still frolicked across Duanphen's skin, but she wasn't nearly as charged as she was a second ago. Ran had taken that from her.

Ran turned to face Duanphen, her fist crackling with electricity.

"This is yours," Ran said.

She opened her palm and a bolt of lightning shot forth, all that electricity Duanphen had pumped into her let loose at once. The jagged streak hit Duanphen in the chest and left her a smoking heap, breathing but unconscious.

Ran had little time to celebrate her discovery. There was a sharp, sizzling pain in her temple. She went down to one knee and grabbed her head. The pain was coming from beneath the little scar where Walker's people had inserted their Inhibitor chip.

It felt like something inside Ran had just burst.

Five's hand wrapped tight around Nigel's throat. Nigel looked up at the Loric boy, at his one eye and blemished face, and saw nothing but unfettered rage. He'd snapped. There was no reason in there.

With a mighty bellow, Kopano shoulder-blocked Five away from Nigel. The two of them got tangled up and rolled to the ground, punching each other, steel fists hitting unbreakable skin.

Kopano. God bless 'im. Always saving Nigel's ass.

As they fought on the ground, Kopano snaked one of his hands up to press against the side of Five's head. For the briefest of moments, it went transparent, Kopano's fingers disappearing beneath Five's steel carapace.

Five reeled backwards with a howl of pain, clutching at his face. "What did you do to me?"

Kopano, still on the ground, turned his head to yell towards the road. "Walker! Use my Inhibitor! WALKER! USE MY INHIBITOR!"

The second time Kopano screamed out his nonsense order to his mysterious ally, Nigel used his Legacy to augment the sound, make it carry. He couldn't do much—beaten up and breathless—but he could do that.

Suddenly, Five's whole body jerked. He lost control of his Legacy, the steel skin turning back to soft, pink flesh. He fell to his hands and knees.

Kopano scrambled to his feet with a triumphant cheer. "It worked! I—"

Five stood back up. His head twitched back and forth,

shaking off the debilitating shock from the Inhibitor that Kopano had snuck inside of him. Smoke rolled out of his mouth when he spoke, but the Beast was still standing.

"Always against me . . . always . . . even when I'm on the right side . . . ," Five murmured, his words slurred. "Let me show you . . . show you what they . . . what they did to me."

Kopano took a frightened step away. Nigel crab-walked backwards to put some distance between him and Five.

His skin changed. Not back to metal like before. The dark blemishes that covered his skin grew wet and expanded, spreading out to cover Five's entire body, every inch of him now the same writhing black oil that he had smashed into Bea's face.

Five held out one of his arms and tendrils snaked forth, writhing and snapping, towards Kopano's face.

"ENOUGH!"

The needle-sharp tentacles stopped just in front of Kopano's eye. Five froze.

Einar stood at the edge of the fray, pale as a ghost, his shirt soaked through with blood. Taylor and Isabela watched from a few steps behind him.

"Not that, Five," Einar said, his voice hoarse, exhausted, like that yell had drained his last bit of energy. "Never that."

Slowly, Five pulled back the oozing mass that was his arm. With an agonized groan, he changed his skin back to normal. Five looked as if he had to fight to do it, like his Legacy wasn't working properly, like he needed to physically contract the dark patches back to their former size.

Einar focused on Five until his breathing slowed, until he unclenched his fists, until he fell to his knees.

"Calm . . . ," Einar said. "You're calm. It's okay."

"I'm sorry," Five said, looking first at Kopano and then at Nigel. A tear streaked down his blood-crusted cheek. "I'm so sorry."

CHAPTER THIRTY-SEVEN

"I DID THIS TO BRING US TOGETHER," EINAR said. "I never wanted us to fight."

"Jesus, Einar," Taylor replied. "Do you ever shut up?"

The small field at the foot of the Alps suddenly felt so peaceful. The sun had just dipped below the horizon, tinting the mountains a deep purple. The abandoned town with all its warm kitchens and empty beds seemed so inviting. Taylor just wanted to pop into one of those houses for a quick nap.

But then she heard the moans. She smelled the acrid smoke of Sydal's burning aircraft.

No time to rest.

Isabela pulled on her arm. "Caleb's hurt bad," she said. "Those Earth Garde girls, too."

Taylor's whole body ached. She didn't know how much energy she had left in her. Healing Einar had taken a lot out of her. She looked at him now, pale and shaky, like a strong breeze would knock him over. He'd need time to recover from the blood loss. They could take him down now, if they wanted.

She looked around. It seemed the fight had gone out of everyone.

"Show me," Taylor said to Isabela, turning her back on Einar.

"You know I'm right, though," Einar rasped at her back, a note of desperation in his voice. "They don't care about us. The Academy can't protect you from what's coming."

"Take your people and go," Taylor said over her shoulder. "But don't even think about touching Bea Barnaby. She's *our* prisoner."

✧ ✧ ✧

Bea looked down at her hands. There were black worms writhing beneath her skin, digging their way towards her veins. The same thing was happening to her face, where Five had smashed her with the vial. It was truly disgusting.

Strange, then, that she didn't feel ill. In fact, she felt more vibrant and healthy than she had in ages, even with the broken nose and assorted bumps and bruises.

"Hello."

Bea looked up to find Kopano standing over her.

"I wanted to introduce myself. My name is Kopano," he said. "I've gathered that you're a bad person and part of the

Foundation. But I wanted to tell you that your son, Nigel, is one of the best people I know. No thanks to you."

Bea snorted but had no response. She looked back down at her hands.

"Also," Kopano continued with a puffed-out chest, "by the power vested in me as a future member of Earth Garde, I hereby place you under arrest. If you tell us everything you know about your Foundation allies, maybe we'll go easy on you."

"Hello, *mabudachi*," Ran said, plopping down in the mud and snow next to Nigel.

He smiled faintly at her arrival, but didn't take his eyes off his mother. Nigel felt disgust just looking at her. He watched her over there, Kopano standing guard on her, and waited for Bea to pull one last trick.

Bea's shoulders were slumped. Kopano helped her to her feet and then walked her over to where Walker kept watch on the Blackstone mercenaries. She didn't even glance over her shoulder to look for Nigel.

Bea was done. They'd gotten her.

Nigel let out a shaky sigh and rested his head on Ran's shoulder.

"Getting bloody embarrassing," Nigel said. "Needing you and Kopano to save me on every mission."

She rubbed his back. "Your moment will come."

Nigel hiccupped. He pressed his eyes against Ran's arm so no one would see the tears. Especially not Bea.

"I always said I hated both of 'em, you know? But I didn't hate them, not really," Nigel said, the words pouring out of him after days, maybe weeks, maybe years of bottling it up. "I just wanted them to be better parents. I wanted *them* not to hate *me*. And now . . . now I find out they're monsters. They're the actual monsters I always pretended they were and I still . . . I still can't hate her. What am I supposed to do with that, Ran?"

Ran wiped her cheeks. "We must be better than them," she said. "That is all you can do."

Nigel sniffed and looked up at her. "Anyway, that's what's new with me. The hell happened with you?"

She touched her temple. "Too much to say, but, Nigel . . ."

There was movement over at the road. Walker and Kopano having words. That ended with Kopano turning his back on Walker and jogging over to where Taylor was healing the Earth Garde members. As Ran watched, Walker waved in Ran's direction, sending Rabiya over towards her and Nigel.

"Holy shit," Nigel said, noticing the teleporter for the first time. "Where'd she come from?"

"Listen to me, Nigel," Ran said hurriedly, ignoring his question. "You are my best friend. I care about you deeply. Please remember that."

"Ran, what're you on about?"

Before she could answer, Rabiya was in front of them. In her hijab and dress, without even the least bit of blood on her, the girl seemed too clean for this mess.

"Walker wants to talk to you," Rabiya said dryly, clearly

letting Ran know she was just the messenger.

Ran tossed her arm around Nigel's neck and squeezed him in a hug. Then, she stood up.

"Right," Nigel said, rubbing his hands across his face. "I'm just going to rest here a bit and contemplate my messed-up origin, if that's bloody okay with everyone."

Ran allowed herself a brief smile before narrowing her eyes at Rabiya. "Let's go."

Moments later, she stood in front of Walker. The agent nodded across the field, where Einar was walking slowly back towards the Skimmer, rubbing his neck like he could still feel the bullet hole. Five was at his side, carrying the unconscious but alive Duanphen.

"There goes our target," Walker said.

"You expect me to go after him?" Ran asked. "Take on Number Five again?"

"I don't want you to get yourself killed," Walker replied. "But I was hoping you'd have an idea."

"Kopano put his Inhibitor inside Five," Ran said. "Why don't you try shocking him? You're fond of that."

Walker took her cell phone out of her pocket and opened the program that controlled the Inhibitors. "The thing's gone offline. They don't exactly work right when you just jam them in someone's head."

Ran nodded, watching Walker closely. "What about mine?" she asked. "I felt something during the fight when that girl shocked me. It felt like an explosion in my head."

Walker glanced down at her phone again. Ran saw it

then—a shadow across the agent's face, a flicker of fear. She made a point of looking Ran right in the eyes.

"Nothing has changed with yours," Walker said. "It's fine."

She was lying. Ran could tell.

It was just like she thought. Duanphen had short-circuited her Inhibitor.

Ran turned to gaze across the battlefield, watching Einar and Five as they neared their ship.

"Perhaps," Ran said, "we should live to fight another day."

Taylor held Caleb's face in her hands. She was pretty sure she'd fixed his broken jaw, but he was just staring up at her, giving no indication that she should take her hands away and stop pumping healing energy into him.

"Caleb?" she asked, finally. "Can you talk?"

"Oh," he said, working his mouth around, testing. "Yeah, guess I can. You done?"

Taylor smirked. "Been done for like a minute." She let her hands drop away and Caleb sat up. "I thought what you did was pretty brave, by the way."

"You did?"

"You stood up to Einar and Five, tried to save lives," Taylor replied. "I think that's what we're supposed to be all about."

"I thought it was stupid," Isabela put in, peering at Caleb over Taylor's shoulder.

Taylor turned around to reply sharply, but instead her face split into a grin.

Kopano bounded towards her.

He scooped her up in a bear hug and spun her around, her legs flailing. Despite the chaos of the last hour and the exhaustion she felt, Taylor found herself laughing. She grabbed Kopano's face and kissed him.

"Where've you been?" she asked. "You're supposed to keep things boring for me."

"So many places," Kopano replied. "I'll tell you, but please kiss me again."

Taylor happily did as he asked. Isabela rolled her eyes and Caleb looked away.

"Okay, okay, put me down," Taylor said to Kopano. "I've still got people to heal."

"I'll help," Kopano declared. "My moral support will boost your healing."

Caleb glanced over at Daniela and Melanie, both badly beaten, both unconscious but alive. Taylor would see to them. They'd recover.

His eyes settled on a loose vial on the ground next to him, one of the ones that had spilled out of Sydal's briefcase when Melanie smashed it on Five's face. Five had gathered all the others before attacking Bea and Nigel, apparently missing only this one. Caleb picked it up and looked at the black rot contained within.

He remembered Patience Creek. There had been a Mogadorian there, a trueborn woman named Phiri Dun-Ra, who had been bonded to this horrific ooze. She'd stabbed parts of it into John Smith and stolen his Legacies, used them to massacre countless soldiers and a few young Garde who had barely discovered their powers.

Who would take possession of this now? Earth Garde? Some other inventor like Sydal? Who could be trusted to keep such a deadly weapon?

Caleb pocketed the vial. Isabela saw him, raised an eyebrow, but said nothing.

As Taylor finished healing Daniela and Melanie, she heard the *whup-whup-whup* of incoming helicopters. They all did. Everyone around the battlefield—tired and dirty and spent—they stood up, expecting more trouble.

A trio of choppers with the UN logo was headed in their direction. At their vanguard was the Loric cruiser that Taylor had seen once before, the one Lexa kept around for use by herself and Professor Nine. Taylor touched her forearm. The chip had worked. They were coming to get her.

Taylor looked across the battlefield. Einar's Skimmer was still there, he and Five lingering on the entrance ramp like they were waiting for something. Why hadn't they left when she gave them the chance?

Now, it was too late.

Before the aerial convoy even had a chance to land, something dropped off from the entryway of the Loric vessel. It hit the ground with an explosion of dirt and snow. Dark hair whipping in the wind, metal arm glinting in the fading light—Professor Nine loved to make an entrance.

And he'd already recognized who was standing on the ramp of the Mogadorian Skimmer.

"FIVE!" Nine shouted.

"Goddamn it," Five muttered. He took a step down the ramp, but Einar stopped him by placing a hand on his shoulder.

They all gathered around Professor Nine. Taylor and Kopano stood to his left, holding hands. Daniela sidled up on his right, nodding in greeting to Nine before turning to glare daggers at Five. Ran and Nigel came to stand at the edge of the group, a glowing stone held in one of Ran's hands. Melanie hung back, still crying a little but trying to keep it together, occasionally touching her face as if to make sure Taylor had healed her properly. Isabela and Caleb stood next to her. Even Rabiya moved to stand with the Academy group, her eyes warily fixed on Einar.

Together, they formed a loose semicircle, facing down the two boys on the Skimmer's ramp.

"Surprised to see you here, big boy," Professor Nine said. "You're supposed to be playing dead on a private island somewhere."

"I'm done with that," Five replied coldly.

"I know someone who'll be interested to hear that."

"Yeah?" Five replied, raising his voice. "Look at me. I've paid my penance. I'm done looking for forgiveness from you assholes. Not even two years since the war and you've already let this world go to shit, failing these kids just like our Cêpans failed us. So you tell *her*. You tell *all* of them. They want me? They can come for me. It'll be the last thing they do."

Nine took a step forward. "We can get started on that right now, tubby."

Five moved forward as well. "First thing I'm going to do is jam that toy arm up your—"

"Stop it!" Taylor snapped. "Jesus. Enough. Enough fighting."

"I agree," Einar added, putting himself in front of Five. "This will get us nowhere."

Nine's brow knit in consternation. "What the hell? You were just letting them leave?"

"Fuck that," Daniela growled.

"They come with us," Nine said, staring down Taylor. "As prisoners. They both have too much to answer for."

"We don't want to fight you," Einar said.

"I do," Five grumbled.

"Kid, I *know* you don't want to fight me," Nine replied, focusing on Einar. "I hear you're supposed to have some sick Legacies and no mercy, but you look half-dead already and I've got years of experience on you. Surrender now and save us some trouble."

"No," Einar replied. He looked around at the gathered Garde and spoke louder. "I know you might not trust me. Might hate me. But this Loric and his Academy cannot protect you. Society wants to control you and he is an instrument of that."

"Bullshit," Nine growled.

"Come with us," Einar continued. "There are safe places, away from their watchful eyes, away from their manipulation. We will take care of you. Grow stronger. And wait to carve out a place in this world free from tyranny and—"

"Blah, blah, blah," Nine interrupted. "Ten on two, by my count. I'm good with that math."

As Nine took a step forward, a glowing rock landed at his feet. He leaped back just in time to avoid the explosion.

"Nine on three," Ran said, as she strode forward to stand beside Einar and Five. She avoided looking at Nigel, unable to bear the hurt expression on his face.

"This is crazy!" Taylor said. "Ran—"

"We were kidnapped from under your watch," Ran said, pointing at Nine. "Your Earth Garde put a chip in my head and forced me to be their assassin."

"Ran . . . ," Nine said. "I swear, I didn't know."

"That is why I will not go back with you," Ran said. She looked at Kopano. "You should come, too."

Kopano shook his head and grabbed Taylor's hand. "No. I will face what is to come, not run from it."

Ran bowed her head. "So be it."

"Goddamn it, Ran," Nine growled. "You know I can't let them leave. I don't want to fight you, but I will."

Nine took another step forward. Daniela joined him. Melanie sniffed defiantly, clenched her fists, and edged forward as well.

"This is moronic," Taylor said, but she nonetheless inched

towards the Skimmer. Kopano came with her, tightening his molecules, anticipating another throw-down with Five.

"I'm sorry, love," Nigel said to Ran as he flanked them as well, his eyes wet. "You know how it is."

Ran inclined her head, her fists aglow. "I understand."

The crowd of Garde suddenly shifted, jostled as three duplicates of Caleb pushed through their ranks in order to join Einar's group. Taylor glanced behind her, saw one Caleb still standing there beside Isabela. The guy was split, as usual.

"Caleb? What the hell?" Daniela asked in a strained voice.

"We took a vote," one of the Calebs said. "Our decision— my decision—is to formally resign from Earth Garde."

Isabela jumped as the Caleb standing beside her vanished. He was fully on the other side now.

"Caleb, man," Nine growled, sensing his authority slipping away. "That's the wrong decision."

"Maybe. But it's *my* decision. In my life, I haven't gotten to make a lot of them." Caleb glanced over his shoulder at Einar. "And if he gets out of line, goes too far, he knows I can stop him."

Einar said nothing, but he touched his cheek, remembering the bruises.

"You're out of the band," Nigel said to Caleb.

"Oh, shit on this."

That was Isabela. She too broke from Nine's group and crossed over to join Einar and the others.

Taylor's mouth hung open. "Isabela . . . don't."

Isabela tossed her hair. "I never belonged in that place, Taylor. You know that. I belong with people like these." Isabela took a deep breath and let go of her Legacy. Her face shifted, the skin tightened and scarred, her terrible burns revealed. "I belong with the freaks."

On one side: Professor Nine, Daniela, Nigel, Taylor, Kopano, Rabiya, and Melanie.

On the other: Einar, Five, Ran, a group of Calebs, and Isabela.

"Now," Ran said, her fists glowing. She looked at Nine. "Do you still want to fight us?"

EPILOGUE

"YOU AREN'T WELCOME HERE, GREGER, NOT AFTER the shit you pulled with Ran and Kopano."

Greger chuckled. He stood casually before Professor Nine, a team of UN Peacekeepers armed with Sydal Corp anti-Garde weaponry at his back. Nine blocked his way into the Academy's faculty building, the fingers on his metallic arm clenching and unclenching with a rhythmic creak.

"Ironic," Greger replied. "Because you are the one who is not welcome."

"Come again?"

The Earth Garde liaison handed Nine a folded piece of paper.

"That letter is from the UN. You have been terminated as headmaster of this training facility."

"Bullshit."

"Don't be dense, Nine," Greger replied. "After everything that's happened, did you honestly expect them to keep you on? You've let this place get out of control. The public has no faith in you."

Nine tore up the letter without reading it.

"You want me out," he snarled, "you're going to need an army."

"That," Greger replied, "can be arranged."

It took every bit of John Smith's willpower to stay silent.

He floated above his old friend Nine, an invisible observer, watching the scene play out. He hadn't come to the Academy that day expecting to find the place in the midst of a power struggle. He was there on other business. Urgent business.

But if he needed to intervene on Nine's behalf, John would. Even if that would be in violation of the treaty they'd signed with the humans.

There needed to be a friendly face in charge of the Academy. Someone John could trust. Especially considering what was coming.

Luckily, Greger's small team of Peacekeepers didn't seem all that keen to take on Nine. Especially not once they noticed Taylor and an assortment of other students standing behind him, arms crossed, ready to defend their professor.

The Earth Garde liaison backed down. Greger led the Peacekeepers away, back to their guard posts at the Academy's entrance, where their guns were now pointed inwards.

He would be back with a stronger force. John knew this.

They would have to fight.

But at the moment, there was something more important to prepare for.

A new arrival.

John floated upward, not turning visible until he was out of sight of the Academy. He cut through the clouds, going higher and higher, until he reached the upper limits of Earth's breathable atmosphere.

He waited there.

John couldn't keep away the chills when it appeared. The urge to flee or fight ingrained in him. No matter how powerful he became, he'd fought for too long to ever be able to get over that feeling.

Not when faced with a Mogadorian warship.

The massive locust-shaped vessel entered Earth's atmosphere and headed straight for John.

He raised a hand and waved.

Then, John led the warship down.

The Academy their destination.

The thrilling finale to the pulse-pounding
Lorien Legacies Reborn series

RETURN
TO ZERO

by PITTACUS LORE

Coming June 2019